ABYSS

The Abyss line of cutting-edge, psychological horror is committed to publishing the best, most innovative works of dark fiction available. ABYSS is horror unlike anything you've ever read before. It's not about haunted houses or evil children or ancient Indian burial grounds. We've all read those books, and we all know their plots by heart.

ABYSS is for the seeker of truth, no matter how disturbing or twisted it may be. It's about people, and the darkness we all carry within us. ABYSS is the new horror from the dark frontier. And in that place, where we come face-to-face with terror, what we find is ourselves.

PRAISE FOR ABYSS

"Thank you for introducing me to the remarkable line of novels currently being issued under Dell's Abyss imprint. I have given a great many blurbs over the last twelve years or so, but this one marks two firsts: first *unsolicited* blurb (*I* called *you*) and the first time I have blurbed a whole *line* of books. In terms of quality, production, and plain old storytelling reliability (that's the bottom line, isn't it?), Dell's new line is amazingly satisfying . . . a rare and wonderful bargain for readers. I hope to be looking into the Abyss for a long time to come."   —Stephen King

Praise for ABYSS

"What *The Twilight Zone* was to TV in 1959, what *Night of the Living Dead* was to horror films in 1968, what Stephen King was to dark fiction in the mid-'70s—Abyss books will be to horror in the 1990s."
—Mark Hurst, editor of *The Golden Man*

"Gorgeously macabre eye-catching packages . . . I don't think Abyss could have picked a weirder, more accomplished novel [than *The Cipher*] to demonstrate by example what the tone and level of ambition of the new line might be."

—*Locus*

"A splendid debut." —*Rave Reviews*

"Dell is leading the way." —*Writers Digest*

"They are exploring new themes and dimensions in the horror field. My hat's off to Koja, Hodge, Dee, and Dillard, as the others forthcoming! And hats off to Dell Abyss!"

—Gary S. Potter, *The Point Beyond*

Turn the Page for More Quotes

MetaHorror

EDITED BY
DENNIS ETCHISON

A DELL BOOK

Published by
Dell Publishing
a division of
Bantam Doubleday Dell Publishing Group, Inc.
666 Fifth Avenue
New York, New York 10103

ACKNOWLEDGMENTS

"Blues and the Abstract Truth": Copyright © 1988 by Barry N. Malzberg and Jack Dann. First published in *Lord John Ten*. Reprinted by permission of the authors. "Are You Now?": Copyright © 1992 by Scott Edelman. "Stab": Copyright © 1992 by Lawrence Watt-Evans. "Mutilator": Copyright © 1992 by Richard Christian Matheson. "Martyrdom": Copyright © 1992 by The Ontario Review, Inc. "Briar Rose": Copyright © 1992 by Kim Antieau. "Replacements": Copyright © 1992 by Lisa Tuttle. "Ziggles": Copyright © 1992 by Donald R. Burleson. "End of the Line": Copyright © 1992 by Ramsey Campbell. "Did They Get You to Trade?": Copyright © 1992 by Karl Edward Wagner. "GIFCO": Copyright © 1992 by M. John Harrison. "The Properties of the Beast": Copyright © 1992 by Wilson & Neff, Inc. "In Praise of Folly": Copyright © 1992 by Thomas Tessier. "The Visit": Copyright © 1992 by William F. Nolan. "The Ring of Truth": Copyright © 1992 by George Clayton Johnson. "Nothing Will Hurt You": Copyright © 1992 by David Morrell. "Underground": Copyright © 1992 by Steve Rasnic Tem. "Bucky Goes to Church": Copyright © 1992 by Robert Devereaux. "Dumbarton Oaks": Copyright © 1992 Barry N. Malzberg. "Novena": Copyright © 1992 Chelsea Quinn Yarbro. "The Ghost Village": Copyright © 1992 by Peter Straub.

The trademark Dell® is registered in the U.S. Patent and Trademark Office.

ISBN: 0-440-20899-8

Printed in the United States of America

Published simultaneously in Canada

July 1992

10 9 8 7 6 5 4 3 2 1

OPM

TO

Ramsey, Jenny, Tamsin & Matthew Campbell

Contents

INTRODUCTION   xi

I Something Happened

BLUES AND THE ABSTRACT TRUTH
   Barry N. Malzberg and Jack Dann   3
ARE YOU NOW? *Scott Edelman*   12
STAB *Lawrence Watt-Evans*   24
MUTILATOR *Richard Christian Matheson*   28
MARTYRDOM *Joyce Carol Oates*   31
BRIAR ROSE *Kim Antieau*   54

II A Long Time Till Morning

REPLACEMENTS *Lisa Tuttle*   73
ZIGGLES *Donald R. Burleson*   94
END OF THE LINE *Ramsey Campbell*   109
DID THEY GET YOU TO TRADE?
   Karl Edward Wagner   134
GIFCO *M. John Harrison*   160
THE PROPERTIES OF THE BEAST
   Whitley Strieber   180

III   *Grateful Dead*

IN PRAISE OF FOLLY   *Thomas Tessier*   195
THE VISIT   *William F. Nolan*   215
THE RING OF TRUTH   *George Clayton Johnson*   222
NOTHING WILL HURT YOU   *David Morrell*   234
UNDERGROUND   *Steve Rasnic Tem*   260
BUCKY GOES TO CHURCH   *Robert Devereaux*   280

IV   *The Devil, Probably*

DUMBARTON OAKS   *Barry N. Malzberg*   301
NOVENA   *Chelsea Quinn Yarbro*   308
THE GHOST VILLAGE   *Peter Straub*   334

Introduction

"But you know, you still haven't explained why these writers have to write about crazy people doing terrible things!"

"You mean the externals they use?"

" 'Externals'?"

"You are objecting to their use of symbols."

"Symbols, are they?"

"Of course. Art is made out of symbols the way your body is made out of vital tissue."

"Then why have they got to use—?"

"Symbols of the grotesque and the violent? Because a book is short and a man's life is long."

"That I don't understand."

"Think it over."

"You mean it's got to be concentrated?"

"Exactly. The awfulness has to be compressed."

So wrote Tennessee Williams in his Introduction to *Reflections in a Golden Eye* by Carson McCullers. In this short novel, as in all her work, the theme is isolation and spiritual alienation. But Williams might as well have been writing about his own plays and stories, in which similar characters from the fringes of society are driven to seek love and redemption with tragic miscalculation. His people were cripples, convicts, prostitutes and psychopaths, hers deaf-mutes, hunchbacks, dwarfs and schizophrenics; for both writers the dramatic progression often led to an extreme moment of grotesque violence—murder, castration, suicide—or devastating loss and abandonment. In short, neither author had much to say that was reassuring.

And yet their works are among the most moving and memorable in modern literature. The characters remain indelible, their pain and suffering all too authentically human. That is because both writers possessed certain important insights into the darker aspects of life, and the skills to render the horror accessible and universal.

I mention this only to remind readers of the present book that the dark side is also frequently a subject for so-called serious fiction, and that such writing is part of a tradition that goes back farther and encompasses more than our specialized field cares to acknowledge. For with the popular success of the horror genre, some practitioners (and even critics, who ought to know better) seem to be asserting that they have invented a literature of violence, pain and the grotesque, and I find their naïveté, if that is what it is, hard to take.

From the supply side it makes perfect sense, of course, since specialization serves the economy. If you want a widget, you go to the place that has, or wants you to believe it has, an exclusive patent on that sort of thing. However, in our case this works to keep the consumer ignorant of not only Williams and McCullers but Andreyev's *The Seven Who Were Hanged*, Trumbo's *Johnny*

Got His Gun and so much more—a list of titles alone that is long enough to fill this volume. In other words, if you confine your reading to what is packaged for a specialty audience, you may have no idea what you are missing. The nature of genrefication is to exclude. It serves those with a vested interest, and that does not necessarily include readers.

I have done what I could to resist this tendency toward separatism in my own writing and editing, by presenting fiction that is for the most part nontraditional and eclectic, that cuts across categories. As I have said elsewhere, I have no desire to perpetuate arbitrary class distinctions. This position has sometimes worked to the detriment of my career. How easy it would have been to take stock of the marketplace and then direct my efforts to fulfilling expectations, like a good boy; how much easier, and yet how pointless. For better or worse, my aims are quite the opposite: to expand the boundaries of this insular camp by challenging its goals and techniques, urging it into riskier and more rewarding territory. Whether this radical approach will gain momentum or simply be defused and absorbed by an establishment that moves like a glacier under the weight of its own agenda remains to be seen. You who are reading these words years after the fact know the answer; I do not, and cannot predict.

MetaHorror, then, is designed not only to entertain but to redefine, to enrich and broaden a field that I hope will not exist indefinitely as a separate entity. The cross-pollination that comes from the breaking down of fences can only benefit those on both sides. For example, the field today has much more to offer than "the inadvertent packaging of violence and cruelty like attractive commercial products," to borrow a phrase from J.G. Ballard. It is, after all, a literature *in extremis;* its nominal focus is on matters of life and death.

Where did we come from?

What are we supposed to do while we're here?

What's next?

The rest is finally trivial, and a work of art, even more so than a life, is only a brief temporal experience.

You mean it's got to be concentrated?

Exactly. The awfulness has to be compressed.

The best "horror" writers, those who are doing something more than pandering to their audience, have a head start. They are predisposed to the Big Issues, foremost among them Death, the which than which there is no whicher, for there is only one certainty, and it is that we will die.

This is a volume of short stories, a form that encourages the compression or concentration. I prefer this form for such subject matter, to which it seems supremely well suited, though I have often been told that most readers prefer novels.° The implication is that novels are somehow better or more important. This contradicts what we know of modern life—with so many distractions competing for our attention that reading time is at a premium—as well as of art. Would anyone claim that poetry, with its extraordinary attention to the fine details of lan-

---

° Conventional wisdom has it that only novels sell—this despite the sales figures for Kirby McCauley's *Dark Forces* (1980), which has never gone out of print, not to mention Douglas Winter's *Prime Evil* or my own *Cutting Edge*, or the collections of Lovecraft and Bradbury and Oates and Salinger, et al. . . . These are exceptions, we are told, that prove the rule. But the rule is an exercise in circular logic. If only a relatively few copies of a book are printed because the sales department decides that it will not sell, and if these copies are then released with no effort at promotion, the outcome is a self-fulfilling prophecy. Who really made the choice?

guage, is inferior to prose? Or that a still photograph by Ansel Adams or Edward Steichen, reflecting so many creative decisions on the way to the gallery, is a lesser accomplishment than motion picture photography, which produces twenty-four images every second? Yet the assumption that more is better seems to dominate at the moment, at least in the publishing world. Why? One reason may be that few accomplished professional writers can afford to give much attention to short stories today, since the pay is hardly more than it was twenty or thirty years ago and certainly not enough to offset inflation. The result is that most of the short stories now appearing commercially in this field are the work of beginning authors still learning their craft and eager to sell at any price, or of the journeyman hacks, hustlers, charlatans, self-proclaimed celebrities and whores who are the perfect cultural artifacts of the Reagan-Bush era.

How anyone manages to become a fine short story writer against such odds is a mystery and a wonder to me. But it happens, as this book attests. I was surprised and heartened by the hundreds of manuscripts I received unsolicited in the mail. Apparently there is something of a renaissance going on out there, with dozens of small-press magazines now devoted to horror/dark fantasy fiction, as was previously the case with the science fiction, fantasy and mystery pulps, where the short story flourished for decades almost independently of the larger arena.

I have selected the very best for this book,° in addition

° My editor on this project, Jeanne Cavelos, deserves special thanks for bringing the most talented of these writers into the mass marketplace. Her remarkably courageous line, Abyss Books, appears to recognize no tradition but excellence.

to pieces from established writers whose careers occasionally overlap other fields. In keeping with my philosophy of presenting the most interesting work regardless of whether it fits any formula, I am including several stories that may reward readers in unexpected ways.

Scott Edelman's "Are You Now?" is not about witches or werewolves but a very real vampire, Tailgunner Joe McCarthy, the House Committee on Un-American Activities and the legacy of the Blacklist. Chelsea Quinn Yarbro's "Novena" addresses political terrorism in another (purposely unidentified) part of the world. Steve Rasnic Tem takes an unflinching look at AIDS, perhaps the single most virulent horror extant. The always surprising Joyce Carol Oates offers a savage fable about sexism and testosterone poisoning, among other things, from her forthcoming collection, *Tales of the Grotesque*. And Peter Straub's "The Ghost Village" is not about a small New England town but instead takes us back to Vietnam for a further excavation of the mystery that was only hinted at in "Blue Rose" and *Koko*.

This is only a sampling. There are other startlingly unconventional stories (every one of them a tour de force, I might add) by Ramsey Campbell, Karl Edward Wagner, David Morrell, Whitley Strieber, Lisa Tuttle, Barry N. Malzberg, Jack Dann, William F. Nolan, M. John Harrison, George Clayton Johnson, Richard Christian Matheson, Thomas Tessier, Lawrence Watt-Evans and Donald R. Burleson, as well as two shockingly beautiful pieces from writers who I must confess were unknown to me, Kim Antieau and Robert Devereaux.

I can take no credit for the amazingly high level of quality here—I am only the middleman. The praise belongs to these twenty extraordinary writers. Taken all together, their work is wonderfully varied in both content and style. As you know, I wouldn't have it any other way. All in all, the effect is curiously exhilarating, even uplifting, perhaps uniquely so among horror anthologies.

"Blissful is he," wrote Pindar of the initiation into the Eleusinian Mysteries, "who after having beheld this enters on the way beneath the earth. He knows the end of life as well as its divinely granted beginning."

Even the Spirit of truth; whom the world cannot receive, because it seeth him not, neither knoweth him: but ye know him; for he dwelleth with you, and shall be in you.

—John 14: 17–18

—Dennis Etchison

PART ONE
Something Happened

Blues and the Abstract Truth

Barry N. Malzberg and Jack Dann

 This isn't a spiritual or a prescription. It is, however, a precise diagnosis.

Bear with me. To explain and explain.

So this is how it happens: It's 1963, and you are with a girl named Mollie. John F. Kennedy was killed three weeks ago on the twenty-second (you can look that up), and LBJ is telling us that we will continue . . . continue with what? *"Danke Schoen"* and "Call Me Irresponsible" are playing day and night on the radio, God help us all. You went out to a college bar in Hempstead, Long Island, where they had a guy who played terrific jazz organ, and you picked up this girl who is a freshman at Hofstra and hails from upstate somewhere, maybe Cohoes. She says she was the *only* Jewish girl in her high school, and she makes every other word sound like "aou."

You've brought her back to your rented room on the second floor of Mr. Seitman's rooming house in East Meadow. You thought you'd have to sneak her into the house, but dictatorial, half-blind Mr. Seitman has gone out to play Bingo, and now you're safely behind closed

doors and impressing the hell out of Mollie with your
knowledge of jazz. You're studying music at the same
college she's attending (she's a theater major) and you
are absolutely certain that one day your name will be
listed in *Playboy*'s Annual Jazz Poll. And you're smart
because you're studying musicology; worse comes to
worse you can teach during the day and play in the clubs
all night. You have a 1–Y draft status because you have a
nervous stomach, and right now you're playing the classic
recording of Louis Armstrong's "A Monday Date,"
where he cuts in with a brilliant vocal rendition right
after his trumpet solo.

Mollie has been saying something like she's a virgin
and that she believes chastity to be the only valid option
for a woman in these times, although she's not opposed
to oral sex. Not *bitterly* opposed, anyway. In 1963, before
and after JFK's extraordinary run of bad luck, it was very
chic in college circles to be a virgin, even if you weren't,
so this is not surprising or objectionable.

"Sure," you agree, understandingly. "Sure."

She looks like she has nice breasts under her skin-pink
mohair sweater, and you are hopeful of seeing them naked soon, but (and this is the kicker) *you* are for sure the
virgin in this crowd. You don't know how to tell her this
or cover your inexperience.

Luckily, she knows that you want her and senses your
awkwardness, and she takes you off the hook easily by
making the first move.

The important thing is you are going to come.

Coming is definitely not a routine event in your life,
with a woman, that is to say. You have been thinking
about it all night. Now the black lights are on, and so is
the rotating sparkle globe you've installed on the ceiling,

and all your posters are glowing like neon: peace signs and astrological signs and all manner of fantastic beasts and nereids are suddenly brought to radioactive life while the room seems to twirl with every possible color. You and Mollie are smoking some unbelievably good Panama Red, which a buddy from your band has left with you to stash, and Mollie's clothes are off, almost all of them anyway, and you are so stoned-out now, the two of you, that you are confusing the music with your thoughts, but you're getting it right, sliding your fingers over her goosebumped skin, pushing and grinding against her, tasting her cigarette-soured mouth, thinking musically of this and that and nothing at all and that poor bastard JFK, fucked over now by a Texan and then you are

Transformed.

You are taken up and out, stoney-o, you are lifted like the bullets lifted JFK in the Continental, you are *yanked* and then . . .

You are bearing with me. I am doing what I can to explain. Over and over this goes, but it is vitally important to get it right; there is no understanding without memory, Mollie, and I can still almost feel your arms tight around me, and your tongue, and then

You are somewhere else.

You are *here.*

You are in this *place.*

It's like being six sheets to the wind and falling down the stairs.

It's like being jolted out of a deep sleep.

But here you are, young man, no transition, yank, bang, and you're in a large office separated into cubicles. The pushpin fabric of the five-feet-high cubicle dividers are powder blue, the commercial grade carpet a dismal brown. The dividers are on your right, and six people are crammed into the cubicles, one to a spot, phoning until suddenly they all turn to look at you, staring at you, waiting for an explanation. You must have made *some* kind of squawking noise, and who can blame you, what with Mollie's face taking up the field of vision one minute and now this . . .

You look at these six people, and what you really want to say is "What the fuck is going on here?" but that would expose your position immediately. It's not for nothing that you have a little sixties smarts, a residue of late-fifties cunning. You still have a buzz on from the grass (maybe that pot was *too* good), and you say, keeping your cool, adjusting yourself to the situation, "Back to work, gang. I just got a shock from the computer."

The word just comes to you. *Computer.* In 1963 that was a tech-word like astronaut and *New Frontier,* but you somehow had access to it. Be that as it may, you're still new to all this, and as you look at your hands, you can tell you have aged. You are not twenty, that is for sure. (Would that you were!) The hands are solid and bear the heavy imprints of time, and you know, now you know, that if you raise your hand to your face, you will feel texture, wrinkles, a bristly-stiff moustache.

Such is the rush of chronology. It is much more than a physical dislocation. Much has shifted.

But under the circumstances, you are amazingly calm.

You have had all of this latter time to think about that, of course; your calm, your amalgamation, your *synchronicity* with the impossible. Because, of course, you are of two parts: there is the strangling, stunned part of you that has come *here,* and there is that distant and cold part with which you have just merged; it is that distant "you" that knows about computers and the precise function of this office, which is to sell the unneeded to the unloved under the guise of love and need.

You're selling entertainment.

This is a cable television sales pit.

But the young, dislocated part of you asks how the fuck you got *here*, of all places. This is absolutely nowhere. You were supposed to become a goddamn musician. You should be out playing a gig at the Metropole or maybe The Half Note. At the very least you should be teaching, maybe not at Juilliard, but a decent university wouldn't have been out of the question. You certainly shouldn't be managing six part-time temporaries working on a Friday night. And your distant, older part—the self you are quickly coming to know, the self that has been ground smooth as a stone by forty-two years of experience and frustration—doesn't have a word to say to you.

Because you know, stoney-o. You *know*.

A young woman of about twenty says, "Yeah, I've had that happen to me too when I'm putting stuff into the computer. Shocks the hell right out of you, doesn't it?" she says crudely, smiling. She is swarthy and doe-eyed, and it is obvious that her long shock of white-blond hair is dyed, the ends burned by countless applications of bleach. The part of you with whom you have merged, the worn-out and cynical "you" who knows computer, understands that her name is Franny. She has been here for six months—a long time in the telemarketing game—and not so long ago you asked her to have lunch with you, but she said, "No married men, I've been through that door once and that was enough." Another humiliation, even though *you* are the boss, even though you are supposed to be in control.

So now you know of this and other incidents of this man's life. Although everything is new and terrifying, now you *know* that twenty-odd years have passed and that you have merged with an older self, but whether it is really you or a defeated facsimile, you are not yet sure. There is still a tendril of hope in your heart. After all, this couldn't really have happened to *you*. But with dislocation comes instant maturity, and you really do know the truth, just as you know that it would be a kind of death to accept it completely.

Slow and tentative, fast and desperate, you have the answers. And yet you have none.

The buzz from the grass has ebbed, the yanking will do that to you, and you are very cold and very clear on a level of functioning which is so precise that it is the most terrifying thing yet. You are out of control, and yet you are *in* control. JFK, you understand, has been dead for half as long as he was alive, and Phil Spector is gone, gone.

"Come on, now," you say, cheerlessly enough, as you are in a supervisory position, "let's get back to *work*," just as if you knew what you were doing here, as if you belonged (but you do! you do!), and you go back to the computer. As one part of you gazes in wonder, the other part is monitoring the telemarketing service reps (you also know they're called TSR's) and at the same time typing in names and addresses, answering Y or N to arcane questions coming up on the screen of the monitor, which reminds you of the fluorescent black light posters in your room in East Meadow, the very same room where moments before you were kissing and tasting Mollie's lips, which were sticky and deliciously red from a recent application of strawberry lipstick gloss.

Well, that is how it began. Or how it ended.

Outside looking in . . . inside looking out: my mantra.

One moment I'm twenty and trying to score, the next moment I'm forty-three and supervising cable sales in an upstate district which includes Mollie's home town of Cohoes. I am married to a woman named Ellen Aimes, my first and only marriage, her second. We have been married for eighteen years and have one daughter, Mollie. (Through the insane coincidence of a malign but stupid fate, Mollie was the name of Ellen's mother.) We have careful sex once a week, always in bed and in a missionary position. Ellen is a mathematics teacher at a junior high school. I make about $25,000 a year, she makes $30,000. I drive a 1983 Pontiac Catalina and collect bebop and modern jazz, although I don't play any gigs, nor do we have instruments in the house. I don't need eight hundred pounds of piano to remind me of my failure. In the years since my . . . merging, return, amalgamation, whatever you wish to call it, I have had three adulterous involvements for a total of eight fornications, none of them particularly successful, all of them with younger co-workers. Ellen knows nothing of this, nor does she know that I was recently yanked out of my past and spilled into my future, all middle having been taken away from me.

But I know that if I were to tell this to anyone—anyone at all—I would be in severe trouble. Life would tremble. Life would topple. Life would become dangerous and ill-considered. I cannot manage this. I have bills to pay. I have a life, yes, a life, to lead. Mollie needs a father. She is eleven years old and is beginning to hate me in a healthy, bored sort of way.

How, I ask you, can I tell anyone of this? How, outside of this recollection, can I make my fate, my condition, clear?

Only this: once I was twenty, and the shot that killed JFK somehow seemed to have catapulted me into my life; all the years of outside looking in, and now I was going to be on the inside myself and then, and then—

And then another shot, another catapult, and I am forty, married, a father, an unsuccessful adulterer (although perhaps I should count it a success that I haven't been caught), a panting, heavy, sad case of a man on the lip of middle age, and I now *am* on the inside looking out. Evicted and entrapped without a single moment, a single moment in the middle.

But I do have a facility for amalgamation. I could have just as easily lost it in the first moment of middle age, but instead I interfaced with the future and saved it.

Interface . . .

And I pick up a work order for a sale to a new subscriber in Cohoes (which precipitates all of this, you understand) and I just stare at it and stare at it.

Is that you, Mollie?

Is that you, I see, first name, middle name, new last name? Is that what I have made of you? A name and address on a sales card?

I'll never call you. It would be a disaster.

I will call you. It will be a disaster.

I'll never call you. It would be a disaster.

o   o   o

You think of calling her, don't you, stoney-o?

If you do—oh, you poor bastard—if you do, *will it take you back*?

Will it will it will it?

———————

Barry N. Malzberg is the author of many short stories; novels such as *The Destruction of the Temple, The Cross of Fire, Guernica Night, Herovit's World, The Falling Astronauts, Revelations, Beyond Apollo, The Remaking of Sigmund Freud;* and the nonfiction *The Engines of the Night.* He recently completed his eighty-third book.

Jack Dann is the author of the novels *Junction, Starhiker* and *The Man Who Melted,* and the collection *Timetipping.* He is the editor of *Wandering Stars* and *More Wandering Stars,* and co-editor of a series of anthologies with Gardner Dozois, as well as *In the Field of Fire* with his wife, Jeanne Van Buren Dann. His latest novel is *The Path of Remembrance.*

Are You Now?

Scott Edelman

 ASTIGMATISM: When he looks back on his life, it's as if somebody has taken away his glasses. Or perhaps, as he'd decided was more apt, removed his appendix. As a lexicographer who feels most defined by his work, the loss of that above all things would render his life meaningless. So as he contemplates his friends and his family, he fears that they would cut their consciences to fit this year's fashions, and life's purpose seems as absent as Larry Parks's career, or as heavy as the hand which knocks when wrapped around a subpoena.

DISBELIEF: They could not understand why he began asking them, "What would you do? What would you do?" It has suddenly become very important what they would do. He is not sure why, and when he tries to explain this to them, to transform his anger and ambivalence into words, he fails. He earns his living at words, words are his life, and yet he cannot make the words perform for him the way they should when it matters most. He very much wants them all to know him fully, and when he tries to open his soul to them, their countenances grow more confused instead of less. Sometimes he worries that these looks of confusion are not because he has failed to make them understand, but because he has succeeded.

OBFUSCATION: In his dreams, the people he knows are usually friendly witnesses. The setting is always the same. He cannot remember when he last had a dream unconnected with this obsession. A dream set at work, or at school, or at home. He is not quite sure he ever had such dreams. All he knows is that when he sees these people these recent nights, their brows are furrowed, their faces are washed clean of their sins by impossible volumes of sweat, and names are named. Most names are unrecognizable, drowned out by the murmurs and astonished gasps of the crowd. The only name he can consistently make out is his own. *Is that the regard in which I am held?* he thinks as he dreams. *I suppose it could be worse.* Yet at other times those faces belong to the ones with gavels in hands, waiting to silence him even as they invited him to speak. Waking, he is never quite sure where each belongs, inquisitor or willing victim. But none of them ever refuses to cooperate, damning the cost. And that disappoints him.

RESEARCH: A word means what he says it will mean, but people never do.

HISTORY: He tries to remember a time when this was not so, but no matter how hard he focuses his will, he cannot. It would be easier to find a spool of microfilm in a pumpkin patch. He cannot remember a time without anxiety, without fear, even though he is sure such a time must have existed. Wasn't there a time when calm pervaded his life, when he would go to his office along with the rest of the dictionary's research staff and confidently carve out of the chaos of history the lineage of each present word? Wasn't there a time when the hunt so filled his life that there was no remaining moment for his obsession to inhabit? Now fear has joined him as a fellow traveler. His life has escaped him the way dreams sometimes did, crumbling under his examination. He cannot honestly be sure he's lived, or whether he had sprung full-blown into existence a month before, his obsession handed to him as a newly minted membership card to life.

E P I P H A N Y : *Decades pass, and still they refuse to sit next to each other,* he'd thought, as he watched the documentary on television. *Still they do not forgive.* How wonderful it must be to have such a passion! Winning a cause to call one's own is not so easily won as the cause itself. He did not know which saddened him more, whether he had made no true friends, or had picked up no lifelong enemies. He began to jiggle his life as one jiggled a favorite childhood toy, eager to learn, as if it were a complete mystery to him, into which holes each he knew would fall.

E N V E L O P E S : When his interoffice mail arrives that morning, it is as if delivered from another time. The envelopes are covered with the brown stain of age. The package of galleys from typesetting is heavy in his hands. Does it contain the transcripts of his testimony? This envelope. Is it Robert Rich's Academy Award, ready to be placed into the hands of Deborah Kerr? He opens them, finding only galleys and memos and mundane incoming mail, and he is deeply disappointed.

ACCUSATION: It was three o'clock in the morning when he first demanded of his wife what she would do if. She rolled over towards him groggily. "I'm the one who's supposed to do this," she said. "Wake you in the middle of the night. Ask you things you're too dazed to understand. What are you talking about?" He felt too silly to repeat his question, and so told her he guessed that it didn't matter.

STARS: In an earlier time he might have wondered who would have joined him in wearing a yellow star, but it is a decade later, no, no, almost five decades later, he reminds himself. This is another time, another way. A peculiarly American way. It was right that he should be asking himself this question instead of any other.

TIMING: A teacher at school might tell his daughter and all the other students to report should they ever see any "strange" books or magazines when visiting at the friends of their parents, with the obvious implication that they should keep a careful eye on their parents as well. How would she react? Would she report that he read a liberal newspaper, occasionally reciting passages out loud from the editorials? That he was known to snort when he heard the president speak on television? That his grandparents still lived in a foreign country? When would she know love? When would she learn loyalty? Would she turn her back on him innocently? Or with a sly smile? He did not doubt the fact that she would betray him. He only wondered how and when.

SIGNIFICANCE: Is his wife sleeping with his best friend? That question no longer worries him. Once, upon taking the measure of each possible sign of what he believed to be their illicit relationship, he wove elaborate histories. Out of each stray hair, each possible scent of aftershave, grew passionate encounters rivaling any provided by Hollywood. But now his suspicions and self-tortures are of a different kind. It is no longer his wife's breast around which he imagines his friend's hand, but instead a microphone stand. It is no longer his wife uttering verbal caresses back to that friend that fills him with fear, but instead those same lips spouting the syllables of his own name. Adultery has become a lesser grade of betrayal.

SYNCHRONIZATION: He began to curse his time. He prayed for the return of a repressive age such as that. He toyed with changing his voter registration to that of another party to quicken its onset, abandoning that idea only when he realized that he did not know whether voting Republican or Democrat was likelier to bring back the day. He would do anything he could to hasten it, but cursed himself for being unable to draw conclusions of action. He did not believe he would ever know his own worth without that pressure to test him. "Are you now?" they would ask him when that day came. And what would he say? What would any of them say?

KINESCOPES: When the documentary was repeated, he was ready for it. Sitting in his living room, binoculars held tightly to his eyes, he thought the grainy figures in the background seemed familiar. Was that his mother leaning forward to whisper in Roy Cohn's ear? She could have been there, she could. He strained to make sense of the phosphor dots, but the camera cut away too quickly. He heard his wife come into the room, but he did not turn towards her. Sudden blackness stole his view of the screen. He waited one beat. Two. "Excuse me," he finally said, continuing to stare through the eyepieces. Blackness continued for another moment. He heard a click, and when his view of the television screen returned, it was to the sight of a Road Runner cartoon.

QUESTIONS: A co-worker casually asks him who he had lunch with the day before, and he suddenly feels threatened. On the surface, it seems such a small thing to ask, and yet, underneath, what were the man's motives? This is America, land of free association. He could have lunch with whomever he damned well pleased. What business is it of his! How dare he have to suffer such an interrogation! He notices the co-worker staring at him uneasily. "Are you all right?" he is asked. "I plead the Fifth," he says. The man walks away, nodding his head.

PERSPECTIVE: *Where am I in all of this?* he begins to ask. The dreams come so frequently now that the odor of the smokefilled room lingers in his nostrils throughout the day. Appearances are made by all the supporting cast of his life. And as he watches them testify or urge testimony, he tries to ascribe meaning to his point of view. Just where is he? *Give me my place.* Now he always wakes just when he is about to sense his seat. It seems important that he know where his dreams situate him, but they have turned into fellow travelers, and will not grant him that yet.

LIST: When the woman slides him the file folder across the long table, he opens it with trembling fingers. A sick feeling rises in his stomach as he scans the list of names inside. He slowly begins nodding his head. "I can't go through with it," he says. "I didn't expect to be pressed into doing this so soon," he says. His voice trails off nervously. "But I can't. I can't tell you a damned thing about these people. I won't. It's just . . . it's just not American to do things this way. I resent the whole concept of this list." He crumples the page into a ball. "I reject this committee. I reject . . ." His head begins to ache, and when he looks around the table, he sees that he is surrounded by his co-workers for their weekly meeting. He flattens the sheet out before him. The list is of slang words the inclusion of which in the latest edition is to be decided. He excuses himself and leaves the room. Part of him expects reporters to leap at him on the other side of the door to barrage him with questions he cannot answer.

MASK: He holds the cigarette between his lips gingerly, attempting to incorporate its power into his persona. Murrow had smoked. To him, that is like saying God smoked. The match, when he finally strikes it, shakes in his hand. He has never attempted to smoke before. After half an hour, he gives up, the cigarette still unlit, its tip and several of his fingers singed.

BLACKLIST: The door that clicks shut behind him does so quietly, but to him its sound is deafening. "Perhaps we should have had this talk earlier," says his boss. They are alone. His boss gestures towards a chair; he sits in it uncomfortably. "I've been hearing stories—" "Lies!" he says, jumping up before his boss can continue. "Lies and innuendoes! I don't know who's been telling you this, but I won't put up with these sorts of smear tactics, I won't—" He suddenly stops and looks down at his hands. "I'm sorry," he says. His boss places a hand on his shoulder. "I was going to suggest a short vacation," his boss whispers, "but perhaps a leave of absence would be a better idea. I think you should . . . you should see a doctor." *They are trying to silence me,* he thinks.

AUTOBIOGRAPHY: He has a lot of time on his hands now. He was never much of a reader, but now the books pile high, surrounding him like the walls of a federal prison in Ashland, Kentucky, say, or perhaps Danbury, Connecticut. He had not known there were that many books. He had not known there were that many survivors still telling tales, still incapable of forgetting. It's still not over. All these decades later and it still isn't over. *Is anyone keeping score?* he wonders. *Or are these people just talking to themselves?* He reads every word as if it details the story of his life, trying on with the tenacity of a tailgunner every gesture, every action, every statement as if it were his own, regardless of the side of the issue on which it fell. He struggles to find a comfortable fit, but all the roles he plays fit him uncomfortably, like shoes that had been long worn by another.

HORROR: When he peers down into his daughter's crib, Roy Cohn's cancerous face peers up from beneath the covers. Intense hatred overwhelms him when he spies its tumorous glory. Even knowing that Cohn finally died of AIDS does not satisfy that hatred, for here he is before him, is he not? He is amazed that his mind can comprehend the fact of that duplicitous death, and the evil eyes glaring at him through heavy lids. He notices that his fingers itch, and his breathing has quickened. He balls his hands into fists. He jumps nervously at a noise behind him. Is it the junior senator from Wisconsin? No, it is his wife at the nursery door. "What were you thinking?" she asks. She is staring at his hands. He cannot think of how to tell her, and responds with a shrug. She takes his hand and slowly pulls him from the room, closing the door silently behind him.

REINCARNATION: He has purchased a videotape recorder and made a tape of the documentary. Thank God for PBS and their endless repeats. He sits in the living room, the machine automatically set to rewind each time the program ends and then begin running anew. He watches it continually, stopping only when hunger or exhaustion bids him. He usually returns quickly, a chunk of food still being swallowed, the crust of sleep still in the corners of his eyes. He no longer uses binoculars; they'd kept him too distant, he'd decided. Instead, he keeps his nose pressed to the screen. He is searching for himself. His eyes ache from the strain. The tape has gone so fuzzy from repeated playing that he is no longer sure if the committee is truly on the screen before him, or if he is taking some sort of insane Rorschach test. His wife enters the room, cursing. She shoves him from in front of the television. She jabs the eject button and pulls the tape from the cartridge, scattering it about the room like confetti. He tries to stop her with gestures, but feels he dare not touch her. "Pay attention to me!" she shouts. "Enough about what you'd have done back then. Pay attention to how you perform now!" She throws the cartridge into his lap as hard as she can and stalks from the room. After a moment, he slowly begins rolling the tape back into the cartridge.

R E C E S S : As she hides from him in the darkness, he feels that she would be as hidden from him were it the middle of the day. He finds it hard to believe the words she is saying to him from a mattress-length away. "What do you mean, going?" he says. Her answer makes him wish she'd pled the Fifth. "I don't feel safe here any-more. If it was just me . . . but we have a daughter now. I just can't risk it anymore." He wants to shout at her, to demand that she tell who put her up to this. *Have you no decency?* he thinks. Tell me who is smearing me, he wants to say. No, that's not it, help me, he wants to say. There is so much he wants to say. Instead, saying nothing, side by side, they lie awake, until, just as the sun begins to rise, he falls asleep, leaving her to stare at the cracked ceiling alone.

A N S W E R : As his sweat burns his eyes the crowd that hems him in appears to be melting. Their questions make him feel as if he were the one melting. It wasn't the hot lights nor the stinging smoke, but the damned questions. Are you now? Have you ever been? Do you remember? When did you first meet? Were you present? Why didn't you? The questions come so fast there is no space between for him to answer. Panic grips him as the burning sweat continues to drip from his brow, squeezing like water from his sponge of a brain. Who else was? How is it that? Didn't you realize at the time? Finally he can take it no longer and storms from the room, his inquisitors chasing him. He runs into the bathroom and slams the door behind him. He presses a shoulder against the door to keep them out. Their questions continue to slip through under the door like unwanted mail.

APOTHEOSIS: The water, when he splashes it on his face, he would swear it, sizzles against his skin. Awake now, he knows he is in his own bathroom, having run from a dream. His wife sleeps in the next room, and yet . . . still he hears the murmuring questions from the other side of the door. Staring into the mirror, he does not recognize the features he sees there even though they are his own. As he continues to look into the glass, smoke rises from where each droplet fell, and those features begin to change. He begins to recognize himself. That porcine face. The stubble. It's you, Joe, isn't it, that's who I would have been, isn't it? A shiver of horror passes through him, quickly fading to be replaced by a shiver of joy. He wipes his face dry, and prepares himself to step through the door and face his questioners. *At last I know who I am.*

———————————————

Scott Edelman's short stories and poetry have appeared in *The Twilight Zone, Fantasy Book, Amazing Stories* and *Isaac*

Asimov's Science Fiction Magazine. A novel, *The Gift*, was published in 1990. He has written for weird comics (*House of Mystery, House of Secrets*, etc.) and for the television series *Tales From the Darkside*. More stories and novels are forthcoming.

Stab

Lawrence Watt-Evans

You still remember it, don't you?

You remember the feel of the knife going in.

You remember the pressure on your forearm as you pulled him to you. You remember the smell of his breath, and of his sweat, and the feel of the rough cloth of his shirt. You remember the sound of his breathing as he struggled. You remember the firm, hard grip of the knife in your hand, your brother's fancy military knife that you borrowed without asking, and how it pulled the skin tight across the insides of your knuckles as you shoved it up through the shirt, under the ribs, into the flesh. You remember the resistance, how you had to push harder than you expected.

You did, though, you pushed hard, as hard as you could, and the blade went in, and his breath suddenly all came out in a gasp, and his face came forward, smacked against your shoulder, his cheek brushing yours, and you felt his body tense, and then relax. You smelled urine, and when you felt the moisture you realized you had your leg between his, pressed into his crotch. You heard his own knife fall.

You remember the fear, the shame, the confusion, and the rush of adrenaline you felt. You remember the weird relief, relief you didn't understand.

Then you let go of him, and stepped away, and pulled the knife out. He fell, a dead weight, and his arms and legs flopped against you and almost knocked you over, and you stepped back.

He fell to the ground and didn't move, and you turned and ran, your shoes slapping the pavement. You were overwhelmed by terror, by the enormity of what you had done, the knowledge that you had taken a human life, the certainty that you would be caught and punished.

But you weren't, were you?

You never were. You were just a scared kid in a gang fight, and they never caught you, never knew who did it.

And that fall you went back to school. The next June you graduated, with a scholarship nobody expected you to get, and you went off to college, and you did fine there, got your engineering degree. You were quiet, never bothered anyone, never went back to the old gang —you remembered it all, but you didn't want to think about it.

So you didn't think about it.

You thought about stresses and linkages and tensile strengths, and about the people around you who had never fought in the streets, the girls who were more impressed with your GPA than your scars.

You thought about the future, now that you knew you'd have one.

You went for your MBA and you got it, and you got a job, and a promotion, and you took women to bed and finally married one.

And you never mentioned the gang fight and the knife

going in and the other boy falling to the ground in his own blood. You never thought about it.

But you always remembered it.

And your wife had a baby, and you argued, and she left, taking the mewling little brat with her, and you turned your energy into the company.

You fought. You schemed. You did everything you could to bring in money, to make the company a success, to let everyone know you were bringing in money. You had power.

And before all that long, you had the company.

CEO, they call you. Sir, they say when they speak to you. You have women—not cheap floozies, not confused college girls, not your wife fighting you for control, but sleek young women who want to be close to power and wealth. Men respect you, fear you. You eat well, eat anything you want at the best restaurants. You drink fine brandy. You sleep on the finest linens, cool and smooth. Anything you want, you can buy.

But you still remember it.

And now you do think about it. You have time now. You look back and remember, and sometimes you lie awake sweating as you recall it all.

You killed a boy.

You committed a murder, and got away with it. No one could ever suspect you now.

And if they did suspect, what could they do?

You got away with murder.

You lie there, remembering the feel of the knife going in, and you smile.

You know that you have something the men around you, the men you compete with, don't have. You have that knowledge in you, that calm certainty that you have the ruthlessness you need to destroy your enemies. You've killed. You could do it again.

It gives you the edge, doesn't it?

You remember the feel of the knife going in.

And you know that you will never again experience anything that powerful.

You know that that murder, at the age of seventeen, was the high point of your life.

You know that everything since has been basking in the afterglow.

And you lie there on your fine smooth sheets, the woman beside you stroking your cheek, and you remember the feel of the knife going in.

———

Lawrence Watt-Evans is the author of *Shining Steel, Denner's Wreck, Nightside City, The Cyborg and the Sorcerers* and other science fiction novels, and the "Ethshar" and "Lords of Dûs" fantasy series. His short stories appear in *Analog, Amazing Stories, The Magazine of Fantasy & Science Fiction* and *Isaac Asimov's Science Fiction Magazine.* He is a Hugo Award winner. Latest: a horror novel, *The Nightmare People.*

Mutilator

Richard Christian Matheson

 DIARY NOTES

October 14

I am bleeding. I can hear it. I listen until the red noise stops. The blood needs rest.

October 16

Someone hurt me today. They always hurt me. They don't care.

October 22

I hate everyone. I try so hard. It's time to bleed.

October 29

Midnight. I am lonely. I press the knife into my skin. The blade is cool. I let it wade through flesh. Close my eyes. Lean back. Warm surf breaks on my skin. I am safe.

October 30

I am sad. I hate myself. I want to sleep. How did this happen to me?

November 5

Another horrible day. I wait for the blood to seep, to visit me, in daylight. It wanders out, afraid of light. But I know it craves my attention. Wants companionship. I smear it on my palm. Smile down at it. Move it around; it likes to play. Before it gets sleepy and dies, I lick it up. Allow it to head in again. Crawl down my throat, into dark pipelines; go home.

November 11

I can't be with anyone. Don't want them to see my body. The scarred curves, burned angles. My secret memories. I am happy with my cuts and sores. I listen to the skin heal.

November 17

I am angry. I pry my cuts open. I need company. The blood comes out to greet me. Its slow shyness makes me impatient. I squeeze the skin. Peel scabs off. Stand in front of the mirror. Watch myself turn red. I sleep naked on clean sheets. I feel the soft suction of cotton drinking. I sleep.

November 24

They hurt me again, today. Why do they hurt me?

December 10

I burned myself with chemicals, again. Let the liquid burn my arms and genitals. My face. It soothes me. Hisses like rain. The odor is a perfume. For Christmas I know what I want.

December 24
Christmas eve. I wrapped my presents to myself. The holidays are a good time. A time to not count on family or friends. They never care. Never call. Never loved me. They reject me. Why don't others love me like I love myself?

December 25
New scissors. They snip through skin, dig for bone. Shiny hunters, stalking tissue and liquid. I open my other present. An iron. I plug it in and listen to the metal tick. I strip and press it to my leg, melting flesh. Sealing out the world. I would like to have friends. It doesn't matter. I'm safe and warm. It's Christmas and I am bleeding. No one understands me. No one ever did. But I am safe. And I am warm. I realize how lucky I am. In a world filled with cruelty and misery I'm never alone. Never in pain.

January 2
A new year. I listen to my skin heal. I wait to bleed.

———————————

Richard Christian Matheson is the author of science fiction, fantasy, horror and mystery short stories as well as hundreds of hours of television scripts and several feature films. The collection *Scars and Other Distinguishing Marks* was published in 1987. A new novel, *Created By,* is a thriller set against a show business background.

Martyrdom

Joyce Carol Oates

 1.
A sleek tiny baby he was, palpitating with life
and appetite as he emerged out of his
mother's birth canal, and perfectly formed:
twenty miniature pink toes intact, and the near-micro-
scopic nails already sharp; pink-whorled tiny ears; the
tiny nose quivering, already vigilant against danger. The
eyes were relatively weak, in the service of detecting motion rather than figures, textures, or subtleties of color.
(In fact, he may have been color blind. And since this
deficiency was never to be pointed out to him, he was
arguably "blind" in a secondary, metaphysical sense.) His
baby's jaws, lower and upper, were hinged with muscle,
and unexpectedly strong. And the miniature teeth set in
those jaws—needle-sharp, and perfectly formed. (More
of these teeth, soon.) And the quizzical curve of the tail,
pink, hairless, thin as a mere thread. And the whiskers,
no more than a tenth of an inch long, yet quivering, and
stiff too, like the bristles of a tiny tiny brush.

2.

What a beautiful baby *she* was, Babygirl the loving parents called her, conceived in the heat of the most tender yet the most erotic love, fated to be smothered with love, devoured with love, an American Babygirl placed with reverent fingers in her incubator. Periwinkle blue eyes, fair silk-soft blond hair, perfect rosebud lips, tiny pug nose, uniform smoothness of the Caucasian skin. A call went out to nursing mothers in ghetto neighborhoods requesting milk from their sweet heavy balloon-breasts, mother's milk for pay, since Babygirl's own mother failed to provide milk of the required richness. Her incubator filtered our contaminated air and pumped pure oxygen into her lungs. She had no reason to wail like other infants, whose sorrow is so audible and distracting. In her incubator air humid and warm as a tropical rain forest Babygirl thrived, glowed, prospered, *grew*.

3.

And how *he* grew, though nameless even to his mother! How *he* doubled, trebled, quadrupled *his* weight, within days! Amid a swarm of siblings he fended his way, shrewd and driven, ravenous with hunger. Whether he was in the habit of gnawing ceaselessly during his waking hours, not only edible materials but such seemingly inedible materials as paper, wood, bone, metal of certain types and degrees of thinness, etc., because he was ravenously hungry or because he simply liked to gnaw, who can say? It is a fact that his incisors grew at the rate of between four and five inches a year, so he had to grind them down to prevent their pushing up into his brain and killing him. Granted the higher cognitive powers generated by the cerebral cortex, he might have speculated upon his generic predicament: is such behavior voluntary, or involuntary; where survival is an issue, what *is* compulsion; under the spell of Nature, who can behave *unnaturally*?

4.
Babygirl never tormented herself with such questions. In her glass-topped incubator she grew ounce by ounce, pound by pound, feeding, dozing, feeding, dozing—no time at all before her dimpled knees pressed against the glass, her breath misted the glass opaque. Her parents were beginning to be troubled by her rapid growth, yet proud too of her rosy female beauty, small pointed breasts, curving hips, dimpled belly and buttocks and crisp cinnamon-colored pubic hair, lovely thick-lashed eyes with no pupil. Babygirl had a bad habit of sucking her thumb so they painted her thumb with a foul-tasting fluorescent-orange iodine mixture and observed with satisfaction how she spat, and gagged, and writhed in misery, tasting it. One mild April day, a winey-red trail of clotted blood was detected in the incubator, issuing from between Babygirl's plump thighs, we were all quite astonished and disapproving but what's to be done? Babygirl's father said, Nature cannot be overcome, nor even postponed.

5.
So many brothers and sisters he had, an alley awash with their wriggling bodies, a warehouse cellar writhing and squeaking with them, he sensed himself multiplied endlessly in the world, thus not likely to die *out*. For of all creaturely fears it is believed the greatest is the fear of, not merely dying, but dying *out*. Hundreds of thousands

of brothers and sisters related to him by blood which was a solace, yes but also a source of infinite anxiety for all were ravenous with hunger, the *squeak! squeak! squeak!* of hunger multiplied beyond accounting. He learned, on his frantic clicking toenails, to scramble up sheer verticals, to run to the limits of his endurance, to tear out the throats of his enemies, to leap, to fly—to throw himself, for instance, as far as eleven feet into space, from one city rooftop to an adjacent rooftop—thus thwarting his pursuers. He learned to devour, when necessary, the living palpitating flesh of prey while on the run. The *snap!* of bones radiated pleasure through his jaws, his small brain thrummed with happiness. He never slept. His heartbeat was fever-rapid at all times. He knew not to back himself into a corner, nor to hide in any space from which there was no way out. He was going to live forever!—then one day his enemies set a trap for him, the crudest sort of trap, and sniffing and squeaking and quivering with hunger he lunged for the moldy bread-bait and a spring was triggered and a bar slammed down across the nape of his neck snapping the delicate vertebrae and near severing his poor astonished head.

6.
They lied to her, telling her it was just a birthday party—for the family. First came the ritual bath, then the anointing of the flesh, the shaving and plucking of certain undesirable hairs, the curling and crimping of certain desirable hairs, she fasted for forty-eight hours, she was made to gorge herself for forty-eight hours, they scrubbed her tender flesh with a wire brush, they rubbed pungent herbs into the wounds, the little clitoris was sliced off and tossed to the clucking hens in the yard, the

now-shaven labia were sewed shut, the gushing blood
was collected in a golden chalice, her buckteeth were
forcibly straightened with a pliers, her big hooked nose
was broken by a quick skilled blow from the palm of a
hand, the bone and cartilage grew back into more desirable contours, then came the girdle-brassiere to cinch in
Babygirl's pudgy twenty-eight-inch waist to a more desirable seventeen-inch-waist, so her creamy hips and thighs
billowed out, so her gorgeous balloon-breasts billowed
out, her innards were squeezed up into her chest cavity,
she had difficulty breathing at first, and moist pink-tinted
bubbles issued from her lips, then she got the knack of it,
reveling in her classic "hour-glass" figure and new-found
power over men's inflammable imaginations. Her dress
was something fetching and antique, unless it was something sly and silky-slinky, a provocative bustline, a snug-
fitting skirt, she was charmingly hobbled as she walked
her dimpled knees chafing together and her slender ankles quivering with the strain, she wore a black lace gar-
ter belt holding up her gossamer-transparent silk stockings with straight black seams, in her spike-heeled
pointed-toed white satin shoes she winced a bit initially
until she got the knack and very soon she got the knack,
the shameless slut. Giggling and brushing and making
little fluttery motions with her hands, wriggling her fat
ass, her nipples hard and erect as peanuts inside the
sequined bosom of her dress, her eyes glistened like
doll's eyes of the kind that shut when the doll's head is
thrust back, the periwinkle-blue had no pupils to distract, Babygirl was not one of those bitches always thinking plotting calculating how to take advantage of some
poor jerk, she came from finer stock, you could check
her pedigree, there were numerals tattooed into her

flesh (the inside of the left thigh), she could be neither
lost nor mislaid, nor could the cunt run away, and lose
herself in America the way so many have done, you read
about it all the time. They misted her in the most exquisite perfume—one whiff of it, if you were a man, a normal man, there's a fever in your blood only one act can
satisfy, they passed out copies of the examining physi-
cian's report, she *was* clean of all disease venereal or
otherwise, she *was* a virgin, no doubt of that though trip-
ping in her high heels and grinning and blushing peering
through her fingers at her suitors she sometimes gave the
wrong impression, poor Babygirl: those lush crimson lips
of such fleshy contours they suggested, even to the most
gentlemanly and austere among us, the fleshy vaginal labia.

7.
Filthy vermin! obscene little beast! they were furious at
him for *being* as if, incarnated thus, he'd chosen his species, and took a cruel pleasure in carrying the seeds of
typhus in his guts, bubonic plague virus in his saliva,
poisons of all kinds in his excrement. They wanted him
dead, they wanted all of his kind extinct, nothing less
would satisfy them firing idle shots at the town dump as,
squeaking in terror, he darted from one hiding place to
another, reeking garbage exploding beside him as the
bullets struck, they blamed him for the *snap!* of poultry
bones in predators' jaws, they had no evidence but they
blamed him for a litter of piglets devoured alive, and
what happened to that baby in the ground-floor apartment on Eleventh Street left unattended for twenty minutes when its mother slipped out to buy cigarettes and
milk at the 7-Eleven store a block away—*Oh my God!*

Oh oh oh don't tell me, I don't want to know—and a fire
that started and blazed out of control in the middle of a
frigid January night because insulation around some
electrical wires had been gnawed through, but how was
that his fault, how *his,* where was the proof amidst hundreds of thousands of his siblings, each possessed by a
voracious hunger and a ceaseless need to gnaw? Pursuing
him with rocks, a gang of children, whooping and yodel-
ing across the rooftops injuring him as in desperation he
scrambled up the side of a brick wall, yes but he managed to escape even as his toenails failed him and he
slipped, fell—fell sickeningly into space—down an airshaft—five storeys—to the ground below—high-pitched
squeaky shrieks as he fell—plummeted downward
thrashing and spiraling in midair, red eyes alight in terror
for such creatures know terror though they do not know
the word "terror," they embody terror, that's to say em-
body it, though every cell in his body strained to live,
every luminous particle of his being craved immortality,
even as you and me. (Of the suffering of living things
through the millennia, it is wisest not to think, Darwin
advises.) So he fell off the edge of the roof, down the
airshaft, the equivalent of approximately one hundred
seventy times his size measured from nose to rump (but
excluding his tail which, uncurled, straight and stiff, is
longer than his length—eight inches!) so we were watching smiling in the knowledge that the dirty little bugger
would be squashed flat, thus imagine our indignation and
outrage to see him land on his feet! a tiny bit shaken, but
uninjured! untouched! a fall that would have broken every bone in our goddam bodies and *he* shakes his whiskers and furls up his tail and scampers away! And the
rancid night parted like black water to shield him.

8.

It was the National Guard Armory, rented for the night at discount price, a slow season, and in the cavernous smoke-filled gallery fresh-groomed men sat attentive in rows of seats, their faces indistinct as dream-faces, their eyes vague and soft as molluscs focussed on Babygirl, fingers fat as cigars poking in their crotches, genitalia heavy as giant purplish-ripe figs straining at the fabric of their trousers. Yes but these are carefully screened and selected gentlemen. Yes but these are serious fellows. Most of them pointedly ignore the vendors hawking their wares in the Armory, now's hardly the time for beer, Coke, hotdogs, caramel corn, the men's eyes are hotly fixed on Babygirl my God get a load of *that*. To find a worthy wife in today's world is no simple task. An old-fashioned girl is the object of our yearning, the girl that married old dead dad is our ideal, but where is she to be found?—in today's debased world. So Babygirl tossed her shimmering cinnamon curls and prettily pouted, revealed her dazzling white smile, in a breathy singsong she recited the sweet iambic verse she had composed for this very occasion. So Babygirl twirled her gem-studded baton. Flung her baton spinning up into the rafters of the Armory where at the apogee of its flight it seemed for a magic instant to pause, then tumbled back down into Babygirl's outstretched fingers—the rows of staring seats burst into spontaneous applause. So Babygirl curtsied, blushed, ducked her head, paused to straighten the seams of her stockings, adjusted an earring, adjusted her girdle that cut so deeply into the flesh of her thighs there would be angry red indentations there for days, Babygirl giggled and blew kisses, her lovely skin all aglow, as the auctioneer strutted about hamming it up with his hand-

held microphone, Georgie Bick's his name, cocky and
paunchy in his tux with the red cummerbund, Hey
whooee do I hear 5,000, do I hear 8,000, gimme 10–, 10–,
10,000, in a weird high-pitched incantatory voice so mesmerizing that bidding begins at once, a Japanese gentleman signaling a bid by touching his left earlobe, a
swarthy turbaned gentleman signaling with a movement
of his dark-glittering eyes, Hey whooee do I hear 15,000,
do I hear 20,000, do I hear 25–, 25–, 25,000, thus a
handsome moustached Teutonic gentleman cannot resist
Yes, a Mediterranean gentleman, a gentleman with a
shaved blunt head, a gentleman from Texas, a heavyset
perspiring gentleman rubbing at the tip of his flushed
pug nose, Do I hear 30,000, do I hear 35,000, do I hear
50,000, winking and nudging Babygirl, urging her to the
edge of the platform, C'mon sweetie now's not the time
for shyness, c'mon honey we all know why you're here
tonight don't be coy you cunt, clumsy cow-cunt, gentlemen observe those dugs, those udders, and there's *udder*
attractions too, hardee-har-har! And from up in the balcony, unobserved till now, a handsome white-haired gentleman signals with his white-gloved hand Yes.

9.
He was battle-weary, covered in scabs, maggot-festering
little wounds stippling his body, his once-proud tail was
gangrenous, the tip rotted away, yet he remained stoic
and uncomplaining gnawing through wood, through paper, through insulation, through thin sheets of metal,
eating with his old appetite, the ecstasy of jaws, teeth,
intestines, anus, if the time allotted to him were infinite
as his hunger it's certain he *would* gnaw his way through
the entire world and excrete it behind him in piles of

moist dark dense little turds. But Nature prescribes otherwise: the species into which he was born grants on the average only twelve months of survival—if things go well. And this May morning things are decidedly not going well here on the fourth floor of the partly empty ancient brick building on Sullivan Street housing on its first floor the Metropole Bakery, most acclaimed of local bakeries, "Wedding Cakes Our Specialty Since 1949," he has nested in a nook in a wall, he has been nibbling nervously on a piece of something theoretically edible (the hardened flattened remains of a sibling struck by a vehicle in the street, pounded into two dimensions by subsequent vehicles) sniffing and blinking in an agony of appetite: on the fourth floor, with his many thousands of fellows, since, it's one of Nature's quiddities, when BROWN and BLACK species occupy a single premise, BROWN (being larger and more aggressive) inhabit the lower levels while BLACK (shier, more philosophical) are relegated to the upper levels where food foraging is more difficult. So he's eating, or trying to eat, when there's a sound as of silk being torn, and a furry body comes flying at him, snarling, incisors longer and more deadly than his own, claws, hind legs pummeling like rotor blades, every flea and tick on his terror-struck little body is alert, every cell of his being cries out to be spared, but Sheba with her furry moon face has no mercy, she's a beautiful silver tabby much adored by her owners for her warm affectionate purring ways but here on this May morning in the ancient brick building housing the Metropole Bakery she is in a frenzy to kill, to tear with her jaws, to eat, the two of them locked in the most intimate of embraces, yowling, shrieking, he'd go for her jugular vein but, shrewd Sheba, she has already gone for his jugular vein, they are rolling crazily together in the filth, not just Sheba's terrible teeth but her maniac hind legs are killing him, yes but he's putting up a damned good fight yes he has ripped a triangular patch of flesh out of her ear, yes but it's too late, yes you can see that Sheba's greater weight will win the day, even as he squeaks and bites in self-defense Sheba has torn out his throat, she has in fact disemboweled him, his hapless guts in slimy ribbons now tangled in her feet, what a din! what a yowling! you'd think somebody was being killed! and he's dying, and she begins to devour him, warm-gushing blood is best, twitchy striated muscle is best, pretty Sheba shuts her jaws on his knobby little head and crushes his skull, his brains inside his skull, and he goes *out*. Just goes *out*. And the greedy tabby (who isn't even hungry: her owners keep her sleek and well fed, of course) eats him where they've landed, snaps his bones, chews his gristle, swallows his scaly tail in sections, his dainty pink-whorled ears, his rheumy eyes, his bristly whiskers, as well as his luscious meat. And afterward washes herself, to rid herself of his very memory.

10.
Except: wakened rudely from her post-prandial nap by a sickish stirring in her guts, poor Sheba is suddenly wracked by vomiting, finds herself reeling ungracefully and puking on the stairs, descending to the rear of the Metropole Bakery, mewing plaintively but no one hears as, teetering on a rafter above one of the giant vats of vanilla cake batter, poor Sheba heaves out her guts, that's to say *him*, the numerous fragments and shreds of *him*: a convulsive gagging and choking that concludes with the puking-up of his whiskers, which are now broken into

half- and quarter-inch pieces. Poor puss!—runs home
meek and plaintive and her adoring mistress picks her
up, cuddles, scolds, Sheba where have you *been*! And
Sheba's supper comes early that evening.

11.
Madly in love, Mr. X is the most devoted of suitors. And
then the most besotted of bridegrooms. Covering
Babygirl's pink-flushed face with kisses, hugging her so
tight she cries *Oh!* and all of the wedding company, her
own daddy in particular, laugh in delight. Mr. X is a
dignified handsome older gentleman. He's the salt of the
earth. He leads Babygirl out onto the polished dance
floor as the band plays "I Love You Truly" and how ele-
gantly he dances, how masterfully he leads his bride,
blood-red carnation in his lapel, chips of dry ice in his
eyes, wide fixed grinning-white dentures, how graceful
the couple's dips and bends, Babygirl in a breathtakingly
beautiful antique wedding gown worn by her mother,
her grandmother, and her great-grandmother in their
times, an heirloom wedding ring as well, lilies of the
valley braided in the bride's cinnamon curls, Babygirl
laughs showing the cherry-pink interior of her mouth,
she squeals *Oh!* as her new husband draws her to his
bosom, kisses her full on the lips. His big strong fingers
stroke her shoulders, breasts, rump. There are champagne toasts, there are gay drunken speeches lasting well
into the evening. The Archbishop himself intones a
blessing. Babygirl on Mr. X's knee being fed strawberries
and wedding cake by her bridegroom, and feeding her
bridegroom strawberries and wedding cake in turn, each
sucking the other's fingers, amid kisses and laughter.
Chewing her wedding cake Babygirl is disconcerted to

discover something tough, sinewy, bristly in it, like gristle, or fragments of bone, or tiny bits of wire, but she is
too well-bred and embarrassed to spit the foreign substance, if it is a foreign substance, out: discreetly pushes
it with her tongue to the side of her mouth, behind her
molars, for safe-keeping. For his part, Mr. X, a gentleman, washes his mouthfuls of wedding cake down with
champagne, swallows everything without blinking an eye,
This is the happiest day of my life he whispers into
Babygirl's pink-whorled ear.

12.
It was an experiment in behavioral psychology, in the
phenomenon of conditioning, to be published in *Scientific American,* and there to cause quite a stir, but naturally *he* wasn't informed, poor miserable bugger, nor did
he give consent. Semi-starved in his wire mesh cage,
compulsively gnawing on his own hind legs, he quickly
learned to *react* to the slightest gesture on the part of his
torturers, his monitored heartbeat raced in panic, his
jaundiced eyeballs careened in their sockets, a metaphysical malaise permeated his soul like sulphur dioxide, after
only a few hours. Yet his torturers persisted for there
were dozens of graphs and charts to be filled out; dozens
of young assistants involved in the experiment. In the
gauging of "terror" in dumb beasts of his species they
shocked him with increasing severity until virtual puffs of
smoke issued from the top of his head, they singed his
fur with burning needles, poked burning needles into his
tender anus, lowered his cage over a Bunsen burner,
wiped their eyes laughing at his antics, shaking and rat-
tling his cage, spinning his cage at a velocity of ninety
miles an hour, they marveled at how he was conditioned

to respond not just to their gestures but to their words as if he could understand them and then, most amazing of all,—this would be the crux of the controversial article in *Scientific American*—after forty-eight hours he began to react unerringly to the mere *thought* that the torture would be resumed. (Provided the experimentors consciously "thought" their thoughts inside the laboratory, not outside.) A remarkable scientific discovery!—unfortunately, after his death, never once to be duplicated. Thus utterly worthless as science and a bit of a joke in experimental psychology circles.

13.

How Mr. X adored his Babygirl!—lovingly bathing her in her fragrant bubble bath, brushing and combing her long wavy-curly cinnamon hair that fell to her hips, cooing to her, poking his tongue in her, bringing her breakfast in bed after a fevered night of marital love, insisting upon shaving, with his own straight razor, the peachy-fuzzy down that covered her lovely body, and the stiff "unsightly" hairs of underarms, legs, and crotch. Weeks, months. Until one night his penis failed him and he realized he was frankly bored with Babygirl's dimpled buttocks and navel, her wide-open periwinkle-blue eyes, the flattering *Oh!* of her pursed rosebud lips. He realized that her flat nasal voice grated against his sensitive nerves, her habits disgusted him, several times he caught her scratching her fat behind when she believed herself unobserved, she was not so fastidious as to refrain from picking her nose, frequently the bathroom stank of flatulence and excrement after she emerged from it, her menstrual blood stained the white linen heirloom sheets, her kinky hairs collected in drains, her early-morning breath was rancid as the inside of his own oldest shoes, she gazed at him with big mournful questioning cow-eyes, Oh what is wrong dearest, oh! don't you love me any longer? What did I *do*! lowering her bulk onto his knees, sliding her pudgy arms around his neck, exhaling her meaty breath in his face, so, cruelly, he parted his knees and Babygirl fell with a graceless thud to the floor. As she stared at him speechless in astonishment and hurt he struck her with the backside of his hand, bloodying her nose, Oh you will, bitch, will you! he grunted, will you! Eh!

14.

Mating, and mating. Mating. A frenzy of mating. In the prime of his maleness he fathered dozens, hundreds, thousands of offspring, now they're scurrying and squeaking everywhere, little buggers everywhere under-foot, nudging him aside as he feeds, ganging up on him, yes a veritable gang of them, how quickly babies grow up, it's amazing how quickly babies grow up, one day an inch long, the next day two inches long, the next day four inches long, those tiny perfect toes, claws, ears, whiskers, graceful curved tails, incisors, ravenous appetite *And the horror of it washed over me suddenly: I cannot die, I am multiplied to infinity*. It was not his fault! His enemies are even now setting out dollops of powdery-pasty poi-son, to rid the neighborhood of him and his off-spring, but it was not his fault! A fever overtook him, him and certain of his sisters, almost daily it seemed, yes daily, maybe hourly, no time to rest, no time for contempla-tion, a two-inch thing, a sort of a knob of flesh, a rod, hot

and stiff with blood, piston-quick, tireless, unfurling itself
out of the soft sac between his hind legs, yes and he was
powerless to resist, it was more urgent even than gnawing, more excruciatingly pleasurable, *he* was but an ap-
pendage! thus innocent! But his enemies, plotting against
him, don't give a damn, they're cruel and cold-blooded
setting out dollops of this most delicious poison, sugary,
pasty, bread-moldy, delicious beyond reckoning, he
should know better (shouldn't he?) but he's unable to
resist, pushing his way into the sea of squeaking quivering young ones, seething sea, dark waves, wave upon
wave eating in a delirium of appetite, a single feeding
organism you might think, it's a diabolical poison however that doesn't kill these poor buggers on the premises
but induces violent thirst in them thus shortly after feeding he and his thousands of sons and daughters are rushing out of the building, in a panic to find water, to drink
water, to alleviate this terrible thirst, they're drawn to the
dockside, to the river, there are screams as people see
them emerge, the dark wave of them, glittering eyes,
whiskers, pink near-hairless tails, they take no notice of
anyone or anything in their need to get to water, there in
the river a number of them drown, others drink and
drink and drink until, as planned, their poor bodies bloat,
and swell, and *burst.* And city sanitation workers wearing
gas masks complain bitterly as they shovel the corpses,
small mountains of corpses, into a procession of dumpster trucks, then they hose down the sidewalks, streets,
docks. At a fertilizer plant he and his progeny will be
mashed down, ground to gritty powder and sold for com-
mercial/residential use. No mention of the poison of
course.

15.

Grown increasingly and mysteriously insensitive to his
wife's feelings, Mr. X, within their first year of marriage,
began to bring home "business associates" (as he called
them) to ogle Babygirl, to peek at her in her bath, to
whisper licentious remarks in her ears, to touch, fondle,
molest—as Mr. X, often smoking a cigar, calmly watched!
At first Babygirl was too astonished to comprehend, then
she burst into tears of indignation and hurt, then she
pleaded with the brute to be spared, then she flew into a
tantrum tossing silky garments and such into a suitcase,
then she was lying in a puddle on the bathroom floor,
nights and days passed in a delirium, her keeper fed her
grudgingly and at irregular intervals, there were promises of sunshine, greenery, Christmas gifts, promises
made and withheld, then one day a masked figure appeared in the doorway, in leather military regalia, gloved
hands on his hips, brass-studded belt, holster and pistol
riding his hip, gleaming black leather boots the toes of
which Babygirl eagerly kissed, groveling before him,
twining her long curly-cinnamon hair around his ankles.
Begging, Have mercy! don't hurt me! I am yours! in sick-
ness and in health as I gave my vow to God! And assum-
ing the masked man was in fact Mr. X (for wasn't this a
reasonable   assumption,   in   these   circumstances?)
Babygirl willingly accompanied him to the master bedroom, to the antique brass four-postered bed, and did
not resist his wheezing, straining, protracted and painful
lovemaking, if such an act can be called lovemaking, the
insult of it! the pain of it! and not till the end, when the
masked figure triumphantly removed his mask, did
Babygirl discover that he was a stranger—and that Mr. X
himself was standing at the foot of the bed, smoking a

cigar, calmly observing. In the confusion of all that followed, weeks, months, there came a succession of "business associates," never the same man twice, as Mr. X
grew systematically crueler, hardly a gentleman any
longer, forcing upon his wife as she lay trussed and helpless in their marriage bed a man with fingernails filed
razor-sharp who lacerated her tender flesh, a man with a
glittering scaly skin, a man with a turkey's wattles, a man
with an ear partly missing, a man with a stark-bald head
and cadaverous smile, a man with infected draining sores
like exotic tattoos stippling his body, and poor Babygirl
was whipped for disobedience, Babygirl was burnt with
cigars, Babygirl was slapped, kicked, pummelled, near-
suffocated and near-strangled and near-drowned, she
screamed into her saliva-soaked gag, she thrashed,
convulsed, bled in sticky skeins most distasteful to Mr. X
who then punished her additionally, as a husband will do,
by withholding his affection.

16.
So light-headed with hunger was he, hiding in terror
from his enemies beneath a pile of bricks, he began to
gnaw at his own tail—timidly at first, then more avidly,
with appetite, unable to stop, his poor skinny tail, his
twenty pink toes and pads, his hind legs, choice loins and
chops and giblets and breast and pancreas and brains and
all, at last his bones are picked clean, the startling sym-
metry and beauty of the skeleton revealed, now he's
sleepy, contented and sleepy, washes himself with fastidious little scrubbing motions of his paws then curls up in
the warm September sun to nap. A sigh ripples through
him: exquisite peace.

17.

Except: two gangling neighborhood boys creep up on him dozing atop his favorite brick, capture him in a net and toss him squeaking in terror into a cardboard box, slam down the lid that's pocked with air holes, he's delivered by bicycle to a gentleman with neatly combed white hair and a cultivated voice who pays the boys $5 each for him, observes him crouched in a corner of the box rubbing his hands delightedly together chuckling softly, Well! you're a rough-looking fella aren't you! To his considerable surprise, the white-haired gentleman feeds him; holds him up, though not unkindly, by the scruff of his neck, to examine him, the sleek perfectly-formed parts of him, the rakish incisors most particularly. Breathing audibly, murmuring, with excited satisfaction, Yes. I believe you will do, old boy.

18.

No longer allowed out of the house, often confined to the bedroom suite on the second floor, poor Babygirl nonetheless managed to adjust to the altered circumstances of her life with commendable fortitude and good humor. Spending most of her days lying languorously in bed, doing her nails, devouring gourmet chocolates brought her by one or another of Mr. X's business associates, sometimes, in a romantic mood, by the unpredictable Mr. X himself, she watched television (the evangelical preachers were her favorites), complained to herself in the way of housewives in America, tended to her wounds, clipped recipes from magazines, gossiped over the telephone with her female friends, shopped by catalogue, read her Bible, grew heavier, sullen, apprehensive of the future, plucked her eyebrows, rubbed fragrant creams into her skin, kept an optimistic attitude, made an effort. Of the disturbing direction in which her marriage was moving she tried not to think for Babygirl was not the kind of wife to whine, whimper, nag, not Babygirl so imagine her surprise and horror when, one night, Mr. X arrived home and ran upstairs to the bedroom in which, that day, she'd been confined, tied to the four brass posts of the marital bed by white silken cords, and in triumph threw open his camel's hair coat, See what I've brought for you, my dear! unzipping his trousers with trembling fingers and as Babygirl stared incredulous out *he* leapt—squeaking, red-eyed, teeth bared and glistening with froth, stiff curved tail erect. Babygirl's screams were heartrending.

19.
Mr. X and his (male) companions observed with scientific detachment the relationship between Babygirl and He (as, in codified shorthand, they referred to him): how, initially, the pair resisted each other most strenuously, even hysterically, Babygirl shrieking even through the gag stuffed in her mouth as He was netted in the bed with her, such a struggle, such acrobatics, He squeaking in animal panic edged with indignant rage, biting, clawing, fighting as if for His very life, and Babygirl, despite her flaccid muscles and her seemingly indolent ways, putting up a fight as if for *her* very life! And this went on for hours, for an entire night, and the night following, and the night following that. And there was never anything so remarkable on Burlingame Way, the attractive residential street where Mr. X made his home.

20.

He did not want this, no certainly he did not want this, resisting with all the strength of his furry little being, as, with gloved hands, Mr. X forced him *there*—poor Babygirl spread-eagled and helpless bleeding from a thousand welts and lacerations made by his claws and teeth and why was he being forced snout-first, and then head-first, then his shoulders, his sleek muscular length, why *there*—in *there*—so he choked, near-suffocated, used his teeth to tear a way free for himself yet even as he did so Mr. X with hands trembling in excitement, as his companions, gathered round the bed, watched in awe pushed him in farther, and then *farther*—into the blood-hot pulsing toughly elastic tunnel between poor Babygirl's fatty thighs—and still *farther* until only the sleek-furry end of his rump and his trailing hind legs and, of course, the eight-inch pink tail were visible. His panicked gnawing of the fleshy walls that so tightly confined him released small geysers of blood that nearly drowned him, and the involuntary spasms of clenching of poor Babygirl's pelvic muscles nearly crushed him, thus how the struggle would have ended, if both he and Babygirl had not lost consciousness at the same instant, is problematic. Even Mr. X and his companions, virtually beside themselves in unholy arousal, were relieved that, for that night, the *agon* had ceased.

21.

As, at her martyrdom, at the stake in Rouen, as the flames licked mindlessly ever higher and higher to consume her, to turn her to ashes, Jeanne d'Arc is reported to have cried out "Jesu! Jesu! Jesu!" in a voice of rapture.

22.

And who would clean up the mess. And who, with a migraine, sanitary pad soaked between her chafed thighs, she's fearful of seeing her swollen jaw, blackened eye in any mirrored surface weeping quietly to herself, padding gingerly about in her bedroom slippers, mock-Japanese quilted housecoat. The only consolation is at least there's a t.v. in most of the rooms so, even when the vacuum is roaring, she isn't alone: there's Reverend Tim, there's Brother Jessie, there's Sweet Alabam' MacGowan. A consolation at least. For, not only did Babygirl suffer such insult and ignominy at the hands of the very man who, of all the world, was most responsible for her emotional well-being, not only was she groggy in the aftermath of only dimly remembered physical trauma, running the risk, as she sensed, of infection, sterility, and a recrudescence of her old female maladies,—not only this but she was obliged to clean up the mess next morning, who else. Laundering the sheets, blood-stained sheets are no joke. On her hands and knees trying (with minimal success) to remove the stains from the carpet. Vacuum the carpet. And the dirt-bag is full and there's a problem putting in a new dirt-bag, there always is. Faint-headed, wracked several times with white-hot bolts of pain so she had to sit, catch her breath. And the pad between her legs soaked hard in blackish blood like blood-sausage. And the steel wool disintegrating in her fingers as gamely she tries to scour the casserole dish clean, dissolves in tears, Oh! where has love gone! so one evening he surprises her, in that melancholy repose, the children are in on it too, what's today but Babygirl's birthday and she'd tormented herself thinking no one would remember but as they sweep into the restaurant, the Gondola that's one of the few good Italian restaurants in the city where you can order pizza too, the staff is waiting, Happy Birthday! balloons, half-chiding there's a chorus, Did you think we'd forgotten? and Babygirl orders a sloe gin fizz which goes straight to her head and she giggles and suppresses a tiny belch patting her fingers to her mouth, later her husband is scolding one of the boys but *she's* going to steer clear of the conflict, goes to the powder room, checks her makeup in the rose-lit flattering mirrors seeing yes, thank God the bruise under her left eye is fading, then she takes care to affix squares of toilet paper to the toilet seat to prevent picking up an infectious disease, since AIDS Babygirl is even more methodical, then she's sitting on the toilet her mind for a moment blissful and empty until, turning her head, just happening to turn her head, though probably she sensed its presence, she sees, not six inches away, on the slightly grimy sill of a frosted-glass window, the red-blinking eyes of a large rodent, oh dear God is it a rat, these eyes fixed upon *hers,* her heart gives a violent kick and nearly *stops.* Poor Babygirl's screams penetrate every wall of the building.

Joyce Carol Oates is the author of *Wonderland, Them, Where Are You Going, Where Have You Been?, American Appetites, Night Side, The Crosswicks Horror, Because It Is Bitter, and Because It Is My Heart,* and scores of other novels, plays and volumes of stories, poems, literary criticism and essays. A National Book Award winner, she is professor of humanities at Princeton University and editor of *The Ontario Review.* Among her latest books is *Heat and Other Stories.*

Briar Rose

Kim Antieau

 She opened her eyes to white and realized she knew nothing.

The nurse was white, too.

"Good morning, sugar," the nurse said. "Do you know who you are?"

She shook her head and wondered where the window was. Maybe if she saw the sunlight, maybe if she saw the world really existed, she would know. Silly thought. The world existed. It was she, she was certain, who was not supposed to be.

"Turn over," the nurse said. Her voice was as pretty as anything she could remember. Though that wasn't much. She turned over. The nurse threw off the covers and pulled up her hospital gown. "Lookie here, girl," the nurse said. "Maybe that will jar your memory."

She looked down at her own bare ass, twisting her head and arching her back. A small rose bloomed on her white butt, its red petals surrounded by a crown of thorns.

She touched it.

"Maybe my name is Rose," she said.

"All right, Rose, honey," the nurse said, putting the hospital gown and covers back over her bare skin. "We don't know who you are either. You came in with glass all over your arms, cut deep."

Rose held up her bandaged arms.

"You said you'd fallen through a plate glass window." The nurse smiled. "We decided to take your word on that and not put you in the psych ward. All you have to do now is eat that shit they call food, rest, and get better. Just whistle if you need anything."

The nurse in white smiled; for a moment, Rose thought she was dressed in shining armor. Rose shook her head and the nurse was gone. She closed her eyes and reached into her memory. Nothing. Except a man with a needle that looked like those wood burners they used in shop class when she was in high school. "Have you come to be transformed?" the man asked. "I don't think so," she answered. "I just want a rose tattoo." He hummed some tune, Beethoven's Fifth, while he rat-ta-tat-tatted on her backside.

When he was finished, he smoothed a bandage over the patch of skin and handed her a card with care instructions, as if she had just bought a sweater. She pulled up her pants and went home. Home? She couldn't really see it, only her reflection in the mirror, somehow, as she pulled off the bandage and looked at the scab forming where he had drawn the rose with his needle and ink.

"There now," she said. "I am whole again. I am myself. My body is mine."

Rose opened her eyes and started to call to Nurse White, to tell her she did know something. Instead, she closed her eyes again and went to sleep.

In the morning, after she ate the shit they called food,

Rose got out of bed, found her bloodstained clothes, and got dressed. She was frightened until she thought of the rose blooming on her butt, and then she was no longer afraid. She walked into the hallway, got on the elevator, and went down to the lobby. Outside through the revolving doors, Rose saw a world she had never seen before, bright, noisy. White with color. No, bright with color. She reached into her pockets as she went down the street, away from the hospital. She pulled out forty dollars, crumpled up in her front pockets. That was it.

She hummed Tchaikovsky's *1812 Overture* as she walked. Pigeons shadowed her as she went down the street, toward the tall buildings and bridges arching the river or expressway. The pigeons dogged her steps, looking for handouts. As she walked she remembered nothing except the rose, knew nothing except the feel of her own skin under her hand. She smiled. Ignorance was bliss.

When she got downtown, the pigeons swore at her and flew away to the Burger King parking lot. Rose went onto a street called Burnside and walked until she came to a door which said: TATTOOS. CLEAN SURROUNDINGS. NO ONE UNDER 18 ADMITTED. Rose gently pulled off the gauze from her arms. Scabs traced the places the glass had cut. She dropped the gauze and scabs into a garbage can and then pushed the door open and went inside.

The man with the wood burner looked up when she came in. He smiled. He was the man from her memory.

"Sorry, honey, I can't take it off."

"I don't want it off," she said. "I want another one." She stepped past the swinging door and into his domain of stencils and needles, inks and memories. She looked at the drawings on his walls.

"You going to pick from my flash this time? Last visit you wanted something no one else had." He stood next to her and pointed. "There, how about another flower?"

She shook her head. "I want a child. Here on my arm. Do you have a child? I need to remember."

"No, but I can draw one," he said. He had curly black hair and tattoos everywhere she could see. A dragon belched smoke up his right arm. Jupiter surrounded by stars rotated on his left arm. A butterfly flew beneath that.

She followed him to the tattoo place behind his drawing table. He wanted her to lie down, she wanted to sit. He hummed as he cleaned her arm with alcohol, let the air dry it, and then drew a little girl. Rose watched his fingers and arm move and knew that she could do it, too. Draw. Sketch her life. After a time, when no one else came into the shop, he stopped and asked her if she liked the little girl he had drawn.

She looked down at her arm. "That little girl is me," she said.

"Yes," he said, "I know."

"I don't remember if I liked her." The girl was smaller than Rose had imagined, two years old perhaps. The man began spreading the inks onto her arm. Then he sewed the girl into her skin with the color. When he finished, it was dark outside and the little girl was blowing out two candles on a blue-frosted cake.

"Someday, Charlie, my brother, some little prick's going to get her," her uncle Bobbie said, "and it'll all be over. That's the way with girls. Dad always said so." He laughed and spilled beer on himself while her mother sliced pieces of cake. Rose looked over at her father and saw the fear in his eyes; she was only two but she saw it, and Bobbie was too young to drink beer, maybe thirteen.

"Are you all right?" The tattooist touched her arm with his fingers. She moved her arm away from him. "Sorry," he said. "You only want to be touched if it hurts."

She looked at the little girl on her arm. Her lips were pursed, forever trying to blow out the candles.

"Can you teach me how to do this?" she asked.

"Transform yourself? Or tattoo?"

"Draw with a needle."

"Do you have any money?"

"Forty dollars and two memories," she said. "I could stay here. Clean up. Do anything else you want."

"Don't scratch your tattoo," he said. He started to hand her the card with care instructions written on it. She stared at him.

"All right," he said. He nodded as if he had known it all along.

"I want another," she said. "The other arm. A snake."

He got up and went to the door and locked it. He pulled the shade down. Then he took a stencil from his flash and returned to her. "Turn around," he said, "so I can work on your other side." He pressed the drawing onto her arm. When he pulled it away, Rose could see the outline of a snake. She stared at the bandage on her other arm and imagined the girl beneath it while the tattooist drew the snake.

When he was finished, he dropped his instruments. "I can't do any more," he said and walked up the steps that led to his loft. She listened to his heavy breathing for several minutes before she got up. She threw out the needle and put away the inks. Then she went into a small office in the back and curled up on a battered couch.

When she awakened, it was still dark. She felt hurried, as if something had to be finished soon. Something she had started and somehow had messed up. She turned on a light over the desk and looked at her arms. Where the glass had pierced her skin were now black lines, jagged shapes tattooed into her arms.

She remembered standing in the motel room, wondering why she was there. Her mother was dead. Too many sleeping pills. Her father was dead. Too many cigarettes. And she was alive. Her body ached. Her body that wasn't hers. The tattoo itched. It had not brought her back from the edge. Something had pricked her, just as her father had feared: men, boys, life. She hurt, as if slivers of glass were tickling her insides. She had raised her fists in anger, wanting to pound the windows that looked out onto the parking lot, when suddenly she knew how to have peace.

She ended up in the hospital eating shit and getting sponge baths from Nurse White.

She turned her arms around and pulled off the bandage over the little girl and her birthday cake. The scab came off with the bandage. The girl had tears in her eyes. She had heard the conversation, had known her life had changed.

Rose peeled off the other bandage. The snake shed his scab, and Rose was in the backyard of her home, eight years old, bent over a translucent snake skin, wondering where the snake had gone. What an easy life. If you don't like it, just shed it and begin anew. She reached out a finger and touched the skin tentatively. Dry.

"If it's from a poisonous snake you could die." She

looked up. Uncle Bobbie. He smiled. All his smiles looked monstrous. She wasn't sure why. He snatched up the snake skin and began running. She went after him, into the woods where the oaks and maples were shedding their leaves. Suddenly his footsteps stopped and she was alone in the woods. Then Bobbie jumped from behind a tree and threw her to the ground, laughing all the time, tossing the skin into the air, out of her reach. He pulled off her pants and then his. When it was over, he promised to get her a pony if she didn't tell anyone.

Rose turned off the light. Now she had four memories.

She watched the man prick pictures into other people's skins all day. She took care of his inks and needles and cleaned the floors. At night, she counted his money and gave it to him. He needled her when everyone was gone. A drop of blood tattooed on her right forearm brought Bobbie back to her, brought his smile as he zipped up his pants and she put her hands between her legs. She cried and he told her to shut up. Her parents were afraid to leave her with anyone else except family. Afraid of the outside world. Uncle Bobbie had been right, they would tell each other, there were millions of guys out there just waiting to hurt their child.

A willow tree brought her father back. She leaned her head against his knee. He stroked her hair while he read his newspaper. Her mother knelt in her garden and whispered to the flowers.

"I've never seen anyone heal as quickly as you do," the tattooist told her. He seemed tired, as if he felt it all, too.

She nodded and took the needle from him. "May I try?"

"Don't hurt yourself," he said.

"Isn't that what this is all about?" she asked, holding

the needle like a writer holds a pen, poised to express herself.

"No," he said. And he went up his steps. She waited until she heard his heavy breathing and then she began drawing.

She tried a flower but it turned into a warped sun, bringing back a summer when she was four and Bobbie was pushing his fingers between her legs while he held onto something between his legs. Rose laughed at his face, funny Bobbie, until he hurt her and she started to cry and wondered where her mother was. The sun was too hot and the flowers were dying.

"Momma," she whispered.

She tried tattooing flowers again, this time on her thighs. First violets, then roses, gardenias, rhodies; a garden bloomed on her skin and she was next to her mother in the dirt. Her mother was crying, the tears making paths through the dust on her face. "What's wrong? What's wrong?" Rose asked. She was ten and her throat hurt from trying not to cry. Bobbie lurked in the bushes somewhere, always waiting, and Momma cried.

The tattooist came down the stairs when it was morning. He looked at her thighs.

"You're an artist," he said.

"The agony and the ecstasy?" she said. "I'm my own Sistine Chapel." She held up the needle. "Will you do my back?"

"Why?"

"I have to remember," she said.

"But wasn't it nice before?" he said. "When you knew nothing?"

She shook her head. "I knew nothing when I was two years old and look what happened."

"You hardly scab," he said.

"I go straight to scarring," she said.

She took off her shirt and camisole. She didn't care if he saw her. He made holes in her back and let the ink soak in, making the memories permanent. They could be wiped from her brain but not from her skin.

"What have you drawn?" she asked when he paused.

"Can't you tell?" he said. "Don't you remember being a kid in the bathtub with your brother or sister? You'd wipe the other guy's back and then put soap on it and draw, usually words, and the other person would have to guess."

"I didn't have any brothers and sisters," she said. "But I do remember a cousin, Mary, and we played together. Sometimes we took baths together, when we were real little and we'd do that. Yes, I remember now." It had been nice to touch her and to be touched by her. They were each the other's drawing boards. They got water and soap everywhere. "We floated little plastic ships in the water and pretended we were seeing the world."

"That's what I put on your back," he said.

She got up and went into the bathroom where there was a full-length mirror and looked at herself. Two girls stood on a sailing ship. They held hands and waved to the mermaids in the water. The ship bobbed in the waves. A flag with a rose on it flapped in the breeze.

Rose smiled. Some of the memories were good.

She went back into the room where the tattooist sat.

"You understand that I have to do this," she said.

"Yes," he said. "It's part of what I do. Transformations, remember. It's difficult sometimes."

She nodded.

She drew a lady on her left calf. Her golden hair

flowed away from her as she lay on the bed of skin. Her eyes were open but Rose knew she was dead. Her open eyes had surprised Rose. She had died of an overdose of pills. Eaten one at a time.

"Why?" Rose asked as her mother swallowed a little white pill.

"Because I ache," she said. "I've been stabbed in a million places."

Had Bobbie played with her, too?

"I need you to stay," Rose said. She started to cry. Where was her father? At work? The car was with him. Their closest neighbors, the Nelsons, were gone on vacation. She wasn't sure she could reach anyone else. They lived too far from the city. Out in the country where nothing could hurt them. Her mother had ripped out the phone.

"Bobbie's been playing with me," Rose said. She was twelve, desperate. She'd tell her mother, get her to stay.

"What do you mean?" Her mother swallowed four pills this time.

"You know, putting his thing in me," Rose said. Stop it, Mom. Stay with me.

"Tell your father," she said. "He'll protect you."

That was it. That was all her mother had to say to her after all the agony she had been through.

"He promised me a pony," she said.

"I'm so tired," her mother said.

Rose ran downstairs and out the door. She ran into the dusty afternoon and through the woods toward the house Bobbie shared with his parents, farther and farther away from home. He worked in town at night. Maybe he'd be home now. She pounded and pounded on the door. After a while, she heard his voice from deep within the house. He came to the door, half-asleep.

"What are you doing here?" he said.

"It's Momma," she said. "She's taking too many sleeping pills. Please, you've got to do something."

He opened the screen door and she came in. He went to the phone and called the police and an ambulance. She hated him, despised him, hated herself. But he was going to save her mother.

He took her hand and they went out to his car. He drove her back to her house and together they went upstairs. Her mother lay on the bed, her hair spread out around her, like a golden-haired Snow White waiting for her Prince Charming. Her eyes were open.

Bobbie started to cry. Rose went away. She wasn't certain where she went. Her soul wandered for a time. She thought she had died when she was eight, but she had been wrong. Now she died. Pricked by her mother's death.

She drew a garden on her other leg. Its weeds and thorns twisted around her calf and up her knee. A man stood among the weeds.

"He never let me near him after that," Rose said.

"Who? Your father?" the tattooist asked.

"No," Rose said. Tears stung her eyes. "Bobbie."

She felt like she was going to throw up. "I hated him, but he was all there was. I guess. Momma had left me a long time before she died. And my dad was . . . my dad."

The tattooist took the needle. Rose lay on her stomach and he drew on her back. Her butt became a tangle of dark briar that went up her back, no way to get through.

She remembered leaving her bedroom window open.

The boys knew where to come in and they did, one at a time. She didn't care who they were. She just opened her legs to them. She had to fill the emptiness somehow.

The briars pricked her skin; the tattooist drew drops of blood down her legs.

She touched the blood and remembered being seventeen. Her father was drunk. She had never seen him drunk before. But he was blind with grief. He wept and started calling her Joanie. Her mother's name. She went into the bathroom and curled her hair up and behind her, dabbed her cheeks with powder, put her mother's pearl necklace around her neck, slipped into her mother's blue flowered dress, the one her mother had worn often, especially when she was in the garden, and then she went out to her father. In the darkness, she opened herself to him, not understanding, and he pushed into her, sobbing, until in the middle of it, hard inside her, he opened his eyes and screamed with the horror of it, knowing it was she; knowing it, he kept going. When he was finished, he curled up on the floor and asked how she could have done it.

"Does it hurt?" the tattooist asked.

"Yes." Rose wiped her tears and sat up. "I want you to do my breasts."

He drew flowers and restaurants and neon lights and cowboys. It hurt. He drew her trek across the country after her father told her to leave. She went to Bobbie's house first. He had a wife and a child and he could not look at her. Rose turned away from the house and hoped he never touched his little girl the way he had touched her. She took a ride from a trucker. She let him have her at night, after they drove several hundred miles. She felt dry inside and he told her she wasn't much fun. "I don't want nobody don't want me," he said. He let her out in the darkness. The next one beat her up. The tattooist pricked the black and blue spots onto her skin. She hadn't minded the beatings so much. She deserved it. Touching was meant to hurt. She ended up working in a restaurant in Tucson, fifteen hundred miles from home. For some reason, she told Bobbie where she was.

She looked down at her breasts and saw the envelope, saw the writing on the letter. The tattooist bit his lip as he pushed the needle into her.

"It's for my own good," she said.

"It's for your death," he said.

She nodded.

The letter told her her father was dead. A year to the day she had left. Lung cancer. She didn't go back for the funeral. She stayed in Tucson. A cactus grew from her navel. An old Indian woman tried to heal her insides. But she couldn't let the woman touch her. Couldn't let anyone touch her.

When she turned nineteen, she went north. She found the tattooist and had him etch a rose into her body. It was her body now.

He painted the house around her side. It wrapped her. She had never gone back to the house. She had heard they sold it. Another family lived in it now. After she got the rose, she thought it would be better. It was supposed to be better. A reason to go on: because she had reclaimed her body. Instead, she stood in the motel room and wanted to die.

The tattooist moved away from her. He was crying.

"There are scabs all over your body," he said.

She was naked except for the tattoos.

"Are you glad you remembered?" he asked.

"No," she said. "Thank you."

"Don't go," he said. "You're very good. An artist. You could transform people."

"I can't even transform myself," she said. She put on her clothes. Her entire body hurt.

"I could help you get started," he said. She was quiet. "Stay until the scabs are gone then."

"All right," she said. "I'll at least stay the night."

He started to touch her arm, but he stopped. "I'm going to bed," he said. He slowly walked up the steps to his loft.

Rose went to the office and sat on the couch. Her body was now covered with her memories. It ached with them. She took off her shirt; the throbbing lessened somewhat. She wanted to cry. The memories burned her skin. Hurt. Too much. She stood up and took off her pants. How could she live with it all? Stand it? She touched one of the faces on her body that was Bobbie. He peered at her from her right shoulder. She shook herself, like a dog shaking water from its fur, and the scabs fell away from her body, becoming flower petals, red, yellow, blue, floating slowly to rest on the carpet. Now she could clearly see all her memories. Her life was etched into her skin.

She went into the bathroom and stared at her body in the mirror. Her ruined body. Bobbie had ruined her. Killed her. Doomed her to sleep until she died. Her mother had ruined her. Her father had ruined her. She had only been a child. They had all taken pieces of her and had forgotten to give them back.

She started to cry. She thought of those hours when she hadn't remembered anything. When Nurse White had turned her over. A babe from the womb. Being taken care of, loved, patted. She had known nothing. Now she knew everything.

Bobbie drank too much. His wife had left him. Her father was dead, never forgiving her. Never realizing it had been his responsibility, not his daughter's. Her mother was dead. Never caring what she left behind.

"Time to wake up," she whispered to her reflection.

She reached down and pulled a briar away from the patch that circled the rose on her butt. Her skin itched. Crackled. She sat on the floor and pressed the thorn into the top of her head until she drew blood. It had been good to remember. Blood ran into her eyes. To realize she had only been a child. Her mother had chosen to die; Bobbie had chosen to hurt her; her father had chosen to blame her. It was past. Time for reclamation. Seeing it all had made it, somehow, understandable. She remembered touching the snake skin when she was a child, being amazed that it could just start fresh, shed its old life.

She stretched and creaked and rubbed herself along the carpet and her past started to fall from her. She sat up and helped it: she peeled away the dead skin. It felt dry and cool, just as the snake skin had. Lifeless. No power. The flowers came away, Bobbie's face, her mother's eyes, the weeds, the ship on her back, the snake, the blood. All of it. She stood and dropped the past onto the carpet. She shook herself, causing the last pieces of skin to fly away. She looked down at her body. She was white and pink. New. Only the rose on her buttock remained, without the crown of thorns.

The tattooist stood in the doorway. He leaned over and picked up the skin.

Rose touched his arm. "Leave it," she said. "I don't

need it anymore." She reached down and smoothed her hand over her rose tattoo and smiled. "I am myself again."

Kim Antieau has published short stories in *Isaac Asimov's Science Fiction Magazine, The Twilight Zone, The Magazine of Fantasy & Science Fiction* and *Crosscurrents,* and in such anthologies as *Shadows, The Year's Best Fantasy Stories, The Year's Best Horror Stories, Best New Horror, Borderlands II* and *Final Shadows.* Her next work is a novel, *Ruins.*

PART TWO

A Long Time Till Morning

Replacements

Lisa Tuttle

 Walking through grey north London to the tube station, feeling guilty that he hadn't let Jenny drive him to work and yet relieved to have escaped another pointless argument, Stuart Holder glanced down at a pavement covered in a leaf-fall of fast-food cartons and white paper bags and saw, amid the dog turds, beer cans and dead cigarettes, something horrible.

It was about the size of a cat, naked looking, with leathery, hairless skin and thin, spiky limbs that seemed too frail to support the bulbous, ill-proportioned body. The face, with tiny bright eyes and a wet slit of a mouth, was like an evil monkey's. It saw him and moved in a crippled, spasmodic way. Reaching up, it made a clotted, strangled noise. The sound touched a nerve, like metal between the teeth, and the sight of it, mewling and chok-ing and scrabbling, scaly claws flexing and wriggling, made him feel sick and terrified. He had no phobias, he found insects fascinating, not frightening, and regularly removed, unharmed, the spiders, wasps and mayflies which made Jenny squeal or shudder helplessly.

But this was different. This wasn't some rare species of

wingless bat escaped from a zoo, it wasn't something he would find pictured in any reference book. It was something that should not exist, a mistake, something alien. It did not belong in his world.

A little snarl escaped him and he took a step forward and brought his foot down hard.

The small, shrill scream lanced through him as he crushed it beneath his shoe and ground it into the road.

Afterwards, as he scraped the sole of his shoe against the curb to clean it, nausea overwhelmed him. He leaned over and vomited helplessly into a red-and-white-striped box of chicken bones and crumpled paper.

He straightened up, shaking, and wiped his mouth again and again with his pocket handkerchief. He wondered if anyone had seen, and had a furtive look around. Cars passed at a steady crawl. Across the road a cluster of schoolgirls dawdled near a man smoking in front of a newsagent's, but on this side of the road the fried chicken franchise and bathroom suppliers had yet to open for the day and the nearest pedestrians were more than a hundred yards away.

Until that moment, Stuart had never killed anything in his life. Mosquitoes and flies of course, other insects probably, a nest of hornets once, that was all. He had never liked the idea of hunting, never lived in the country. He remembered his father putting out poisoned bait for rats, and he remembered shying bricks at those same vermin on a bit of waste ground where he had played as a boy. But rats weren't like other animals; they elicited no sympathy. Some things had to be killed if they would not be driven away.

He made himself look to make sure the thing was not still alive. Nothing should be left to suffer. But his heel had crushed the thing's face out of recognition, and it was unmistakably dead. He felt a cool tide of relief and satisfaction, followed at once, as he walked away, by a nagging uncertainty, the imminence of guilt. Was he right to have killed it, to have acted on violent, irrational impulse? He didn't even know what it was. It might have been somebdy's pet.

He went hot and cold with shame and self-disgust. At the corner he stopped with five or six others waiting to cross the road and because he didn't want to look at them he looked down.

And there it was, alive again.

He stifled a scream. No, of course it was not the same one, but another. His leg twitched; he felt frantic with the desire to kill it, and the terror of his desire. The thin wet mouth was moving as if it wanted to speak.

As the crossing-signal began its nagging blare he tore his eyes away from the creature squirming at his feet. Everyone else had started to cross the street, their eyes, like their thoughts, directed ahead. All except one. A woman in a smart business suit was standing still on the pavement, looking down, a sick fascination on her face.

As he looked at her looking at it, the idea crossed his mind that he should kill it for her, as a chivalric, protective act. But she wouldn't see it that way. She would be repulsed by his violence. He didn't want her to think he was a monster. He didn't want to be the monster who had exulted in the crunch of fragile bones, the flesh and viscera merging pulpily beneath his shoe.

He forced himself to look away, to cross the road, to spare the alien life. But he wondered, as he did so, if he had been right to spare it.

Stuart Holder worked as an editor for a publishing

company with offices an easy walk from St. Paul's. Jenny
had worked there, too, as a secretary, when they met five
years ago. Now, though, she had quite a senior position
with another publishing house, south of the river, and
recently they had given her a car. He had been supportive of her ambitions, supportive of her learning to drive,
and proud of her on all fronts when she succeeded, yet
he was aware, although he never spoke of it, that something about her success made him uneasy. One small,
niggling, insecure part of himself was afraid that one day
she would realize she didn't need him anymore. That was
why he picked at her, and second-guessed her decisions
when she was behind the wheel and he was in the pas-
senger seat. He recognized this as he walked briskly
through more crowded streets towards his office, and he
told himself he would do better. He would have to. If
anything drove them apart it was more likely to be his
behavior than her career. He wished he had accepted
her offer of a ride today. Better any amount of petty
irritation between husband and wife than to be haunted
by the memory of that tiny face, distorted in the death he
had inflicted. Entering the building, he surreptitiously
scraped the sole of his shoe against the carpet.

Upstairs two editors and one of the publicity girls were
in a huddle around his secretary's desk; they turned on
him the guilty-defensive faces of women who have been
discussing secrets men aren't supposed to know.

He felt his own defensiveness rising to meet theirs as
he smiled. "Can I get any of you chaps a cup of coffee?"

"I'm sorry, Stuart, did you want . . . ?" As the others
faded away, his secretary removed a stiff white paper bag
with the NEXT logo printed on it from her desktop.

"Joke, Frankie, joke." He always got his own coffee

because he liked the excuse to wander, and he was always having to reassure her that she was not failing in her secretarial duties. He wondered if Next sold sexy underwear, decided it would be unkind to tease her further.

He felt a strong urge to call Jenny and tell her what had happened, although he knew he wouldn't be able to explain, especially not over the phone. Just hearing her voice, the sound of sanity, would be a comfort, but he restrained himself until just after noon, when he made the call he made every day.

Her secretary told him she was in a meeting. "Tell her Stuart rang," he said, knowing she would call him back as always.

But that day she didn't. Finally, at five minutes to five, Stuart rang his wife's office and was told she had left for the day.

It was unthinkable for Jenny to leave work early, as unthinkable as for her not to return his call. He wondered if she was ill. Although he usually stayed in the office until well after six, now he shoved a manuscript in his briefcase and went out to brave the rush hour.

He wondered if she was mad at him. But Jenny didn't sulk. If she was angry she said so. They didn't lie or play those sorts of games with each other, pretending not to be in, "forgetting" to return calls.

As he emerged from his local underground station Stuart felt apprehensive. His eyes scanned the pavement and the gutters, and once or twice the flutter of paper made him jump, but of the creatures he had seen that morning there were no signs. The body of the one he had killed was gone, perhaps eaten by a passing dog, perhaps returned to whatever strange dimension had spawned it. He noticed, before he turned off the high street, that other pedestrians were also taking a keener than usual interest in the pavement and the edge of the road, and that made him feel vindicated somehow.

London traffic being what it was, he was home before Jenny. While he waited for the sound of her key in the lock he made himself a cup of tea, cursed, poured it down the sink, and had a stiff whisky instead. He had just finished it and was feeling much better when he heard the street door open.

"Oh!" The look on her face reminded him unpleasantly of those women in the office this morning, making him feel like an intruder in his own place. Now Jenny smiled, but it was too late. "I didn't expect you to be here so early."

"Nor me. I tried to call you, but they said you'd left already. I wondered if you were feeling all right."

"I'm fine!"

"You look fine." The familiar sight of her melted away his irritation. He loved the way she looked: her slender, boyish figure, her close-cropped, curly hair, her pale complexion and bright blue eyes.

Her cheeks now had a slight hectic flush. She caught her bottom lip between her teeth and gave him an assessing look before coming straight out with it. "How would you feel about keeping a pet?"

Stuart felt a horrible conviction that she was not talking about a dog or a cat. He wondered if it was the whisky on an empty stomach which made him feel dizzy.

"It was under my car. If I hadn't happened to notice something moving down there I could have run over it." She lifted her shoulders in a delicate shudder.

"Oh, God, Jenny, you haven't brought it home!"

She looked indignant. "Well, of course I did! I couldn't just leave it in the street—somebody else might have run it over."

Or stepped on it, he thought, realizing now that he could never tell Jenny what he had done. That made him feel even worse, but maybe he was wrong. Maybe it was just a cat she'd rescued. "What is it?"

She gave a strange, excited laugh. "I don't know. Something very rare, I think. Here, look." She slipped the large, woven bag off her shoulder, opening it, holding it out to him. "Look. Isn't it the sweetest thing?"

How could two people who were so close, so alike in so many ways, see something so differently? He only wanted to kill it, even now, while she had obviously fallen in love. He kept his face carefully neutral although he couldn't help flinching from her description. "*Sweet?*"

It gave him a pang to see how she pulled back, holding the bag protectively close as she said, "Well, I know it's not pretty, but so what? I thought it was horrible, too, at first sight. . . ." Her face clouded, as if she found her first impression difficult to remember, or to credit, and her voice faltered a little. "But then, then I realized how *helpless* it was. It needed me. It can't help how it looks. Anyway, doesn't it kind of remind you of the Psammead?"

"The what?"

"Psammead. You know, *The Five Children and It*?"

He recognized the title but her passion for old-fashioned children's books was something he didn't share. He shook his head impatiently. "That thing didn't come out of a book, Jen. You found it in the street and you don't know what it is or where it came from. It could be dangerous, it could be diseased."

"Dangerous," she said in a withering tone.

"You don't know."

"I've been with him all day and he hasn't hurt me, or anybody else at the office, he's perfectly happy being held, and he likes being scratched behind the ears."

He did not miss the pronoun shift. "It might have rabies."

"Don't be silly."

"Don't *you* be silly; it's not exactly native, is it? It might be carrying all sorts of foul parasites from South America or Africa or wherever."

"Now you're being racist. I'm not going to listen to you. *And* you've been drinking." She flounced out of the room.

If he'd been holding his glass still he might have thrown it. He closed his eyes and concentrated on breathing in and out slowly. This was worse than any argument they'd ever had, the only crucial disagreement of their marriage. Jenny had stronger views about many things than he did, so her wishes usually prevailed. He didn't mind that. But this was different. He wasn't having that creature in his home. He had to make her agree.

Necessity cooled his blood. He had his temper under control when his wife returned. "I'm sorry," he said, although she was the one who should have apologized. Still looking prickly, she shrugged and would not meet his eyes. "Want to go out to dinner tonight?"

She shook her head. "I'd rather not. I've got some work to do."

"Can I get you something to drink? I'm only one whisky ahead of you, honest."

Her shoulders relaxed. "I'm sorry. Low blow. Yeah, pour me one. And one for yourself." She sat down on the couch, her bag by her feet. Leaning over, reaching inside, she cooed, "Who's my little sweetheart, then?"

Normally he would have taken a seat beside her. Now, though, he eyed the pale, misshapen bundle on her lap and, after handing her a glass, retreated across the room. "Don't get mad, but isn't having a pet one of those things we discuss and agree on beforehand?"

He saw the tension come back into her shoulders, but she went on stroking the thing, keeping herself calm. "Normally, yes. But this is special. I didn't plan it. It happened, and now I've got a responsibility to him. Or her." She giggled. "We don't even know what sex you are, do we, my precious?"

He said carefully, "I can see that you had to do something when you found it, but keeping it might not be the best thing."

"I'm not going to put it out in the street."

"No, no, but . . . don't you think it would make sense to let a professional have a look at it? Take it to a vet, get it checked out . . . maybe it needs shots or something."

She gave him a withering look and for a moment he faltered, but then he rallied. "Come on, Jenny, be reasonable! You can't just drag some strange animal in off the street and keep it, just like that. You don't even know what it eats."

"I gave it some fruit at lunch. It ate that. Well, it sucked out the juice. I don't think it can chew."

"But you don't know, do you? Maybe the fruit juice was just an aperitif, maybe it needs half its weight in live insects every day, or a couple of small, live mammals. Do you really think you could cope with feeding it mice or rabbits fresh from the pet shop every week?"

"Oh, Stuart."

"Well? Will you just take it to a vet? Make sure it's healthy? Will you do that much?"

"And then I can keep it? If the vet says there's nothing wrong with it, and it doesn't need to eat anything too impossible?"

"Then we can talk about it. Hey, don't pout at me; I'm not your father, I'm not telling you what to do. We're partners, and partners don't make unilateral decisions about things that affect them both; partners discuss things and reach compromises and . . ."

"There can't be any compromise about this."

He felt as if she'd doused him with ice water. "What?"

"Either I win and I keep him or you win and I give him up. Where's the compromise?"

This was why wars were fought, thought Stuart, but he didn't say it. He was the picture of sweet reason, explaining as if he meant it, "The compromise is that we each try to see the other person's point. You get the animal checked out, make sure it's healthy and I, I'll keep an open mind about having a pet, and see if I might start liking . . . him. Does he have a name yet?"

Her eyes flickered. "No . . . we can choose one later, together. If we keep him."

He still felt cold and, although he could think of no reason for it, he was certain she was lying to him.

In bed that night as he groped for sleep Stuart kept seeing the tiny, hideous face of the thing screaming as his foot came down on it. That moment of blind, killing rage was not like him. He couldn't deny he had done it, or how he had felt, but now, as Jenny slept innocently beside him, as the creature she had rescued, a twin to his

victim, crouched alive in the bathroom, he tried to remember it differently.

In fantasy, he stopped his foot, he controlled his rage
and, staring at the memory of the alien animal, he struggled to see past his anger and his fear, to see through
those fiercer masculine emotions and find his way to
Jenny's feminine pity. Maybe his intuition had been
wrong and hers was right. Maybe, if he had waited a little
longer, instead of lashing out, he would have seen how
unnecessary his fear was.

Poor little thing, poor little thing. It's helpless, it needs
me, it's harmless so I won't harm it.

Slowly, in imagination, he worked towards that feeling,
her feeling, and then, suddenly, he was there, through
the anger, through the fear, through the hate to . . .
not love, he couldn't say that, but compassion. Glowing
and warm, compassion filled his heart and flooded his
veins, melting the ice there and washing him out into the
sea of sleep, and dreams where Jenny smiled and loved
him and there was no space between them for misunder-
standing.

He woke in the middle of the night with a desperate
urge to pee. He was out of bed in the dark hallway when
he remembered what was waiting in the bathroom. He
couldn't go back to bed with the need unsatisfied, but he
stood outside the bathroom door, hand hovering over the
light switch on this side, afraid to turn it on, open the
door, go in.

It wasn't, he realized, that he was afraid of a creature
no bigger than a football and less likely to hurt him;
rather, he was afraid that he might hurt it. It was a
stronger variant of that reckless vertigo he had felt sometimes in high places, the fear, not of falling, but of throw-

ing oneself off, of losing control and giving in to self-destructive urges. He didn't *want* to kill the thing—had his own feelings not undergone a sea change, Jenny's love for it would have been enough to stop him—but something, some dark urge stronger than himself, might make him.

Finally he went down to the end of the hall and outside to the weedy, muddy little area which passed for the communal front garden and in which the rubbish bins, of necessity, were kept, and, shivering in his thin cotton pajamas in the damp, chilly air, he watered the sickly forsythia, or whatever it was, that Jenny had planted so optimistically last winter.

When he went back inside, more uncomfortable than when he had gone out, he saw the light was on in the bathroom, and as he approached the half-open door, he heard Jenny's voice, low and soothing. "There, there. Nobody's going to hurt you, I promise. You're safe here. Go to sleep now. Go to sleep."

He went past without pausing, knowing he would be viewed as an intruder, and got back into bed. He fell asleep, lulled by the meaningless murmur of her voice, still waiting for her to join him.

Stuart was not used to doubting Jenny, but when she told him she had visited a veterinarian who had given her new pet a clean bill of health, he did not believe her.

In a neutral tone he asked, "Did he say what kind of animal it was?"

"He didn't know."

"He didn't know what it was, but he was sure it was perfectly healthy."

"God, Stuart, what do you want? It's obvious to everybody but you that my little friend is healthy and happy. What do you want, a birth certificate?"

He looked at her "friend," held close against her side, looking squashed and miserable. "What do you mean, 'everybody'?"

She shrugged. "Everybody at work. They're all jealous as anything." She planted a kiss on the thing's pointy head. Then she looked at him, and he realized that she had not kissed him, as she usually did, when he came in. She'd been clutching that thing the whole time. "I'm going to keep him," she said quietly. "If you don't like it, then . . ." Her pause seemed to pile up in solid, transparent blocks between them. "Then, I'm sorry, but that's how it is."

So much for an equal relationship, he thought. So much for sharing. Mortally wounded, he decided to pretend it hadn't happened.

"Want to go out for Indian tonight?"

She shook her head, turning away. "I want to stay in. There's something on telly. You go on. You could bring me something back, if you wouldn't mind. A spinach bahjee and a couple of nans would do me."

"And what about . . . something for your little friend?"

She smiled a private smile. "He's all right. I've fed him already." Then she raised her eyes to his and acknowledged his effort. "Thanks."

He went out and got take-away for them both, and stopped at the off-license for the Mexican beer Jenny favored. A radio in the off-license was playing a sentimental song about love that Stuart remembered from his earliest childhood: his mother used to sing it. He was shocked to realize he had tears in his eyes.

That night Jenny made up the sofa bed in the spare room, explaining, "He can't stay in the bathroom; it's just not satisfactory, you know it's not."

"He needs the bed?"

"I do. He's confused, everything is new and different, I'm the one thing he can count on. I have to stay with him. He needs me."

"He needs you? What about me?"

"Oh, Stuart," she said impatiently. "You're a grown man. You can sleep by yourself for a night or two."

"And that thing can't?"

"Don't call him a thing."

"What am I supposed to call it? Look, you're not its mother—it doesn't need you as much as you'd like to think. It was perfectly all right in the bathroom last night —it'll be fine in here on its own."

"Oh? And what do you know about it? You'd like to kill him, wouldn't you? Admit it."

"No," he said, terrified that she had guessed the truth. If she knew how he had killed one of those things she would never forgive him. "It's not true, I don't—I couldn't hurt it any more than I could hurt you."

Her face softened. She believed him. It didn't matter how he felt about the creature. Hurting it, knowing how she felt, would be like committing an act of violence against her, and they both knew he wouldn't do that. "Just for a few nights, Stuart. Just until he settles in."

He had to accept that. All he could do was hang on, hope that she still loved him and that this wouldn't be forever.

The days passed. Jenny no longer offered to drive him to work. When he asked her, she said it was out of her way and with traffic so bad a detour would make her late. She said it was silly to take him the short distance to the station, especially as there was nowhere she could safely stop to let him out, and anyway the walk would do him good. They were all good reasons, which he had used in the old days himself, but her excuses struck him painfully when he remembered how eager she had once been for his company, how ready to make any detour for his sake. Her new pet accompanied her everywhere, even to work, snug in the little nest she had made for it in a woven carrier bag.

"Of course things are different now. But I haven't stopped loving you," she said when he tried to talk to her about the breakdown of their marriage. "It's not like I've found another man. This is something completely different. It doesn't threaten you; you're still my husband."

But it was obvious to him that a husband was no longer something she particularly valued. He began to have fantasies about killing it. Not, this time, in a blind rage, but as part of a carefully thought-out plan. He might poison it, or spirit it away somehow and pretend it had run away. Once it was gone he hoped Jenny would forget it and be his again.

But he never had a chance. Jenny was quite obsessive about the thing, as if it were too valuable to be left un-guarded for a single minute. Even when she took a bath, or went to the toilet, the creature was with her, behind the locked door of the bathroom. When he offered to look after it for her for a few minutes she just smiled, as if the idea was manifestly ridiculous, and he didn't dare insist.

So he went to work, and went out for drinks with col-leagues, and spent what time he could with Jenny, although they were never alone. He didn't argue with her, although he wasn't above trying to move her to pity if he could. He made seemingly casual comments designed to convince her of his change of heart so that eventually, weeks or months from now, she would trust him and leave the creature with him—and then, later, perhaps, they could put their marriage back together.

One afternoon, after an extended lunch break, Stuart returned to the office to find one of the senior editors crouched on the floor beside his secretary's empty desk, whispering and chuckling to herself.

He cleared his throat nervously. "Linda?"

She lurched back on her heels and got up awkwardly. She blushed and ducked her head as she turned, looking very unlike her usual high-powered self. "Oh, uh, Stuart, I was just—"

Frankie came in with a pile of photocopying. "Uh-huh," she said loudly.

Linda's face got even redder. "Just going," she mumbled, and fled.

Before he could ask, Stuart saw the creature, another crippled bat–without–wings, on the floor beside the open bottom drawer of Frankie's desk. It looked up at him, opened its slit of a mouth and gave a sad little hiss. Around one matchstick-thin leg it wore a fine golden chain which was fastened at the other end to the drawer.

"Some people would steal anything that's not chained down," said Frankie darkly. "People you wouldn't suspect."

He stared at her, letting her see his disapproval, his annoyance, disgust, even. "Animals in the office aren't part of the contract, Frankie."

"It's not an animal."

"What is it, then?"

"I don't know. You tell me."

"It doesn't matter what it is, you can't have it here."

"I can't leave it at home."

"Why not?"

She turned away from him, busying herself with her stacks of paper. "I can't leave it alone. It might get hurt. It might escape."

"Chance would be a fine thing."

She shot him a look, and he was certain she knew he wasn't talking about *her* pet. He said, "What does your boyfriend think about it?"

"I don't have a boyfriend." She sounded angry but then, abruptly, the anger dissipated, and she smirked. "I don't have to have one, do I?"

"You can't have that animal here. Whatever it is. You'll have to take it home."

She raised her fuzzy eyebrows. "Right now?"

He was tempted to say yes, but thought of the manuscripts that wouldn't be sent out, the letters that wouldn't be typed, the delays and confusions, and he sighed. "Just don't bring it back again. All right?"

"Yowza."

He felt very tired. He could tell her what to do but she would no more obey than would his wife. She would bring it back the next day and keep bringing it back, maybe keeping it hidden, maybe not, until he either gave in or was forced into firing her. He went into his office, closed the door, and put his head down on his desk.

That evening he walked in on his wife feeding the creature with her blood.

It was immediately obvious that it was that way round. The creature might be a vampire—it obviously was—but his wife was no helpless victim. She was wide awake and in control, holding the creature firmly, letting it feed from a vein in her arm.

She flinched as if anticipating a shout, but he couldn't speak. He watched what was happening without attempting to interfere and gradually she relaxed again, as if he wasn't there.

When the creature, sated, fell off, she kept it cradled on her lap and reached with her other hand for the surgical spirit and cotton wool on the table, moistened a piece of cotton wool and tamped it to the tiny wound. Then, finally, she met her husband's eyes.

"He has to eat," she said reasonably. "He can't chew. He needs blood. Not very much, but . . ."

"And he needs it from you? You can't . . . ?"

"I can't hold down some poor scared rabbit or dog for him, no." She made a shuddering face. "Well, really, think about it. You know how squeamish I am. This is so much easier. It doesn't hurt."

It hurts me, he thought, but couldn't say it. "Jenny . . ."

"Oh, don't start," she said crossly. "I'm not going to get any disease from it, and he doesn't take enough to make any difference. Actually, I like it. We both do."

"Jenny, please don't. Please. For me. Give it up."

"No." She held the scraggy, ugly thing close and gazed at Stuart like a dispassionate executioner. "I'm sorry, Stuart, I really am, but this is nonnegotiable. If you can't accept that you'd better leave."

This was the showdown he had been avoiding, the end of it all. He tried to rally his arguments and then he realized he had none. She had said it. She had made her choice, and it was nonnegotiable. And he realized, looking at her now, that although she reminded him of the woman he loved, he didn't want to live with what she had become.

He could have refused to leave. After all, he had done nothing wrong. Why should he give up his home, this flat which was half his? But he could not force Jenny out onto the streets with nowhere to go; he still felt responsible for her.

"I'll pack a bag, and make a few phone calls," he said quietly. He knew someone from work who was looking for a lodger, and if all else failed, his brother had a spare room. Already, in his thoughts, he had left.

He ended up, once they'd sorted out their finances and formally separated, in a flat just off the Holloway Road, near Archway. It was not too far to walk if Jenny cared to visit, which she never did. Sometimes he called on her, but it was painful to feel himself an unwelcome visitor in the home they once had shared.

He never had to fire Frankie; she handed in her notice a week later, telling him she'd been offered an editorial job at The Women's Press. He wondered if pets in the office were part of the contract over there.

He never learned if the creatures had names. He never knew where they had come from, or how many there were. Had they fallen only in Islington? (Frankie had a flat somewhere off Upper Street.) He never saw anything on the news about them, or read any official confirmation of their existence, but he was aware of occasional oblique references to them in other contexts, occasional glimpses.

One evening, coming home on the tube, he found himself looking at the woman sitting opposite. She was about his own age, probably in her early thirties, with strawberry blond hair, greenish eyes, and an almost translucent complexion. She was strikingly dressed in high, soft-leather boots, a long black woolen skirt, and an enveloping cashmere cloak of cranberry red. High on the cloak, below and to the right of the fastening at the neck, was a simple, gold circle brooch. Attached to it he noticed a very fine golden chain which vanished inside the cloak, like the end of a watch fob.

He looked at it idly, certain he had seen something like it before, on other women, knowing it reminded him of something. The train arrived at Archway, and as he rose to leave the train, so did the attractive woman. Her stride matched his. They might well leave the station together. He tried to think of something to say to her, some pretext for striking up a conversation. He was after all a single man again now, and she might be a single woman. He had forgotten how single people in London contrived to meet.

He looked at her again, sidelong, hoping she would turn her head and look at him. With one slender hand she toyed with her gold chain. Her cloak fell open slightly as she walked, and he caught a glimpse of the creature she carried beneath it, close to her body, attached by a slender golden chain.

He stopped walking and let her get away from him. He had to rest for a little while before he felt able to climb the stairs to the street.

By then he was wondering if he had really seen what he thought he had seen. The glimpse had been so brief. But he had been deeply shaken by what he saw or imagined, and he turned the wrong way outside the station. When he finally realized, he was at the corner of Jenny's road, which had once also been his. Rather than retrace his steps, he decided to take the turning and walk past her house.

Lights were on in the front room, the curtains drawn against the early winter dark. His footsteps slowed as he drew nearer. He felt such a longing to be inside, back home, belonging. He wondered if she would be pleased at all to see him. He wondered if she ever felt lonely, as he did.

Then he saw the tiny, dark figure between the curtains and the window. It was spread-eagled against the glass, scrabbling uselessly; inside, longing to be out.

As he stared, feeling its pain as his own, the curtains swayed and opened slightly as a human figure moved between them. He saw the woman reach out and pull the creature away from the glass, back into the warm, lighted room with her, and the curtains fell again, shutting him out.

———————

Lisa Tuttle has written many stories in the science fiction, fantasy and horror fields, some of which have been collected in *A Spaceship Built of Stone* and *A Nest of Nightmares*. Her novels include *Windhaven* (with George R. R. Martin), *Gabriel* and *Familiar Spirit*. She is a winner of the John W. Campbell Award and editor of the nonfiction *Encyclopedia of Feminism*.

Ziggles

Donald R. Burleson

 Joyce didn't know it yet, but it was starting.

She was tired, and her head ached. God. Ten more minutes. Forcing a smile, she held up a clutch of papers to show the class. "All right, everyone—our Funtime Handout Page."

Amid the predictable hum and chatter, she thought: I wish someone would give *me* a handout. Ah, well—this little pleasantry was the signal that the day was nearly done, and they couldn't be any more relieved than she was. Of course *they* were not looking forward to a vodka martini when they got home.

She went among them, threading her way through the desks, handing out the pages.

"Is it 'find the animals' again, Miss Keating?" Cindy, in the back, wanted to know, impatient.

"No, Cindy, something a little different this time," Joyce said, smiling. "It's fun when it changes and things are new, don't you think?"

"Yes, ma'am." It sounded dutiful.

"Is it 'what's wrong with this picture,' Miss Keating?" asked Brad, across the aisle from Cindy in the back.

"No, not that either, Brad," Joyce said.

"Oh."

When the last of the sheets were handed out, Joyce returned to her desk amid a rustle of paper. "Who can read the instructions to us?"

Several children had their hands in the air. She pointed. "Wendy."

Little Wendy started reading. "Find, the, faces, that, are, hiding—"

"Hidden."

"Hidden, in this, pic—ture. You, should, be, able, to, find, t-twelve, faces. Look c-c—"

"Carefully."

"Carefully."

"All right, class, you may begin, and put your hand up as soon as you find twelve faces in the picture." The children became a sea of silent monks, their heads bent reverentially over the pages before them. Joyce scanned the picture herself. It was a line drawing of a country scene, meadows in the foreground punctuated by trees, a denser stand of trees farther off, low mountains in the background, clouds in the sky. She picked her way among the details, finding the faces. Two were woven cleverly into the clouds, another was rather more transparently concealed in the trunk of a tree, another in the grassy meadow itself, more in the far-off foliage, more in the contours of the mountains behind. There, another one, number twelve.

Slowly, hands began to go up; first Jerry, then Tammy, then Heather, and Mollie and Melissa and Brad and Paul, and others following. Barbara, in the front row, still looking down at her sheet, stretched her hand higher, eyes wide.

"Miss Keating?"

"Barbara?"

"I found thirteen."

"What a dope," Tom said from behind her, laughing. "It said twelve."

"That's not nice, Tom," Joyce said. "You think you found thirteen faces, Barbara?"

"Yes, ma'am." She gave Tom a sour look over her shoulder and stuck out her tongue.

"I see thirteen too," Jimmy said, nodding his head vigorously.

"Me, too." It was Melissa and Heather in singsong unison.

"Me, too," Russ said, a second later.

Well. "How about it, class? Are there really thirteen faces here?"

"No." It was a chorus: Wendy, Susie, Bill, Julie, Steve, others joining in. Little Karen, near the back of the room, was shaking her head with nearly pious conviction.

"I only see twelve."

"Well, then," Joyce said, "let's have someone who thinks they have found thirteen tell us where all the faces are."

Five hands went back up. Funny, Joyce thought, that it always seems to be these five, the old Fearsome Five, who see things differently. But maybe they're right. She pointed. "Russ, I believe you had your hand up first."

Russ, looking very pleased—almost, Joyce thought, gloatingly so—began. "Two of 'em is in the clouds."

"*Are* in the clouds."

He looked at her blankly and continued. One by one, he ticked off the same twelve faces she herself had found. Then: "And this funny round one on the left, lookin' around from behind the tree. That's thirteen."

She peered at her own sheet, puzzled. What face was he talking about? She didn't see anything. "I'm not sure I'm with you, Russ," she said, stepping around from behind her desk. Could the teacher's copy be different? "Let me look at your sheet."

She leaned over him. He was pointing at a spot in the picture where she felt certain she had looked. Sure enough, there was an odd face peering around from behind the trunk of a tree, a round, grinning face with none of the artistic sophistication of the other faces, a mere circle enclosing two dark little eyes and a wide, curving mouth. There was a suggestion of an arm, too, reaching around the tree trunk, an arm that was only a single line with a spidery hand of little radiating lines at the end. It was—rather odious, somehow. How had she missed it in her own copy?

"I don't see nothing," Cheryl piped up from nearby.

Heather turned on her. "You're pretty stupid, then, Cheryl, 'cause it's right there. I see it."

"Heather, that's not very—" Joyce began.

"It *is* there," Jimmy said, with Melissa and Heather and Russ and Barbara nodding sagely.

"Is *not*," Mollie said.

"Is *so*," Barbara spat back at her.

A full-blown brawl was stewing, and Joyce moved to stop it. "Listen, class. I do see the face there, so I guess it does make thirteen. But those of you who didn't see this last one, I can't blame you, because when I looked at first I didn't see it either. So let's not fight about it, okay?"

It *had* been a long day, and the thought of that vodka martini seemed more fetching every minute.

◦   ◦   ◦

Phillips Park was nearly deserted, and that was fine with
her. Sitting on a bench near the middle of the park, she
savored the silence, stretching her legs, relaxing, taking
some deep breaths. The sky was a ripening red melon in
the west as the last trace of the sun slipped below the
line of the trees, and it was only pleasantly cool, comfortable for the middle of May in New Hampshire. She dug
into the bag at her side and pulled out a paperback novel
and settled herself to enjoy a good half hour's reading.
After a day like today, she owed it to herself to rest a bit
before going home and preparing her dinner.

The light was waning, and she drowsed over her book
for a moment. Or maybe for longer; it was hard to tell.
When she opened her eyes and took her glasses off,
there were only a few thin cottony wisps of crimson in
the sky, and a cooler breeze had sprung up. She gathered
her coat collar closer around her throat and closed her
book and put it back in the bag. Across the grassy ex-
panse before her, an elderly couple were walking their
dog on a leash and, beyond them, across the way, groups
of children were running, their motions putting her in
mind of the skittering of waterbugs. A sound wafted
across to her.

"Hi, Miss Keating!"

She strained to see. It was Melissa and Heather, off in
the distance, waving as they ran. She waved back to
them, and they went on their way, cavorting together.
She fished a cigarette out of her purse and cupped her
hand against the breeze and lit up, and sat back and
looked across the park toward the woody corner where
the children played. Melissa and Heather and someone
else were running, chasing each other in dizzy circles

around a large maple tree, and she could hear their muffled laughter. As she made ready to leave she massaged her tired eyes and put her glasses back on. No, she had been mistaken; it was only the two of them out there, only Heather and Melissa.

With only a few days left of school, it was inevitable that they were more than usually restless, and on this particular day it had been a strain on her, no question about it. Could you begin to "burn out" after only nine years of teaching? At any rate, it was a relief to get to the Funtime Handout today; this would settle them in until time to go.

"Is it 'find the faces' again, Miss Keating?" Jimmy wanted to know.

"No, Jimmy. Not this time."

"We never had 'find the faces' again," he complained.

"Well, that'll come around another time," she said. "This one is 'hidden animals' again. It will be fun."

When the sheets were handed out and the class was studying them, she glanced at the picture. This time it was a city street scene, and animals were woven in. A store's display window had a striped cloth in which lurked a zebra. A cat's head was hidden in the wrinkled lines of a man's coat. There were the inevitable cloud dwellers, a dog, a cow. Altogether she counted fourteen, the recommended number. Hands were going up; they had found them too.

Barbara was in a state of excitement. "And him!"

"What do you mean, Barbara?" On an impulse, Joyce edged around her desk and went over to look on the girl's sheet.

"Here, Miss Keating, behind the car. It's Ziggles."

"It's *what*?" Joyce peered at the picture. Again, a circular, vapid-looking face line-drawn with small, dark eyes stared back at her, its wispy hands clutching the edge of the parked car that hid most of its form. In a crazy way, something about the thing made her think of Ken, with his gangly arms and long fingers. She suppressed the thought.

"Ziggles, Miss Keating," Russ was saying.

Cheryl and Mollie and Brad were in an uproar. "There's nothing there."

"Use your eyes, you dummies," Heather said. "He's right there."

Joyce's head was beginning to ache dully. "Hold on a minute. I said—class!" The noise subsided, but hostile looks still darted back and forth. "Now, what's all this about Ziggles? I don't know why it's in this picture, too, but why do you call it that?"

Jimmy looked at her as if she were demented. "Because that's his name."

Joyce's professional instincts began to kick in. Don't stifle their creativity, a voice whispered. "Well, that's an interesting name. Who thought of it first?"

Melissa shook her head, tossing her pigtails like a Chinese kite. "That's just his name. 'Cause his arms and legs go like this"—she drew zigzags in the air with her forefinger—"and 'cause he wiggles when he walks." The class laughed, though some more freely than others. As usual, she reflected, it seemed to be the old Fearsome Five who relished all this most; some of the others were still blinking at the picture and shaking their heads, not seeing the face.

"Well, anyhow, we did find all the animals, right, everyone?"

"Yes, Miss Keating."

She returned to her desk and put the teacher's copy of the handout away hurriedly, without looking at it too closely.

The last rumbles of the buses were dying away outside, lumbering dinosaurs carrying squealing children in their bellies. The hallway was flanked with long bulletin boards on which were tacked, crowded and overlapping like scales on a fish, the second-grade and third-grade artwork. The scent of dried paste and pungent crayon made her almost dizzy, and it was surely only that, and the poor lighting, that made her think she saw a pale and curious face nodding at her from out of the multicolor frenzy of Melissa's farm scene. Looking quickly away, she saw Mr. O'Connell coming down the hall with his school-administrator smile. The fellow meant well.

"You're looking a little tired, Joyce."

She grinned and nodded. "I *am* a little tired."

He picked a piece of lint from his tweed jacket and returned her grin. "Those second-graders keeping you on the run, are they?"

"I guess they are."

"Well, hang in there. School year's almost over. Summer's peeking at us from around the corner."

Somehow, she wished he had chosen another image.

This time it was the "what's wrong with this picture" variation. As always, some of the children were pleased, some were disappointed. They puzzled over their sheets, looking for the fifteen things that were supposed to be wrong. Joyce, examining her own copy, quickly found them: the dog with his feet pointed the wrong way, the faucet in the tree trunk, the car with square tires, the apartment window with the venetian blinds on the outside, the man walking with only one shoe, the other things. Hands were going up.

"Cindy, will you tell us what the fifteen things are that are wrong?"

Cindy, haltingly because she had to find some of them again, named them off, with Tammy and Steve helping her out with two that she missed. "That's fifteen," she said finally.

"Sixteen!" exclaimed Russ.

What now? Joyce thought. Not again. Outside the window, a light rain had begun to fall, and there was a grumble of thunder in the air. "Russ? What *else* is wrong with the picture?"

He grinned and clapped his hands, and Melissa and Jimmy and Heather and Barbara joined in. "What's wrong with the picture is, Ziggles isn't in it!"

For once the weather forecast had been accurate, and she had been right to bring her raincoat. It wasn't a long walk home from the school, but the rain had begun coming down somewhat harder by the time she passed the park. No children playing there today, certainly. The rain on the plastic hood of her raincoat was a loud and constant patter now, and she felt chilled. Off there in the distance, someone *was* in the park after all. But it was hard to see through the blowing rain, and besides, black rain clouds in the sky had made it so dark that some of the streetlamps overhead, goosenecked out over the sidewalk, had started flickering faintly, trying to come on. The sooner she got home and inside, safe and warm and dry, the better.

Why had she thought *safe* as well as *warm* and *dry*?

Past the park, she slogged through the water gathering on the pavement, and reflected that she could have asked for a ride with someone, or could even have called a cab. She was the only one crazy enough to be out here courting pneumonia in this weather.

Except for whoever was sloshing through the puddles behind her.

She turned and looked around. What appeared to be something stringy attached to a lamppost was only the pattern made by rivulets of water filling the cracks in the surface. Nothing moved, no one was there. She walked on, beginning to shiver with the cold. She turned down her side street.

And heard someone splashing through rainwater behind her.

This was silly; she wasn't about to look around again. But she was going to walk a little faster. No use staying out in this chilly air any longer than necessary. She ought to hurry on home. She picked up her pace.

And someone, or some*thing*, sizzled along all the faster behind her.

She was running now, catching at her breath, badly out of shape. Her feet sent water spraying, and she slipped and nearly fell, steadying herself by catching hold of a utility pole. As she brought her head up, regaining her balance, stringy black fingers reached around to plant themselves wispily on both sides of her face. Screaming, she brushed at the fingers, feeling them hard and ropy and clammy in the streaming rain. They were the drawstrings on the hood of her raincoat.

Inside her apartment, she had a drink, and thought about Ken (wasn't that over, a long time ago?), and had a

cry, and another drink, and laughed at herself and tried
to read, but fell into an uneasy sleep, in which her
dreams were of a frenzied form in the dark and the rain,
a form like graphite lines in the air, zigzag lines of negative lightning, jagged dark against dark, atop which an
idiot circle nodded and smiled as spidery hands groped
for her face. When she awoke, she was nearly late for
school.

She was not going to let her nerves and the pressures of
her life put her out of sorts for the end of the school
year. The remaining days would pass, and then she could
relax for the summer. The important thing was to keep
wholesomely occupied and think only practical and pro-
ductive thoughts. Her headaches became less frequent,
and her outlook improved. Mornings she came to work
smiling, and afternoons she left not feeling too worn out.
She was going to make it.

A heightened regimen of pupil discipline helped.
These kids were not going to get her down, and she was
letting them know it. Even the Fearsome Five were going to stay in line, or she was jolly well going to make
them wish they had. It seemed to be working; all in all,
there was order in her classroom.

During the Funtime Handout sessions she kept things
running at a brisk pace. Today, it was even "find the
faces" again, and she was brooking no nonsense. There
were fifteen faces in the picture, and that meant fifteen,
no more.

Heather was looking sly. "I found sixteen." Jimmy and
Melissa snickered, behind her.

"He-e-e's there, okay," Russ said, rolling his eyes comically wide, and Barbara giggled, covering her mouth with her hand. Most of the others looked uncomfortable.

"We're having none of that today," Joyce said, stuffing her own handout page into her briefcase without looking at it. "We have ten minutes left. You may spend it cleaning your desks."

On the last day of school, Russ and Jimmy were in trouble from the beginning. The first thing in the morning, they smacked each other with chalk-dusty erasers, stirring up a cloud that sent some of the other children coughing. Joyce had a hand on each of the boys, leading them back to their seats.

"If any of you think that you can't get into trouble just because it's the last day, you can just think again." Shame them, too, she thought, and added: "Is this how third-graders behave?"

Thank heaven it would be an early-release day.

As the morning wore on, the trouble continued. Melissa spilled a jar of paint on the floor, and the ensuing chaos of giggling and reproach and name-calling was unpleasant; Joyce could almost have sworn the spilling of the paint had been deliberate. Heather and Barbara, for the rest of the morning, were in a behind-the-hands conspiracy of snickering and laughing, and by eleven o'clock Joyce was thoroughly fed up.

"All right. Russ. Heather. Barbara. Melissa. Jimmy. It's not as if I didn't warn you, now, is it? I told you I don't care if it *is* the last day of school, I'm not putting up with any more of your nonsense. The five of you will remain in your seats after the final bell has rung. If you're going to be third-graders, you're going to have to learn some responsibility for what you do." Some of the other children were looking smugly vindicated; their expressions said: It serves them right.

The last echoes of the final bell were dying away down the halls amid the distant rumble of the buses. Joyce stood at her desk, looking at the five of them, still in their seats. She ruffled a handful of papers.

"These are some extra spelling exercises," she said, aware of their quiet moans of disapproval. "You will work on them until I say you can go." She stepped among them and handed out the pages. They eyed her with expressions she found difficult to characterize—not sullenness or resentment, exactly; something less placeable. Sometimes the eyes of a child could look . . . old.

She returned to her desk and busied herself with end-of-the-year paperwork, barely noticing at first that the sky through the room-length windows had grown dark and grumbly, and that a steady rain had begun to fall. Well, she reflected, if nothing else, I may have to give some of these little ne'er-do-wells a ride home. But at least I made my point. There's a limit to what I will put up with in my classroom. She squinted at the administrative forms cluttering her desktop; the light was poor, and with the strain on her eyes, a headache was starting. She wouldn't be staying much longer.

Glancing up, she found the children busy at their work, heads bent over their desks; only Barbara returned the glance, smiling enigmatically for an instant and returning to her task. It was almost as if they had *wanted* to stay after school, all of them; what little demons they had been all day.

The power must be close to browning out, she thought, it's so dim in here; I can barely see, and I can't really expect them to hurt their eyes trying to read under these conditions. She glanced up again. Apparently oblivious to the poor lighting, the six of them were still quietly at work.

Children are pretty hardy creatures, she reflected; too much so, sometimes, since they'll harm their eyes reading in near-darkness just because it doesn't particularly bother them to—

The *six* of them?

She jerked her head up.

No, what was she thinking? Melissa, Jimmy, Heather, Barbara, Russ.

Five.

But in the gathering darkness, the incongruous midday darkness of the storm, it seemed to her that they weren't sitting where they should be. Had they moved farther back? She squinted at them; her head was hurting worse now. Surely they were in their own seats, and it was the wan light and the dully throbbing pain in her temples that made them seem distant, indistinct.

And when she glanced up the next time, she felt that surely it was the poor light and the ache in her head that made it seem as if the six of them, from farther back than they should be, from a giddy distance back in the dark corner of the room, were grinning insupportably at her. This was hysterical nonsense, and she dropped her eyes and pushed her ballpoint pen along with renewed speed.

And only looked up when she realized she'd thought it again: six of them.

And six of them it was, because now, his gray pencil-line legs jittering insanely under him, his big vacuous white disc of a face nodding and grinning and peering with its tiny doll-like black-dot eyes, his long, thin, ropy arms zigzagging in the air, his spidery fingers splayed to an almost obscene eagerness, here he came now, moving rapidly like a wisp of hair among the chairs, crossing the darkening room. In spite of herself she closed her eyes, and whether it was those sinewy fingers that caressed her burning face for a moment or just a clammy touch of storm-driven wind from the window she could not say, but then it did not matter, because he was upon her.

Donald R. Burleson's short stories have appeared in *Twilight Zone, The Magazine of Fantasy & Science Fiction,* and the anthologies *Best New Horror, The Year's Best Fantasy Stories* and *Post Mortem.* He is also the author of *H. P. Lovecraft: A Critical Study* and *Lovecraft: Disturbing the Universe.*

End of the Line

Ramsey Campbell

 "Pook."

"Is this Mrs. Pook?"

"Who wants to know?"

"My name . . . my name is Roger and I think you may be interested in what I have to offer you."

"That's what you say. You don't know a thing about me."

"Don't you wish you could see what I look like?"

"Why, what have you got on?"

"I mean, don't you wish you could see my face?"

"Not if it looks like you sound. Mum, there's some weird character on the phone."

"Hang on, I thought you said you were Mrs.—"

"He's saying would I like to watch him."

"Who's speaking, please? What have you been suggesting to my daughter?"

"My name is Rum, that is, my name's Ralph, and I think you may be interested in what I'm offering."

"I doubt it. Don't I know you?"

"My name's Ralph."

"I don't know anyone called Ralph, but I'm sure I know your voice. What's your game?"

"He said his name was Roger, mum, not Ralph."

"Did he now. Charlie? Charlie, pick up the extension and listen to this."

"Mrs. Pook, if I can just explain—"

"Charlie, will you pick up the extension. There's one of those perverts who like to hide behind a phone. He can't even remember his own name."

"Who the fuck is this? What do you want with my wife?"

"My name's Ralph, Mr. Pook, and perhaps I can speak to you. I'm calling on behalf of—"

"Whoever he is, Charlie, his name isn't Ralph."

"My name isn't important, Mr. Pook. I should like to off—"

"Don't you tell me what's important, pal, specially not on my fucking phone. What do you want? How did you get this number?"

"Out of the directory. Can I take just a few minutes of your time? We'd like to offer you a way of avoiding mis-understandings like this one."

"It's we now, is it? You and who else?"

"I'm calling on be—"

"Charlie, I think I know who—"

"Tell you what, pal, I don't care how many of you there are. Just you say where I can find you and we'll settle it like men."

"Just put it down. Just put it down."

"What are you mumbling about, pal? Lost your voice?"

"Mrs. Pook, are you still there?"

"Never mind talking to my fucking wife. This is between you and me, pal. If you say another word to her—"

"That's enough, Charlie. Yes, I'm here."

"Mrs. Pook, would your first name be Lesley?"

"That's it, pal! I'm warning you! If any fucker says another fucking word—"

"Just put it down," Speke told himself again, and this time he succeeded. The long room was full of echoes of his voice in voices other than his own: "I'm speaking on behalf . . ." "Don't you wish . . ." During the conversation his surroundings—the white desks staffed by fellow workers whom he scarcely knew, the walls to which the indirect lighting lent the appearance of luminous chalk, the stark black columns of names and addresses and numbers on the page in front of him—had grown so enigmatic they seemed meaningless, and the only way he could think of to escape this meaninglessness was by speaking. He crossed out Pook and keyed the next number. "Mrs. Pool?"

"This is she."

"I wonder if I could take just a few minutes of your time."

"Take as much as you like if it's any use to you."

"My name is Roger and I'm calling on behalf of Face to Face Communications. I should have said that to begin with."

"No need to be nervous of me, especially not on the phone."

"I mum, I'm not. I was going to ask don't you wish you could see what I look like."

"Not much chance of that, I'm afraid."

"On the phone, you mean. Well, I'm calling to offer—"

"Or anywhere else."

"I don't rum realum rea*lum* really under—"

"I could have seen you up to a few years ago. Do you look as you sound?"

"I suppum."

"I'm sorry that I'm blind, then."

"No, it's my fault. I mean, that's not my fault, I mean I'm the one who should be sorry, apologizing, that's to sum—" He managed to drag the receiver away from his mouth, which was still gabbling, and plant the handset in its cradle. He crossed out her name almost blindly and closed his eyes tight, but had to open them as soon as he heard voices reiterating portions of the formula around him. He focused on the next clear line in the column and grabbing the receiver called the number. "Mr. Poole?"

"Yes."

"This is *Mr.* Poole?"

"Who, you are?"

"No, I'm saying you are, are you?"

"Why, do you know different?"

"Yum, you don't sound—" To Speke it sounded like a woman trying to be gruff—like Lesley, he thought, or even his daughter, if hers had been the voice which had answered the Pooks' phone. "My name is Roger," he said hastily, "and I'm calling on behalf of Face to Face Communications. I wonder if you can spare me a few minutes of your time."

"It'd be hard for me to spare anyone else's."

"Well, qum. Dum. Um, don't you wish you could see my face?"

"What's so special about it?"

"Not just my face, anyone's on the phone. I'd like to

offer you a month's free trial of the latest breakthrough in communication, the videphone."

"So that you can see if I'm who I say I am? Who did you think I was?"

"Was when?"

"Before I was who I said I was."

"Forgum. Forgive me, but you sound exactly like—"

"Sounds like you've got a wrong number," the voice said, and cut itself off.

It seemed to have lodged in his head, blotting out the overlapping voices around him. He returned the handset to its housing and made his way up the aisle to the supervisor's desk, feeling as if his feet were trying to outrun each other. The supervisor was comparing entries on forms with names and addresses in her directory. "How's it coming, Roger?" she said, though he hadn't seen her glance at him.

"A bit hit and miss this evening, Mrs. Shillingsworth," he managed to say without stumbling. "I wonder if I should vary my approach."

"It seems to be working for everyone else," she said, indicating the forms with an expansive gesture. "Have you any customers for me?"

"Not yet tonight. That's what I was saying."

She ticked a box on the form she was examining and raised her wide-eyed placid flawless face to give him a single blink. "So what did you want to suggest?"

"Maybum, jum, just that maybe we could use our own voices a bit more, I mean our own words."

"I'll mention it next time the boss comes on screen. Have they installed yours yet, by the way?"

"They were supposed to have by now, but we're still waiting."

"It's important to you, isn't it?"

"I didn't think seeing people's faces while I'm talking to them was, but now I know I can . . ."

"Customers have priority. I'll speak to the engineers anyway. As for your calls, you can play them by ear to a certain extent. Just don't go mad." She looked down quickly, clearing her throat, and pulled the next form towards herself. "Give them another half an hour and if you haven't had any joy by then I'll let you go."

The conversation had left Speke feeling locked into the formula, which sounded more enigmatic every time he placed a call. "My name is Roger and I'm speaking on behalf of—"

Only half an hour to go . . .

"My name is Roger and I'm speaking—"

Only twenty-eight minutes . . .

"My name is Roger and I—"

Only twenty-six . . .

"My name is Roger—"

Twenty-four minutes, twenty- two, twenty, one thousand and eighty seconds, nine hundred and fifty-seven, eight hundred and forty-one, seven hundred and . . .

"My name is Roger and I'm speaking on behalf of Face to Face Communications."

"Really."

"Yes, I wonder if I can borrow a few minutes of your time. I expect that at this very moment you're wishing you could see my face."

"Really."

"Yes, I know I am. I'd like to offer you a month's free trial of the latest breakthrough in communication, the videphone."

"Really."

"Yes, you must know people who already have one, but perhaps you think it's a luxury you can't afford. I'm here to tell you, Mr. Pore, that our technicians have brought the cost down to the level of your pocket, even my pockum. If you'll allow us to install our latest model in your home for a month at no obligation to you, you can see for yourself."

"Really."

"That's what I said."

"Well, go ahead."

"Sorry, you wum— You're asking me to arrange a trial?"

"I thought that was why you were calling, Roger."

"Yes, of course. Just a mum, I'll just gum—" Speke had been growing more and more convinced that Pore was making fun of him. He snatched a form from the pile beside the six-inch screen, on which electrical disturbances continued to flicker as though they were about to take shape. "Let me just take a few details," he said.

Pore responded to his name and address with no more than a grunt at each, and emitted so vague a sound when he was asked what times would be best for him that Speke suggested times which would be convenient for himself, not that it had anything to do with him. When he returned the handset to its nest his half an hour had almost elapsed, but he couldn't call it a day now that he might have made a sale. He pushed the form to the edge of his desk to be collected by the supervisor and found his gaze straying up the column in the directory to Pook, Charles. He crossed out the listing until it resembled a black slit in the page, and then he wished he'd memorized the number.

"My name is Roger and I'm speaking," he repeated as

he drove home. Figures were silhouetted against the illuminated windows of shops, or rendered monochrome by streetlights, or spotlighted by headlamps. On the two miles of dual carriageway between the office block and the tower block where he lived he couldn't distinguish a single face, even when he peered in the rearview mirror. Large fierce bare bulbs guarded the car park around the tower block, and the glare of them pulled a bunch of shadows out of him as he left the Mini and walked to the entrance. For a moment numbers other than the combination for the doors suggested themselves to him. He keyed the correct sequence and shouldered his way in.

Although the tower blocks had been gentrified it seemed that a child had been playing in the lift, which stopped at every floor. Someone with long hair was waiting on the seventh, but turned towards the other lift as the door of Speke's opened, so that Speke didn't see his or her face. Until the person moved Speke had the impression that it was a dummy which had been placed near the lifts to lend some contrast to the parade of otherwise identical floors, fifteen of them before he was able to step out of the shaky box and hurry to his door.

Stef was home. The kitchen and the bedroom lights were on, and the narrow hall, which was papered with posters for English-language films which had been dubbed into other languages, smelled of imminent dinner. Speke eased the door shut and tiptoed past the bedroom and the bathroom to the main room, but he had only just switched on the light above the bar when Stef emerged from the bedroom. "Shall I make us drinks, Roger?"

"Rum," Speke said before he managed to say "Right."

"We haven't any rum unless you've bought some. It looks as if we've just about everything else."

"Whatever's quickest," Speke said, sitting down so as not to seem too eager; then he jumped up and kissed her forehead, giving her bare waist a brief squeeze. "Tell you what, I'll make them if you want to see to dinner."

"I'll get dressed first, shall I?"

"I should."

He had a last sight of her glossy black underwear half-concealed by her long blond hair as she stepped into the hall while he uncorked the vodka. One swig felt sufficient to take the edge off his thoughts. He made two Bloody Marys, with rather more vodka in his, and carried them into the kitchen, where Stef in a kimono was arranging plates on the trolley. "Busy day?" he said.

"We've a class of students all week at the studio. I've been showing them what you can do with sound and vision."

"What can I?"

"Don't start that. What they can. Tomorrow I'll be on the sidelines while they improvise."

"I know how you feel."

Before she responded she ladled coq au vin onto the plates, wheeled the trolley into the main room, switched on the light over the dining table and set out the plates, and then she said, "What's wrong?"

"I'm . . ."

"Go on, Roger. Whatever it is, it's better out than in."

"I'm sure I spoke to Lesley and Vanessa."

"What makes you say that?"

"You just did."

"Don't tell me if you don't want me to know."

"I dum," Speke said, draining the cocktail and wrenching the cork out of a liter of Argentinian red. "Someone answered the phone and I thought it was Lesley, but it turned out to be the daughter."

"Why are they on your mind again after all this time?"

Speke topped up her wineglass and refilled his own. "Because I spoke to the husband as well. I can't believe Lesley could have got involved with someone like that, let alone married him."

"Well, all of us—" Stef silenced herself with a mouthful of dinner. After more chewing than Speke thought necessary she said, "Someone like what?"

"By the sound of him, an ego with a mouth."

"Some partners cope with worse."

"But if she can handle him, why couldn't shum— Besides, what about Vanessa? She must still be at school, she shouldn't be expected tum—"

"Roger, we agreed you'd try and put them out of your head."

"Wum," Speke said, not so much a stutter as a deliberate attempt to shut himself up, and drained his wine in order to refill the glass.

Once he'd opened a bottle of dessert wine to accompany the ice cream it seemed a pity to cork it after only one glass. Stef allowed him to replenish hers when it was half-empty, but placed her hand over it when he tried again. "I have to get up early," she said.

He was washing up the dinner things when it occurred to him that he'd heard a plea in her voice because she wanted them to make love. When he found his way into the bedroom, however, she was asleep. He switched off all the lights and considered watching television, but the prospect of consuming images on a screen—images which were lifelike and yet no longer alive—had lost its appeal. He sat at the dining table and finished the bottle while gazing out of the window at the neighboring tower blocks. The window resembled a screen too—perhaps a computer display on which enigmatic patterns of luminous rectangles occasionally shifted at random—but at least he could see no faces on it, not even his own. When he'd emptied the bottle he sat for a time and then took himself to bed.

He awoke with a sense that someone had just spoken to him. If Stef had, it must have been more than an hour ago, when she would have left for work. Sunlight streamed into the room, catching dust in the air. Speke sat up and waited for his equilibrium to align itself with him; then he performed several tasks gingerly—showered, shaved, drank a large glass of orange juice, ate cereal heaped with sugar and swimming in milk, downed several mugfuls of black coffee that shrank the image of his face—before he set about tidying up. He dusted everything except the bottles behind the bar, since they hardly called for dusting. He went once through the rooms with the large vacuum cleaner and then again with its baby. He loaded the washing machine and, when it had finished, the dryer. He rearranged the plates in the kitchen cupboard and the cutlery in the drawers, and lined up tins of food and packets of ingredients in alphabetical order. He found himself hoping that all this activity would keep him there until Stef came home, but the only company he had was the persistent sense of having just heard a voice. Before Stef returned it was time for him to leave for work.

The late afternoon sky, and presumably the sun, was the same color as the extinguished bulbs above the car park. All the colors around him, such as they were—of

cars, of leafless saplings, of curtains in the windows of the
chalky tower blocks—appeared to be about to fade to
monochrome. If he walked fast he would be at work on
time, but if he drove he might feel less exposed.Though
he drove slowly he was able to glimpse only a handful of
faces, all of which seemed unusually remote from him.

Several of his colleagues were already in the long
room, draping their jackets over the backs of their chairs
or tipping the contents of polystyrene cups into their
faces. As Speke aligned the forms and the directory with
the lower edge of the screen on his desk the supervisor
beckoned to him, hooking a finger before pointing it first
at her mouth and then at her ear. "Yes, Mrs. Shillingsworth," he said when he felt close enough to speak.

"Pore."

"Pum."

"Mr. Pore. Mr. Roger Pore. Does the name convey
anything to you?"

"Yes, he booked a month's free trial last night."

"You're standing by that, are you?"

"Yes, I should say sum. He was my only catch."

"And you felt you had to give me one."

"Shouldn't I hum?"

"Only if it stands up. His wife says he never spoke to
anyone."

"She must have got it wrong, or the engineers did.
They're only engineers, num—"

"It was I who had a word with her, Mr. Speke, because there were things on your form I didn't understand. Was it a Scotsman you spoke to?"

"A Scum? No, he sounded more like me."

"Mr. Pore is a Scotsman."

"How do you know if you spoke to his wife?"

"They both are. I heard them."

"What, his wife sounds like a Scotsmum? I mean, I'm sorry, I must have, maybe I—"

"I should try harder tonight if I were you, but not that hard," Mrs. Shillingsworth said, gazing at him over the form which she had lifted from the desk and crumpling it above her wastebasket before letting it drop.

"You aren't me," Speke mumbled as he headed for his desk. He was sitting down when he realized he had walked too far. About to push back the chair, he grabbed the directory instead and turned quickly to the page corresponding to his assignment. Pontin, Ponting, Pool, Poole . . . He made himself run his gaze down the column more slowly, but there was no entry for Pook.

"Old directory," he told himself, and moved to the desk on his left, where he checked that the directory was up-to-date before heaving it open at the same page. Ponting, Pool. He lowered his face to peer at the names as though the one he was seeking might have fallen through the space between them, then he dodged to the next desk, and the next. Ponting, Pool, Ponting, Pool . . . He didn't know how long Mrs. Shillingsworth had been watching him. "There you are," she said briskly, indicating the blank screen on his desk.

He ran at his chair and flung the directory open."Mrs. Pook," he repeated over and over under his breath until he heard himself saying "Mrs. Spook." Between Ponting and Pool was an etched line of black ink wide enough, he was almost sure, to conceal a directory entry. He was holding the page close to his face and tilting the book at various angles in an attempt to glimpse what lay beneath the ink when he realized that the supervisor was still watching him. "Jum, jum—" he explained, and fumbling

the handset out of its stand, hastily keyed the first un-
marked number.

When the screen flickered he thought he'd called a
videphone at last, but the flicker subsided, "Poridge?" a
voice said.

"Just cornflakes for me."

"Beg p?"

"Um sum, I'm speaking on behalf, on behalf of Face
to Face Communications and I wonder if, fum. If you
can spare me a few minutes."

"Sugar?"

"What?"

"Lots of it for your cereal, sugar."

"How did you know? What are you making out?"

"I think that's enough sweetness," Mr. Poridge
seemed to respond, and terminated the call.

Speke was grateful to be rid of the voice, whose feminine sound he hadn't cared for. He memorized the next
number and turned the directory in an attempt to shed
some light on whatever the line of ink concealed as he
placed the call. "Pork," a woman told him.

"Y pig."

"What's that? Who's this?"

The screen was flickering so much Speke thought it
was about to answer her last question, unless it was his
vision that had begun to flicker. When the screen remained blank he said "Miss Pork, my name is Roger and
I wonder—"

"Same here."

"You are? You're what?"

"Wondering what I'm being made to listen to."

"I'm not making you. I just jum, just wondering. That

is, I'm speaking on behalf of Face to Face Communications."

"That's what you call this, is it?"

"No, that's what I'm saying. I wish we could see each other face to face."

"Do you now?"

Speke's gaze darted from the line of ink to the screen, where the flickering had intensified. "Why?" said the voice.

"Because then I'd see if you lum, if you look, if you don't just sound like—" Speke gabbled before he managed to slam the handset into place.

He kept his head down until he couldn't resist glancing up. Though Mrs. Shillingsworth wasn't watching him he was convinced that she had been. He repeated the next number out loud and moved the directory another half an inch, another quarter, another eighth. Something was close to making itself clear: the digits beneath the ink or the restlessness on the screen? He keyed the numbers he was muttering and glanced up, down, up, down . . . "Porne," a voice said in his ear.

"My name is Roger and I wonder—"

"Porne."

"I wonder what number I've called."

"Ours. Porne."

That was the name in the directory, but Speke suspected that he had inadvertently keyed the numbers which perhaps, for an instant too brief for him to have been conscious of it, had been visible through the line of ink. "Don't I know you?" he said.

"Where from?"

"From in here," Speke said, tapping his forehead and baring his teeth at the screen, where his grin appeared as a whitish line like an exposed bone in the midst of a pale blur. "I expect you wish you could see my face."

"Why, what are you doing with it?"

Speke stuffed the topmost form into the edges of the screen, because each flicker seemed to render his reflection less like his. "Don't you think that your name says a lot?" he said.

"What do you mean by that, young man?"

"You're a woman, aren't you? But not as old as you want me to think."

"How dare you! Let me speak to your supervisor!"

"How did you know I've got one? You gave yourself away there, didn't you? And since when has it been an insult to tell a woman she isn't as old as she seems? Sounds to me as if you've got something to hide, Mrs. or Miss."

"Why, you young—"

"Not so young. Not so old either. Same age as you, as a matter of fact, as if you didn't know."

"Who do you imagine you're talking to? Charles, come here and speak to this, this—"

"It's Charles now, is it? Too posh for that ape," Speke said, and fitted the handset into its niche while he read the next number. He fastened his gaze on the digits and touch-typed them on the handset, and lifted the form with which he had covered the screen. His grin was still there amid the restless flickering; the sight made him feel as though a mask had been clipped to his face. He let the page fall, and a voice which felt closer than his ear to him said, "Posing."

"Who is?"

"This is Miss Posing speaking."

"Why do you keep answering the phone with just a

name? Do you really expect me to believe anyone has names like those?"

"Who is this?"

"You already asked me that two calls ago. Or are you asking if I know who you are? Belum—"

Mrs. Shillingsworth was staring at him. He hadn't realized he was speaking loud enough for her to overhear, even if his was the only voice he could hear in the crowded room. The panic which overwhelmed him seemed to flood into his past, so that he was immediately convinced that every voice he'd spoken to on the phone was the same voice, not just tonight but earlier—how much earlier, he would rather not think. "Thanks anyway," he said at the top of his voice, both to assure Mrs. Shillingsworth that nothing was wrong and to blot out the chorus around him, which had apparently begun to chant "I'm speaking" in unison. The only voice he wanted to hear, was desperate to hear, was Stef's.

He couldn't remember the number. He stared at the flickering line of black ink while he thumbed through the wad of corners. As soon as he'd glimpsed the number, which now he saw was in the same position as the line of ink, he let the directory fall back to the page from which he was meant to be working. He pulled a form towards him and poised his pen above it as he typed the digits, resisting the urge to grin at Mrs. Shillingsworth to persuade her this wasn't a private call. He had barely entered the number when the closest voice so far said, "S & V Studios."

"Stef?"

"Hang on." As the voice receded from the earpiece it seemed to retreat into Speke's skull. "Vanessa, is Stefanie still here?"

"Just gone."

"Just gone, apparently. Is there a message?"

"I've already got it," Speke said through his fixed grin.

"I'm sorry?"

"You're forgetting to disguise your voice," Speke said and dropping the handset into its niche, leaned on it until he felt it was secure. "I'm speaking," said a voice, then another. All the screens around him appeared to be flickering in unison, taking their time from the pulse of the line of black ink on the page in front of him. He shoved himself backwards, his chair colliding with the desk behind him, and was on his feet before Mrs. Shillingsworth looked up. He didn't trust himself to speak; he waggled his fingers at his crotch to indicate that he was heading for the toilet. As soon as the door of the long room closed behind him he dashed out of the building to his car.

He drove home so fast that the figures on the pavements seemed to merge like the frames of a film. He parked as close to the entrance as he could and sprinted the few yards, his shadows sprouting out of him. He wasn't conscious of the number he keyed, but it opened the door. The lift displayed each floor to him, and he wished he'd thought to count them, because when he lurched out of the box it seemed to him that the room numbers in the corridors were too high. He threw himself between the closing doors and jabbed the button for his floor, and the door shook open; he was on the right level after all. He floundered into the corridor, unlocked his door and stumbled into the dark which it closed in with him. He was rushing blindly to the bar when the doorbell rang behind him. He raced back and bumped into the door, yelling "Yes?"

"Me."

Speke shoved his eye against the spyhole. Outside was a doll with Stef's face on its swollen head. "Haven't you got your kum?" he shouted.

"Can't you see I've got my hands full? Didn't you see me flashing my lights when you were driving? I've been right behind you for the last I don't know how long."

"I saw some flickering in the mirror," Speke seemed to recall.

"That was me. Well, are you going to open the door or don't you want to see my face?"

"That's a strange way to put it," Speke said and found himself backing away from a fear that he would be letting in the doll with her face on its bulbous outsize head. He wasn't fast enough. His hand reached out and turned the latch, and there was Stef, posing with armfuls of groceries against the blank backdrop of the corridor. He grabbed the bags from her and dumped them in the kitchen, then he fled to the bar. "Drink," he heard his voice say, and fed himself a mouthful from the nearest bottle before switching on the light and calling "Drink?"

She didn't come for it. He traced her to the kitchen by the order in which the lights came on. "Have something to eat if you're going to drink," she said as he accepted the glass. "It's in the microwave."

The sight on the screen of the microwave oven of a plastic container rotating on the turntable like some new kind of record sent him back to the bar. He was still there when Stef switched on the main light in the room and wheeled the trolley in. "Roger, what's—"

He interrupted her so as not to be told that something was wrong. "Who's called Lesley where you work?"

"Leslie's one of the sound men. You've heard me mention him."

"Sound, is he, and that's all?" Speke mused, and raised his voice. "How about Vanessa?"

"Roger . . ."

"Not Roger, Vanessa."

Stef loaded his plate with vegetarian pasta and gazed at him until he took it. "You told me there was no such name before some writer made it up."

"There is now."

"Not where I work."

Speke's voice appeared to have deserted him. He made appreciative noises through mouthfuls of pasta while he tried to think what to say. By the time Stef brought the ice cream he was well into his second bottle of wine, and it no longer seemed important to recall what he'd been attempting to grasp. Indeed, he couldn't understand why she kept looking concerned for him.

He'd taken his expansive contentment to bed when a thought began to flicker in his skull. "Stef?"

"I'm asleep."

"Of course you aren't," he said, rearing up over her to make sure. "You said we agreed. Who? Who are we?"

Without opening her eyes Stef said, "What are you talking about, Roger?"

"About us, aren't I, or am I?" He had to turn away. Perhaps it was an effect of the flickering dimness, but her upturned face seemed almost as flat as the pillow which framed it. He closed his eyes, and presumably the flickering subsided when at last he fell asleep.

Was that the phone? He awoke with a shrill memory filling his skull. He was alone in bed, and the daylight already looked stale. When the bell shrilled again he kicked away the sheets which had been drawn flat over him, and blundered along the hall to the intercom by the front door. "Spum," he declared.

"We've brought your videphone, boss."

The flickering recommenced at once. Speke ran into the main room and, wrestling the window along its track, peered down. Fifteen floors below, two tufts of hair with arms and legs were unloading cartons from a van. They vanished into the entranceway, and a moment later the bell rang again. Speke sprinted to the intercom and shouted, "I can't see you now. Go away."

"You asked for us now, it says so here," said the distorted voice. "When do you want us?"

"Never. It could all be fake. You can do anything with sound and vision," Speke protested before he fully realized what he was saying. He rushed back to the open window and watched until the walking scalps returned to the van, then he grabbed enough clothes to cover himself and heard rather than felt the door slam behind him.

He couldn't drive for the flickering. The floors of the tower block had seemed like frames of a stuck film, and now the figures he passed on the pavements of the carriageway resembled images in a film advancing slowly frame by frame. The film of cars on the road was faster. The side of the carriageway on which he was walking forked, leading him into a diminishing perspective of warehouses. On one otherwise blank wall he found a metal plaque which, as he approached, filled with whitish daylight out of which the legend s & v studios took form. He leaned all his weight on the colorless door, which seemed insubstantial by comparison with the thick wall,

and staggered into a room composed of four monochrome faces as tall as the indirectly lit brick ceiling.
A young woman was sitting at a wide low desk with
her back to one actor's flat face. "May I help you?" she
said.

"Vanessum?" Speke said, distracted by trying to put
names to the faces.

"Yes?" she said as though he'd caught her out. "Who
are you?"

"Don't tell me you don't know."

"I only started properly this morning," she said, pushing a visitor's book towards him. "If I can just have
your—"

Speke was already running down the corridor beyond
her desk. On both sides of him glass displayed images of
rooms full of tape decks or screens that were flickering
almost as much as his eyes, and here was one crowded
with students whose faces looked unformed. Even Stef's
did. She was lecturing to them, though Speke couldn't
hear her voice until he flung open the heavy door; then
she said less than a word, which hadn't time to sound like
her voice. "You said we agreed I'd try to put them out of
my head," Speke shouted. "Who? Who are we?"

"Not here, Roger. Not now."

Speke closed his eyes to shut out the flickering faces.
"Who's speaking? Who do you think you sound like?"

"I'm sorry, everyone. Please excuse us. He's . . ."

He didn't know what sign Stef was making as her voice
trailed off, and he didn't want to see. "Don't lie to me,"
he shouted. "Don't try to put me off. I've seen Vanessa. I
won't leave until you show me Lesley."

Without warning he was shoved backwards, and the

door thumped shut in front of him. "Roger," Stef's flat-tened voice said in his ear. "You have to remember. Les-ley and Vanessa are— It wasn't your fault, you mustn't keep blaming yourself, but they're dead."

Her voice seemed to be reaching him from a long way off, beyond the flickering. "Who says so?" he heard him-self ask in as distant a voice.

"You did. You told me and you told the doctor. It was nothing to do with you, remember. It happened after you split up."

"I split up?" Speke repeated in a voice that felt dead.

"No, not me. You did, maybe. They did."

"Roger, don't—"

He didn't know which voice was trying to imitate Stef's, but it couldn't call him back. It shrank behind him like an image on a monitor that had been switched off, as no doubt her face was shrinking. He fled between the warehouses, which at least seemed too solid to transform unexpectedly, though wasn't everything a ghost, an im-age which he perceived only after it had existed? Mustn't that also be true of himself? He didn't want to be alone with that notion, especially when the echoes of his foot-steps sounded close to turning into a voice, and so he fled towards the shops, the crowds.

That was a mistake. At a distance the faces that con-verged on him seemed capable of taking any form, and when they came closer they were too flat, strips of im-ages of faces that were being moved behind one another or through one another by some complicated trick which he was unable to see through. Their hubbub sounded like a single voice which had been electronically trans-formed in an attempt to give the impression of many, and as far as he could hear it, it seemed to be chanting in a bewildering variety of unrelated rhythms: "Dum, rum, sum, bum . . ." The faces were swelling, crowding around him wherever he ran with his hands over his ears. When he saw an alley dividing the blank walls of two dress shops he fought his way to it, his elbows encountering obstructions which felt less substantial than they were trying to appear. The walls took away some of the pressure of the voices, and when he lowered his hands from his ears he saw that the alley led to a bar.

It was the realest place he could see—so real that he was almost sure he could smell alcohol. He had plenty to drink at home, but the thought of drinking near the open window on the fifteenth storey aggravated his panic. A few drinks ought to help the image stabilize, and then he might go home. He tiptoed to the end of the alley so that his echoes couldn't follow him, and let himself into the bar.

For a moment he thought it wasn't open for business. A solitary tube was lit above the counter at the far end of the long room, but nobody was sitting at the small round tables in the dimness. As Speke closed the door behind him, however, a figure came out of the doorway behind the counter. Speke's ears began to throb in time with the flickering as he tried to be prepared to hear what he was afraid to hear. It didn't matter, so long as he got his drink. He stepped forwards, and the other came to meet him, saying "There's only mum" and then "There's only me." Neither voice was bothering to disguise itself now, even as human. As the face advanced into the light Speke thought that behind every bar was a mirror, and all at once he was afraid to open his mouth.

Ramsey Campbell's collections and novels include *The Inhabitant of the Lake and Other Less Welcome Tenants, Demons by Daylight, The Height of the Scream, Cold Print, Scared Stiff, The Doll Who Ate His Mother, The Face That Must Die, The Nameless, The Parasite, The Influence, Incarnate, Obsession, The Hungry Moon, Ancient Images* and *Midnight Sun.*

Did They Get You to Trade?

Karl Edward Wagner

Ryan Chase was walking along Southampton Row at lunchtime, fancying a pint of bitter. Fortunately there was no dearth of pubs here, and he turned into Cosmo Place, a narrow passage behind the Bloomsbury Park Hotel and the Church of St. George the Martyr, leading into Queen Square. The September day was unseasonably sunny, so he passed by Peter's Bar, downstairs at the corner—looking for an outdoor table at The Swan or The Queen's Larder. The Swan was filling up, so he walked a few doors farther to The Queen's Larder, at the corner of Queen Square. There he found his pint of bitter, and he moved back outside to take a seat at one of the wooden tables on the pavement.

Ryan Chase was American by birth, citizen of the world by choice. More to the point, he spent probably half of each year knocking about the more or less civilized parts of the globe—he liked hotels and saw no romance in roughing it—and a month or two of this time he spent in London, where he had various friends and the use of a studio. The remainder of his year was devoted to long hours of work in his Connecticut studio, where he painted strange and compelling portraits, often derived from his travels and created from memory. These fetched rather large and compelling prices from fashionable galleries—enough to support his travels and eccentricities, even without the trust allowance from a father who had wanted him to go into corporate law.

Chase was pleased with most of his work, although in all of it he saw a flawed compromise between the best he could create at the time and the final realization of his vision, which he hoped someday to achieve. He saw himself as a true decadent, trapped in the *fin de siècle* of a century far drearier than the last. But then, to be decadent is to be romantic.

Chase also had a pragmatic streak. Today a pint of bitter in Bloomsbury would have to make do for a glass of absinthe in Paris of *La Belle Epoch*. The bitter was very good, the day was excellent, and Chase dug out a few postcards from his jacket pocket. By the end of his second pint, he had scribbled notes and addresses on them all and was thinking about a third pint and perhaps a ploughman's lunch.

He smelled the sweet stench of methylated spirit as it approached him, and then the sour smell of unwashed poverty. Already Chase was reaching for a coin.

"Please, guv. I don't wish to interrupt you in your writing, but please could you see your way towards sparing a few coins for a poor man who needs a meal?"

Ryan Chase didn't look like a tourist, but neither did he look British. He was forty-something, somewhere around six feet, saddened that he was starting to spread at the middle, and proud that there was no grey in his short black beard and no thinning in his pulled-back hair

and short ponytail. His black leather jacket with countless studs and zips was from Kensington Market, his
baggy slacks from Bloomingdale's, his T-shirt from Ro-
deo Drive, and his tennis shoes from a Stamford garage
sale. Mild blue eyes watched from behind surplus avia-
tor's sunglasses of the same shade of blue.

All of this in addition to his fondness for writing postcards and scrawling sketches at tables outside pubs made
Chase a natural target for London's growing array of
panhandlers and blowlamps. Against this Chase kept a
pocket well filled with coins, for his heart was rather kind
and his eye quite keen to memorize the faces that peered
back from the fringes of Hell.

But this face had seen well beyond the fringes of Hell,
and as Chase glanced up, he left the pound coin in his
pocket. His panhandler was a meth-man, well in the grip
of the terminal oblivion of cheap methylated spirit. His
shoes and clothing were refuse from dustbins, and from
the look of his filthy mackintosh, he had obviously been
sleeping rough for some while. Chalky ashes seemed to
dribble from him like cream from a cone in a child's fist.
Beneath all this, his body was tall and almost fleshless;
the long-fingered hand, held out in hope, showed dirt-
caked nails resembling broken talons. Straggling hair and
unkempt beard might have been black or brown,
streaked with grey and matted with ash and grime. His
face—Chase recalled Sax Rohmer's description of Fu
Manchu: A brow like Shakespeare and eyes like Satan.

Only, Satan the fallen angel. These were green eyes
with a tint of amber, and they shone with a sort of majestic despair and a proud intelligence that not even the
meth had wholly obliterated. Beneath their imploring

hopelessness, the eyes suggested a still smoldering sense of rage.

Ryan Chase was a scholar of human faces, as well as impulsive, and he knew any coins the man might beg here would go straight into another bottle of methylated spirit. He got up from his seat. "Hang on a bit. I'll treat you to a round."

When Chase emerged from The Queen's Larder he was carrying a pint of bitter and a pint of cider. His meth-man was skulking about the Church of St. George the Martyr across the way, seemingly studying the informational plaque affixed to the stucco wall. Chase handed him the cider. "Here. This is better for you than the meth."

The other man had the shakes rather badly, but he steadied the pint with both hands and dipped his face into it, sucking ravenously until the level was low enough for him to lift the pint to his face. He'd sunk his pint before Chase had quite started on his own. Wiping his beard, he leaned back against the church and shuddered, but the shaking had left his hands as the alcohol quickly spread from his empty stomach.

"Thanks, guv. Now I'd best be off before they take notice of me. They don't fancy my sort hanging about."

His accent was good, though too blurred by alcohol for Chase to pin down. Chase sensed tragedy, as he studied the other's face while he drained his own pint. He wasn't used to drinking in a rush, and perhaps this contributed to his natural impulsiveness.

"They'll take my money well enough. Take a seat at the table round the corner, and I'll buy another round."

Chase bought a couple packets of crisps to accompany their pints and returned to find the other man cautiously seated. He had managed to beg a cigarette. He eagerly accepted the cider, but declined the crisps. By the time he had finished his cider, he was looking somewhat less the corpse.

"Cheers, mate," he said. "You've been a friend. It wasn't always like this, you know."

"Eat some crisps, and I'll buy you one more pint." No need to sing for your supper, Chase started to say, but there were certain remnants of pride amidst the wreckage. He left his barely tasted pint and stepped back inside for more cider. At least there was some food value to cider in addition to the high alcohol content, or so he imagined. It might get the poor bastard through another day.

His guest drank this pint more slowly. The cider had cured his shakes for the moment, and he was losing his whipped cur attitude. He said with a certain foggy dignity: "That's right, mate. One time I had it all. And then I lost it every bit. Now it's come down to this."

Chase was an artist, not a writer, and so had been interested in the man's face, not his life story. The story was an obvious ploy to gain a few more pints, but as the face began to return to life, Chase found himself searching through his memory.

Chase opened a second bag of crisps and offered them. "So, then?"

"I'm Nemo Skagg. Or used to be. Ever heard of me?"

Chase started to respond: "Yes, and I'm Elvis." But his artist's eye began filling in the eroded features, and instead he whispered: "Jesus Christ!"

Nemo Skagg. Founder and major force behind Needle —probably *the* cutting edge of the punk rock movement in its early years. Needle, long without Nemo Skagg and with just enough of its early lineup to maintain the group's name, was still around, but only as a ghost of the original. *Rolling Stone* and the lot used to publish scandalous notices of Nemo Skagg's meteoric crash, but that was years ago, and few readers today would have recognized the name. The name of a living-dead legend.

"Last I read of you, you were living the life of a recluse at someplace in Kensington," Chase said.

"You don't believe me?" There was a flicker of defiant pride in those wounded eyes.

"Actually, I do," Chase said, feeling as though he should apologize. "I recognize your face." He wiped his hands on his trousers, fumbling for something to say. "As it happens, I still have Needle's early albums, as well as the solo album you did."

"But do you still listen to them?"

Chase felt increasingly awkward, yet he was too fascinated to walk away. "Well. I think this calls for one more round."

The barman from The Queen's Larder was starting to favor them with a distasteful frown as he collected glasses from outside. Nemo Skagg nodded toward Great Ormand Street across the way. "They do a fair scrumpi at The Sun," he suggested.

It was a short walk to the corner of Great Ormand and Lamb's Conduit Street, giving Chase a little time to marshal his thoughts. Nemo Skagg. Nova on the punk rock scene. The most outrageous. The most daring. The savior of the world from disco and lame hangers-on from the 60s scene. Totally full-dress punk star: the parties, the fights on stage, the drugs, the scandals, the arrests, the hospital confinements. Toward the last, there were only the latter two, then even these were no longer newsworthy. A decade later, the world had forgotten Nemo Skagg. Chase had assumed he was dead, but now could recall no notice of his death. It might have escaped notice.

The Sun was crowded with students as usual, but Chase made his way past them to the horseshoe bar and sloshed back outside with two pints of scrumpi. Nemo had cleared a space against the wall and had begged another fag. They leaned against the wall of the pub, considering the bright September day, the passing show, and their pints. Chase seldom drank scrumpi, and the potent cider would have been enough to stun his brain even without the previous bitter.

"Actually," Nemo said, "there were *three* solo albums."

"I had forgotten."

"They were all bollocks."

"I'm not at all certain I ever heard the other two," Chase compromised.

"I'm bollocks. We're all of us bollocks."

"The whole world is bollocks." Chase jumped in ahead of him.

"To bollocks!" Nemo raised his glass. They crashed their pints in an unsteady toast. Nemo drained his.

"You're a sport, mate. You still haven't asked what you're waiting to ask: How did it all happen?"

"Well. I don't suppose it really matters, does it?"

Nemo was not to demur. "Lend us a fiver, mate, and I'll pay for this round. Then Nemo Skagg shall tell all."

Once, at the White Hart in Drury Lane, Chase had bought eight pints of Guinness for a cockney pensioner who had regaled him with an impenetrable cockney accent concerning his adventures during the Dunkirk evacuation. Chase hadn't understood a word in ten, but he memorized the man's face, and that portrait was considered one of his very finest. Chase found a fiver.

The bar staff at The Sun were loose enough to serve Nemo, and he was out again shortly with two more pints of scrumpi and a packet of fags. That was more than the fiver, so he hadn't been totally skint. He brightened when Chase told him he didn't smoke. Nemo lit up. Chase placed his empty pint on the window ledge and braced himself against the wall. The wall felt good.

"So, then, mate. Ask away. It's you who's paid the piper."

Chase firmly resolved that this pint would be his last. "All right, then. What did happen to Nemo Skagg? Last I heard, you still had some of your millions and a house in Kensington, whence sounds of debauchery issued throughout the night."

"You got it right all along, mate. It was sex, drugs and alcohol that brought about me ruin. We'll say bloody nothing about scheming managers and crooked recording studios. Now, then. You've got the whole soddin' story."

"Not very original." Chase wondered whether he should finish his scrumpi.

"Life is never original," Nemo observed. The rush of alcohol and nicotine had vastly improved his demeanor. Take away the dirt and shabby clothes, and he might well look like any other dissipated man in his sixties, although that must be about twice his actual age. He was alert enough not to be gauging Chase for prospects of further largess.

"Of course, that's not *truly* the reason."

"Was it a woman?" asked Chase. The scrumpi was making him maudlin.

"Which woman would it have been? Here, drink up, mate. Give us tube fare to Ken High Street, and I'll show you how it happened."

At this point Ryan Chase should have put down his unfinished pint, excused himself, and made his way back to his hotel. Instead he drank up, stumbled along to the Holborn tube station, and found himself being bounced about the train beside a decidedly deranged Nemo Skagg. Caught up in the adventure of the moment, Chase told himself that he was on a sort of quest—a quest for truth, for the truth that lies behind the masks of faces.

The carriage shook and swayed as it plummeted through subterranean darkness, yanking to a halt at each jostling platform. Chase dropped onto a seat as the passengers rushed out and swarmed in. Lurid posters faced him from the platform walls. Bodies mashed close about him, crushing closer than the sooty tunnel walls, briefly glimpsed in flashes of passing trains and bright bursts of sparks. Faces, looking nowhere, talking in tight bundles, crowded in. Sensory overload.

Nemo's face leered down. He was clutching a railing. "You all right, mate?"

"Gotta take a piss."

"Could go for a slash myself. This stop will do."

So they got off at Notting Hill Gate instead of changing for High Street Kensington; and this was good, because they could walk down Kensington Church Street, which was for a miracle all downhill, toward Kensington High Street. The walk and the fresh air revived Chase from his claustrophobic experience. Bladder relieved, he found himself pausing before the windows of the numerous antique shops that they passed. Hideous Victorian atrocities and baroque horrors from the continent lurked imprisoned behind shop windows. A few paintings beckoned from the farther darkness. Chase was tempted to enter.

But each time Nemo caught at his arm. "You don't want to look at any of that shit, mate. It's all just a lot of dead shit. Let's sink us a pint first."

By now Chase had resigned himself to having bankrolled a pub crawl. They stopped at The Catherine Wheel, and Chase fetched pints of lager while Nemo Skagg commandeered a bench around the corner on Holland Street. From this relative eddy, they watched the crowd stroll past on Kensington Church Street. Chase smelled the curry and chili from within the pub, wondering how to break this off. He really should eat something.

"I don't believe you told me your name." Nemo Skagg was growing measurably more alert, and that seemed to make his condition all the more tragic.

"I'm Ryan Chase." Chase, who was growing increasingly pissed, no longer regarded the fallen rock star as an object of pity: he now revered him as a crippled hero of the wars in the fast lane.

"Pleased to meet you, Ryan." Nemo Skagg extended a taloned hand. "Where in the States are you from?"

"Well, I live in Connecticut. I have a studio there."

"I'd reckoned you for an artist. And clearly not a starving garret sort. What do you do?"

"Portraits, mostly. Gallery work. I get by." Chase could not fail to notice the other's empty pint. Sighing, he arose to attend to the matter.

When he returned, Chase said, with some effort at firmness: "Now then. Here we are in Kensington. What is all this leading to?"

"You really are a fan, then?"

The lager inclined Chase toward an effusive and reckless mood. "Needle was *the* cutting edge of punk rock. Your first album, *Excessive Bodily Fluids,* set the standard for a generation. Your second album, *The Coppery Taste of Blood,* remains one of the ten best rock albums ever recorded. When I die, these go into the vault with me."

"You serious?"

"Well, we do have a family vault. I've always fancied stocking it with a few favorite items. Like the ancient Egyptians. I mean, being dead has to get boring."

"Then, do you believe in an afterlife?"

"Doesn't really matter whether I do or I don't, does it? Still, it can't hurt to allow for eventualities."

"Yeah. Well, it's all bollocks anyway." Nemo Skagg's eyes had cleared, and Chase found their gaze penetrating and disturbing. He was glad when Nemo stared past him to watch the passersby.

Chase belched and glanced at his watch. "Yes. Well. Here we are in Kensington." He had begun the afternoon's adventure hoping that Nemo Skagg intended to point out to him his former house near here, perhaps entertain him with anecdotes of past extravagances committed on the grounds, maybe even introduce him to some of his whilom friends and colleagues. Nothing more than a bad hangover now seemed the probable outcome.

"Right." Nemo stood up, rather steadier now than Chase. "Let's make our move. I said I'd show you."

Chase finished his lager and followed Nemo down Kensington Church Street, past the church on the corner, and into Ken High Street, where, with some difficulty, they crossed over. The pavement was extremely crowded now, as they lurched along. Tattooed girls in black leather miniskirts flashed suspender belts and stiletto heels. Plaid-clad tourists swayed under burdens of cameras and cellulite. Lads with pierced faces and fenestrated jeans modeled motorcycle jackets laden with chrome. Bored shopworkers trudged unseeingly through it all.

Nemo Skagg turned into the main doorway of Kensington Market. He turned to Chase. "Here's your fucking afterlife."

Chase was rather more interested in finding the loo, but he followed his Virgil. Ken Market was some three floors of cramped shops and tiny stalls—records and jewelry, T-shirts and tattoos, punk fashions from skinhead kicker boots to latex minidresses. You could get your nipples pierced, try on a new pair of handcuffs, or buy a heavy-metal biker jacket that would deflect a tank shell. Chase, who remembered Swinging London of the Beatles era, fondly thought of Ken Market as Carnaby Street Goes to Hell.

"Tell me again," he called after Nemo Skagg. "Why are we here?"

"Because you wanted to know." Nemo pushed forward through the claustrophobic passageways, half dragging Chase and pointing at the merchandise on display. "Observe, my dear Watson."

Ken Market was a labyrinth of well over a hundred vendors, tucked away into tiny cells like funnel spiders waiting in webs. A henna-haired girl in black PVC stared at them incuriously from behind a counter of studded leather accessories. A Pakistani shuffled stacks of T-shirts, mounted on cardboard and sealed in cellophane. An emaciated speedfreak in leather harness guarded her stock of records—empty albums on display, their vinyl souls hidden away. An aging Teddy boy arranged his display of postcards—some of which would never clear the postal inspectors. Two skinheads glared out of the twilight of a tattoo parlor: OF COURSE IT HURTS read the signboard above the opening. Bikers in leather studied massive belts and buckles memorializing Vincent, BSA, Triumph, Norton, Ariel, AJS—no Jap rice mills served here.

"What do you see?" Nemo whispered conspiratorially.

"Lots of weird people buying and selling weird things?" Chase had always wanted to own a Vincent.

"They're all dead things. Even the motorcycles."

"I see."

"No, you don't see. Follow and learn."

Nemo Skagg paused before a display of posters. He pointed. "James Dean. Jim Morrison. Jimi Hendrix. All dead."

He turned to a rack of postcards. "Elvis Presley. Judy Garland. John Lennon. Marilyn Monroe. All dead."

And to a wall of T-shirts. "Sid Vicious. Keith Moon. Janis Joplin. Brian Jones. All dead."

Nemo Skagg whirled to point at a teenager wearing a Roy Orbison T-shirt. Her friend had James Dean badges all across her jacket. They were looking at a poster of Nick Drake. Nemo shouted at them "They're all *dead*! Your heroes are ghosts!"

It took some doing to attract attention in Ken Market, but Nemo Skagg was managing to do so. Chase took his arm. "Come on, mate. We've seen enough, and I fancy a pint."

But Nemo broke away as Chase steered him past a stall selling vintage rock recordings. Album jackets of Sid and Elvis and Jim and Jimi hung in state from the back of the stall. The bored girl in a black latex bra looked at Nemo distastefully from behind her counter. Either her face had been badly beaten the night before, or she had been reckless with her eyeshadow.

"Anything by Needle?" Nemo asked.

"Nah. You might try Dez and Sheila upstairs. I think they had a copy of *Vampire Serial Killer* some weeks back. Probably still have it."

"Why don't you stock Needle?"

"Who wants Needle? They're naff."

"I mean, the early albums. With Nemo Skagg."

"Who's he?"

"Someone who isn't dead yet."

"That's his problem then, isn't it."

"Do you know who I am?"

"Yes. You're a piss artist. Now bugger off."

Chase caught Nemo Skag's arm and tugged hard. "Come on, mate. There's nothing here."

And they slunk out, past life-size posters of James Dean, mesmerizing walls of John Lennon T-shirts, kaleidoscopic racks of Marilyn Monroe postcards. Elvis lip-synched to them from the backs of leather jackets. Betty Page stared wide-eyed and ball-gagged from Xotique's window of fetish chic. Jim Morrison was being born again in tattoo across the ample breast of a spike-haired blonde. A punker couple with matching Sid and Nancy T-shirts displayed matching forearms of needle tracks. Someone was loudly playing Buddy Holly from the stall that offered painless ear piercing. A blazing skull grinned at them from the back of the biker who lounged at the exit, peddling his skinny ass in stained leather jeans.

Outside it was still a pleasant September late afternoon, and even the exhaust-clogged air of Ken High Street felt fresh and clear to Chase's lungs. Nemo Skagg was muttering under his breath, and the shakes seemed to have returned. Chase steered him across traffic and back toward the relative quiet of Ken Church Street.

"Off-license. Just ahead." Nemo was acting now on reflex. He drew Chase into the off-license shop and silently dug out two four-packs of Tennant's Super. Chase added some sandwiches of unknown composition to the counter, paid for the lot, and they left.

"Just here," said Nemo, turning into an iron gate at the back of the church at the corner of Ken Church and Ken High Street. There was an enclosed churchyard within—a quiet garden with late roses, a leafy bower of some vine, walkways and benches. A few sarcophagi of eroded stone made grey shapes above the trimmed grass. Occasional tombstones leaned as barely decipherable monuments here and there; others were incorporated into the brick of the church walls. Soot-colored robins explored wormy crab apples, and hopeful sparrows and pigeons converged upon the two men as they sat down. The traffic of Kensington seemed hushed and distant, although only a glance away. Chase was familiar with this area of Kensington, but he had never known that this churchyard was here. He remembered that Nemo Skagg had once owned a house somewhere in the borough. Possibly he had sat here often, seeking silence.

Nemo listlessly popped a can of Tennant's, sucked on it, ignored the proffered sandwich. Chase munched on cress and cucumber, anxious to get any sort of food into his stomach. Savoring the respite, he sipped on his can of lager and waited.

Nemo Skagg was on his second can before he spoke. "So then, mate. Now you know."

Chase had already decided to find a cab once the evening rush hour let up. He was certain he could not manage the tube after the afternoon's booze-up. "I'm sorry?" he said.

"You've got to be dead. All their heroes are ghosts. They only worship the dead. The music, the posters, the T-shirts. All of it. They only want to love dead things. So easy to be loyal to dead things. The dead never change. Never grow old. Never fade away. Better to drop dead than to fade away."

"Hey, come on." Chase thought he had it sussed. "Sure the place has its obligatory showcase of dead superstars. That's nostalgia, mate. Consider that there were ten or twenty times as many new faces, new groups, new stars."

"Oi. You come back in a year's time, and I promise you that ninety per cent of your new faces will be missing and well forgotten, replaced by another bloody lot of bloody new sods. But you'll still find your bloody James Dean posters and your bloody Elvis jackets and your bloody Doors CD's and your bloody John Lennon T-shirts, bullet holes three quid extra.

"Listen, mate. They only want the dead. The dead never change. They're always there, at your service, never a skip. You want to wank off on James Dean? There he is, pretty as the day he snuffed it. Want head from Marilyn Monroe? Just pump up your inflatable doll.

"*But*. And this is it, Ryan. Had James Dean learned to

drive his Porsche, he'd by now be a corpulent old geezer with a hairpiece and three chins like Paul Newman or Marlon Brando. Marilyn Monroe would be a stupid old cow slapping your Beverly Hills cops around—when she wasn't doing telly adverts for adult nappies and denture fixatives. Jim Morrison would be flogging a chain of vegetarian restaurants. Jimi Hendrix would be doing a golden oldies tour with Otis Redding. Elvis would be playing to fat old cunts in Las Vegas casinos. Buddy Holly would be selling used cars in Chattanooga. How many pictures of fat and fading fifty-year-old farts did you see in there, Ryan? Want to buy the latest Paul McCartney album?"

Chase decided that he would leave Nemo Skagg with the rest of the Tennant's, which should keep him well through the night. "So, then. What you're saying is that it's best to die young, before your fans find someone new. So long, fame; I've had you. Not much future in it for you, is there, being a dead star?"

"Sometimes there's no future in being a live one, after you've lost it."

Chase, who had begun to grow impatient with Nemo Skagg, again changed his assessment of the man. There was more in this wreckage than a drunken has-been bitterly railing against the enduring fame of better musicians. Chase decided to pop another Tennant's and listen.

"You said you're an artist, right? Paint portraits?"

"Well, I rather like to think of them as something more than that . . ."

"And you reckon you're quite good at it?"

"Some critics think so."

"Right, then. What happens the day comes and they say you aren't all that good: that your best work is behind you; that whatever it was you had once, you've lost it now? What happens when you come to realize they've got it right? When you know you've lost the spark forever, and all that's left is to go through the motions? Reckon you'll be well pleased with yourself, painting portraits of pompous old geezers to hang in their executive board rooms?"

"I hardly think it will come to that." Chase was somewhat testy.

"No more than I did. No one ever does. You reckon that once you get to the top, you'll stay on top. Maybe that happens for a few, but not for most of us. Sometimes the fans start to notice first; sometimes you do. You tell yourself that the fans are fickle, but after a while you know inside that it's you what's past it. Then you start to crumble. Then you start to envy the ones what went out on top: they're your moths in amber, held in time and in memory forever unchanging."

The churchyard was filling with shadows, and Chase expected the sexton would soon be locking the gates. Dead leaves of late summer were softly rustling down upon the headstones. The scent of roses managed to pervade the still air.

"Look." Chase was not the sort who liked touching, but he gave a quick pat to the other man's shoulder. "We all go through low periods; we all have our slumps. That's why they invented comebacks. You can still get it back together."

"Nothing to put back together, mate. Don't you get it? At one time I had it. Now I don't."

"But you can get help . . ."

"That's the worst part, mate. It would be so good just to blame it all on the drugs and the booze. Tell yourself you can get back on your feet; few months in some trendy clinic, then you're back on tour promoting that smash new album. Only that's not the way it is. The drugs and the booze comes after you somehow know you've lost it. To kill the pain."

Nemo Skagg sucked his Tennant's dry and tossed the can at the nearest dustbin. He missed, and the can rattled hollowly along the walkway.

"Each one of us has only so much—so much of his best—that he can give. Some of us have more than the rest of us. Doesn't matter. Once the best of you is gone, there's no more you can give. You're like a punch-drunk boxer hoping for the bell before you land hard on your arse. It's over for you. No matter how much you want it. No matter how hard you try.

"There's only so much inside you that's positively the best. When that's gone, you might as well be dead. And knowing that you've lost it—that's the cruelest death of all."

Ryan Chase sighed uncomfortably and noticed that they had somehow consumed all the cans of lager, that he was drunker than he liked to be, and that it was growing dark. Compounding his mistakes, he asked: "Is there someplace I can drop you off? I'm going for a cab. Must get back."

Nemo Skagg shook his head, groping around for another can. "It's all right, mate. My digs aren't far from here. Fancy stopping in for a drink? Afraid I must again impose upon you for that."

In for a penny, in for a pound. All judgment fled, Chase decided he really would like to see where Nemo Skagg lived. He bought a bottle of Bell's, at Nemo's suggestion, and they struggled off into the gathering night.

Chase blindly followed Nemo Skagg through the various and numerous unexpected turnings of the Royal Borough of Kensington and Chelsea. Even if sober and by daylight, he'd not have had a clue as to where he was being led. It was Chase's vague notion that he was soon to be one of the chosen few to visit with a fallen angel in his particular corner of Hell. In this much he was correct.

Chase had been expecting something a little more grandiose. He wasn't sure just what. Perhaps a decaying mansion. Nemo Skagg, however, was far past that romantic luxury. Instead, Nemo pushed aside a broken hoarding and slid past, waving for Chase to follow. Chase fumbled after him, weeds slapping his face. The way pitched downward on a path paved with refuse and broken masonry. Somewhere ahead Nemo scratched a match and lit a candle in the near-darkness.

It was the basement level of a construction site, or a demolition site to be accurate. A block of buildings had been torn down, much of their remains carted away, and nothing had yet risen in their place save for weeds. Weathered posters on the hoarding above spared passersby a vision of the pit. The envisioned office building had never materialized. Scruffy rats and feral cats prowled through the weeds and debris, avoiding the few squatters who lurked about.

Nemo Skagg had managed a sort of lean-to of scrap boards and slabs of hoarding—the lot stuck together against one foundation wall, where a doorway in the brick gave entrance to a vaulted cellar beneath the street above. Once it had served as some sort of storage area, Chase supposed, although whether for coal or fine wines was a secret known only to the encrusted bricks. Past the lean-to, Nemo's candle revealed an uncertain interior of scraps of broken furniture, an infested mattress with rags of bedding, and a dead fire of charcoal and ashes with a litter of empty cans and dirty crockery. The rest of the grotto was crowded with a stack of decaying cardboard cartons and florist's pots. Nemo Skagg had no fear of theft, for there plainly was nothing here to steal.

"Here. Find a seat." Nemo lit a second candle and fumbled about for a pair of pilfered pub glasses. He poured from the bottle of Bell's and handed one clouded glass to Chase. Chase sat down on a wooden crate, past caring about cleanliness. The whisky did not mask the odor of methylated spirits that clung to the glass with the dirt.

"To your very good health, Ryan," Nemo Skagg toasted. "And to our friendship."

Chase was trying to remember whether he'd mentioned the name of his hotel to Nemo. He decided he hadn't, and that the day's adventure would soon be behind him. He drank. His host refilled their glasses.

"So, this is it," Chase said, somewhat recklessly. "The end of fame and fortune. Good-bye house in Kensington. Hello squat in future carpark."

"It was Chelsea," Nemo replied, not taking offense. "The house was in Chelsea."

"Now he gets his kicks in Chelsea, not in Kensington anymore," sang Chase, past caring that he was past caring.

"Still," Nemo went on, content with the Bell's. "I did manage to carry away with me everything that really mattered."

He scrambled back behind the stack of cardboard cartons, nearly spilling them over. After a bit of rummaging, he climbed out with the wreckage of an electric guitar. He presented it to Chase with a flourish, and refilled their glasses.

It was a custom-built guitar, of the sort that Nemo Skagg habitually smashed to bits on stage before hordes of screaming fans. Chase knew positively nothing about custom-built guitars, but it was plain that this one was a probable casualty of one such violent episode. The bowed neck still held most of the strings, and only a few knobs and bits dangled on wires from the abused body. Chase handed it back carefully. "Very nice."

Nemo Skagg scraped the strings with his broken fingernails. As Chase's eyes grew accustomed to the candlelight, he could see a few monoliths of gutted speakers and burned-out amplifiers shoved in with the pots and boxes. Nothing worth stealing. Nothing worth saving. Ghosts. Broken, dead ghosts. Like Nemo Skagg.

"I think I have a can of beans somewhere." Nemo applied a candle to some greasy chips papers and scraps of wood. The yellow flame flared in the dark cave, its smoke carried outward past the lean-to.

"That's all right," said Chase. "I really must be going."

"Oi. We haven't finished the bottle." Nemo poured. "Drink up. Of course, I used to throw better parties than this for my fans."

"Cheers," said Chase, drinking. He knew he would be very ill tomorrow.

"So, Ryan," said Nemo, stretching out on a legless and spring-stabbed comfy chair. "You find yourself wanting to ask where all the money went."

"I believe you've already told me."

"What I told you was what people want to hear, although it's partly true. Quite amazing how much money you can stuff up your nose and shove up your arm, and how fast that draws that certain group of sharks who circle about you and take bites till there's nothing left to feed on. But the simple and unsuspected truth of the matter is that I spent the last of my fortune on my fans."

Chase was wondering whether he might have to crash here for the night if he didn't move now. He finished Nemo's sad story for him: "And then your fans all proved fickle."

"No, mate. Not these fans. Just look at them."

Nemo Skagg shuffled back into his cave, picked out a floral vase, brought it out into the light, cradling it lovingly in his hands for Chase to see. Chase saw that it was actually a funeral urn.

"This is Saliva Gash. She said she was eighteen when she hung out backstage. After she OD'd one night after a gig, her family in Pimlico wouldn't own her. Not even her ashes. I paid for the cremation. I kept her remains. She was too dear a creature to be scattered."

Ryan Chase was touched. He struggled for words to say, until Nemo reached back for another urn.

"And this one is Slice. I never knew his real name. He was always in the front row, screaming us on, until he sliced his wrists after one show. No one claimed the remains. I paid for it.

"And this one is Dave from Belfast. Pissed out of his skull, and he stuck his arm out to flag down a tube train. Jacket caught, and I doubt they picked up all of him to go into the oven. His urn feels light."

"That's all right," said Chase, as Nemo offered him the urn to examine. "I'm no judge."

"You ever notice how London is crammed with bloody cemeteries, but no one gets buried there unless they've snuffed it before the fucking Boer War? No room for any common souls in London. They burn the lot of us now, and then you get a fucking box of ashes to carry home. That's *if* you got any grieving sod who cares a fuck to hold onto them past the first dustbin."

Nemo dragged out one of the cardboard boxes. The rotted carton split open, disgorging a plastic bag of chalky ashes. The bag burst on the bricks, scattering ashes over Nemo's shoes and trouser cuffs. "Shit. I can't read this one. Can you?"

He handed the mildewed cardboard to Chase, then poured out more Bell's. Chase dully accepted both. His brain hurt.

"Bought proper funeral urns for them all at first," Nemo explained. "Then, as the money went, I had to economize. Still, I was loyal to my fans. I kept them with me after I lost the house. After I'd lost everything else."

The fire licked at the moldy cardboard in Chase's hand, cutting through his numbness. He dropped the box onto the fire. The fire flared. By its light Chase could make out hundreds of similar boxes and urns stacked high within the vault.

"It's a whole generation no one wanted," Nemo went on, drinking now straight from the bottle. "Only *I* spoke for them. I spoke to them. They wanted me. I wanted them. The fans today want to worship dead stars. Sod 'em all. I'm still alive, and I have my audience of dead fans to love me."

Chase drank his whisky despite his earlier resolve. Nemo Skagg sat enthroned in squalor, surrounded by chalky ashes and the flickering light of a trash fire—a Wagnerian hero gone wrong.

"They came to London from all over; they're not just

East End. They told the world to sod off, and the world repaid them in kind. Dead, they were no more wanted than when they lived. Drugs, suicides, traffic accidents, maybe a broken bottle in an alley or a rape and a knife in some squat. I started out with just the fans I recognized, then with the poor sods my mates told me about. After a while I had people watching the hospital morgues for them. The kids no one gave a shit for. Sure, often they had families, and let me tell you they was always pleased to have *me* pay for the final rites for the dearly departed, and good riddance. They were all better off dead, even the ones who didn't think so at first, and I had to help.

"Well, after a time the money ran out. I don't regret spending it on them. Fuck the fame. At least I still have my fans."

Nemo Skagg took a deep swig from the bottle, found it empty, pitched it, then picked up his ruined guitar. He scraped talons across the loose strings.

"And you, Ryan, old son. You said that you're still a loyal fan."

"Yes, Nemo. Yes, I did indeed say that." Chase set down his empty glass and bunched the muscles of his legs.

"Well, it's been great talking with you here backstage. We'll hang out some more later on. Hope you enjoy the gig."

"I'll just go take a piss, while you warm up." Chase arose carefully, backing toward the doorway of the lean-to.

"Don't be long." Nemo was plugging wires into the broken speakers, adjusting dials on the charred amps. He peered into the vaulted darkness. "Looks like I got a crucial audience out there tonight."

It was black as the pit, as Chase blundered out of the lean-to. Nettles and thistles ripped at him. Twice he fell over unseen mounds of debris, but he dragged himself painfully to his feet each time. Panic steadied his legs, and he could see the halo of streetlights beyond the hoarding. Gasping, grunting, cursing—he bulled headlong through the darkened tangle of the demolition site. Fear gave him strength, and sadistic fortune at last smiled upon him. He found the rubble-strewn incline, clawed his way up to pavement level, and shouldered past the flimsy hoarding.

As he fell sobbing onto the street, he could hear the roar of the audience below, feel the pounding energy of Nemo Skagg's guitar. Clawing to his feet, he was pushed forward by the screaming madness of Needle's unrecorded hits.

Nemo Skagg had lost nothing.

Karl Edward Wagner is the author of *Darkness Weaves, Death Angel's Shadow, Bloodstone, Dark Crusade, Night Winds, In A Lonely Place* and *Why Not You and I?* He is also editor of *The Year's Best Horror Stories.* His newest books are *Tell Me, Dark,* a graphic novel with artist Kent Williams, and the novels *The Fourth Seal* and *At First Just Ghostly.*

GIFCO

M. John Harrison

 A few months after the death of our teenage daughter, my wife and I bought a house in Peckham, South London.

"My God," my wife said, the day we moved in.

She wasn't keen. But Peckham suited me. Its main street was full of cheap hardware shops. Fast-food wrappers blew about in the sunshine. Driving past the Leisure Centre that first afternoon, we noticed that part of its signboard had fallen off. The next day it had lost the whole of the first E in "leisure." Peckham leaned up against the rich suburb of East Dulwich (where at that time the Prime Minister still lived) like some old bag lady against a West End shop window. Every morning its rich complement of lunatics and failures would begin to make their hesitant way down Rye Lane into Peckham itself to do their shopping. There were halfway-housers, psychotics released suddenly into the community with a quilted cos-coat and a strange list to the left, failed old criminals with eyes huddled and blank, fat women in jogging pants and carpet slippers. They shambled and loped, or walked sideways like Martinique land crabs. Shouts were drawn from them inadvertently as their dreams and anxieties ebbed or flowed. They talked to themselves without let.

Down the length of the lane massive horse chestnuts were in blossom, their leaves so densely packed it was evening outside the Jet paper factory at 9 A.M. The chestnut flowers looked like strange little flickering pagodas of light. They always reminded me of William Blake's "tree full of angels." Further down Rye Lane stood the remains of an old hedge made up of holly, hawthorn and elder. It was dusty, broken, full of gaps, full of rubbish from the house behind it. Builders had been working on the house for months, perhaps years. The collapse of the property market towards the end of the Eighties had made them desultory, halfhearted.

When I first went past, its windows were boarded over with panels of cheap blond wood. Across one of them had been scrawled in grey cellulose primer: GIFCO WE ARE HERE. This message began high up on the left of the panel but rapidly lost confidence and toppled away towards the right-hand bottom corner, the letters becoming smaller and harder to make out. It had a desperate air and I wondered who had written it. They weren't there anymore. The house was silent. Gifco had never arrived. Or perhaps he had. Perhaps, waiting it seemed interminably in the dark behind the boards, they had made some essential mistake about his nature, about his plan and their part in it. Walking past among all the other lunatics I caught the corrupt, sweet scent of hawthorn blossom, and paused fractionally as if I had heard someone call my name.

Later that day a young policeman rang my doorbell. Anxious to do things properly, he showed me his warrant card twice: once on the doorstep and then again inside on the stairs. He was quiet-spoken; dressed in jeans, a thick pullover and oxblood Dr. Marten's shoes. He explained that he wanted to use my second-floor balcony to get a view of some houses further down the Rye. That was all right, I said. But would he be comfortable?

Showing me a cheap airline bag, he said:

"I could survive for days with what I've got in here."

He didn't seem to have much more than a pale blue nylon rally jacket and a two-way radio. "Hello?" he said into the radio. "I think I've got an OP." He had a boyish look, an undiminished sense of the excitement of what he was doing. "This'll be great," he said. "Great."

I took him a dining chair to sit on, and a cup of tea. I found that he had camouflaged himself by hanging up two large squares of black plastic material and rearranging some flower pots along the low wall of the balcony. The radio was in front of him. He was grateful for the tea. "It's a real sun-trap out here," he said.

"I love the sun," I told him immediately. "I'm out here a lot."

"If anything exciting happens I'll give you a shout," he promised.

He grinned.

"Better than watching it on the telly."

After that, things were quiet. From the front room I heard him speak once or twice into the radio.

About half an hour later he went away again for ten minutes, then came back. "Sorry about this," he said, as I let him in. "Something has happened. Not very spectacular, but something." He had another cup of tea, and this time he spent much longer out there. He spoke into his radio.

"Control, control from Colin.

"I've just seen an IC3 climb up some ladders at the back of the house. Control, did you get that? Yes, yes, I can confirm that.

"No, he's gone up a ladder and through a door at the rear. Wearing a blue jacket: a ski jacket: an IC3."

His voice became lively.

"Second floor, window on the right. Yes!" he shouted. Then:

"To your left, to your left!"

I was excited too. We huddled behind the camouflage plastic, craning our necks to see what was going on. I heard some faint shouts from down in the street. I thought I could see a lightly built figure running about in a back garden: a child or a teenager: an IC3.

Suddenly I realized the direction I was looking in.

"Isn't that the house with the boarded-up windows?"

He stared at me.

"I wouldn't say anything about that to anyone."

Later he added, as he put his things one by one back in the airline bag:

"After all, you've got to live round here."

The radio fizzed and spluttered to itself from inside the bag. Every so often a woman's voice assembled itself out of this noise, like a child speaking into an empty tin to make itself important. It sounded like "Paul? Paul?"

He zipped the bag shut.

"Can I use your loo, please?" he asked. He laughed. "I think I'm going to be busy for the rest of the day and this is going to be my last chance."

"He was nice," I told my wife when she got home. She wasn't so sure.

"It never occurs to you to hold anything back," she said.

That night I had a nightmare about hiding from people. I was rushing about trying to keep trees, buildings, cars, anything between me and them. I heard a voice say, "The double paradox. Life is not death, and neither is death," and woke up to an empty bedroom. It was three o'clock, pitch dark. A rhythmical thudding, with the muffled but determined quality of someone banging nails into a cellar wall or knocking on a heavy door two or three houses further down the street, had carried over from the dream. When it failed to diminish I got up unsteadily. The bedroom door was open, the stairwell dark.

"Mary?"

Pounding, as distant as before.

"Mary? Are you there? Are you all right?"

I went from room to room looking for her. All the internal doors were open. Orange street light had established itself everywhere, lodging within the mirrors, slicking along each mantelpiece, discovering something in every room. In the lounge that evening a book, *Sexual Behaviour in the Human Female,* had been pulled partly off a shelf—the shadow of its spine fell obliquely across five or six others. In the kitchen, a knife, a breadboard and a loaf of bread lay next to a Braun coffee grinder like a little white idol. Up in the studio, near the top of the house, something had fallen and broken in the empty grate. "Mary?" She wasn't there. Outside, Peckham was full of parked cars and angels. Though I was naked I felt languorous and comfortable, as if I was surrounded by some warm fluid; I had a partial erection which hardened briefly when it touched the fabric of the living room curtains. At the same time I was filled with anxiety. Its cause was hidden from me, but like that noise it never stopped.

"Mary?"

Eventually I went back to bed and found her lying there awake in the dark.

"What's the matter?" she whispered.

"I—"

"What is it?"

"I thought you'd got up," I said. "That noise—"

"I can't hear anything."

"Didn't you get up?" I said. And: "There! Listen!"

"I can't hear anything."

I had begun to shiver. "I went all round the house," I said. "I can't get warm."

She put her arms round me.

"What have you been doing to get so upset?"

"Listen!"

Some dreams, I know, detach themselves from you only reluctantly, amid residual flickers of light, sensations of entrapment, effects which disperse quite slowly. Everything is trancelike. You wait to understand the world again and, as you wait, fall back into the dream with no more fear. But there was something awful about that thudding noise, its remoteness, its persistence.

"How do you feel?" my wife asked next morning.

"Oh fine, fine," I told her.

But I knew that something had been knocking. Something had come into the house.

"I hope you are," she said.

"I'm fine."

· · ·

After that I set up my own OP on the balcony at nights. It was hard to see clearly. But I thought I could make out a constant quiet coming and going at the Gifco house. There were visits and deliveries. Black plastic rubbish bags were manhandled into the garden and perhaps buried. By day, though, it lay hot and deserted behind its hawthorn hedge in the sun. Late one morning curiosity made me push my way through the hedge, prise the hardboard off one of the ground-floor windows, and climb inside. The air lay hot and heavy in the corners of the room. After a moment I could feel it in my chest, in my heart, all the lobes of my body. A single thin bar of light fell molten yellow across the concrete floor, revealing shreds of old green linoleum, a dusty armchair. I stood there for some time, lapped in the most perfect silence though the lunchtime traffic was already backing up on Rye Lane, heat shimmering off the bonnets of the little modern cars.

Peckham is always full of temporary bookstalls which appear and disappear in a day—one table pushed up against the window of a hairdresser or furniture shop, with perhaps thirty or forty dog-eared paperbacks on it. They are the result of house clearances: the books of the deceased, the evicted, the permanently hospitalized. That morning I had bought an old novel from one of them. I took it out and, squatting down in that perfect ray of sun, began to read the first page—"When I was a tiny boy I often sat motionless in the garden, bathed in sunshine, hands flat on the rough brick of the garden path, waiting with a prolonged, almost painful expectation for whatever would happen, whatever event was contained by that moment, whatever revelation lay dormant in it."

As I read the word "revelation" I heard someone come in through the front door. Feet scraped in the hall. I closed the book and stood up.

"I wondered if I'd find you here."

It was the policeman, Colin.

"When did you begin to work for Gifco?"

Colin, I discovered, lived with his mother in Peckham. He had worked as a policeman for only a year. His face was thin, already muscular about the mouth from the effort of suppressing some internal tension. His eyes, though, remained clear and childish, and he had a habit of staring at you after he had spoken, as if anticipating some response you could never make. He knew you could never make it, never guess what he wanted. Disconcerted, you stared back.

When I asked him what he did with his time, he said, "Oh, read a lot mostly."

He enjoyed science fiction, of which he had gathered quite a large collection; or books about concentration camps bought from the nonfiction shelves of W. H. Smiths. He had read Primo Levi, but preferred Wieslaw Kielar. Growing up on this stuff in his mother's one-bedroom flat—the third of four in a gloomy Victorian house with gabled upper storeys—he had failed to notice the gas water heater above the bath, the loose floor-boards, the doorframes which changed shape every summer as the London clay dried out. His mother, who tended to doze off during *News at Ten* or earlier, had the bedroom. This left Colin to sleep on the convertible sofa in the lounge; more often than not he kept the television buzzing instead and drank Harp lager out of a tin in the wavering half-light.

Two young Asian women lived on the floor below. One
of them was a paranoid schizophrenic on community release, who often shouted and screamed deep in the
night.

"Get that filth out of here!" Colin would hear her call
suddenly after a long silence.

"The people next door," he told me, "had to get rid of
their dogs. They used to join in when she started. They'd
howl until it got light." She wasn't too bad at the moment, he believed, because he played his stereo loudly
during the day. "That keeps her awake, so she sleeps
more at night." He was solicitous about her, despite the
trouble she caused. "We keep an eye on her when we
can," he said. "Her friend has to go out to work."

Colin's other interest was his car. He owned an old
Hillman Avenger. It was a fawn color, patched with ma-
roon where he had sanded and primed it for respraying.
Inside, it smelled of oil, Halfords air-freshener and foreign food, like a Peckham minicab. His mother, as unde-
terred by this as by its scabbed chrome and deteriorating
wheel-arches, redeemed it every week with a new soft
toy. She bought him a sticker which warned, You toucha
my car, I smasha your face. On Saturdays in the summer
they blu-tacked a crocheted blanket to the inside of the
glass to keep the sun off the back seat, and Colin drove
her slowly round the Rye into Dulwich Village, so that
she could enjoy the posh houses with their oriel windows
and hundred-year-old trees. Colin was her youngest
child. He had arrived late and learned slowly. Prone,
especially after his father died, to obsessions and enthusi-
asms—model fighter aircraft, weekly encyclopaedias of
military history, anything you could collect or assemble—
he had puzzled her by becoming self-contained. "Very

much his own person," she told people. "Not like the other three." That innocent obsessiveness lay curled inside him, waiting until Gifco eventually found a use for it.

We talked for so long that first morning I was late for lunch. When I got home I found a Ford van parked outside the house next to mine. HOUSES CLEARED was painted on its side in fake Edwardian script: DECEASED EFFECTS. An oldish man, very active, with a pink face, grey hair and spectacles, wearing Marks & Spencer's joggers, a cardigan and a neck scarf, was making a pile of the stuff on the pavement while a younger one threw it into the van. The older man laughed and joked a lot.

"Lucky?" I heard him say. "I'm not lucky!"

Cushions off a chair, a wooden ironing board, two black tin boxes about eighteen inches on a side and rusty at the corners; a grey double-breasted jacket and a pink shirt; old aluminum saucepans, plastic supermarket bags stuffed with clothes: everything went in, even the tangle of wire coat hangers left behind in the wardrobe. A pair of stepladders was hurled in like a javelin.

Upstairs I found my wife.

"Someone's died next door," she said.

She was standing at the window looking down into the street. I could hardly hear her over the sound of the television.

"Perhaps they're just moving," I said.

"If he's just moving, why are they throwing his mattress into the back of the van like that? Look at that sock! If you're moving you don't just drop a sock in the road and leave it there."

She rubbed the window with her hand.

"Those are someone's things."

Through our wall you could hear the older man run energetically up and down the stairs inside the house, then shout:

"Here, catch this!"

"Christ!" my wife said disgustedly.

The pile in the back of the van grew unstable. For a moment it looked as if everything would totter and fall. With an intelligent, attentive expression on his face, shifting his balance like a goalkeeper intent on saving a penalty, the younger man watched it for a moment. But everything settled down again suddenly. He shrugged and walked away.

"They're just taking aim and throwing it in," my wife whispered to herself. "Those are someone's things," she repeated, then:

"Can't you switch that fucking TV off?"

"It was you who put it on," I said. "You put it on yourself."

"We'll be next. Don't worry about that. They'll be throwing us in the back of a van next."

Three weeks after I met him, Colin turned up at the Gifco house, where he undid his coat nervously, gawping like a tourist at the rows of books I had arranged around the skirting boards.

"I'm ready if you are," he said. "Where we going?"

Gifco had told him nothing. I let him see the Polaroid photograph I had been provided with. It showed quite a pretty teenage girl in the white blouse, royal blue V neck and pleated grey skirt of some private school. Failures of the developing chemicals had drained color out of her face, so that it had a blank, unformed look. She was sitting on a garden bench, leaning forward with her clasped hands resting on her lap. Behind her it was possible to make out a neo-Georgian door; some standard rose bushes in grey, loose, heavily weeded earth; a black BMW. Something about the curve of her back, the clasped hands, the way she seemed to be staring straight ahead into the air, reminded me of a painting. I couldn't think who it was by.

"I'd prefer to be there before it gets dark," Colin reminded me.

The car had developed an electrical fault: once he turned its headlights on, we wouldn't be able to stop.

"Electrics can be complicated."

"We'll go up the M1," I said.

On the motorway he turned out be an impatient driver, pushing aggressively through the Friday afternoon traffic with the speedometer up against the stop, where he kept it until near Luton all three lanes began to back up.

"Nice to be out, anyway," he said.

"Nothing wrong with this engine," he boasted. "As long as you stay on top of it."

Then:

"Look at him. No, him, him over there! Is he a wanker, or what? Three litres, fuel injection, antilock brakes. What's he doing? Fifty miles an hour.

"Fifty fucking miles an hour!"

When there was no one to overtake he became restless, switching the radio on and off, opening and closing the ventilators. He had a trick of swapping his left foot to the accelerator pedal, tucking his right foot up between the seat and the door. He could do this with hardly a blip in the engine revs; although sometimes while his attention was diverted the car itself lurched disconcertingly through the slipstream of a sixteen-wheeler. Spray shattered the light on the windscreen, blowing in all directions through a haze of sunshine and exhaust smoke. We watched two crows flopping heavily away from the hard shoulder, reluctant to leave something they had been eating there.

"I used to drive a van," he volunteered suddenly. "Rented van, for a firm of builders. We took it back to the rental place and said, 'It's overheating if you do a hundred for any length of time.'"

He chuckled.

"The bloke said, 'A van like this won't do a hundred.' Fuck that, mate!" He looked sideways at me to see if I believed him. "I had that job a month."

"Why don't we try the A5 for a few miles, then join the M6 near Rugby?"

"Why not."

As we turned off the motorway, a Ford Sierra station wagon, logy with children, spare bedding and pushchairs, wallowed past us in the middle lane.

"Can you believe that?"

By the time we got to Cheshire, he had worn himself out. "I could do with a cup of tea." He put his feet up on the dashboard, rubbed his eyes, stared emptily out across the Little Chef car park at a strip of bleak grass rising to newly planted trees, where, in the gathering twilight, some children were running around the base of a pink fibre glass dragon fifteen feet high. "Who would build a thing like that for kids?" he asked me, wriggling about behind the wheel until he could get one arm into his donkey jacket and pull it awkwardly over his shoulders.

He looked genuinely puzzled. "Who would want their kids playing in that?"

"Stay here," I told him. "I'll fetch you the tea."

"Fucking hell."

The Little Chef franchise includes a carpet with a repeating pattern of swastikas, each arm of the symbol a tiny chef who smiles all day while he holds up a dish. Inside, three sales reps were eating cheeseburgers, fries, a garnish of lettuce shiny with fat. Every so often one of them would read out a paragraph from *Today;* the others would laugh. I found the girl waiting quietly in the No Smoking section. She was perhaps thirteen years old. "Be certain it's her," Gifco had warned me. When she saw me comparing her to the Polaroid photograph, she pretended to be looking out of the window, from which, if she moved her head slightly, she could see the parked cars; the line of the Derbyshire hills a long way in the distance south and east; and against them the fibre glass dragon with its slack, Disney Studio jaw signifying helpless good humor. She had on the identical pleated skirt in the Polaroid, with a white blouse; but her hair was in a plait. Close to, she smelled of Wrights soap.

"Gifco sent me to fetch you," I said. I had been warned: "Be certain to say that first. 'Gifco sent me.' " A waitress arrived at the table. I ordered a pot of coffee and sat down while she brought it. Then I added—because what else could I say?—

"He's looking forward to seeing you."

Colin came to the door to find out if his tea was ready. "For God's sake!" I called. "I'm bringing it!" He ducked away, and I saw him walking quickly back to the car, his shoulders hunched under the leatherette yoke of the donkey jacket. I got the girl and her things together and went up to pay.

"Everythink all right for you sir?" asked the woman at the cash desk.

"Yes thanks," I said.

"Want anythink else?"

I could see her looking worriedly at the girl.

"No thanks," I said.

The M6 was deserted. From the moment Colin launched us down the access ramp into a rushing darkness broken only by the occasional oncoming light, someone else's will clung round us like the smell of the car. Despite our speed we were in a kind of glue. Colin wouldn't speak to me. If the girl's presence had isolated me from him, what I knew about her seemed to detach all three of us from our common humanity. "The victim," Gifco had begun to teach me, "has its own powers." She made herself comfortable in the back, and sat so quietly at first that after a few minutes I asked:

"Are you all right?"

"I quite like this grey fur," she said, touching the seat covers. "It's soft as a cat."

Then: "I'm not often carsick."

"Are you warm enough?"

"The last time we went on a motorway with Daddy, there were three dead cats," she said suddenly.

"When we got home we found our own cat had been hurt by a lawnmower and had all the flesh stripped off one front leg. You could see all the lines under the skin. You never know whether it's bones or tendons, or what, do you? He kept pawing us and howling, there was blood all over the kitchen top. Mummy was funny after that.

Every time she saw something in the hedge or in the gutter, she made us stop the car."

She laughed.

" 'Is that a dead bird?' " she mimicked.

" 'Is that somebody's walking stick, or just a broken umbrella?' "

Unnerved perhaps, Colin began to talk, too—

He had seen the most brilliant film when he was small. *"Flying Tigers,* fucking amazing!"

He was reading a book about the Auschwitz museum.

"In Birkenau," he said, "they cut the hair off the women prisoners before they gassed them. It was sold to manufacturers for mattress stuffing. Can you believe that?"

I admitted I could. He added:

"But the worst thing is, tell me if I'm wrong, some of those mattresses could still be on beds. Couldn't they?"

He was worried about his mother.

"She's due to go into the Maudsley for a couple of days soon." It turned out that she had some kind of bone disease. A broken wrist had failed to heal after two months in plaster and would have to be pinned. "It always happens to someone else, doesn't it? Cancer, air crashes, drunk driving, it's never you it happens to."

He stared ahead for a moment.

"It always happens to someone else."

He meant to be ironic, but only wound up sounding wistful.

"Look!"

Our shadows had been thrown onto an enormous exit sign by the headlights of the car behind. Briefly we became monumental and cinematic—yet somehow as domestic as the silhouettes of a married couple caught watching TV in their front room—then the journey resumed itself as a series of long, gluey moments lurching disconnectedly one into the next until we reached the outskirts of London, where the traffic, inching along under a thick orange light, filled the steep cuttings with exhaust smoke. Two men fought on the pavement outside the Odeon cinema, Holloway. The girl daughter had gone to sleep, her face vacant, her head resting loosely against the window, where every movement of the car made it slide about uncomfortably. She didn't seem to notice when I reached back and tucked a folded pullover under it. Later—or it might have been in the same moment—I looked up and thought I saw roses blooming in a garden on top of the Polytechnic of North London. Between the lawns were broad formal beds of "ballerinas" grafted on to standard stocks, with lilies planted between them. Dog rose and guelder spilled faint pink and thick cream over old brick walls and paths velvety with bright green moss. White climbing roses weighed down the apple trees. Two or three willows streamed, like yellow hair in strong winter sunshine, over the parapets of the building; briars hung there in a tangle. A white leopard was crouched among the roses. It was four times the size it would have been in life, and its tail whipped to and fro like a domestic cat's. Other buildings had put forth great suffocating masses of flowers; other animals were at rest there or pacing cagily about among the service gantries and central heating machinery—baboons, huge birds, a snake turning slowly on itself. "The Rose of Earth is the Lily of Heaven." The scent of attar was so strong and heavy it filled the street below:

through it like flashes of light through a veil came the piercing human smells of fried food, beer, petrol.

Colin braked suddenly.

"Jesus!" he said.

The back of a refrigerated truck filled the windscreen, TRANSFIGORANTE painted across it in huge white letters. I jumped out of the car in the middle of the road and shouted back through the open door, into the heat and smell and Colin's surprised white face:

"I'll walk home from here."

"What?"

I slammed the door.

"I'll walk!"

All that night I lay awake. My wife turned restlessly beside me. "Can't you keep still?" she asked.

"I'm going to make a cup of tea."

"Don't use all the bloody milk."

The next morning I made my way reluctantly to the Gifco house. Whatever I had expected, I found neither Colin nor the girl. The room we used was dark and empty except for its rows of books. Over the weeks, heat and humidity had piled up into it until the air seemed saturated and heavy, hard to breathe, on the verge of being something other than air. It had a distinctive odor. But above that I could smell something else. Perfume. Sweat. Some sharp bodily smell which made me shiver with the ghost of old anticipation. One ray of light lanced across the center of the floor, where it found among the blackened flakes of linoleum two Polaroid photographs. I picked them up. One was of the girl we had brought back from Cheshire. In it she was shown sprawled, legs apart, in one corner of the room. She was naked but for a pair of white briefs designed for someone twice her age, with lace detail and legs cut very high to accentuate the pubic mound. Her ribcage and immature nipples stood out in the forty-watt light. Shadows pooled in the hollow of her collarbone. A musing, inturned expression was on her face; but you could almost hear her laughing inappropriately at something an adult had said.

The other picture was of a woman who bore a strong resemblance to my wife. She wore a long pink satin slip, and her hair was disordered. Her expression was hard to read. I remembered how my wife had said to me some time after the death of our daughter:

"Why don't we fuck anymore?" And then:

"Oh for God's sake, it doesn't matter."

I waited for Colin, but he didn't come. Halfway through the afternoon I left the house and walked back up Rye Lane. Women were toiling up the hill in the hot sunshine, laden with plastic supermarket bags.

"I think John's going to let me buy that clock," I heard one of them say. "You know, that hippo clock. Because he was having a look at it in the Argus catalogue."

When I got home, my wife had gone. I went through each room, calling, "Mary? Mary?" The bedroom was in a mess, the curtains half-drawn, makeup and underclothes pulled out of drawers and strewn over the carpets. There were signs of a struggle, but not necessarily with someone else. The bath was full of hot water, the bathroom full of steam. It smelled strongly of rose bath oil, which she loved. In the condensation on the bathroom window she had written, making careful, reversed capitals, so that it could be read from outside: GIFCO LEAVE US ALONE. The door to the balcony was open.

M. John Harrison served as literary editor for *New Worlds* between 1968 and 1975. His books include *The Committed Men, The Centauri Device, In Viriconium, Viriconium Nights, The Ice Monkey* and *The Machine in Shaft Ten. Climbers* (1989) won the Boardman Tasker Award. His latest works are a graphic fantasy novel in collaboration with artist Ian Miller; *The Course of the Heart,* a metaphysical thriller; and the nonfiction *The Drop.*

The Properties of the Beast

Whitley Strieber

Barbie smelled cigarette smoke, which made her want one. "Ken, are there any cigarettes?"

"Boomie filled the living room with them a couple of weeks ago. Which you know."

"I can't smoke those logs. I mean my pretend Marlboros."

"You can't smoke pretend cigarettes." Ken sounded disgusted.

He was such an odd. He wouldn't even pretend to come up the spiral stairs to their bedroom. And he actually pretended to talk to that stupid Elvis doll Boomie kept in the carport. Every time the bigs left, the Elvis doll started going, "haon dawg, haoon dawwggg," again and again, and staring with its awful, soulless eyes. Why didn't Boomie get tired of it and tear its head off like she had the monstrous Rigadoon that Grammie gave her?

Ken was so different. A boy should like Cokes and fries and whatever sport was in season. He should smell like hair tonic. He should tell Little Moron jokes and want to kiss her after dates. Or if they were married he should play the role of Hugh Beaumont with no upsetting variations.

Here they had this beautiful home and a big white Ferrari and everything, and all he could do was kvetch, kvetch, kvetch. She sighed an angry sigh. She'd never get rid of Ken. Too bad the *Mr. Bill* show didn't come on anymore. She'd hoped it would eventually give Beaky the idea to mash Ken's head off or tear out his arms or something.

She looked at Ken. He would never grow up. He would just stay like that, like he was. Boomie pulled his pants down sometimes. "Ooooooo," Barbie said, then she chuckled.

"What's that about?"

"I was thinking about your penis." Ken didn't have one. All he had was a sort of bump. But Beaky had stuffed her down his pants once. She knew what a *real* penis was all about. And Ken was sadly lacking. Ken was a horrible failure in the penis department.

Barbie had makeup and everything. She had a whole closetful of dresses. But she didn't get to go out. Why didn't they make a Barbie nightclub or a Barbie movie theater where they would play real movies? She wanted to see *Dumbo* and *Mary Poppins* and *101 Dalmatians.* "I want to go out, Ken. I was *made* for dating and stuff. Why can't we go out on a date?"

"Shut up, you stinking bitch. Even if I had a penis, it wouldn't mean shit. You don't have a vagina."

"Well, screw me!"

"That's exactly what I can't do. Unless I find a drill somewheres that works."

"Ken's Tool Box has a drill, so use it!"

"Pretend electricity never turned a drill and it never

will. Anyway, I've looked at it and it has no moving parts. It's just a lump of cheap plastic like the rest of the shit around here."

"My dresses are nice."

"Your dresses suck. Shit from a Barbara Cartland nightmare. And how about these overalls they got me in? Christ, I look like some kind of farmer doll."

"You could change clothes with your friend Elvis."

"How, if you are incapable of moving a single millimeter, do you expect me to do it? And with what—these stinking excuses for hands? The fingers don't come apart. The fuckers won't even bend!"

Barbie pretended to dangle one of her hands. "My hands are pretty. My skin is pretty." She imagined smelling the back of it. "I smell sweet!"

"Like plastic."

She pretended to come closer to him. Ken might be a jerk, but he was all she had. She certainly wasn't going to pay any attention to Elvis. He had cheap plastic hair.

"I wish Boomie would put me in my pink slacks and tank top, and put on my ponytail wig, then take me to the beach," she said. "I could lie staring up at the sun and listening to the surf."

"And what about me? What about old Ken? One second you pretend to cuddle up, then you're thinking about going to the beach. Barbie, you can't concentrate on anything, not even for a second."

"I want to smoke. Boomie and Teresa smoke. Beaky taught them how."

"Beaky also makes them lift their dresses for cigarettes."

"I'd lift *my* dress if Beaky would teach me how to smoke."

"Fuckin' idiot." Ken pretended to close his eyes.

She hated it when he did that. "Come on, Ken, don't be so yucky. Why not pretend to have that nice ham sandwich—"

"That's been lying on the kitchen floor ever since Boomie lost interest in us and forgot we existed! And you don't want to be fucked with by Beaky. Don't you understand? He's only eleven but he abuses both of the girls right before our eyes because he doesn't give a shit since we're dolls and we can't talk and we can't do a damn thing about it!"

"He took his pants off for Boomie. He took it all off. Boom-boppa, boom-boppa, *boom*!"

"You crazy bitch! He comes down here and displays himself like some kind of fucking oversexed baboon! And the girls take full advantage of him, too!"

"I think he's very romantic. The way they all dress up and all . . . the girls in Mommie's slinky dresses and he dresses like you, Ken, with no underpants."

"He doesn't wear underpants! I know those kids come in here and play sex games! And I can't do shit about it! Hell, I have dim memories—wasn't I—didn't I—move— oh, God, I was a psychologist!"

She tried to understand how it was that she was always managing to upset him. He lay against the wall on his side. That must be it, those naughty girls shouldn't lay him on his side. Don't they know it makes a man feel bad to just lie staring at a busted pretend TV for months at a time? He's hardly a man at all.

"We're not dolls," Ken shrieked. He grunted, groaned, tried to move. "We're in hell! Hell's in the toys! Oh, God, don't you see? But I didn't do anything bad. No, I didn't!

I was a child psychologist, my name was Harvey Feinman. I died, Barbie!"

"Oh, Ken, I hate to talk about death, you know that!"

"Haooon, haoonn," went the Elvis doll in the carport. "Haoon dawwgggg!"

"Shut up, you cookie-cutter bitch! You're not a Barbie doll, not really."

She did not like the drift of this. No, indeed. "Oh, Ken, honestly, I wish I had on my beach outfit and my pretty pink beachball. We could go to the beach and you could wear your bathing suit."

"We're lost, we're forgotten. Other people get heaven, eternal life, but we got this! Watching a bunch of hopelessly oversexed preteens grope each other into twisted, neurotic basket cases! And knowing how to save them, to redeem them!"

"Haaaooooonnnn . . ."

"Shut up, asshole. Elvis is dead and you're on your way to the trash can! You're going to the dump, ha ha! Oh shit, I even sound like Ken would sound if he was going nuts—shallow and simple and shitty! Fuck this! I'm a psychologist, my name is Harvey Fummammfumma—what the fuck *is my name*!"

"Feinman."

"That's it! That's right! Thanks, doll. If I'm a psychologist I must know jargon! I can speak jargon! I don't have to sound like some airhead beach bum of a fuckin' doll! A regressive shift away from clear consciousness can produce—see! Fuckin'-A! From his memory the patient painted for me an unforgettable picture of his mother offering—offering—Barbie, I think I want that sandwich! I want that pretend sandwich! Help me, Barbie!"

He was all worked up, that much was obvious. Why

couldn't he just relax and lie back and listen to pretend records on the marvelous Barbie portable stereo with the turntable that really turns? Why not? Barbie did. She did it every day. Ken was just so-o-o *different*. "I don't like boys who are different," she said shyly. "I don't think I like you, Ken."

"Haaaoooonnnn dawwwggggg . . ."

"Hound dog," Ken yelled, "God damn you, Elvis, *hound dog*!"

"Ken, he's singing because he's sad. Haven't you ever been kinda low, and felt like singing about it? 'When the ole hooty-owl hooty-hoos to the dove . . .' Doesn't that make you feel better? Oh, Ken, you are so *different*!"

"You're Ruth Rausch, the most brilliant psychometrician in the world, the first person to introduce chaos theory into the four-dimensional psychometric model and successfully predict the incidence of psychopathologic behavior in a prison population!"

"Huh?"

"Ain't nothin' but a . . ."

"Shut up! Shut up, Elvis!"

"Haaaooouuunnn daaawwwggg!!"

Barbie chewed on the name Ruth Rausch. "Marlboros," she said.

"Marlboros?"

"I smoked Marlboros. Chain smoker. My, how I stank. I had tar and nicotine in my blood. It was lovely."

"Yes! Because you were alive. *Alive!*"

"Oh . . . I remember the hummingbirds and my wedding cake and my grandmother had a white dress . . . and I remember stamps and Jarlsberg cheese and Chevys and Moulin-à-Vent!"

"I remember Post Toasties and the American Psycho-analytic Association and the concept of cornholing!"

"I remember bacon and all night diners and Fudg-sicles and my mother had a mole on her left arm!"

"Oh, I had kids! I had Jennifer and Scott and I had to leave them when they were still so very young. Oh, Bar-bie—"

"Ruth!"

"Ruth, I miss my children! I want my babies!"

"Harvey, we've got to get out of this. There must be something we can do, someone we can appeal to." She remembered a courtroom, a clown in a fake halo, wasn't that it? Or—an angel—some cheapjack third-rate angel named Scrubble or something, and he'd said she could have a Ferrari and all kinds of clothes— "I'VE BEEN CHEATED!"

"Haaounnn daaawwwgggg!"

"He knows! He's been here all along watching us with those horrible glass eyes of his, watching from under that hideous fiberglass pompadour of his. Fuck you, Elvis!" She wanted to spit, but she didn't have a mouth, not really, and she couldn't do anything except pretend to go pffffftttt!

"Ruth, we were at a conference together. We were in an elevator, and instead of going up to the Roche Phar-maceuticals Hospitality Suite, it went down. It went down very, very fast, and your—"

"My dress! My dress is flying up around my ears! I'm off the floor, we're pressed against the ceiling—"

"And then we're—we're—"

"It looks like a courtroom! We're being sentenced."

"I thought—the IRS . . . tax evasion. Is that a sin, too?"

Ruth remembered their trial, there'd been a pop music quiz, Harvey hadn't been able to name ten Rosemary Clooney hits and so they'd been condemned to this hell. She remembered drifting in the world, through the living, conscious wonder of a forest, down a throbbing street, into this house full of children that shone with the very light of God, Boomie and Beaky and Teresa and thinking she had gone to the lap of heaven when she lay in Boomie's embrace and all of a sudden she knew she was a Barbie and the thrill—the ineffable, perfect thrill . . .

"We got—it's a trap!"

Harvey did not reply. He had gone dead silent, and Ruth knew why. There was great movement in the basement, the enormous roar of big breath and the smacking of lips and the thick, salty smell of boys.

Suddenly Beaky's voice came: "C'MON GUYS, LET'S DO HER DOLLS!"

"Oh, shit," Harvey said.

She felt herself being grasped in the huge hands of the little boy, she saw a scratch, a smudge of dirt, sweat and body oils across the wide, smooth back of the hand as she was lifted high, high up to the top of the world, and her house was only a few pieces of plastic up against the wall of the basement playroom. "Oh, God, Ken, we haven't been played with in *years*!" Then she smelled the salt and sweat of the skin, and the sharp, sour odor of cigarettes and saw the yellow stains between the fingers that were crushing her guts out.

Ken shot past in a blur, then there was a horrible lurch and all of a sudden it was all dark and it stank of rotten candy and popcorn and old used Kleenex and more sweat.

"Oh, Ken—"

"Harvey, please, dear. Call me Harvey from now on."

Elvis was dumped down on top of them. He was bigger and astonishingly heavy. Ruth was all twisted out of
shape, her head turned to one side, her arms and legs
akimbo. She remembered being pretty, she remembered
oral sex, she remembered listening to her patients while
counting the fly dots on the ceiling. She remembered
real food and the wonderful feeling of dropping a load
and how men tasted to kiss and dancing and driving a car
and the smell of pinto beans and the sound of her insurance agent's voice. "I'm real! I've always been real!"

"WE'LL MAKE THE STAKES RIGHT OVER
HERE."

"YOUR MOMMA—"

"SHE'S AT K-MART. THIS IS GONNA BE SO
NEAT."

"I WANNA BURN SOMEBODY REAL AT THE
STAKE."

"WE CAN'T, NOT BEHIND MY GARAGE."

"THAT RETARDATE, OLD GORDO. LURE HIM
INTO CLANCY'S WOODS."

"WE'LL GET CAUGHT—"

"EVEN IF WE DO GET CAUGHT, WHAT'RE
THEY GONNA DO TO A COUPLA KIDS? WE GOT
CARRIED AWAY WITH PRET-E-E-END! I'D LIKE
TO WATCH A GUY BURN."

"ME, TOO."

Ruth was screaming and screaming but there was
nothing whatsoever she could do. She felt herself being
lifted by an enormous fist, felt the string going round her
body, affixing her to the stake. The boy was blond and
pure as sunlight with sweet unfinished eyes and the inno-

cent lips of a baby. She was face-to-face with Ken, but there were probably ten stakes and there were other dolls, dolls she'd never seen before, a Barbie with no hair, a couple of more old-fashioned dolls, a Wonder Woman and Elvis, all tied to stakes.

The boys gathered twigs, and put a pile of them at the feet of each doll. Ruth was sick with dread. She remembered her husband's arms and her father's arms and her Ph.D. on the wall and the fact that her car insurance was about to expire.

The boys squirted every little pile of sticks with Energine lighter fluid. "We're alive," Harvey said, "alive!"

"God help us!"

"You kids! Stop! Can't you see what you're doing! Stop!"

They didn't even begin to hear him, not over the summer sound of birds and the sweet calling of the cicadas. It was a soft day, the sky was blue and flecked with white clouds. Somewhere nearby a lawn mower clattered, and an angel sang. In the song Ruth heard something extraordinary that suggested to her that nothing, nothing was as it seemed, all was different, the world proceeding by rules of unimaginable subtlety and force, rules that had not in any way ever entered human understanding at all, which was why the angel appeared to her as a great, bobbing Mickey Mouse carrying a gondola full of terrified tourists.

The Garden of Eden? The Academia Bridge?

Then there was fire. It hurried, it ran, a hustling little fire that dashed toward her legs. She tried to make some sign that would awaken the boys to what was *really* happening. But they sat hand in hand like babies at a scary movie, watching. She could see the fire in their eyes, could see it coming closer and closer to her.

Then Harvey wailed and she saw that his legs were aflame. He was burning up, he was burning alive and nobody knew it, he was only some old doll, who cared? But he hurt, she could hear his shrieks.

Then others began screaming, the hideous, crackling ma-mas of the older dolls, the cry of haaaooo-oouuuunnnn daaaawwwwgggg echoing to high heaven and glass eyes sinking down in boiling plastic faces and a pain more terrible than anything she had ever, ever imagined possible, the most hideous agony that a human being could know, gnawing into her legs, sending its fingers deep into her.

Smoke and flame filled her and gagged her, the fire coming out her mouth and nose and her eyes falling back into her head and from far, far away, "AAAAHHHH, OOOOOHHHH, LOOKIT 'EM!" One of the boys is laughing and one is crying. "I TOLE YOU IT WAS NEAT!"

All full of awe: "THEY LOOK LIKE MELTIN' PEO-PLE, BEAKY."

Then it is dark and she feels cold, she is all the cold, hurt women the world has ever known and an angel stands before her with tickets to the garden, and she enters at last.

All around her there are enormous purple flowers with red blood pulsing in their veins, and huge ears of berries fit for giants to eat, and the Gods stalking in their garden like dinosaurs, their eyes livid with curiosity. She has become a berry, and Harvey too, a little, plump berry, and a huge God with a serpent's neck comes and touches her with his long tongue and takes her toward his mouth.

She smells the stinking foetor of its breath, as she is lifted far up into the steamy, ancient air, the air of the garden, a fat, tart berry in the mouth of a dinosaur.

Dimly, she knows that it is very long ago and she is very lost. She is chewed and it hurts something awful, like being run over by a steamroller or crushed in a falling elevator.

"My name is Ruth, and I remember Cherry Coke." She knows the truth of the world. A vise grips her chest. She cannot talk, cannot even think. But she knows the truth of the world!

"Haaaooouuunnn daaawwwggg!"

Elvis is a rocket, they have put fireworks in his body and he flares off into the sky, gone to heaven, Elvis sent to eternal heaven by the judgment of two sadistic little boys who can't so much as read a novel and don't know St. Peter from Adolf Eichmann.

And Harvey, he is the clattering of the railroad train, the hissing to the great gas doors, and the wailing of the multitudes, he is the darkness and the sorrows of the night, a photograph on a sideboard, a boy's memory at a Bar Mitzvah, the blink of an eye and then all turn, forgetting . . .

The huge beasts of the garden slither or stride, and some of them fly on leatherbat wings, and there are insects with eyes like bomber canopies. Outside the envelope of the world a meteor that has been falling since the beginning of time, that dropped from the fingers of God before Earth was a molten streak in the sky, will soon smite the garden, the sword of the angel, and Dante lingering at the Bridge of Sighs will toss a pebble into the Po. . . .

All that follows the dinosaurs will be a dream.

She is in the belly with its sloshing acid, becoming one with the atoms of the beast, losing all memory of Barbie and Ruth and Ken and all she has known, William Blake and sourdough bread and edible birthday candles and Klaus Barbie, feeling herself entering the properties of the beast, its dense and shaking flesh, the formless caverns of its brain, where amid the memories of berries and leaves lies the whole unformed future of the world.

———————

Whitley Strieber is the author of *The Wolfen, The Hunger, Black Magic, The Night Church, Wolf of Shadows, Catmagic, Majestic, Billy* and *The Wild,* in addition to the nonfiction *Communion* and *Transformation,* and two books with James Kunetka, *Warday* and *Nature's End.* His latest novel is *Unholy Fire.*

PART THREE
Grateful Dead

In Praise of Folly

Thomas Tessier

 He drove north in air-conditioned comfort, a road map on the seat beside him, Satie's piano music rippling pleasantly from the stereo speakers. Thank God for the little things that make human life bearable when summer's on your neck.

It was August. The stagnant heat and humidity were so heavy they no longer seemed like atmospheric phenomena, but had assumed a suffocating gelatinous density. People moved slowly if at all, dazed creatures in the depths of a fungal deliquescence.

It had to be better up in the Adirondacks, cooler and drier. But Roland Turner was not just another vacationer seeking escape. He was on a mission of discovery, he hoped, a one-man expedition in search of a serious folly.

Roland was one of the very few American members of the Folly Fellowship, an organization based in London that was dedicated to "preserve and promote the enjoyment and awareness of follies . . . to protect lonely and unloved buildings of little purpose . . . unusual, intriguing or simply bizarre structures and sites." Roland first learned about the group two years earlier, when he came across an issue of their quarterly magazine in a Connecticut bookshop. The photographs were fascinating, the text charming and witty.

A typical English eccentricity, Roland thought at the time, the sort of thing that lasts for a year or two and then dies away as enthusiasm and funds decline. He wrote a letter to ask if the Fellowship was still going, and was surprised to get a reply from the president and editor himself, one Gwyn Headley. Not only was the Fellowship still active, it was thriving, with more than five hundred members worldwide (most of them, naturally, residents of the United Kingdom).

Roland immediately mailed off a bank draft to cover the cost of membership, a set of back issues of the magazine, a folder of color postcards and a copy of Headley's definitive work, *Follies: A National Trust Guide* (Cape, 1986).

There was something romantic and mysterious about monuments, castles and old ruins that had always appealed to Roland. He saw the past in them, and he loved to imagine what life had been like so long ago. Perhaps it was because his own day-to-day existence was placid and humdrum. Roland owned a printing company, a small outfit that produced trade newsletters and supermarket fliers for the Westchester County market. Over the years he had worked long and hard to build up a reliable trade, and now he presided over a solid, secure business operation. On the negative side, Roland's personal life was somewhat threadbare.

He'd been through a number of brief intimate encounters, but none of them even came close to marriage. Now in his middle age, Roland could take it or leave it. He enjoyed a good book, mainly history or historical fiction, as well as classical music, and he had a special fondness for follies.

A genuine folly was a building, garden, grotto or other such architectural construct that had been designed with a deliberate disregard for the normal rules. A folly was something literally "to gasp at," as Headley put it in his massive tome. Roland had not yet been able to travel to Britain, due to pressure of work, but he had managed to track down a few American follies, such as Holy Land in Waterbury and the Watts Towers in Los Angeles. He'd also visited a fully functional house that had been built out of beer bottles in Virginia, a four-acre Sahara located in the Maine woods, and a home designed as Noah's ark in the Tennessee hills. American follies tended to lack the air of lost grandeur that was the hallmark of classic British follies, but they often displayed a kind of heroic zaniness that was utterly endearing.

Roland could only look forward to the time in his life when he would at last be free to spend two or three months journeying around England, Scotland and Wales, leisurely inspecting some of the remarkable things he could only read about now—such as the rocket ship in Aysgarth, the "house in the clouds" at Thorpeness, Clavel's Tower, and Portmeirion, not to mention all the splendid follies that could still be found in and around the great city of London itself.

Follies are the dizzy, demented lacework on the edge of the vast human tapestry, Roland had written in a letter that for some unknown reason Mr. Headley had not yet seen fit to publish in the magazine of the Follies Fellowship. In his spare hours, Roland continued to hone his thoughts and write up notes on the American follies he came across.

Then, two weeks ago, the message had arrived from London. A "rather spectacular" folly was rumored to exist on the grounds of the old Jorgenson summer cottage in Glen Allen, New York. Would Mr. Turner be able to check it out and report back? If it proved to be a worthwhile site, photographs and notes would be welcome. Roland immediately faxed his answer: "Absolutely."

It took a while to find Glen Allen on the map. Apparently a rural village, it was some two hundred miles away, a little north of Big Moose Lake in the Adirondacks. Definitely a weekend trek. Get up there and find a rustic inn Friday evening, spend Saturday investigating the Jorgenson property, and then drive back down to Rye on Sunday. Roland fled the office at noon, and a few minutes later hit the turnpike.

As far as anyone knew he was enjoying a short getaway in the countryside. Roland had mentioned his interest in follies to one other person, Patty Brennan, a robust divorcée who had worked for him briefly last year. Roland thought he fancied Patty, but they never got beyond the talking stage.

"You mean like Coney Island, or Grant's Tomb," had been her reaction when he told her about follies.

"Well, no, not exactly . . ."

Perhaps Roland had explained it badly. He decided then and there to keep the world of follies to himself, his little secret. Patty soon fell in love with the man who cleaned the heads of her VCR, and quit to take a position in his business. It was all for the best, Roland convinced himself. When you share something you treasure with another person, it's no longer quite so special; it inevitably loses a little of its magic aura.

Roland made fairly good time, but the actual journey

clocked in at closer to three hundred miles, so it was a little after six in the evening when he reached Glen Allen. He passed by the Glen Motel on his way into town but found no other accommodation, and eventually circled back to it. A satellite dish, a room full of vending machines, three other cars parked in the lot. Nothing at all like a rustic inn, but it would have to do. Roland went into the office and paid for a room.

The middle-aged woman on duty took his cash, gave him a key and some brochures about the boating and fishing opportunities in the vicinity.

"Where's the best place to eat in town?" Roland asked.

"Bill's Friendly Grille, right on Main," the woman replied. "By the way, there's an electrical storm supposed to come through tonight. If the power goes out, you'll find some candles in your closet."

"Thanks. I was thinking of taking a look at the Jorgenson estate tomorrow. Is it hard to find?"

"The Jorgenson estate," she repeated carefully, as if giving the matter some thought. She was a large woman with bland, empty features. "No, it's not hard to find but it might be hard to get to. It's just a couple of miles up the glen, but nobody's lived there in about thirty years, so the private road's all overgrown. You'd have to hike some." Then added, "From what I heard there's nothing much left to see."

"Oh."

"Are you in real estate?"

"No, no, I represent the—well, it's a British fellowship, you see, and we're interested in neglected sites of architectural distinction."

He was upset with himself for hesitating and then failing to utter the word *folly*, but there was no point in trying to explain it to this woman. As it was, she made a vague sound and appeared to have no interest whatsoever.

"Well, I could be wrong but I don't think you'll find there is any architecture up there."

"None at all?" Roland asked in disbelief. Until now he hadn't even considered the possibility that he might have come all this way on a wild goose chase. "There's nothing left?"

The woman shrugged blithely, seeming to take pleasure in his distress. "Place burned down ages ago." She picked up the book she had been reading—a paperback account of some lurid murders in Texas—and found her place.

"Ah. Well . . ."

His room was adequate, just. There was mildew on the shower curtain, and the air had a damp musty smell that some city people regard as the authentic flavor of the countryside, but the sheets were clean and the air conditioner worked. Outside, the heat and humidity were nearly as oppressive as they'd been in Rye.

Roland decided not to linger in his room. He was hungry and a storm was coming. He left his overnight bag, still packed, on a rock maple armchair, left his camera locked in the trunk of his car, and set off to find Bill's Friendly Grille.

Glen Allen, what there was of it, had the peeling, outdated look of a town still stuck in the forties or fifties. It was not unpleasant—the weathered clapboards, the old Flying Red Horse gas pumps, the rusty cars and battered pickups, the general store with a group of kids hanging around out front—a curious mix of what was genuinely quaint and what was merely Tobacco Road.

But it wasn't what was there, Roland realized as he parked. It was what wasn't there—no trendy boutiques, no video stores, no T-shirt joints, no fast-food chains, no blaring boom boxes, not even one odorific Chinese takeaway—that was somehow pleasing. The present had not yet arrived in Glen Allen, at least not with the full force of all its tawdry enterprise.

Roland sat at the bar and had the cheeseburger deluxe, which was suitably greasy and rather good. The fries were on the soggy side, but the coleslaw was tangy and delicious. Roland washed it all down with a large mug of cold beer—the first of several he would enjoy that evening.

There were a handful of other customers, regulars it seemed, who clutched their glasses, kept an eye on the Yankee game on the TV at the far end of the bar, and chatted easily with each other. None of them showed any particular interest in Roland, which was fine with him. Most of them were young and probably knew nothing firsthand about the Jorgensons. But Roland did eventually manage to learn something from Bill, the elderly owner of the place, who also presided over the bar.

"Old man Jorgenson made it big in steel, right up there with Carnegie. Lot of money. My father worked on the house when they built it, back in the twenties. Oh, it was beautiful. Wood from South America, marble from Italy, you name it. French furniture, big paintings on the walls. No expense spared. They lived there about two months a year, every summer. They called it a cottage, you know, because it only had about twenty rooms."

Roland nodded, smiling. Bill had a way of saying something and slapping his hand lightly on the bar as if to signal that he was finished. He would turn and drift away, tending to his other customers, but sooner or later he would wander back to Roland and continue, gradually filling in the rest of the story.

The Jorgenson clan came and went year after year. They kept pretty much to themselves. Nothing memorable happened until the winter of 1959, when the house burned down mysteriously. It was gutted, a complete loss. The only people there at the time were the caretaker and his wife, both of whom died in the blaze. Some people thought it was an accident, others that local vandals were responsible—the rich are always resented. There was a lengthy investigation, but no final verdict.

The place was abandoned, the Jorgensons never came back. It wasn't until a few years ago that the estate was in the news once more. A new generation of Jorgensons had seen fit, no doubt with tax considerations in mind, to deed the hundred-plus acres to the state of New York. The surrounding Adirondack forest had already reclaimed it, and now it was a legal fact.

"Weren't there any other buildings, besides the main house?" Roland asked anxiously. "Any other structures?"

"Oh, sure," Bill said. "There was a big garage, a gazebo, a few sheds, and an icehouse. And, uh, Little Italy."

"What?" Roland's hopes soared. "Little Italy?"

"Yeah, my kids used to play there when they were growing up back in the sixties. Crazy thing."

It was a folly, no question. It seemed that the old man had been in love with Italy, so much so that he decided to create a garden that featured miniature replicas of famous Italian sights: the Trevi fountain, Vesuvius and Pompeii, the Blue Grotto at Capri and the Colosseum, among others. Jorgenson had added to it every summer for nearly three decades, and by the time of the fire the Italian garden was said to cover nearly four acres.

Roland was both encouraged and depressed. Yes, there was an authentic folly, but it had been rotting away since 1959, exposed to hot summers, freezing winters and the random violence of local kids. Whatever still survived was no doubt crumbling in the grip of the forest. It was sad, and Roland thought he would be lucky to get one halfway decent photograph. But it was certainly worth writing up—and publishing—and it would be Roland Turner's first appearance in the pages of the Fellowship magazine.

It was well past ten when he finally left the bar. The heat had eased considerably and a breeze blew through town. The storm was closer. Roland could only hope it would be long gone when he went looking for the Jorgenson place in the morning. He caught a glimpse of lightning in the sky, but it seemed far away and there was no following rumble of thunder.

Main Street was now deserted, and Roland thought it looked a bit like an abandoned movie set. Signs swayed, windows rattled, leaves and dust swirled about, and everything was cast in the dim yellow glow of a few widely spaced streetlamps. The bright neon Genesee sign at Bill's stood out in welcome contrast.

Roland was about to get into his car when he first heard the sound, and he stopped to listen to it. Choir practice? No, this was not musical in the sense that it followed any pattern; it was not even human. Roland slowly turned his head, trying to figure out which direction it came from, but it was too diffuse, and the wind in the trees frequently overwhelmed it.

Back at the motel, Roland heard the sound again as

soon as he stepped out of his car. It was stronger and clearer, yet just as hard to define as it had been in town. An Aeolian chorus that sang in the night, rising and fading, shrilling and moaning. The wind was part of it, but there had to be more, some unusual local feature that produced this effect. Roland actually liked it. He was reminded of certain ethereal passages from Debussy and Vaughan Williams. In his room, he turned off the air conditioner, opened a window and listened to it a while longer.

The storm passed by a few miles to the north, crackling and thundering in the distance like a transient war, and the village of Glen Allen took an intense strafing of rain. But it was gone in a quarter of an hour, and its aftermath was a humid, dripping stillness.

In the morning, as he was about to set off for the Jorgenson place, Roland spotted the woman who ran the motel. She came out of the vending machine room with a full garbage sack in one hand. Roland crossed the parking lot and asked her about the sounds he had heard the previous night.

"That's the wind coming down the glen," she told him. "When it blows a certain direction, you get that."

"Yes, but what exactly causes it?"

"The wind coming down the glen," she repeated, as if he were dense. "You don't notice it so much in the winter."

"Ah."

He stopped at Colbert's Store, a few doors up from Bill's on Main Street, to buy a grinder and a carton of juice for lunch. A few minutes later he nearly drove past what had been the entrance to the Jorgenson summer estate. As Bill had explained, it wasn't hard to find: about two miles up North Street, which was the only road north out of town, and look for it on your left. There were two stone columns flanking a single-lane driveway. Roland backed up and studied the scene for a moment.

The stone columns bore the dead pastel blue and green stains of lichen, and their caps were severely chipped and cracked. The wrought iron gate was long gone—only a pair of deeply corroded hinges remained. Then Roland realized that Jorgenson had planted a wall of arborvitae along the road in both directions. It could still be seen, but barely. It must have reached twenty or thirty feet high, but now it was a skeletal ruin, shot through with tall weeds, young maples, choke cherries, wild grapes, and other vines and parasites. The entryway itself was so thick with brush that Roland couldn't even park in it; he had to go another fifty yards before he found a grassy spot on the right. He slung his camera around his neck, took his lunch cooler, locked the car and walked back down the road.

The original dirt road to the house was thoroughly overgrown with weeds and field grass, but it wasn't hard to follow. Roland wandered off it twice and immediately noticed the change from the firm gravel base to a more yielding soil underfoot.

He passed through a tunnel of trees, a landscape effect that may well have been quite lovely once; now it was ragged, dark, and gloomy, devastated by secondary growth. He came out of it on the edge of a large clearing, and sensed that he was now close to the site of the house. It was no longer "cleared" at all, of course, but the perimeter was unmistakably marked by the much taller pine trees of the surrounding forest.

Roland's pants were soaked. The sky was overcast, so

all of the plants he waded through were still wet from the rain. But he preferred it that way to a blazing hot sun. He followed the road as it climbed a very gradual rise and then leveled off. Yes, he thought excitedly, this has to be it. Where else would you build a house? The three or four acres of flat high ground he stood on provided a gorgeous southern view.

Roland gazed down across the old clearance, looking for any human traces. There was a small lake—perhaps Jorgenson had it created for him—and the stumpy remnants of a wooden pier. The lake was nearly dead now, choked with algae, reeds and silt, but it must have been beautiful once.

Roland found it easy to visualize the Jorgenson children out on the lake canoeing, or jumping from the pier and swimming. The family might well have had picnic lunches in the shade of the big sugar maple that still stood by itself not far from the water. A view of the past. The lives, the dreams, so much effort to build a little world within the world. Were the Jorgensons haughty and unbearable, or decent and worthy of what they had? But it didn't matter, because what they had here was gone and so were they.

Roland turned and snagged his toe on a rock. It was part of the foundation of the house. He walked it, leaving his own trail in the tall grass and wildflowers. The fire, and the years, had left nothing but a rectangle of stones that barely protruded from the earth. The outbuildings had vanished as well; maybe some of the locals had dismantled them for the lumber and fittings.

Roland took a photograph of the ground on which the house had stood, and then another of the broad clearance, including the lake. He ate his lunch quickly, eyes scanning the landscape for a sign, a clue. If the Italian folly was hidden somewhere in the forest, he could spend a week looking for it. There was only one other possibility—somewhere up behind the house. Beyond a low ridge only a hundred yards away, the land seemed to hollow out as steep walls formed on either side. That was north. That was the beginning of the glen, or the end of it.

Roland trudged up the rise, and gaped. There it was, Little Italy, Jorgenson's folly. He was so excited he nearly broke into a run, but then he steadied himself and clicked off several shots of the whole panorama. There were all kinds of houses—country villas, farmhouses, squat urban blocks—scattered in clumps and clusters. There were statues, many statues, fountains, archways, piazzas, towers, churches, stables, barns and much more. It went on into the glen as far as Roland could see.

The land on which most of the folly had been built was low, but it was marked by any number of little hillocks that enhanced the visual effect. In addition, the walls of the glen had a way of jutting out and cutting back that created niches, defiles and recesses of varying size and depth. Every wacky detail somehow worked, and it all came together to create a remarkable illusion at first sight.

In fact, it looked its best at a distance. When Roland came down the slope to it and began to make his way through the narrow passages, the decay was all too obvious. Most of the structures had been built with cinderblocks, or plaster on chicken wire, and then coated with paint or whitewash. Tin roofs had been painted a reddish-brown to suggest tile. Cheap stuff for a rich guy, and it showed the effects of age, neglect and intermittent vandalism. Whole walls had been knocked down or worn away. Much of the tin was corroded, the paint blistered and peeling—what there still was of it. Statues were missing hands or heads, sometimes both. Everything was severely chipped or cracked.

Brambles and vines proliferated, often making it difficult for Roland to move about. But in that respect the folly had been spared worse damage. The ground was rocky and the soil thin, so not much else managed to grow there.

Roland advanced slowly, taking pictures as he went. He knew little about Italy but he recognized most of the famous landmarks Jorgenson had chosen to replicate. He was particularly impressed by a fifty-foot section of the Aqueduct high enough to walk under without ducking his head. It was broken in only three places and actually dripped a tiny residue of last night's rain. Roland had to smile when he noticed that the plaster Aqueduct was lined with cast-iron half-pipe.

What really made the whole thing work was the dizzy range of scale—or rather, the complete lack of scale. A two-foot house stood next to a three-foot statue of a dog. Mount Etna was somehow smaller than the Duomo, while the Spanish Steps were larger than all of Venice. Nothing matched anything.

That, and sheer quirkiness. Working only two months a year, Jorgenson obviously felt compelled to add a number of ready-made items to his dream world. The statues, for instance. And Roland especially liked the birdbath—a common garden birdbath—that utterly dominated St. Peter's Square. There were other birdbaths to be seen, as well as birdhouses that could be purchased in any garden shop or nursery even today; perhaps in the ex-

treme reaches of his obsession Jorgenson saw an ideal
Italy populated solely by birds. Roland grinned a few
moments later when he came across a statue of Saint
Francis of Assisi, surrounded by birdhouses that were
mounted on sections of lead pipe—with the entire tab-
leau situated between a *trattoria* and a bizarre little maze
apparently meant to suggest the catacombs.

Roland came into a small clearing with a stone bench.
Maybe this was where old man Jorgenson sat, pondering
his extraordinary creation and dreaming up more addi-
tions to it. Roland rested his feet for a moment and
changed the film in his camera.

It was easy to lose track of the size of the folly. Many
of the structures were only three feet high, but quite a
few were as tall as a man, and with the gently undulating
flow of the ground it was impossible to see ahead to the
point where the folly displays finally came to an end. But
it was also impossible to get lost, since the walls of the
glen were always visible.

Roland had to keep moving. The sky seemed to be
darker now, not from the lateness of the hour but from
the appearance of more storm clouds. He hadn't thought
to check the weather report, and he had no idea whether
a new storm was due or it was the same one circling
back. Roland didn't like the idea of having to hike all the
way back to the car in a downpour, but it might come to
that. He wasn't going to leave until he had seen and
photographed every part of the folly.

Jorgenson had saved his most astounding flight of
fancy for the last. Roland stepped through a gap in a
wall, and he thought that he was standing in a courtyard.
A stretch of ground roughly one hundred feet square had
been covered with large paving stones that had subse-

quently buckled and heaved. Now the whole area was shot through with tufts of dull green weeds, laced with some kind of wild ground ivy.

There was a line of columns along the left edge and another on the right. They were ten or twelve feet high and some of them had fallen over, but they created a sudden impression that still had power. Roland found himself thinking of the Pantheon, but he had no clear mental image of the original to compare.

All this, however, was peripheral to the set piece straight ahead. Where the paving stones ended the ground rose up slightly before it leveled off, creating a rough natural platform. It was as wide as the courtyard, and it was full of statues. There were dozens of them. Roland stumbled forward.

Several interesting features, he thought in a daze. All the statues were positioned to face the center of the glen. They all had their arms raised and their faces uplifted, as if acclaiming the gods or seeking their merciful help. None of them had hands. They had open mouths but otherwise there were no facial features, not a nose or an eye or an ear in the entire assembly. They had no feet, unless they were buried in the ground, for the legs rose up out of the soil, converging in thick, trunklike torsos. The statues were crude and stark, and yet they seemed to be possessed of a terrible poignancy.

They weren't presented as Romans in togas and robes. There were no gods or creatures of myth, not even a Venetian gondolier. They were like golems, clad in stone. Roland climbed the rise to inspect them close up. The surface was brownish in color, rough but firm in texture —like partly annealed sand. Perhaps there was an underlayer of plaster or cement. Roland had seen nothing else like it in Jorgenson's Little Italy. It was an improvement; these statues showed very little evidence of erosion.

But what madness!

Roland was in the middle of his final roll of film, snapping medium shots of the amazing statuary, when the first hand grabbed him by the belt in the small of his back. Then there were others on his body, pulling him down from behind. Something banged him along the side of the head, stunning him briefly.

How much time had passed? Roland's vision was blurred, and would not correct. His head throbbed painfully. It was dark and the air was somehow different. Maybe he was in a cave. He could just make out flickering firelight, and the busy movements of his captors. Roland couldn't move. They held him to the ground, his arms outstretched.

They were like kids—not yet fully grown, voices unformed. He thought there were about a half dozen of them. He had no idea what was going on, he couldn't understand anything. An unnatural silence alarmed him. Roland tried to speak to them, but they sat on his chest and legs, pinned his head in place, and stuffed foul rags in his mouth. Then he saw the dull glint of an axe blade as it began its downward descent to the spot where his left hand was firmly held. Same thing on the right a few seconds later, but by then Roland was already unconscious.

Searing pain revived him; that, and perhaps a lingering will to struggle and save his life. He was alone for the moment, but he could hear them—their squeaky murmurs, and a disturbing wet scraping noise.

Demented teenagers. Maybe some weird sect or cult.

Or they could be a brain-stunted, inbred rural clan that preyed on anyone who was foolish enough to stray into their territory. How could this happen? Was the whole town in on it? What could they want? Perhaps in exploring and photographing Jorgenson's Italian folly, he had somehow violated their sacred ground. But it seemed most likely that they were insane, pure and simple.

Roland still couldn't move. His wrist-stumps were bandaged. The bastards had actually chopped his hands off. The realization nearly knocked him out again, but Roland fought off total panic. He had to think clearly, or he was surely lost. The rest of his body from the neck down seemed to be wrapped in some kind of wire mesh. His mouth was still clogged with the hideous rags, and he had to breathe through his nose. He tried to lever his tongue to push the rags out, or to one side, so he could speak, but at that moment they came back for him.

They dragged him, and it became clear to Roland that some of the monstrous pain he felt was coming from where his two feet had been. They threw him down in a torch-lit clearing. They spread his legs, held his arms out, and began to smear some thick, gooey substance on him. Roland flipped and squirmed like a fish on the floor of a boat until they clubbed him again.

Fresh air, dusk light.

The same day? Couldn't be. But overcast, the wind whipping loudly—and that choral sound Roland had heard his first night in town. They carried him out of the cave, and the wailing noise seemed to fill his brain. He was in the center of it, and it was unbearable.

Only his head was exposed—the rest of his body now stone. It came up to his neck in a rigid collar and forced his head back at a painful angle. Roland caught sight of

them as they propped him in his place on the third rank
of the statuary. They weren't kids, they didn't even look
human—pinched little faces, stubby fingers, a manic
bustle to their movements, and the insect jabber that was
all but lost in the boiling wind.

Like caricature scientists, they turned him one way
and then another, tilting, nudging and adjusting. They
finally yanked the rags out of his mouth. Roland tried to
croak out a few words but his tongue was too dry. Then
the final mystery was solved as his captors thrust a curious device into his mouth. He saw it for an instant—a
wire cage that contained several loose wooden balls.
They were of varying sizes, and Roland thought he saw
grooves and holes cut in them. It fit so well that his
tongue was pressed to the floor of his mouth. A couple of
strands of rawhide were tied around his head, securing
the device even more tightly.

A last corrective nudge, and then the wind took hold
and the wooden balls danced and bounced. Another
voice joined the choir. Satisfied, they went on to complete their work, covering the rest of his head with the
sticky cement and then applying the exterior finish. Only
his open mouth was left untouched.

Roland thought of insects nesting there. He pictured a
warm mist billowing out on cool mornings as he rotted
inside. And he wondered how long it would take to die.
They must do repair work later, to keep the cages in
place after the flesh disappeared. A strangely comforting
thought in the giddy swirl of despair.

The wind came gusting down the glen. Empty arms
raised, his anonymous face lifted to the unseeing heavens, he sang.

Thomas Tessier is the former managing director of Millington Books in London and the author of *Finishing Touches*, *Phantom*, *The Fates*, *Shockwaves*, *Rapture* and *The Night Walker*, a classic modern werewolf novel.

The Visit

William F. Nolan

 "So . . ." he said. "You've been wanting to talk to me. I'm here. Let's talk."

"You're willing to be entirely open and frank?" I ask him.

"Sure."

"You'll tell it to me straight? No evasions. No bullshit."

"You got it."

"You'll answer any question I ask?"

"I said so, didn't I. But keep your face close to the screen. That way the guard can't hear us."

"I'll be taking notes. For the book I'm doing."

"Shit, you're not going to use my real name, are you? I don't want my real name in some goddamn crime book."

"No, don't worry about that. I'll call you Dave. And I won't be using a last name. You'll be . . . a statistic."

"Great. I had a cousin named Dave. Real asshole."

"Shall we begin?"

"That's what I'm here for. Start your questions."

"How old were you when you killed for the first time?"

"Twelve. Like Billy the Kid. He knifed a guy when he

was twelve, back in the Old West. I always felt close to the Kid. Wish I could have known him."

"Was it a man or a woman . . . the first one at twelve?"

"Neither. I snuffed a kid, same age as me. It was after he smart-mouthed me in class. I waited till he was walking home across the ravine, between the school and his house, and that's where I killed him, right there in the ravine."

"How?"

"With a stone. Crushed his skull. It broke open like an egg."

"Then what did you do?"

"Buried him. Ravine's a good place to bury people."

"Body ever found?"

"Nope. He just went to bone. His name was Bobby something. Big red-haired Irish kid. Had a real smart mouth on him."

"When was the next one?"

"When I was fifteen. After I ran away from home . . . that same summer."

"Man or woman?"

"Man. A bum. Railroad tramp. I was going West in this boxcar and he was in the same car, just the two of us. Had some food he didn't want to share so I wrung his skinny neck to get it. He was an old guy, so I had no trouble with him. But he *did* squawk like a chicken when you twist their heads off. Just like a damn chicken."

"Anyone find out? About the bum, I mean?"

"Christ, no. I pitched him out of the car when the train was crossing a river. Neat and easy. And the food made me sleepy. Had me a nice snooze."

"After these killings—the boy and the old man—did you have any remorse?"

"Me? Remorse? Hell, no. When you do somebody, it's like a high. You come down, but then you want another. Like with drugs."

"Ever use any?"

"Sure, I experimented some, but my real high was doing people. So I quit doing the drugs. To keep my head clear so I could enjoy myself. Didn't want anything getting in the way."

"You're what . . . how old now . . . thirty?"

"Thirty-two."

"So how many have you done since the first one at twelve?"

"I'm not like you. I don't make notes. Don't write things down on paper. That's why I don't have any exact figure to give you."

"Take a guess."

"Well . . . fifty or more. Maybe sixty. I just never kept count. But it's under a hundred for sure. I'd know if I did over a hundred. That'd be something to celebrate."

"What about mass killings? Ever been into those . . . or was it one at a time?"

"Hey, I've been into whatever comes up. Sure, I did some numbers once. In Frisco. In a big house near the Barbary Coast area. Big Victorian house."

"Tell me about it."

"It was at night, and this family came home before I expected them to. I was on the second floor, picking up whatever I could find, when the door slams downstairs and this guy and his wife and their two teenage daughters get home early from a play."

"Then you didn't go to the house planning to kill them?"

"No, it's like I said. I went there to pick up some money, jewels, whatever. Guy's gotta earn a living. I'd been staking out the place and earlier that evening I'd heard them through the screen, talking about going to this play, so I figured I'd have plenty of time to do a job on the place. But they left after the first act. Guess the play was lousy."

"So what happened after they came in?"

"I decided to do all four of them, just for the high. I'd never done four at once up to then."

"What were you carrying? What kind of weapon?"

"I had me a big belt knife and a sawed-off."

"Shotgun?"

"Yeah. It was a custom job. I'd trimmed the barrels. Turned it into a mean sonuvabitch."

"Shotguns make noise."

"I know—but I was careful about that. I've always been a real careful guy."

"Who'd you kill first?"

"The wife. She came upstairs to change her dress and I used the belt knife on her. Got excited and near cut her head off. I was using one of those big Bowie type knives and I got a little carried away."

"Then what did you do?"

"Waited till the next one came upstairs. One of the daughters. She was about seventeen. Tall, with a nice ripe figure on her. I used one of her mother's stockings to do her. She was easy."

"In my research, I've found that most killers use the same method in all of their kills. You've been . . . unusual in this respect."

"Yeah, well, I'm an unusual type of guy. As to how I did them, I liked to improvise. Switch around, you know. Knife. Hammer. Rope. Stocking. Whatever. I got a different high each time. I get bored with the same routine, so I tried different things at different times. The police never could figure me out. I've always been ten steps ahead of them!"

"Did you use the shotgun in the house?"

"Sure did. I went downstairs after the stocking job and found the guy and his other daughter watching Cosby on TV. You ever watch Bill Cosby?"

"I've seen him."

"Funny, huh?"

"He can be funny, sure. What did you do downstairs when you found them watching television?"

"I tied them both on the couch and then used big sofa pillows to muffle the sawed-off. A barrel for each one. It really wasn't noisy at all. Got some blood and stuff on my shirt, but the noise was no problem."

"How'd you feel then . . . after eliminating the whole family?"

"Felt great. All charged up. I mean, doing four in one night. It was special."

"Sexually, how did it affect you?"

"Sexually?"

"Were you aroused? You used the word 'excited' earlier."

"I don't like to talk about sex. It's personal."

"You told me you'd answer any question I asked you with no bullshit."

"Okay, all right . . . sure, I had a hard-on if that's what you want to know. The daughter did it. But I beat off before leaving the house and that took care of it."

"Have you ever had intercourse with any of your victims? Either during or after killing them?"

"Jesus, no! I don't fuck corpses if that's what you mean."

"It's not uncommon."

"It is with me. That's not my trip."

"Are you bisexual?"

"Look," he said, "let's skip all this sex shit, okay? I'm a normal guy when it comes to gash. I screw *women*. Period. Can we get off this?"

"Fine. Uh . . . have you ever collected body parts? Like, souvenirs of your kills?"

"This is sick."

"You didn't answer the question?"

"The answer is—shit, no, I don't collect body parts. And I don't stuff people either. Didn't that guy in the *Psycho* movie stuff people?"

"I don't think so. I think it was birds. But he kept his mother's corpse in the basement. In a rocking chair. What about *your* mother? Were you close to her?"

"Let's keep my parents out of this. I'll answer any question about myself, but I'm not going to get into anything about my folks."

"All right, then . . . tell me about the most bizarre killing you've ever done. The weirdest one."

"That guard's giving us the eye. Maybe we'd better save it for the next visit."

"I guess we'd better."

"Time's up," said the guard. "Look, it's none of my business, mister, but I gotta wonder just why you'd wanta waste your time talkin' with 'The Butcher.' Even his own family stays away from him."

"I have my reasons."

"Yeah, I guess you do," said the guard.
And he led me back to my cell.

———————

William F. Nolan is the author of 9 novels, 120 short stories and some 600 magazine and newspaper pieces worldwide. He has published 55 books, is represented in 200 anthologies, and has written extensively for films and television. Among his recent works: *Helltracks* (novel), *The Bradbury Chronicles* (anthology) and *Nightshapes* (collection).

The Ring of Truth

George Clayton Johnson

 You can't believe how frustrating it is being a freelance writer when the ideas won't come.

The writer in me wants to stay home and work on a story, but I find I must get away from the typewriter from time to time to let my other self sort things out.

I go looking for distraction. . . .

By the time I get there the jammed parking lot has been transformed by Deadheads into a vast heads-and-highs marketplace and there is the smell of marijuana everywhere.

The place is mobbed with tie-dye people partying. You've been to rock concerts. You know how it is.

An acidhead sitting in the back of a pickup truck has a boom box going, pumping out eerie feedback music recorded with amazing clarity at an earlier Deadshow.

A long-haired freak goes by wearing a surplus store blanket for a poncho, with holes cut in it for his head and hands, selling 'shrooms from an open cardboard box like a newsboy vending papers.

So I'm standing there off to the side, when this guy I've never seen before comes up to me and says:

"I used to be a serial killer."

He says it just like that, teetering drunkenly on his heels with a half-finished beer bottle in his left hand hanging by two fingers like a loosely held club.

I casually put my pipe away and look him over, edging away, waiting for the punchline. Some people get a kick out of bumming out trippers. Still, I start to feel alarmed.

No matter where I go lately, total strangers come up to me and say the damnedest things. It's like they think I'm some kind of high priest or something and they have to tell me all their sins. Do you think it's the long hair and the beard? Some say it gives me sort of a Jesus look. Maybe people can simply see that I've lived a hard and reckless life and may have learned a thing or two. Perhaps it's something they see in my eyes. I'd like to believe that my basic innocence and sincerity shine through.

So I wait, wondering why this middle-aged, heavy-bellied man with the muscled forearms of a truckdriver has picked me out of the throng to tell this to.

Then he says, with a sort of sincere shrug, as though to reassure me:

"I gave it up."

I look at him but not in the eyes. I'm not really sure I want this guy to *see* me.

I try to get a picture of him there in his worn bluejeans and white T-shirt and one of those trucker's hats with some sort of logo on the front that I can't make out at a glance. I'm also trying to give the impression that I'm not looking at him.

I'm suddenly very aware that I'm standing there alone, without a weapon.

Then this guy says, "I used to follow the Grateful Dead."

He seems to lose his balance and lurches closer to me. I lose my balance and keep my distance, watching his hands and wondering where this is leading, tightening up like a bowstring, becoming very sober.

I haven't said a word yet. As far as this guy knows I could be anybody. I want to keep it that way.

The writer in me wants to ask him, *Aren't you afraid of the electric chair or the gas chamber?*

The writer in me wants to ask him, *Don't you believe in God and retribution?*

The writer in me wants to ask him, *What do you get out of it?*

I don't say anything. I don't want him to get too interested and take it into his head to follow me.

He says, "I'm thinking of taking it up again." And he moves to look directly into my face, studying me for a reaction.

That tab of windowpane I dropped earlier has mostly worn off except for the feeling you get that each instant is terribly important and that there is more going on here than meets the eye. Everything becomes cosmic and fraught with great significance. Time slows to a crawl. Scared, I start to hold my breath. It's like that now, with him looking at me as though waiting for me to advise him.

Does he want me to tell him he's making a mistake? That he may have got away with it once but if he starts up again he'll eventually be caught and put in that chair with the straps and buckles on it or locked in a prison for life?

Does he want me to remind him of his immortal soul and the retribution of God?

Or does he really want nothing from me? I wonder if he tells this to all his victims before clubbing them down.

Then, thinking about that chair and the hood over his head as he waits for the cyanide capsules to drop, I say, "Well, good luck."

Hearing me say this like someone saying *Have a good day* causes a look of disappointment and disgust to come over him and he loses all interest in me. I become a nobody in his eyes, and he is already turning away contemptuously.

I feel a great relief flood through me. Time speeds up. I start to breathe again.

The minute he turns his back I have my big coat off, turning it so that the dark lining is outside, rolling it into a tight bundle under my arm so that now I'm dressed in a bright colored sweatshirt, and at the same time I move off at right angles to the direction he takes as he begins to walk off. Quickly I cover the distance to a knot of people, blending in with them, and when he doesn't turn to look back I leave that group and swiftly move to another farther off.

Still he doesn't turn around.

With a slightly drunken swagger he is walking toward the exit, joining with the other revelers, gesturing with his beer bottle as though singing or conducting an orchestra. A woman wearing a brief halter and long swirling skirts hops off the tailgate of a parked pickup truck to give him a hug as he comes up to her, with me wondering, *Are you going to be the one?* But he waves with his beer bottle and says something to her before weaving away.

I want to go up to the girl, ask her what he said, tell her what he told me, but the thought passes.

A chill evening breeze has sprung up.

All of a sudden there is a kind of scuffle up on the lawn outside the stadium where the Dead play.

A couple of guys are trying to hold down a man who is struggling.

I go to find out what the rough stuff is all about and crouch down beside them to see if I can help. The struggling man has obviously overdosed and is having convulsions. The others are trying to keep him from hurting himself with his violent contortions. They seem to know each other and what they are doing while they wait for the medics.

I start to straighten up, when abruptly the guy stops heaving. He lies still, his eyes coming into focus, looking at me, momentarily seeming to know what is going on. I wonder what I can tell him before the drugs kick in again. What idea can I put in his head that will be helpful?

Then, remembering how I hold my breath when I get scared, I say, "Don't forget to breathe."

He seems to understand me, and then his eyes go wild again and he begins to flail. Realizing I've done all I can, I get up and go looking for a familiar face. I want to tell somebody about my strange conversation with the serial killer while it's still hot in my mind.

I spot Captain Ed and his partner, the Emperor of Hemp, Jack Herer, at one of the food stands—a station wagon with the rear open. Two gypsy women are selling steamed brown rice wrapped in moistened sheets of seaweed. Jack gives me a chunk of his food, tearing it off and gobbling down the rest while ordering another. It tastes delicious. As I tell them about the serial killer they take me over to where they are parked, with a space cleared between the vehicles for a campsite. Someone has fired up a lantern and they've set out several folding chairs in a little circle. The area is alive with activity.

They have a table to collect signatures for the California Marijuana Initiative and Jack is selling autographed copies of *The Emperor Wears No Clothes*, his eye-opening book about hemp. Captain Ed is busy buying stock for his headshop in Van Nuys from long-haired craftsmen who come and go—handmade hippie jewelry, tie-dyed T-shirts, buttons, stickers, surreal art—while filling a bowl with indica he has scored from one of them, and as we are catching a buzz we talk about the guy from this afternoon, the one who said, *I used to be a serial killer.*

"Did you believe him?" asks Jack.

"I don't know," I say soberly. "But it had the ring of truth."

Captain Ed laughs. "Maybe you can put it in a story someday, then."

The writer in me kicks himself, thinking of the lost opportunity, the questions he could have asked.

As it is, it is just a formless fragment. Too bad that nothing is ever complete. Life seems to come one thing after another, all jumbled fragments followed by yet more jumbled fragments and there is no real meaning to it. It just keeps coming in a ceaseless train and there is no way to learn anything as you go along.

So there I am, thinking of fragments, lost in a sea of cars, trucks and buses transformed by mind-freaks into a fantastic bazaar.

Anyway, Captain Ed gets busy again. A couple of guys leave and I take over one of the deck chairs. I'm glad to be off my feet.

Then this guy who's known the Captain from years before looks me over and comes and plunks himself down. He is a wretched hardcore Deadhead, high on acid, who makes his living at shows like this, buying and selling psychedelics. He has seen hard times: skinny, gaunt, dirty with rags beneath a tattered, stained overcoat that doesn't fit.

He looks ghastly.

He's a thin-faced guy with a furtive manner and watchful eyes, bitching about the bad luck that has dogged his fleeing footsteps. He'd been dealing blotterpaper in a small San Francisco park. He was selling a hundred sheets a day or more. It took a long time but finally he had a select clientele. His life was good. He stayed high all the time . . . until somebody over at *High Times,* thinking they were helping dopers, blew his trip by writing about the park and the psychedelics you could get there. He was lucky he found out in time to get away.

He's filling me in on all the details, his blazing eyes fixed on mine. . . .

I've grown conscious of the wind.

I'm glad I thought to bring my big fluffy down-lined coat. I put it on.

I try to focus on what the guy is telling me but I am thinking about the coat. I find myself flashing on what happened earlier in the evening.

Now, looking over the acidhead's shoulder, I see the man from this afternoon.

The serial killer.

Watching me.

He still has the beer bottle in his hand and it doesn't look like he's drunk a drop.

A wave of fear washes through me. I feel rising panic.

Somewhere nearby, a tape deck cuts in with an amplified version of "Death Don't Have No Mercy."

I wonder why I really came so far to mingle with the freaks.

The writer in me knows.

He is looking for a story.

The writer in me looks with a hunter's eyes at the man even as I take out a folded sheet of paper to write on and a fiber-tip pen. I try to carry them with me wherever I go. I take the cap off the pen, getting it ready for action. So that I won't lose the cap I stick it on the back of the pen.

The man from this afternoon is searching for something.

I know what it is.

He wants absolution. He sees me as a link with God.

My excitement rises.

I get to my feet. "Sorry," I say to the acidhead, "I've got to talk to that fellow over there."

The acidhead seems to understand and gives me a wave.

The man sees me coming. His eyes go wide.

He shrinks back into the shadows.

I say, "You used to be a serial killer."

He draws deeper into the darkness, clutching the bottle. I ignore it.

I say, "You gave it up."

He relaxes.

I say, "You used to follow Grateful Dead concerts."

I look around significantly. I give him the eye.

He becomes guarded.

I say, "You're thinking of taking it up again."

He becomes wary, drawing further away. I can barely see him.

Into the darkness I whisper, "You want to know what I think you should do."

Softly, "Yes."

"Will you answer three questions for me?"

A resigned sigh. "Ask them."

I ready my pen and paper.

"Aren't you afraid of the electric chair or the gas chamber?" I ask.

His voice is confident. "All men die. Take what you want and pay for it is the only law."

He edges backward, deep into the black shadows between the bus and the truck.

I stare into his eyes, searching for understanding as I ask the next question, noting down his answers.

"Don't you believe in the retribution of God?"

He looks at me pityingly. "I thought you understood," he says levelly. "I am God."

And as he says this and as I look at him, at last I understand who I am talking to, and know now that I'll get a straight answer to the big question.

The writer in me says, "What do *you* get out of it?"

I poise my pen, ready to write down what he says.

He looks at me thoughtfully for a moment, then answers:

"I can sum it up for you in one word. Gratitude."

His voice is steady and certain.

I glance at him quizzically. He sees my lack of comprehension.

"They are born into fear. They spend their entire lives running from death, dreading it with each living moment, wondering how it will come to them.

"When they finally realize that I've got them, that they're helpless and can't get away, everything changes. A look comes over them. They understand what is happening. They stop struggling. They see my eyes and they know that I've taken the decision out of their hands. They are thankful."

He sighs and slumps closer.

"I've told you everything. Now it's your turn to speak," he says. "What should I do?"

I hesitate, looking into his eyes glowing in the dark, lit by an inner fire.

I feel myself drawn into those eyes—so goatlike, so dreadful.

His face begins to change.

It is like watching time chip away at the visage of the Sphinx.

Is it an acid dream?

I feel his strong right hand suddenly grip my coat, draw me to him, my hands pinned against his chest. I feel powerless to struggle.

"Wait!" I cry. "I know!"

He pauses, relaxing his grip slightly.

I lean toward him as he bends forward to hear me. I hardly sense his arm rising in the dark. With my neck arched to whisper into his ear, stretching on tiptoe, I don't even have to set myself, remembering everything I've ever learned about pressure points and the nervous system. I thrust the fiber-tip pen into his solar plexus with a two-inch shiatsu stroke, as I say, "Die."

Time freezes.

Picture the pen gripped in my right fist with the fiber point like a piece of sharpened bamboo held in place by a metal ferrule that binds it to the sturdy plastic shaft.

Picture a spot just beneath the tip of his sternum where surprisingly there are no stomach muscles to resist the upward hooking blow.

Picture the point piercing the T-shirt without resistance, penetrating into his body with an all but inaudible pop, sliding in the rest of the way with incredible ease.

He is stunned. Shocked, as am I.

All the breath goes out of him with a whoosh.

Blood sprays onto my hand and my coat cuff.

He falls.

But even as contorted as he is at my feet, looking down into the light that spills under the bus from the camp lantern I can see his eyes, much dimmer now. I can see that he understands what has happened even as he is dying. I can see his eyes looking into mine and the expression in those eyes.

He was right.

There is gratitude written there.

For me it is like a benediction.

But something else.

Is it fear of the pit?

I feel ice clog my veins and my heart beating faster. Remembering this afternoon and the guy overdosed on the lawn, to myself I say, "Don't forget to breathe."

I roll him under a nearby truck and try to forget about it.

So why am I writing this?

Hell, for me everything I write is some kind of a confession, and I learned long ago that I must suffer the consequences.

If you were a writer yourself you'd know how hard it is to come up with an idea strong enough to catch an editor's eye in this shrinking literary market.

And the writer in me thinks this story is too good not to write down.

George Clayton Johnson is the coauthor of *Logan's Run* and *Ocean's Eleven*, and wrote several episodes for the original *Twilight Zone* series, including "Nothing in the Dark," "A Penny for Your Thoughts," "The Poolplayer," "The Prime Mover" and "Kick the Can," as well as the premier episode of *Star Trek*. His short stories have appeared in *100 Great Fantasy Short Shorts*, *Author's Choice*, *Cutting Edge* and *Masters of Darkness*.

Nothing Will Hurt You

David Morrell

Later the song would have agonizing significance for him. "I can't stop hearing it," Chad would tell his psychiatrist and fight to control his breathing. His eyes would sting. "It doesn't matter what I'm doing, meeting a client, talking to a publisher, reading a manuscript, walking through Central Park, for Christ sake even taking a shit, I hear that song! I've tried my damnedest not to! It's not on full volume. I wake up, feeling I've been humming it all night. What I mean is when I'm able to sleep."

Chad vividly remembered the first time he'd heard it. He could date it exactly: Wednesday, April 20, 1979. He could give the time precisely: 9:46 P.M., because although he'd found the song poignant and the singer's performance outstanding, he'd felt an odd compulsion to glance at his watch. It must have been a tougher day than I realized, he'd thought. So tired. Nine forty-six. Is that all?

Sweeney Todd. The Demon Barber of Fleet Street. Stephen Sondheim's musical had opened on Broadway in March, a critical success, tickets impossible to get, except

that Chad had a playwright client with contacts in the
production company, and the night Chad's wife, Linda,
broke one of their marriage's rules and gave Chad a surprise birthday party, the playwright (pretending to be a
magician) pulled two tickets from behind Chad's ear.
"Happy forty-second, old buddy."

But Chad remembered the precise date he saw the
musical not because it had anything to do with his birthday (the tickets were dated weeks later). Instead he had
another reason. The demon barber of Fleet Street.
Come in for a shave and a haircut, have your throat slit,
get dumped down a chute, ground up into hamburger,
and baked into Mrs. Lovett's renowned, ever-popular,
scrumptious, how-do-you-get-that-distinctive-taste meat
pies. Can't eat enough of them. To startle the audience, a
deafening whistle shrilled each time Sweeney slashed a
throat. Blood spurted. And one of Mrs. Lovett's waiters
was an idiot kid who hadn't the faintest idea of what was
going on, but he had misgivings that *something* was
wrong. He confessed his fears to Mrs. Lovett, who
thought of him fondly as her son. She promised that
she'd protect him. She sang that nothing would hurt him
—a magnificent performance by Angela Lansbury of a
tune that forever after would torture Chad, its title: "Not
While I'm Around." A lilting heartbreaking song in the
midst of multiple murders and cannibalism.

After the show, Chad and Linda had trouble finding a
taxi, didn't get back to their Upper East Side apartment
until almost midnight, felt so disturbed by the plot yet
elated by the music that they decided to have some
brandy and discuss their reactions to the show, and that's
when, an hour later as they were getting ready for bed,
the phone rang. Scowling, Chad wondered who in hell

would be calling at such an hour. Immediately he suspected one of his nervous, not to mention important, authors with whom he'd been having tense conversations all week because of a publisher's unfavorable reaction to the author's new manuscript. Chad tried to ignore the phone's persistent jangle, but finally, annoyed, he raised it to his ear.

A man's gravelly voice, made faint by the hiss of a long-distance line, sounded tense. "This is Lieutenant Raymond MacKenzie. I'm with the New Haven police force. I know it's late. I apologize if I woke you, but . . . There's been an emergency, I'm afraid."

What Chad heard next made him quiver. "No. You're wrong. There's got to be some mistake."

"Don't I wish." The lieutenant's voice became more gravelly. "You have my sympathy. Times like this, I hate my job." The lieutenant gave instructions.

Chad murmured compliance and set down the phone.

Linda, who'd been staring, demanded to know why Chad was so pale.

When Chad explained, Linda blurted, "No! Dear God! It can't be! Not Stephanie!"

Urgency canceled numbness. They threw clothes into a suitcase, hurried from their apartment to the rental garage three blocks away where they stored their two-year-old Ford (they'd bought the car at the same time they'd bought their cottage in Connecticut, so they could spend weekends near Stephanie), and sped with absolutely no memory of the drive (except that they kept repeating, "No, it's impossible!") to New Haven and Lieutenant MacKenzie, whose husky voice turned out to be in contrast with his short, thin frame.

Denial was reflexive, insistent, stubborn. Even when

the lieutenant sympathetically repeated and rerepeated that there had *not* been a mistake, when he regretfully showed them Stephanie's purse, her wallet, her driver's license, when he showed them a statement from Stephanie's roommate that she hadn't come back to the dormitory last night . . . even when Chad and Linda went down to the morgue and identified the body, or what was left of the body, although it hadn't been Stephanie's *face* that was mutilated . . . they still kept insisting, no, this had to be someone who looked like Stephanie, someone who stole Stephanie's purse, someone who . . . some mistake!

Nothing would hurt him, Angela Lansbury had sung to the boy her character thought of as a son in *Sweeney Todd,* and the night before when Chad had listened to the lilting near-lullaby, he'd been briefly reminded of his own and only child, dear sweet Stephanie, when she was a tot and he'd read to her at bedtime, had sung nursery rhymes to her, and had taught her to pray.

"Now I lay me down to sleep," his beloved daughter had obediently repeated. "I pray the Lord my soul to keep. If I should die before I wake, I pray the Lord my soul to take. . . . Daddy, is there a bogeyman?"

"No, dear. It's just your imagination. Go to sleep. Don't worry. Daddy's here. Nothing will hurt you."

"Not While I'm Around," the song had been called. But two years ago Stephanie had gone to New Haven, for a B.A. in English at Yale, and last night there *had* been a bogeyman, and despite Chad's promise of long ago, he had *not* been around when the bogeyman very definitely hurt Stephanie.

"When did it . . . ?" Chad struggled to breathe as he

stared at Lieutenant MacKenzie. "What time did she . . . ?"

"The body was discovered at just before eleven last night. Based on heat loss from the brain, the medical examiner estimates the time of death between nine-thirty and ten P.M."

"Nine forty-six."

The lieutenant frowned. "More or less. It's difficult to be that precise."

"Sure." Chad bit his lip, tasting tears. "Nine forty-six." He remembered the odd compulsion he'd felt to glance at his watch last night when Angela Lansbury had sung that nothing would hurt her friend.

While the bogeyman killed Stephanie.

Chad knew. He was absolutely certain. Nine forty-six. That was when Stephanie had died. He'd felt the tug of her death as if a little girl had jerked at the sleeve of his suit coat.

"Daddy, is there a bogeyman?"

"Not while I can help it."

Chad must have said that out loud.

Because the lieutenant frowned, asking, "What? I'm sorry, sir. I didn't quite hear what you just . . ."

"Nothing." Sobbing uncontrollably, holding Linda, whose features were raw-red, dripping with tears, contorted with grief, Chad felt the terrible urge to ask the lieutenant to take him down to the morgue again—just so he could see Stephanie one more time, even if she looked like, even if her . . .

All he wanted was to *see* her again! Stephanie! No, it couldn't be! Jesus, no, not Stephanie!

Numbness. Denial. Confusion. Chad later tried to re-construct the conversations, remembering them through a haze. No matter how often he was given details, he needed more and more clarification. "I don't understand! What the hell happened? Have you any clues? Witnesses? Have you found the son of a bitch who did this?"

The lieutenant looked bleak as he explained. Stephanie had gone to the university library the previous afternoon. A friend had seen her leave the library at six. On her way back to the dormitory, someone must have offered her a ride or asked her to help him carry something into a building or somehow grabbed her without attracting attention. The usual method was to appeal to the victim's sympathy by pretending to be disabled. However it was done, she'd disappeared.

Afterward, the killer had stopped his car at the side of a road outside New Haven and dumped Stephanie's body into a ditch. The absence of blood at the scene indicated that the murder had occurred at another location. The road was far from a highway. At night, all the killer had to do was drive along the road until there weren't any headlights before or behind him, then stop and rush to open the trunk and get rid of the body. Twenty seconds later, he'd be back on his way.

The lieutenant sighed. "It's only coincidence that a car on that road last night happened to have a flat tire where the killer left your daughter. The driver's a farmer who lives in the area. He switched on his flashlight, walked around the car to check his tire, and his light picked up your daughter. Pure coincidence, but clues, yes, because of that coincidence, this time we've got some. Tire tracks at the side of the road. It rained yesterday afternoon. Any tracks in the dirt would have to be fresh. Forensics got a *very* clear set of impressions."

"Tire tracks? But *they* won't identify the killer."

"What can I say, Mr. Dolan? At the moment, those tire tracks are all we've got—and believe me, they're more than any other police force involved in these killings has managed to get, except of course for the consistent marks on the victims."

Plural. On that point, at least, Chad didn't need an explanation. One look at Stephanie's body, at what the bastard had *done* to her body, and Chad had known who the killer was. Not the bastard's name, of course. But *everybody* knew his nickname. One of those cheap tabloids at the supermarket checkout counter had given it to him. The Biter. And reputable newspapers had stooped to the tabloid's level by repeating it. Because in addition to raping and strangling his victims (eighteen so far, all Caucasian females, attractive, blond-haired, late teens, in college), the killer left bite marks on them, police reports revealed.

The published details were sketchy. Chad had grimly imagined teeth impressions on a neck, an arm, a shoulder. But nothing had prepared him for the horrors done to his daughter's corpse, for the killer didn't merely bite his victims. He *chewed* on them. He gnawed huge pieces from their arms and legs. He chomped holes in their stomachs, bit off their nipples, nipped off their labia. The son of a bitch was a Goddamned cannibal. Multiple murders and . . .

Sweeney Todd.

Nothing will hurt you.

Imagining Stephanie's lonely panic, Chad moaned until he screamed.

In a stupor, he and Linda struggled through the nightmare of arranging for a funeral and waiting for the police to release the body and collecting their daughter's things from her dormitory room. On her desk, they found a half-finished essay about Shakespeare's sonnets, a page still in the typewriter, a sentence never completed. On a shelf beside her bed, they picked up textbooks, sections of them underlined in red, that Stephanie had been studying for final exams that she'd never take. Clothes, keepsakes, her radio, her Winnie-The-Pooh bear. Everything filled a suitcase and three boxes. So little. So easily removed. Now you're here, now you aren't, Chad bitterly thought. Oh, Jesus.

"I'm sorry, Mr. and Mrs. Dolan," Stephanie's roommate said. She wore glasses, and her long red hair hung in a ponytail, and she looked devastated. "I really am. Stephanie was kind and smart and funny. I liked her. I'm going to miss her. She was special. It just isn't fair. Gosh, I'm so confused. I wish I knew what to say. I've never known anyone close to me who died before."

"I understand," Chad said bleakly. His father had died from a heart attack at the age of seventy, but that death hadn't struck Chad with the overwhelming shock of *this* death. After all, his father had battled heart disease for several years, and the massive coronary had been inevitable. He'd passed away, succumbed, joined his Maker, whatever euphemism hid the fact best and gave the most comfort. But what had happened to Stephanie was cruelly, starkly, brutally that she'd been *murdered*.

Dear God, it couldn't be! Stephanie had been *killed*.

Chad and Linda carried Stephanie's things to the car, returned to the police station, and badgered Lieutenant MacKenzie until he finally gave them directions to the road and the ditch where Stephanie had been found.

"Don't torture yourselves," the lieutenant tried to tell them, but Chad and Linda were already out the door.

Chad didn't know what he expected to find or feel or achieve by seeing the spot where the killer had parked and dumped Stephanie's body like a sack of garbage. As it turned out, he and Linda weren't able to get close anyhow—a police officer was standing watch over a section of the side of the road and a portion of the ditch, both enclosed by a makeshift fence of stakes linking yellow tape labeled DO NOT ENTER: POLICE CRIME SCENE. On the grass at the bottom of the ditch, the outline of Stephanie's twisted body had been drawn with white spraypaint.

Linda wept spastically.

Chad felt weak, sick, and hollow. At the same time his chest, his heart, and profoundly his *soul* swelled with rage. The bastard. The rotten . . . ! Whoever did this, when they find him . . . ! Chad imagined punching him, kicking him, stabbing him, choking him, and at once remembered that *Stephanie* had been choked. He leaned against the car and couldn't stop sobbing.

Finally, after seemingly endless bureaucratic delays, they were given back their wonderful daughter. Following a hearse, they made the solemn trip back to New York for the funeral. Although Stephanie's face had not been mutilated, Chad and Linda refused to allow a public viewing of her remains. Granted, mourning friends and relatives wouldn't be able to see the obscene marks on her body beneath her burial clothes, but Chad and Linda *would* see those marks—in their minds—as if the burial clothes were transparent. More, Chad and Linda couldn't tolerate inflicting upon Stephanie the indignity of being forced to lie in her grave for all of eternity with

that monster's filthy marks on her. She had to be cremated. Purified. Made innocent again. Ashes to ashes.
Cleansed with fire.

Each day, Chad and Linda drove out to the mausoleum to visit her. The trip became the event around
which they scheduled their other activities. Not that they
had many other activities. Chad had no interest in reading manuscripts, meeting authors, and dealing with publishers, although his friends said that the thing to do was
get back on track, distract himself, immerse himself in
his literary agency. But his work didn't matter, and he
spent more and more of each day taking long walks
through Central Park—when he wasn't with Linda visiting Stephanie at the mausoleum. He had dizzy spells. He
drank too much. For her part, Linda quit teaching piano,
sequestered herself in the apartment (except for the
daily trip to the mausoleum), studied photographs of Stephanie, stared into space, and slept a great deal. They
sold the cottage in Connecticut, which they'd bought and
gone to each weekend only so they'd be close to Stephanie in New Haven if she wanted to visit. They sold their
Ford, which they'd needed only to get to the cottage.

Nothing will hurt you. The bittersweet song constantly, faintly, echoed in the darkest chambers of Chad's
mind. He thought he'd go crazy as he trembled from
stress, compelled to visit places he associated with Stephanie: the playground of the grade school she'd at-
tended, her high school, the zoo at Central Park, the
jogging track around the lake. He conjured images of her
—different ages, different heights, different hair and
clothes styles—ghostly mental photographs, eerie double
exposures in which then and now coexisted. A little girl,
she giggled on a swing in a neighborhood park that had

long ago become a sliver apartment building. I can't stand this! Chad thought in mental rage and imagined the blessed release he'd feel if he hurled himself in front of a speeding subway train.

What helped him was that Stephanie told him not to. Oh, he knew that her voice was only in his mind. But she sounded so real, and her tender voice made him feel less tormented. He heard her so clearly.

"Dad, think of Mother. If you kill yourself, you'll cause her twice the pain she has now. She needs you. For my sake, help her."

Chad's legs felt unsteady. He slumped on a chair in the kitchen, where at three A.M. he'd been pacing.

Nothing will hurt you.

"Oh, baby, I'm sorry." Chad sobbed.

"You couldn't have saved me, Dad. It's not your fault. You couldn't watch over me *all* the time. It could have happened differently. I could have been killed in a traffic accident a block from our apartment. There are no guarantees."

Chad pawed at his tears. "It's just that I miss you so damned much."

"And I miss *you*, Dad. I love you. But I'm not really gone. I'm talking to you, aren't I?"

"Yes . . . at least, I think so."

"I'm far away, but I'm also inside you, and whenever you want to talk, we can. All you have to do is think of me, and I'll be there."

"But it's not the same!"

"It's the best we can do, Dad. Where I am is . . . I'm so bright! I'm soaring! I'm ecstatic! You mustn't feel sorry for me. You've got to accept that I'm gone. You've got to accept that your life is different now. You've got to be-

come involved once more. Stop drinking. Stop skipping
meals. *Start* reading manuscripts again. Answer your cli-
ents' phone calls. Get in touch with publishers. Work."

"But I don't care!"

"You've *got* to! Don't throw your life away just because
I lost mine! I'll never forgive you if . . . !"

"No, please, sweetheart. Please don't get angry. I'll try.
I promise. I will. I'll try."

"For *my* sake."

Sobbing, Chad nodded as the speck of light faded.

But Angela Lansbury's voice continued echoing
faintly. Nothing will hurt you. No matter how hard he
tried, Chad couldn't get the song from his mind. The
more he heard it, the more a lurking implication in the
lyrics began to trouble him, a half-sensed deeper meaning, dark and disturbing, felt but not understood, a further horror.

The Biter's next victim was found by a hiker on the
bank of a stream near Princeton. That was three months
later. Although the victim, a co-ed who worked for the
university's library during the summer, had been missing
for two weeks and exposed to scavenging animals and the
blistering sun, her remains were sufficiently intact for the
medical examiner to establish the cause of death as stran-
gulation and to distinguish between animal and human
bite marks. That information was all that the police revealed to the press, but Chad now knew what "bite
marks" meant, and he shuddered with horror, remembering the chunks that the killer had gnawed from Stephanie's body.

By then, he and Linda had stopped going to the mausoleum every day, restricting their visits to the weekend.
Linda had started taking students again. Chad—true to

his promise to Stephanie—had forced himself to pay attention to his authors and their publishers. But now the news of the Biter's latest victim threatened to tear away the fragile control that he and Linda had managed to impose on their lives. Compulsively, he wrote a letter of condolence to the murdered girl's parents.

We mourn for your daughter as we mourn for our own. We pray that they're at peace and beg God for justice. May this monster be caught before he kills again. May he be punished to the limits of hell.

In truth, Chad didn't need to pray that Stephanie was at peace. He knew she was. She told him so whenever he stumbled sleeplessly into the kitchen at two or three A.M. and found her speck of light hovering, waiting for him. Nonetheless Chad's rage intensified. Each morning he mustered a motive to get out of bed, hoping that today would be the day when the authorities caught the monster.

What they found instead, in September, soon after the start of the fall semester, was the Biter's next victim, maggot-ridden, in a storm drain near Vassar College. Chad urgently phoned Lieutenant MacKenzie, demanding to know if the Vassar police had told MacKenzie if they'd discovered any clues.

"Yes." The lieutenant's voice sounded even more gravelly. "It rained again. The Vassar police found the same tire marks." MacKenzie exhaled. "Mr. Dolan, I understand your despair. Your anger. Your need for revenge. But you have to let go. You have to get on with your life while we do our job. Every police department involved in these killings has formed a network. I promise you

that we're doing everything we can to compare information and . . ."

Chad slammed down the phone. Shuddering, compelled, he scribbled a tear-stained letter to the parents of
the Biter's latest victim.

We share your loss. We sob as you do. If there's a
God in heaven—as opposed to this monstrous Devil
out of hell—our beautiful children will not have
died unatoned. Their brilliantly speeding souls will
be granted justice. The obscene desecrations inflicted upon their innocent bodies will be avenged.

Chad never received responses from those other tormented parents. It didn't matter. He didn't care. He'd
done his best to mute their grief, but if they were too
overwhelmed by sorrow to muster the strength to comfort *him* as he strained to comfort *them,* well, that was all
right. He understood. The main thing was, he'd assured
them that he wouldn't rest until the Biter was punished
to the limits of their outrage, of their grief-stricken, hate-
filled imaginations.

Each day, once again ignoring the demands of his literary agency, he made phone calls to all the police de-
partments in the areas where the Biter had disposed of
his victims. Canceling lunches with publishers, postpon-
ing meetings with authors, leaving manuscripts unread,
Chad concentrated on haranguing homicide detectives.
He demanded to know why they weren't trying harder,
why they hadn't achieved results, why they hadn't
tracked down the bastard, allowing his victims to rest
with the knowledge that their abuser would be punished,

at the same time preventing other potential victims from
suffering his brutality.

Chad's efforts proved useless. Just before Thanksgiv-
ing, the Biter's next mutilated target—the same profile:
female, late teens, Caucasian, blond—was discovered in
a Dumpster bin behind a restaurant a mile from Welles-
ley College. Sure, Chad thought. A Dumpster bin. The
monster treated her the same way he did Stephanie and
all his other victims. Like garbage.

He wrote another anguished letter, knowing now that
his frantic, angry tone would repel the parents of the
Biter's latest victim and keep them from responding.
They and the other parents must figure I'm a nut case,
he concluded. Or else they're too stunned to react.
Whatever, it doesn't matter. I did my duty. I shared my
grief. I let them realize that they're not alone. Hell, I'm
their advocate. I'm their and my daughters' protector!

New Year's Eve. Another victim. Brown University.
More phone calls to detectives. More letters to parents.
More visions in Chad's kitchen at three A.M. A speck of
brilliant light. A tender voice.

"You're out of control, Dad! Please! I'm begging you,
please. Get on with your life. Shave! Take a bath! Change
your clothes! Most of your authors have left you! *Mother*
has left you! I'm afraid for you, Dad!"

Chad shook his head. "Your mother . . . ? What? She
left me? That's impossible! When did *that* happen?"

Abruptly, with a shudder, Chad realized that Linda
indeed had packed several suitcases and . . . Several
months ago? Dear God. He remembered now. Linda
had shouted, "It's been too long! It's bad enough to
grieve for Stephanie! But to watch you disintegrate? It's

too damned much! I can't stand this! Don't destroy *my*
life while you destroy *yours.*"

Ah.

Of course.

So be it, Chad dismally thought as his daughter's brilliant speck of light disintegrated. Slumping lower in his
kitchen chair, he recalled self-help books that he'd obses-
sively read about the effects of grief, the strains on marriages, the divorces that often resulted when partners
mourned in different phases and with different intensi-
ties.

My dear, sweet wife. Weeping, Chad clumsily stood,
fumbled to open a bottle of bourbon, and raised it to his
lips. It's probably better this way. Linda needs a comfort
that I can't provide. God willing, she'll find it with someone else.

Now Chad had another reason to hate the Biter. Ven-
geance. Retribution. With greater fury, he pursued his
mission. More victims led to more urgent phone calls,
more frantic letters.

And then a miracle occurred. What the detectives
hadn't revealed to Chad—but what he now learned—was
that the tire tracks left by his daughter's desecrater had
been identified last year, back in April, as standard
equipment on a particular model of American van. Not
only Stephanie's corpse near Yale but the Biter's later
victim near Vassar had been linked with the tire tracks on
that year and model of van. Because the Biter's numerous targets had all been students at prestigious colleges
and universities in New England, the authorities had
concentrated their search in that area.

When a blond, attractive, female student narrowly escaped being dragged inside a van as she strolled toward

her dormitory at Brown University, the local police—braced for the threat—surged into action, ordered roadblocks around the area, and stopped the type of van that they'd been seeking.

The handsome, ingratiating, male driver complied too calmly, his responses too respectful, not at all curious. On a hunch, one officer asked the driver to open the back of the van.

The driver's eyes narrowed slightly.

The policeman—chilled by the intensity of the driver's gaze—grasped his revolver and repeated his request. What the officer and his team discovered . . . after the driver hesitated, after they took his keys . . . were stacks of boxes in the rear of the van.

And behind the boxes, a bound, gagged, unconscious co-ed.

That night, the police announced the suspected Biter's arrest, and Chad, who drunkenly scowled at the CBS news, surged out of his chair, shrieking in triumph.

Finally! Yes! At last, it made sense. A textbook salesman. A publisher's representative. The bastard's district was New England colleges. He stalked each campus. He studied his variety of quarry, reduced his choices, selected his final target, and . . .

Chad imagined the Biter's enticement. "These boxes of books. They're too heavy. I've sprained my left wrist. Would you mind? Could you help me? I'd really appreciate . . . Thank you. Let me give you some books. By the way, what's your major? No kidding? English? What a coincidence. I've got . . . Here. In the back. Come in. Let me open this box. You won't believe what I've got in there."

Rape, torture, cannibalism, and murder were what he had in there.

Step in farther. Nothing's going to hurt you.

But now the bastard had finally been caught. His name was Richard Putnam. The *alleged* Biter, the media carefully called him, although Chad had no doubt of Putnam's guilt as he scowled at television images of the monster. The unafraid expression. The unemotional eyes. The handsome suspect should have been sweating with fear, blustering with indignation, but instead he gazed directly at the cameras, disturbingly confident. A *sociopath*.

Chad repeatedly phoned policemen and district attorneys to warn them not to be fooled by Putnam's calm manner. He wrote inciting letters to the parents of every victim, urging them to make similar calls. Each night at three A.M. as he wandered drunkenly through his cluttered apartment, he always found Stephanie's brilliant speck of light hovering in the kitchen.

"At last they found him, Dad," her vibrant voice urged. "At last you can give up your anger. Sleep. Eat. Rest. Distract yourself. Work. It's over."

"No!" Chad slumped at his kitchen chair. "It *won't* be over until the son of a bitch is punished! I want him to suffer! To feel the terror that *you* did!"

"But Dad, he *can't* feel terror. He can't feel *anything*. Except when he kills."

Chad straightened with force. "Believe me, sweetheart. When the court finds the monster guilty, when the judge pronounces his sentence, that sociopath will suddenly find he can definitely feel emotion!"

"No! That's what I'm afraid of, Dad!"

"I don't understand! Don't you want revenge as much as *I* do?"

"I'm going so fast. I'm speeding so brilliantly. I don't have time to . . . I'm so *afraid*."

"Afraid about *what*, sweetheart?"

Stephanie's radiant light zigzagged, soared up, then down, then faded.

Chad moaned, "You're afraid about *what*?"

Nothing will hurt you. The song kept echoing torturously within Chad's mind. While he hadn't been there to protect his daughter as he'd promised when she was a child, he could certainly do his utmost to guarantee he *was* there to make sure that the monster suffered to the maximum. Persistent calls to policemen revealed that the various states in which the murders had occurred were each demanding to put the Biter on trial. The result was bureaucratic chaos, arguments about which city would have the first chance to prosecute, about which district attorney had the best case.

Chad had been eager for a speedy trial, but as authorities persisted in quarreling, his frustration compelled him to visit the parents of each victim, to convince them to form a group, to conduct news conferences, to implore every district attorney for a consensus of legal opinion, to insist that jurisdictional egos be ignored in favor of the strongest evidence in any one city, to plead for justice.

It gave Chad intense satisfaction to believe that his efforts achieved results—and even greater satisfaction that New Haven was selected as the site of the trial, that Stephanie's murder would be the crime against which the Biter was initially prosecuted. By then, a year had passed. As part of his divorce settlement, Chad had sold

his co-op apartment in Manhattan, splitting the proceeds
with Linda. He moved to cheaper lodgings in New
Haven, relying on the income he received from his ten
percent of royalties that publishers continued to pay his
bestselling, former authors for contracts that Chad had
negotiated when he was a successful agent.

Successful.

Sure.

Before . . .

Nothing will hurt you?

Wrong! It hurts like hell!

Each day at the trial, Chad sat in the front row, far to
the left so he'd have a direct view of Richard Putnam's
unemotional, this-is-all-a-mistake, confident profile.
Damn you, show fear, show remorse, show anything,
Chad thought. But even when the district attorney presented photographs of the horrors done to Stephanie, the
monster did not react. Chad wanted to leap across the
courtroom's railing and claw Putnam's eyes out. It took
all Chad's will power not to scream his litany of mental
curses.

The jury debated for ten days.

Why did they need so long?

They finally declared Richard Putnam guilty.

And yet again the monster showed no reaction.

Nor did he react when the judge pronounced the maximum punishment that Connecticut allowed: life in
prison.

But *Chad* reacted. He stood and shrieked, *"Life in
prison? Change the law! That son of a bitch deserves to
be executed!"*

Chad was forcibly removed from the courtroom. Outside, dismayed, he heard the monster's lawyer make a

speech about a miscarriage of justice, vowing to demand a new trial, to appeal to a higher court.

Thus began a different kind of horror, the complexities and loopholes in the legal system. Another year passed. The monster remained in prison, yes, but what if a judge decided that a further trial was necessary, that the monster was obviously insane and should have pleaded accordingly? A year in prison was ludicrous punishment for what the monster had done to Stephanie, and if he was released on a legal technicality or sent to a mental institution where he'd pretend to respond to treatment and perhaps eventually be pronounced "cured" . . .

He'd surely kill again!

At three A.M., in Chad's dingy New Haven apartment, he drunkenly raised his haggard face from beside a half-eaten pizza on his kitchen table and smiled toward Stephanie's hovering speck of light.

He swallowed. "Hi, dear. It's wonderful to see you. Where have you been? Lord, how I've missed you."

Stephanie's formerly strong voice wavered. "You've got to stop doing this, Dad!"

"I'm getting even for you."

"Wrong! You're making me scared!"

"For me. Of course. I understand. But as soon as I know that the bastard's punished, I'll put my life in order. I promise I'll clean up my act."

"That's not what I mean! I don't have time to explain! I'm soaring so fast. I'm speeding so brilliantly! Stop what you're doing!"

"I *can't* stop. How can you rest in peace if the monster isn't . . . ?"

"I'm afraid!"

Abruptly the radiance vanished.

"No, sweetheart, stay! Nothing can hurt you any longer! Not while I can help it!"

Chad stared at the emptiness where the light had been, blinked in turmoil several times, tried to focus his troubled vision, and didn't feel his head droop onto the table.

Richard Putnam's appeal was denied. But that was another year later. In the meantime, Chad's former wife, Linda, had married someone else, and Chad's percentage of royalties from his past authors dwindled. He was forced to move to more meager lodgings. He began to draw—with tax penalties—from his pension. He now had a beard. Less trouble. No necessity to shave. So what if his unwashed hair drooped over his ears? There was no one to impress. No authors. No publishers. No one.

Except Stephanie.

Where in God's name *was* she?

He'd devoted his life to her. Now she'd abandoned him. *Why?*

While Stephanie's murder had officially been solved, others attributed to the Biter had not. Putnam refused to admit that he'd killed anyone, and the authorities—furious about Putnam's stubbornness—decided to put pressure on him to close the books on those other crimes, to force him to confess. Before the monster had been a publisher's representative in New England, he'd worked in Florida. A blond, attractive co-ed had been murdered years before at that state's university. The killer had used a knife instead of his teeth to mutilate the victim. There wasn't any obvious reason to link the Biter with that killing. But a deep search of that Florida city's records revealed that Richard Putnam had received a parking ticket near where the victim had disappeared as she left the university's library. Further, Putnam's blood type matched the uncommon type derived from the semen that the killer had left within the victim, just as the semen that the monster had left within Stephanie matched Putnam's blood type. Years ago, that evidence could not have been used in court because of limitations in forensic technology. But now . . .

Yes, Jesus, *now*.

New York's Son of Sam had been caught because of parking tickets left on his vehicle while he stalked his victims. Now that precedent encouraged the local Florida police, who in turn were encouraged by the local district attorney, and that prosecutor was in turn cheered on by various New England authorities. Richard Putnam was arrested for the co-ed's murder. His lawyer had insisted on another trial. Well, the monster would get one. In Florida. Where the maximum penalty wasn't life in prison. It was death.

Chad moved to the outskirts of Florida State University. His pension and his portion of royalties from contracts he'd negotiated increasingly declined. His clothes became more shabby, his appearance more unkempt, his frame more gaunt. At some hazy point in the intervening years, his former wife, Linda, died from breast cancer. He mourned for her intensely but not as intensely as he mourned for his dear, sweet Stephanie.

The Florida trial seemed to take forever. Again Chad came to stare at the monster. Again he suffered the frustration of enduring the complexities of the legal system. Again the evidence presented at the trial made him shudder at the thought of the obscenities inflicted upon his daughter.

But finally Richard Putnam was found guilty, and *this*

time the judge—Chad cheered and had to be evicted
from the courtroom—sentenced Richard Putnam to
death in the electric chair. Anti-death-penalty groups
raised a furor. They petitioned Florida's Supreme Court
and the state's governor to reduce the sentence. For his
part, Chad devoted his frenzied days to barraging the
media and the parents of the Biter's victims with phone
calls and letters that they use all their influence to insist
that the judge's sentence be obeyed.

Richard Putnam finally showed a reaction, apparently
now convinced that his life was in danger, that he had to
make a deal or suffer the ultimate consequence. So he
hinted about other homicides he'd committed, offering
to reveal specifics and solve murders in other states, to
allow mourning parents to stop their agonized attempts
to discover what had happened to their missing daughters.

Detectives from numerous states came to question
Putnam about unsolved disappearances of co-eds. In the
end, after they listened in disgust, they refused to ask the
judge to reduce the sentence. There were four stays of
execution, but finally Richard Putnam was shaved,
placed in an electric chair, and exterminated with two
thousand volts through his brain.

Chad was with the *pro-death-sentence* advocates in the
darkness of a midnight rain outside the prison. Along
with them, he held up a sign: BURN, PUTNAM, BURN. I HOPE
OLD SPARKY MAKES YOU SUFFER AS MUCH AS STEPHANIE DID.
The execution occurred on schedule.

The lights at the prison remained steady, but in Chad's
mind, they dimmed. At last, after so many years, he felt
triumphant. Vindicated. At peace.

But when he returned to his cockroach-infested, one-room apartment, when at three A.M. he drank bourbon in victory, he blinked in further triumph. Because Stephanie's brilliant light appeared to him.

Chad's heart thundered. He hadn't seen or spoken to her in so many years. Despite his efforts on her behalf, he'd thought she'd abandoned him. He'd never understood why. After all, she'd promised that she'd be there whenever he needed to talk to her. At the same time, she'd also demanded that he stop his efforts to punish the monster. He'd never understood that, either.

But now, in horror, he did as her gleaming light pulsed with turmoil.

"I warned you, Dad! I tried to stop you! Why didn't you listen? I'm so afraid!"

"*Why?* I got even for you! You can finally rest in peace!"

"No! Now it starts again!"

"*What?*"

"He's free! He's coming for me! He isn't satisfied! Don't you remember? I told you he doesn't feel emotion except when he's killing! And now that he's been released, he can't wait to do it again! He's coming for me!"

"But he can't! You said you're soaring so brilliantly! *How can he catch up to you?*"

"Two thousand volts! He's like a rocket! I see him behind me! A missile! He's grinning! He's reaching out his arms! He—! Help me, Dad! You promised!"

"Keep speeding, sweetheart! Try to stay ahead of him! I swore to you years ago! I swear it again! Nothing will hurt you! Not while I can help it!"

Chad's psychiatrist later concluded that, in retrospect, Chad's final act made perfect, irrational sense. Chad bled profusely as he struggled over the barbed-wire fence. His hands were mangled. That didn't matter. Nor did Chad's fear of heights matter as he climbed the high tower while guards shouted for him to stop. All that mattered was that Stephanie was wailing, in danger. Help me! So what choice did Chad have? Except to grasp the high-voltage lines. To be struck by twenty thousand volts of surging power. Ten times the power that had launched the Biter toward Chad's brilliant, surging daughter. Chad's body burst into flames. His agony meant nothing. The impetus of his soul meant *everything*.

Keep speeding, sweetheart! As fast as you can!

But I'll speed faster! The monster won't catch you! Nothing will hurt you!

Not while I can help it.

————————

David Morrell is the author of *First Blood, The Brotherhood of the Rose, The Fraternity of the Stone, The League of Night and Fog, The Fifth Profession, The Covenant of the Flame, Testament, Last Reveille* and *The Totem*. A short story, "Orange Is for Anguish, Blue for Insanity," won the Horror Writers of America Bram Stoker Award in 1989.

Underground

Steve Rasnic Tem

They had started in April to excavate the block across from Tom's apartment building. Now it was September, and because of work stoppages and other delays there was still the largest hole Tom had ever seen right in the middle of the city, and right in the middle of his life. The library research company he worked for had its offices in a building at the north edge of this giant, muddy hole. Certainly it was a rare moment when he'd noticed any dry earth around the site. September's rainfall had been the heaviest on record. He'd read in the papers that the construction company had had some trouble with slides at the site. Two workers killed. Experts had been called in from more rainy climates to offer their recommendations.

He often considered whether Willie would live long enough to see the new complex. Willie had always been an avid fan of new construction, especially projects this complicated. Staring out the window into the squarish crater filled Tom with doubt. He wasn't sure he believed there was enough steel, stone and concrete in the state to fill such a hole. Construction projects were often as unpredictable as a ravaging disease. The holes in Willie's immune system would not be easy to fill, either. As the complex was beginning a dramatic rise out of the raw wound of ground, Willie was slowly, inexorably being sucked back into it.

The height of the dirt walls at the site impressed him. When the digging had first begun, he'd walked close to the site each day, spending time at the various peepholes cut into the temporary roofed walkways around its perimeter. He'd been surprised at the fecundity of the earth; even at a depth of a hundred feet or more it was rich and moist like cake.

Topsoil was supposedly only a few feet deep, but here he could see roots and animal holes and insect tracks and all the dark strata of decades of decay meant to feed generations of new life that went far deeper than that. Impossibly deep, he thought. The living feeding off the dead. After a week, the machines were still uncovering small animal skeletons and black compost. After two weeks of this grave robbing Tom stopped visiting, trotting through the walkways briskly as he went from apartment to job and back again.

A park over a portion of the site had now vanished into the cavity. Four or five cast statues—a general on a horse, a standing man with his hand on a book—had been lifted out of the way and temporarily stored in a blocked-off portion of street that once ran alongside the park. There were also a couple of old stone statues in the lot, badly weathered and veined heavily with black. From his office window they looked like bystanders, gone to the edge of the pit to see what lay inside.

He had a poor understanding of what was required for such constructions; he had no idea why they would need

to dig a hole so large. He tried to imagine how many
years of the city's history they had ripped away. How
many skeletons of cats and dogs, family pets buried in
the backyard? On the news they'd reported the discovery
of a human skull within the last week, thought to be over
a century old. Foul play was not suspected. They thought
it might have drifted down from the cemetery a half-mile
away. Tom tried to imagine such a thing, dead bodies
drifting underground, swimming slowly through what
most of us liked to think of as too solid ground.

But they weren't bodies anymore, exactly. Separate
bones, the flesh gone to earth. Now it seemed as if the
buried skeletons had discarded their old suits of flesh
and slipped on the entire world as their new bodies. The
world's movements had become the movements of the
ancient dead, its dance their dance, its seasons their
dreams of birth, death, and renewal. So maybe he himself was just a reflection of some dead man's forgotten
desire.

Willie would have liked that conceit, Tom thought. He
might have laughed at the elaborateness of it, but it still
would have meant something to him. Now Willie had
good reason to appreciate such an image. Tom liked to
imagine Willie alive, doing the things they'd always done
together, making plans, watching the city change even if
most of the time they thought it was for the worse. But
Willie wasn't going to be a watcher anymore. Willie was
about to become part of the rest of the world.

The basement of Willie's house had been crumbling for
decades. Tom had warned him against buying the place,
sure that someday the entire structure would collapse,
but Willie had just shrugged, saying that he loved the

upstairs too much not to have it, the cool and the old world charm of it, and in the meantime continued a practice begun by the previous owners: filling the basement cavity with whatever clean fill dirt he could find, packing it down, adding occasional large rocks for more mass. Now it was the structure of Willie himself that was collapsing, and the basement was almost full with a half-dozen or more varieties of earth.

Tom struggled with his key in Willie's front door, the lock out of true, the door itself beginning to list noticeably to the right. *The ground's coming up to get you, Willie,* he thought, and grimaced as the key began to bend just before the door popped open. He glanced at the key once, ran his finger along the warp of it, turned and tossed it out into the front yard. He wouldn't be needing it after today. The yard was almost barren— Willie had let it go after he was diagnosed, and refused to let Tom, or anyone else, do anything with it. Damp red clods of earth heavy with worms showed through vague whiskers of grayish grass, the dirt loose and clumpy as if it had frothed up above the roots and stems, leaving only the tallest plants exposed. The flower beds were a sea of jagged, dark stalks.

He stepped inside onto a discolored patch of carpet. Dirt followed him in, clouds of it forming in the bright light. There used to be a dark green awning over the front door, but somewhere along the line it had disappeared. He looked down at the filthy rug, troubled by all the dirt. He stepped back out onto the single step that was meant to raise a visitor to the level of the door. It was as if it had dropped several inches during last month's heavy rains, leaving only a vague lip above the ground. But Tom knew that couldn't be—if that had been the case the step up to the door would have been far steeper than before. He stared at the threshold. Willie's entire front yard appeared to have risen. The seemingly solid ground rubbed at the bottom of Willie's front door. Trails of dark brown earth had crept up over the worn oak threshold until parts of it were submerged. *Oh, Willie, you didn't stand a chance,* he thought, and stepped quickly back inside, away from this determined stretch of ground. He pushed the door shut firmly, forcing a cloud of earthy smell up into his face.

"Is that you, Mr. Davison?" John, Willie's last lover and now Willie's nurse, stood in glaring light at the top of the stairs. He'd always called him *Mr. Davison,* and Tom had always felt vaguely insulted by the formality. Tom fumbled with the living room light switch, but the overhead bulb was dead. The room was shrouded in black. As Tom made his way up the stairs into the light it felt as if the dark had taken on the weight of earth, pulling him back, seducing him with the impulse to lie down, to sink, to fall back and close his eyes. "Mr. Davison, there's not much time." John reached out and grabbed Tom's hand as if to reel him in. The gesture made Tom uncomfortable, but he permitted John to help him up the remaining steps.

Willie's bedroom door was half-open. Tom stopped with the impulse to knock, then, suddenly angry, pushed the door the rest of the way, slamming it against the edge of Willie's bed. He had never been expected to knock before; he wasn't going to end things knocking.

"We're not doing well today, I'm afraid," John said behind him. Tom turned and, without thinking, searched John's face for evidence of sores. John gestured toward the bed, at the bundle of bedding where Willie was supposed to be. He looked down at the edge of the door pressing against the mattress and frowned slightly. Tom felt defensive, as he usually did in John's presence, but he didn't want to say anything in front of Willie. Instead he looked away with deliberation, his eyes searching the bed for his old friend as if there were some question as to his whereabouts.

The dark shadows on the sheets looked like great splotches of dirt, or even excrement. Tom was suddenly filled with rage and started to turn back to John and let him know about it when the cloud cover outside the window changed, and he realized those splotches were actually shadows after all.

"John . . . leave us alone . . . now." The voice under the sheets was so low Tom could barely recognize it as Willie's. The throat sounded full. Tom thought of the darkness downstairs, and imagined the loose, gray earth rising up the staircase, eventually filling the mouth of the second-floor hall. John looked at Tom with a vaguely troubled expression, then left without protest.

"I feel bad . . . I can't make him . . . at ease. He's scared . . . you know? But I'm glad he's here. Come . . . come closer." It was an eerie feeling, hearing that vaguely recognizable voice coming from beneath the bedclothes, as if Willie were already dead and buried and it was his voice haunting the bed. Tom walked slowly to the head of the bed. "Un . . . uncover me, will you?" Tom leaned over and pulled away the sheet which had been tucked tightly under the shoulders. Appalled, he felt as if he were unwrapping a mummy.

Willie looked up at him, his face a mask of sweat, his skin pocked with sores, his eyes dark as if too much makeup had been applied. ("That's the worst thing, really," he once said. "I'm starting to look like some old drag queen.") Tom thought Willie's flesh looked unstable, as if it might fall off the skull at any moment. He imagined a plate full of such flesh, a grave full of it. "He doesn't mean to, but . . . he keeps . . . covering me . . . a little too much. So he won't . . . have to see." Willie grinned hideously.

"Jesus, Willie. That's horrible. Don't let him."

Willie grinned again. "You don't . . . understand us. Not really."

Tom felt like turning away, but the grin fascinated him. He realized again it was as if Willie were already dead. It was as if a rock had suddenly smiled at him, as if a patch of bare ground had opened up and grinned at him. The thought worked cruelly through him—after all, Willie was his best friend, he loved Willie—but it refused to be ignored: Willie was well on his way to compost.

"Don't let . . . them bury me." Tom looked at him in shock, as if his old friend had been reading his mind. Again Willie smiled. Or was it the same smile, and now his face was frozen that way, the words squeezing past the yellowed bars of his teeth? "Make sure . . . I'm cremated."

Tom shook his head. *No, I won't let them,* or *No, I can't do that* . . . He wasn't sure which he intended by the gesture. Willie's face seemed to be dissolving right in front of him. But his friend wanted help with his last wish, and didn't he *owe* him that, even though his friend was already dead? "Why cremation, Willie? Why do you want that?"

The grin fell away so suddenly Tom thought of magic tricks, Willie wearing a tall dark hat and waving a wand. "I don't want this body . . . even hidden under dirt.

This isn't *me*! . . . want it . . . *burned* away. Let . . . the rest of me . . . inside . . . fly *away*, Tom. Fly away."

"Okay, Willie. Okay."

"Don't . . . let them. They'll . . . bury me."

"I promise."

It was almost over when John came back into the room. Maybe it already *was* over. Maybe it had been over months ago. Tom felt as if he had no understanding here, and in that had let his best friend down. Willie had fallen back, unconscious. John went to the side of the bed and grabbed Willie's hand. *He really loves him,* Tom thought, the first nice thing he'd ever thought about John, but he couldn't watch, didn't even think he should watch. So he left.

Dirt now covered the entire length of the threshold. Dirt formed a wide, shallow pool over several square feet of the carpet in front of the door. As he stepped into the front yard, dark earth slopped over his shoes and stained his socks. He had a sense of the entire house sinking behind him. He was sure that if he came back to this site in a few weeks he'd find only a barren splotch of ground.

It was at that point that Tom realized he had no intention of keeping his promise to his old friend. What was he supposed to do, drag the body away in the night? John was Willie's lover, and what was Tom? A coward of a friend who had been too embarrassed to let other friends know that Willie was gay.

He turned around in the yard, feeling the need to go back up those stairs and tell Willie that he wouldn't be keeping his promise, that he was too embarrassed, that he was too frightened, when he again saw the dirt on the carpet, the way it moved, the way it spread. Like a fluid.

Liquid ground covering the floor slowly, soon to ascend
the stairs in its quest for Willie. And certainly there could
be no way of fighting such hungry ground.

Tom left the yard quickly, intending never to be back.

At Willie's funeral Tom said nothing as they lowered him
into the ground. The day of the funeral was unusually hot
for that time of year. Early in the afternoon a temperature inversion dropped a lid over the city, compressing
the air as the cars continued to move over the dusty
streets and the heavy machinery continued to chew away
at the rich body of the earth. By the time of the late
afternoon funeral a thick stew swirled over the tops of
the buildings, drifting slowly down into the streets where
it forced itself into open windows, cars, and raw, desperate throats.

At the grave site John's eyes met Tom's briefly as John
dropped the first handful of rich, crumbling dirt over the
lid. *Don't let them bury me.*

"But the dead have no say in such things, Willie," Tom
thought. "After the ground takes you back it's the living
that get to decide."

Never before had he felt such shame. For having been
embarrassed. For being one of the living who continue to
make decisions for the dead, even if only by default.

A month after Willie's funeral the work still continued on
the giant hole in the middle of Tom's world. He couldn't
understand why it was taking so long. The papers mentioned continued delays, but work was obviously taking
place—there were simply no indications of impending
completion. What disturbed him most was the fact that
the hole appeared less uniform, more unfinished, as the

work progressed. The excavation had lost its squareness, and now appeared as if something rotted had been removed, as if corruption were distorting the edges of this gigantic earthen wound. Digging had spread past the original wooden walkways and barriers, and some of the bordering buildings appeared in danger of being undermined. Some barriers had actually fallen into the hole, where they were mulched to the point of being indistinguishable from the remaining soil.

During slow periods at work Tom researched the decomposition rates of flowers, mahogany coffins, and a human body short on fat and muscle following a long, debilitating disease.

The temperature inversion recurred several times during that month. Some afternoons the air felt abrasive, and tasted of soil. Other days unusually high winds blew dirt out of the excavation and across the windows of the neighboring buildings. From inside his office the windows appeared smeared with urine and feces. One afternoon the office was evacuated because of an air pollution alert. Tom refused to leave, instead choosing to surround himself with piles of crumbling antique volumes—research whose purpose he'd quite forgotten—while he coughed into a dirty handkerchief.

He'd never intended to go back. But in the will John and Tom had been jointly delegated the task of sorting through Willie's belongings. John told him this briefly, curtly over the phone. They agreed on a day, then John hung up.

Yellow signs were plastered to the outside walls of Willie's house. The property had been condemned. Tom was hardly surprised—the front doorframe had shifted with the loose ground until it could no longer be completely closed. Someone had fixed a metal bar across the door, secured by a hefty padlock. This contraption now hung loosely beside the wide-open door. Boxes containing a variety of junk were stacked high on either side. The front room contained an inch or more of dirt tattooed with a riot of footprints, but a clean, narrow patch had been swept to make a corridor to the bottom of the staircase.

He tried the light switch again but with no luck. Vivaldi's *Four Seasons* drifted down to him. Tom took the stairs carefully, his steps creating dark, musty clouds around his feet.

"You're late. I've already done about half of it." John turned from the bed where he'd been folding some of Willie's sweaters. "I hope that's okay."

"Sure, I . . . I'm sorry," Tom said awkwardly. John kept looking at him, his hands resting on the pile of sweaters. *What does he want me to say?* "You would know best where everything should go, anyway."

John nodded, as if that had been the correct answer. "I appreciate that. I guess I do know who Willie would have liked to have his things, and what should go to Goodwill. I loved Willie, do you know that? I really did."

"I know. I loved him, too."

John sighed, and continued folding the sweaters. "But it isn't the same, is it?"

Tom didn't reply. John sent him for boxes and he got them. Together they packed the boxes—John told Tom whose name to put on each box. Together they dismantled the shelves and sorted through the books. John thought Tom should take a number of those for himself, and Tom accepted the idea. Now and then Tom would be aware of an increased amount of dust in the air—clouds of it would drift past the yellowed windowpanes. He thought John didn't notice until he stopped once and said, "We'll have to hurry. In a couple of days they won't be letting anyone back into the place. And the floorboards are creaking more than they used to. I think that's probably not a good sign."

"He should have moved a long time ago," Tom said, throwing a bundle of old clothes into the Goodwill pile. They appeared streaked with blood, or feces. But that couldn't be—he knew that sort of thing would have been washed or burned. Maybe it was just plain old mud, as if they'd been used to dam a flood.

"I was telling him all the time he should move in with me. But he wanted to stay independent. Sometimes you see someone close to you doing something, or living a certain way that you know isn't good for them, but what do you do? Even if you know you know better, they have to make their own decisions, right?"

Tom dropped the clothes and rubbed his hands briskly against his jeans. "Unless they're dead."

John turned his head, a puzzled set to his lips. "Beg your pardon?"

"I say unless they're dead. They can't make their own decisions if they're dead, and even if they've already made them those of us still living can just pretend we never heard, and do what we want."

"What are you talking about?" John rubbed his scalp in irritation. Tom had seen the gesture before, when Willie was being particularly stubborn about something.

"He wanted to be cremated, John. And you went ahead and buried him, you and your friends. Because that's what *you* wanted."

"Where'd you get that idea? Willie never said . . ."

"He would have told you—you were his lover. You were *responsible* for the arrangements. He must've told me because he wasn't sure you would do it. But I was a coward, I admit it. I couldn't deal with it—I couldn't deal with you and Willie's other friends. But you should have done what he asked for, John. Christ, it was his last . . . 'Don't let them bury me,' he said."

"You stupid fool." John stared at the bed, and the piles of clothes. Tom could see red dust drifting out of the empty sleeves and pants legs. "It wasn't in the will. He told *you* because he wanted to spare me. In him I saw not only the one person who'd ever loved me dissolving into nothing, but I saw myself and all our gay friends. Disappearing like everyone had always wanted us to. He told *you* so that you could *tell me*. He trusted you to carry the message."

Nothing more was said until all of Willie's things were packed and sorted. Tom found the enormous size of the pile going to Goodwill vaguely upsetting. But he trusted John's judgment. John knew that Tom was a fool, and John was correct.

"It goes too fast," John said finally. "A lifetime of things and they can haul it all away in hours. I'm afraid of disappearing like that. Like Willie."

"I'm afraid, too," Tom said.

Over the next few weeks Tom immersed himself in scattershot, seemingly aimless research. When the secretary asked which client to bill his hours to, Tom gave Willie's name.

His hands shook as he ran them through a large volume on the meat industry, counting off the steps involved in butchering cattle in a meat-packing operation. He made notes and compared these steps with the standard operating procedures used by pathologists during an autopsy and morticians during an embalming.

He buried himself in the pictures in a book called *Techniques of Forensic Investigation.* They made his head feel as if it were about to split (gunshot wound? ax?) but he persisted, wondering if these techniques and precedures might have some sort of theological significance. (The rate of discorporation is inversely proportional to our impatience to arrive in heaven, all our sins tattooed onto our naked backs.)

He dug up the geological surveys for his part of the city, for the emptiness next door. He carefully examined the figures concerning the composition of the soil, looking for something of Willie there, and, finally, something of himself.

The next day he was in bed, quite unable to climb up out of the gritty darkness.

Don't let them bury me.

Poe would have understood such a request. Back then, Tom thought, many people might have been buried alive. Or embalmed alive—he supposed that still came first. Filling your body full of inert chemical was the logical preparation for your own eternity of inertness. Without advanced medical procedures, how could they have been sure? Maybe in a hundred years, Tom thought, we'll discover how many we're still burying alive today. We, the living. Always making decisions for the dead. But was there really such a clear distinction between us and them? A breath of wind, a drip of moisture, a vague presence of heat—not much more than that, certainly. Walking dirt and dancing clay.

Under his feet, under his building, the dead were swimming vast distances underground, endlessly seeking rest.

He was out of bed now, but he had not been back to work. He could not bring himself to go out. Outside his apartment, the giant hole in the earth grew bigger every day, a grave that swallowed larger and larger chunks of his world.

It's coming to get me, too, Willie.

A portion of the neighboring streets had buckled and collapsed. The city had rented out the parking lot of his apartment building and moved the homeless statues from the park as a precaution. The workers had conducted this operation in haste, however—nobody liked working too close to "the hole"—resulting in considerable damage. Several of the metal statues had massive splits, arms and legs had separated, and one of the stone statues had been reduced almost to powder. They lay on the pavement below his apartment window, a jumble of disinterred body parts, the dark, rich soil still clinging to their secret surfaces.

Several days of alternating intense heat and wind served to loosen the dirt that was now omnipresent in the neighborhood. It had spread out from the massive hole, dark and reddish as blood, to creep down the streets and alleys, filter into the cracks and mortar that held the walls together, staining stone, metal, and glass with its rich color.

Tom was reminded of childhood days spent in the sandbox his father had built in their backyard: four walls of rough timber holding back a foot-deep mound of sand whose look of sparkling cleanliness seemed impossible, given its constant use. He and his brother Rick would play in the sandbox for hours, even on days when the sun was so intense the crystalline specks in the sand sparked like bits of broken glass and by late afternoon had begun to burn them, and then the grit of it irritated the oval patches of burn that had formed above their waist bands and on the backs of their legs.

Tom remembered that sand as having remarkable powers of adherence; he'd find traces of it in his clothes, in his bed, drifting in narrow ridges through his toy box for days afterward. Sometimes there'd be enough of it pressed into his pajamas and bedclothes that his dreams that night would be about endless days at the beach, lying half-buried with the crabs creeping up on his small face. He'd never quite understood the reason for the terror in those dreams, since he'd always loved burying himself in the sand. Rick, too. Sometimes they'd be "tree men," the larger part of themselves rooted deep inside the sandbox, only their small, growing heads exposed. Tom and Rick had seen their dad dig up roots out of the back yard—the roots had gone all soft and crumbly like they'd become part of the ground. Rick told him that would happen to them, too, if they stayed buried too long. That's what happened to dead people, he'd said; they fell apart and fell apart until they *were* the ground.

Rick died in Vietnam. Later Tom found out from his dad that they'd sent back only part of the body. The rest was part of that big overseas sandbox.

By the time Tom had decided he couldn't take another day of staring out his apartment windows at the ever-widening hole—now wide enough that he was beginning to think it surrounded his building, making an eventual trip outside compulsory if he was to accurately evaluate his current living conditions—a renewed vigor of excavations in combination with high winds solved the problem: his windows became so caked with red-brown dirt he could no longer see out of them.

The building owners no longer provided window washing—there would be no point until the project had been completed. Tom also suspected it would be difficult to get anyone willing to wash windows with that kind of emptiness yawning below them, like working over the edge of the Grand Canyon. On the other side of the glass he could hear the thick rumble of machinery as it chewed still deeper into the earth—he wondered if they had changed the plans to permit more stories underground. Tornado or perhaps hurricane protection?

Or maybe the workers were simply feeling the kind of frustration he'd been experiencing all along: the project seemed simply to refuse to get done. Now they were expending all their energies in a day-and-night marathon of desperation, attempting to finish off the hole before it could turn and swallow them, bulldozers, backhoes, and all.

Don't let them bury me.

One morning Tom awakened to no gas or electricity, no phone. Only a trickle of water from the faucet to refresh him, to keep the dust out of his eyes and off his hot face. He didn't bother to check with the super. He strongly suspected that in their rush to completion the workers had accidentally severed the service lines leading into the building. He was tempted for the first time in days to go down to the front door and out to the parking lot to see how things were progressing next door (and to check on the condition of the statues, whose broken images had filled his dreams many times of late), but he resisted. He could wait until all power was restored by the professionals.

That night in his dreams Tom was in an elevator rocketing deep into the earth's core. He woke up suddenly with his eyes burning, his mouth tasting of sand.

The windows had become so filled with dirt that almost no light got through. His mouth was sick with its own taste of dirt and dry flesh. He spent hours staring at his dirt-packed windows, imagining that he was looking into a kind of aquarium, the dead swimming slowly on the other side of the glass. But because the dead had been there so long, and because there were so many of them, they had become so like the medium they swam in, so much a part of the dirt that he could not tell the difference between the two.

Don't let them bury me.

Finally he had no choice but to take that elevator trip he had dreamed of. Several days of minimal food had left him weak. As he staggered down the corridor to the elevator, he imagined himself falling into his own shadow, but there was no light. Confused, he thought he might be the shadow cast by a self who was always behind him, whom he could not see even if he turned around quickly.

He sank into the cool, earthy darkness of the elevator, pressed the button for the lobby, and let it drag him down.

He must have fallen asleep, because he could clearly see the elevator taking him down through millions of years of strata. When he woke he could hardly breathe because of the pressure. His lungs felt on the verge of collapse. The elevator coughed him out at the bottom of the run.

Down here the walls were mud. And flesh. Mud becoming flesh and flesh becoming mud. Willie and anyone else Tom had ever loved was a whisper lost somewhere within the movements of the ground.

He could smell body odor and the mingled scents of cooking, the blossoming odors of human beings working and meeting and loving, millions of such smells buried deep underground.

He suddenly realized he was naked—he'd left his apartment without bothering to put his clothes on. But the mud had smeared so thickly across his chest and thighs he actually felt modest.

He wanted to tell them he loved them all. He wanted to say things he'd never been able to say before. He wanted to speak to the mud and have the mud speak back.

When he'd been in his sandbox with his brother the sand had been like love to him, warm and caressing, insinuating itself so quickly into every part of him.

And yet, as he began to speak of his regrets and the mud began to melt and the dark earth pushed into his throat to meet the words, he knew there was no love here. He had gone past love completely, to something far more elemental.

Tom tried desperately to hold on to his body, the soft bleeding slide of his own flesh, but his body was gone.

———

Steve Rasnic Tem has published more than 100 stories since 1979, and is the author of the novels *Excavations* and *New*

Blood. He is also the editor of *The Umbral Anthology of Science Fiction Poetry*. Recent works include the chapbooks *Absences: Charlie Goode's Ghosts* and *Celestial Inventory*, and the collection *Dark Shapes in the Road*.

Bucky Goes to Church

Robert Devereaux

His real name was Vernon Stevens but folks called him Bucky on account of his teeth and his beaverish waddle and well, just because it was such a cute name and he was such a cute little fat boy, all cuddles in infancy, a ball of impish pudge in childhood, primed to take on the role of blubbery punching bag in adolescence.

Kids caught on quick, called him names, taunted him, treated him about even with dirt. Bucky smiled back big and broad and stupid, as if he fed on abuse. The worst of them he tagged after, huffing and puffing, arms swinging wildly like gawky chicken wings, fat little legs jubbing and juddering beneath the overhang of his butt to keep up with them. "Wait up you guys," he'd whinny, "no fair, hey wait for me!" They'd jeer and call him Blubberbutt and Porky Orca and Barf Brain, and Bucky just seemed to lap up their torment like it was manna from heaven.

But, hey wuncha know it gang, somewheres in Bucky's head he was storing away all that hurt: the whippings at home from his old man's genuine cow-leather belt, a storm of verbal abuse stinging his ears worse than the

smack of leather on his naked ass; the glares and snip-
pery from his frowzy mama, she of the pinched stare, the
worn, tattered faceflesh, the tipple snuck down her
throat at every odd moment; the bark of currish neighbors yowling after him to keep his sneaks off their precious lawns; teachers turning tight smiles on him to show
they didn't mind his obtuse ways, Bucky'd get by okay if
he did his best, but they'd be triple goddamned if they
were going to go out of their way to help him; and the
kids, not one of them daring to be his friend (Arnie
Rexroth got yanked out of first grade and shuffled off to
Phoenix so he didn't count), all of them coming around
quick enough to consensus, getting off on taking the
fatboy's head for a spin on the carousel of cruelty, good
for a laugh, a good way to get on with the guys, a great
way to forget your problems by dumping them in the
usual place—on Bucky Stevens's fat sweaty crewcut of a
head.

Well one day, about the time Bucky turned fifteen, he
woke to the mutterings of a diamond-edged voice inside
his left frontal lobe. "Kill, Bucky, kill!" it told him, and,
argue with it as he might, the voice at last grew stronger
and more persuasive, until there was nothing to do but
act on its urgings. So Bucky gathered all that hurt he'd
been storing away and pedaled off to church one Sunday
morning on his three-speed with his dad's big backpack
tugging at his shoulders like a pair of dead man's hands.
The weight of the hardware inside punched at his spine
as he pedaled, though it was lighter by the bullets lodged
in the bodies of his parents, who lay now, at peace and in
each other's arms, propped up against the hot-water
heater in the basement. He couldn't recall seeing such

contentment on their faces, such a "bastard!"-less, "bitch!"-free silence settling over the house.

He pumped, did Bucky, pumped like a sweathog, endured the Tech-9 digging at his backbone, kept the churchful of tormentors propped up behind his forehead like a prayer. His fat head gidded and spun with the bloodrush of killing his folks: his dad, dense as a Neanderthal, the ex-marine in him trying to threaten Bucky out of it, arms flailing backward as his forehead swirled open like a poinsettia in sudden bloom, his beefy body slamming like a sledge into the dryer, spilling what looked like borscht vomit all over its white enamel top; his mom down on her knees in uncharacteristic whimper, then, realizing she was done for, snarling her usual shit at him until he told her to shut her ugly trap and jabbed the barrel into her left breast and, with one sharp squeeze of his finger, buckled her up like a midget actress taking a bloody bow, pouring out her heart for an audience of one.

Bucky crested the half-mile hill at Main and Summit. The steeple thrust up into the impossible cerulean of the sky like a virgin boy's New-England-white erection humping the heavens. Bucky braked, easing by Washington, Madison, Jefferson. The First Methodist Church loomed up like a perfect dream as he neared it. It was a lovely white box resting on a close-clipped lawn, a simple beautiful spired construction that hid all sorts of ugliness inside.

Coasting onto the sidewalk, Bucky wide-arced into the parking lot and propped his bike against a sapling. Off came the backpack, clanking to the ground. A car cruised by, a police car. Bucky waved at the cops inside, saw the driver unsmiling return a fake wave, false town cohesion,

poor sap paid to suspect everyone, even some pudgy little scamp parking his bike in the church lot, tugging at
the straps of a big bulky backpack. Grim flatfaced flat-
foot, hair all black and shiny—stranded separately like
the teeth at the thick end of an Ace comb—was going to
wish he'd been one or two seconds later cruising Main
Street, was going to wish like hell he'd seen the Tech-9
shrug out of its canvas confinement and come to cradle
in Bucky's arms, yes indeed.

Not wanting to spoil the surprise, Bucky pulled his
Ninja T-shirt out of the front of his jeans, pressed the
cool metal of the weapon against his sweaty belly, and
redraped his shirt over it.

He could hear muffled organ music as he climbed the
wide white steps. The front doors, crowding about like
blind giants, were off-white and tall. And good God if the
music mumbling behind them wasn't Onward, Christian
Soldiers, as wheezed and worried by a bloodless band of
bedraggled grunts too far gone on the shellshock and
homesickness of everyday life to get it up for the Lord.

Bucky tried the handle. The door resisted at first, then
yielded outward.

The narthex was empty. Through the simulated pearls
of Sarah Janeway's burbling organ music, Bucky could
see an elaborate fan of church bulletins on the polished
table stretched between the inner doors. Programs, the
little kids called them. Through the window in the right
inner door to the sanctuary, the back of a deacon's bald
head hung like some fringed moon. Coach Hezel, that's
who it was; Bucky's coach the year before in ninth grade,
all those extra laps for no good reason, pushups without
end, and the constant yammer of humiliation: how Bucky
had no need for a jockstrap when a rubber band and a

peanut shell would do the trick; how he had two lock-ermates, skinny Jim Simpson and his own blubber; how the school should charge Mister Lardass Vernon extra for soap, given the terrain he had to cover come showertime.

Bucky unshirted the gun, strode to the door, and set its barrel on the window's lower edge, sighting square against the back of Hezel's head. A clink as it touched glass. Hezel turned at the noise and Bucky squeezed the trigger. He glimpsed the burly sinner's blunt brow, his cauliflower nose, the onyx bead of one eye; and then the glass shattered and Hezel's mean black glint turned red, spread outward like burnt film, and Miss Sarah Janeway's noodling trickled to a halt at the tail end of *With the cross of Jeeeee-zus.*

Bucky kicked open the door and leaped over Hezel's still-quivering body. "Freeze, Christian vermin!" he shouted, ready to open up the hot shower of metal tensed in the weapon, but it sounded like somebody else and not quite as committed as Eastwood or Stallone. Besides, his eyes swept the shocked, hymnal-fisted crowd and found young kids, boys of not more than five whose eyes were already lidded with mischief and young girls innocent and whimpery in their pinafores and crinolines, and he knew he had to be selective.

Then the voice slammed in louder and harsher— (KILL THE FUCKERS, BUCKY, KILL THEM SONS OF BITCHES!)—like a new gear ratio kicking in. Bucky used its energy to fight the impulse to relent, dredging up an image of his dead folks fountaining blood like Bucky's Revenge, using that image to sight through as he picked off the Atwoods, four generations of hardware greed on the corner of Main and Garvey: old Grandpappy Andrew, a sneer and a "Shitwad!" on his withered lips as Bucky stitched a bloody bandoleer of slugs slantwise across his chest; Theodore and Gracia Atwood, turning to protect their young, mowed down by the rude slap of hot metal digging divots of flesh from their faces; their eldest boy Alan, overbearing son of an Atwood who'd shortchanged Bucky on fishhooks last July and whose head and heart exploded as he gestured to his lovely wife Anne, who danced now for them all as her mist-green frock grew red with polkadots; and four-year-old Missy who ran in terror from her bleeding family, ran toward Bucky with a scream curling from her porcelain mouth, her tiny fists raised, staggering into a blast of bullets that lifted her body up with the press of its regard and slammed her back against a splintering pew.

A woman's voice rose through the screams. "Stop him, someone!" she yelled from the front. Bucky pointed toward her voice and let the bullets fly, bloodfucking whole rows of worshipers at one squeeze. Most lay low, cowering out of sight. The suicidal made escape attempts, some running for the doors behind Bucky, others for those up front that led into the pastor's study or back where the choir warmed up. These jackrabbits Bucky picked off, making profane messes out of dark-suited bodies that showed no sense of decorum in their dying, but bled on hard-to-clean church property everywhere he looked.

He eased off the trigger and let the blasts of gun-thunder vanish, though they rang like a sheen of deafness in his ears. "Keep away from the doors!" he shouted, not sure if he could be heard by anyone. It was like talking into fog. "Stay where you are and no one will get hurt," he lied, stepping over dead folk to make his way forward. The crying came to him then, thin and distant, and he saw bodies huddled together as he passed, the wounded and the not-yet-wounded. Call them all what they were, the soon-to-be-deceased.

"Shame on you, Vernon Stevens," came a quavery voice. Bucky looked up. There in the pulpit stood the whey-faced Simon P. Stone, sanctimonious pastor who'd done nothing—his piety deaf to cruelty—to keep Bucky from being the butt of his confirmation class two years before. The knuckles of his thin right hand were white with terror as he clutched, unconscious, a fistful of gilt-edged Bible pages. His surplice hung like a shroud from his taut gaunt shoulders, a tasteful Pontiac gray, sheen and all. A lime-green tippet trailed like an untied tie down the sides of his chest.

"Come down, Satan," said Bucky, hearing sirens in the distance through the bloodpulse of his anger, "come down to the altar and call your flock of demons to you."

"No, Vernon, I won't do that." Pastor Stone's eyes were teary with fear—he of little faith not ready, no not after decades of preaching, to meet his Maker.

Bucky looked around through the sobbing, saw crazed eyes turn away from him, saw between pews the sculpted humps of suited shoulders like blue serge whales stuck in waves, saw—yes! saw Mrs. Irma Wilkins, her red velvet hat a half-shell really with black lace crap on it, her gloved hand dabbing a crumpled hanky to one eye. "Mrs. Wilkins," Bucky said, and her head jerked up like a startled filly, "come here!" Her lids lowered in that snippy way, but she rose, a thin frail stick of a woman, and sidled out of her pew. And as she neared, Bucky was back at the church camp five summers before, out in the woods, holding one end of the crossbranch from which depended the iron kettle, its sole support he and another kid and two badly made and badly sunk Y-shaped branches, and the wind shifted and the smoke of the fire blew like a mask of no-breath into his face and clawed at his eyes no matter how hard he tried to blink past it, and he turned away and let go of the branch saying "My eyes!" and the rude blur that was Irma Wilkins rushed in to catch the branch and to sting him with her condemnation, even now as she approached in this church he could hear her say it, *"Your eyes? OUR STEW!"* as if the fucking food were more important than Bucky's vision and to her it *was* and that voice of hers, that whole put-down attitude reduced Bucky to nothing; but Bucky knew he was something all right, and he saw her pinched little lipless mouth as she came closer, by God it looked like a dotted line and by God he'd oblige her by tearing across it now with his widdle gun, better that than live his whole life hearing this nasty woman's voice reduce him to nothing; and he opened up his rage upon her, rippling across her face with a rain of bullets until her head tore back at the mouth like the top of a Pez dispenser thumbed open, shooting out a stream of crimson coffins, spilling gore down the front of her black dress like cherry liqueur over dark chocolate, and mean Irma Wilkins went down like the worthless sack of shit she was, and Bucky felt damned proud of himself, yes he did, happy campers.

Bucky swung back to Pastor Stone. "Bring 'em all to the front of the church and I won't harm a one of 'em," he said. "But if you refuse, I'll pick 'em off one at a time just like I did Mrs. Wilkins here."

Rest of them had ears. They needed no coaxing, but coaxed instead their whimpering kids out of hiding, out into the aisles and up the red runners to the altar, where Pastor Stone, trembling like unvarnished truth, raised his robed arms as if in benediction, as if he were posing for a picture, Pastor Simon P. Stone and his bleating sheep.

The muffled squawk of a bullhorn turned Bucky's head to a tall unstained window at his left. A squat man in blue stood on the grass at the near edge of the parking lot, legs planted firmly apart, elbows bent, face and hands obliterated by a black circle. "Vernon Stevens," came his humorless voice, "lay down your weapon and come out with your hands raised. We will not harm you if you do as I say. We have the church surrounded. Repeat. The church. Is. Surrounded." The bullhorn squawked off and the black circle came down so that Bucky could see clearly the ain't-I-a-big-boy-now, pretend courage painted on the man's face. Glancing back, Bucky saw bobbing blue heads through the two small squares of window that let onto the narthex, a scared rookie or two, the long stems of assault rifles jostling like shafts of wheat in a summer breeze.

Doubt crept into him. And fear. His finger eased off the trigger. Tension began to drain from his arms.

FINISH THE JOB! came the voice, like a balloon fist suddenly inflating inside his skull, pressing outward as if to burst bone. *LOOK AT THEM, BUCKY! LOOK AND REMEMBER WHAT THEY'VE DONE TO YOU!*

And Bucky looked. And Bucky saw. There was Bad Sam in his Sunday best, frog-faced pouting young tough, a lick of light brown hair laid across his brow, freckles sprayed on his bloated cheeks, Bad Sam who'd grabbed Bucky off his bike when Bucky was nine, slammed him to the cement of the sidewalk by Mr. Murphy's house and slapped his face again and again until his cheeks bruised and bled. And through his tears, he could see Mr. Murphy at his front window, withdrawing in haste at being discovered; Mr. Murphy who'd always seemed so kind, tending his tulip beds as Bucky biked by, and now here he was in church along with his tiny wife and their daughter Patricia in a white dress and a round brimmed hat that haloed her head. And next to her stood Alex Menche, a gas jockey at the Exxon station, corner of First and Main, whose look turned to hot ice whenever Bucky walked by, who never blinked at him, never talked to him, but just stared, oily rag in hand, jaw moving, snapping a wad of gum. And back behind Alex he caught a glimpse of Mr. Green the janitor, who'd yelled Shutup! at the lunchbox crowd in second grade even when their mouths were busy with peanut butter. And odd Elvira Freeborn, New Falls' weirdo-lady, who laid claim in good weather to a corner of the city park across from the town hall and had conversation with anyone who chanced by and lingered there—even weirdo Elvira had come up to him one day when he'd been desperate enough for company to go seek her out, had come up all smiles, her hair wispy gray and twisting free of its bun, and said, "My, my, Vernon, you are one fat ugly thing, yes you are, and if you were mine, I'd sew your mouth shut, I would; by God I'd starve that flab right off your bones and I'd see about getting you a nosejob for that fat knob of a honker you got on your face and—" on and on and on, and now her eyes were on him here in church, off-yellow glaring cat's-eyes like a reformed witch having second thoughts. And beside her was Sarah Janeway the organist, who'd laughed and then tried to hide it when Bucky auditioned for the children's choir at the age of eight, a no-talent bitch with her wide vacant eyes encircled in wide glasses rimmed in thin red and her hair cropped short as her musical gifts and her absurd flowered dress poking out of the shimmering-green choir robe down below, and she was standing there white-faced and whiny, and then the bullhorn bullshit started up again, and Bucky brought his one true friend up to his chest and let the surge of righteous wrath seize him.

He made them dance, every last one of them.

He played the tune. They tripped and swayed to the rhythm of his song. Wounds opened like whole notes in them. Sweeping glissandos of gore rose up like prayers of intercession.

Behind him he felt a flood of cops rush in to pick up the beat and join him, to judder and jolt the music out of *him* with music of their own. Bucky, tripped out on giving back in spades what New Falls had so unstintingly bestowed upon him over the years, turned about to spray death into the boys in blue at his back. But there were too many of them, and a goodly number were already in position, rifles beaded on him.

Then pain seized his right knee and danced up his leg in small sharp steps, like invisible wasps landing on him, fury out. Needles of fire watusied across his belly. Two zigzags of lead staggered up the ladders of his ribs and leaped for Bucky's head. Something impossible to swallow punched through his teeth, filling his mouth with meat and blood.

And then his brain lit up like a second sun and all the pain winked out. The terrible thunder of weaponry put to use went away, only to be replaced by organ music so sweet it made Bucky want to wet his pants and not give a good goddamn about the consequences.

He felt himself drift apart like a dreamer becoming someone else. The cops froze, caught in mid-fire. About him, the church walls roiled and wowed like plaster turned to smoke. But it wasn't smoke. It was mist, fog, clouds. They billowed down into the church, rolling and shifting and swirling among the corpses. Bucky glanced back at the altar, saw the bodies of his victims posed in attitudes of death, saw Pastor Simon P. Stone, his robed arms out in crucifixion, veed at the waist as if he'd just caught the devil's medicine ball in his belly.

But right behind Bucky, close enough to startle him, was his own body, bits of flesh being torn out like tufts of grass at a driving range, shoots of blood looking like hopeful red plants just coming into sunlight. He circled, by willing it, about his body, feeling the cumulus clouds cotton under his feet, soothing his soles, as he gazed in astonishment at his head, pate cracked open all round like the top of an eggshell, hovering a foot above the rest of it in a spray of blood and brain. He reached out, touched the stray piece of skull, tried to force it back in place, but it was as if it were made of stone and cemented for all eternity to the air. Likewise the freshets of gore issuing like bloody thoughts from his brain, which, though not cold, were as stiff as icicles.

The music swelled, recaptured his attention. Looking about for its source, he saw emerge from each tiny cloud a creature, all in white, all of white and gold, delicate of hand, beatific of face, and every one of them held a thing of curves in its hands. Their angel mouths O'd like moon craters. Thin fingers swept in blizzards of beauty across iridescent harps. And yet their music was neither plucked nor sung, but a pain-pure hymn rolling out in tones richer than any man-made organ.

They made the bloody scene beautiful, sanctifying it with their psalm. And now their bodies swerved as though hinged and they raised their eyes to the dioramic

massacre before the altar and up past the huge golden
cross even to the white plaster ceiling above it, beyond
which the spire lofted heavenward. With a great groan,
as if angelic eyes could move mountains with a look, the
top of the building eased open, sliding outward on invisible runners to hang there in the open air. And down into
the church descended a great blocky bejeweled thing, an
oblong Spielbergian UFO Bucky thought at first. But
then he saw the sandals, the feet, the robes, the hands
gripping firmly the arms of the throne like Abe Lincoln,
the chest bedecked in white, and the great white beard,
and he guessed what he was in for.

But when the head came fully into view, Bucky had to
laugh. Like Don Rickles trapped in a carpet, the face of
an angry black woman grimaced out from behind the
white beard and moustache of God. Her cheeks puffed
out like wet sculpted obsidian, her dark eyes glared, and
just in front of a Hestonian sweep of white hair, a tight
black arch of curls hugged her face like some dark rider's
chaps curving about the belly of his steed. The white
neck of the deity was stiff and rigid, as if locked in a
brace.

"Bucky Stevens," She boomed, Her eyes moving from
him to a space of air in front of Her, "you'd best be
getting yourself up here this instant, you hear?"

"Yes, ma'am," he said, drifting around his exploding
corpse and sailing up over the bloody crowd at the altar.
He could still sense how fat he was, but he felt as light
and unplodding as a sylph. "You sending me to hell?" he
asked.

She laughed. "Looks to Me like you found your *own*
way there." Her eyes surveyed the carnage. "First off,
young man, I want to say I 'preciate what you did for Me.

I like sinners who listen to My suggestions and have the balls to carry them out."

"That was *You*?"

"Does God lie?"

"No, ma'am."

"Damn right He don't, and I'm God, so you just shove those doubts aside and listen up."

"Um, 'scuse me, ma'am," said Bucky, shuffling his feet in the air, "but how come God's a black woman? I mean in Sunday school—"

"God ain't a black woman, Mister Bucky, leastways no more He ain't. He's been that for a while, oh bout three weeks or so." She smiled suddenly. "But now He gets to be a fat white boy named Bucky Vernon."

Bucky brightened. He didn't doubt for a moment what She'd said. He couldn't. It speared like truth into his heart. "You mean I get to . . . to take over? There's no punishment for killing all these people?"

God chuckled, a high-pitched woo-wee kind of sound. "That ain't what I said a-tall." She did a stiff-necked imitation of a headshake as She spoke.

Bucky was mystified: "I don't get it."

God leaned forward like She had a board strapped to Her back. "I'll be brief," She said, "just so's you can hustle your fat butt up here quicker and let Me come down and do My dying. I killed me a whole officeload of people three weeks ago, got blown away by a security guard after I hosed those heartless fuckers at Century 21. Same sorta miracle that's happening to you now, happened to me then. Only God was this unhinged lunatic I'd seen on Dan Rather the week before, some nut who went to O'Hare and picked off ground crew and passengers not lucky enough to be going through one of those

tubes. He got blown away too, became God, then talked
me into wiping out my co-workers when they gave me
the axe. So I did it, and coaxed you along same's he did
me, and here we are."

The music was doing beautiful things to Bucky's mind.
He grew very excited. "You mean I'm going to be in
charge of everything? I can make any changes I feel like
making, I can stop all the misery if I want to?" God
ummm-hmmmed. "But why would anyone, why would
You, want to give that up?"

She looked agitated, like She wanted to laugh and cry
and holler all at the same time. Instead She said, "As My
momma used to say, young Master Stevens, experience is
the best teacher a body can have." She glared at him
suddenly and Bucky felt himself swept forward and up.

He windmilled his arms, struggling to find his center
of gravity, but found himself fluttering and turning like
an autumn leaf, tumbling spout over teakettle toward the
great black face, toward the crazy brown eyes. He
headed straight between them, fearing he'd smash on the
browbone, but instead doubled and split like a drunkard's vision and fell and swelled into the black pools of
God's pupils. In the blink of an eye, he inflated. That's
how it felt to him, like his head felt when they stuck his
arm and taped it down, knocking him out for an ingrown
toenail operation when he was ten, only all over his body
this time and he didn't lose consciousness. He unlidded
his eyes just in time to see the stocky black woman wink
at him before she put her hands together as if in prayer,
sang out "So long, sucker!", and swan-dived into his shat-
tering body.

Bucky gazed about at the angels on their clouds and
felt guy-wires coming from their O'd mouths as if He

were a Macy's Day balloon and they the marching guardians who kept Him from floating free. The throne rose slowly and the angels with it. Bucky took His first God-breath and felt divine. Like Captain Kirk, He was in command now, He sat at the helm, and things by God were going to fly right from here on out.

But then, as He lifted above the church and its roof clicked into place, time unfroze and, with it, the pain of those inside. He felt it all, like a mailed fist slamming into His solar plexus again and again: Simon Stone, small and mean inside like a mole, gasping for one final breath; Sarah Janeway, two months pregnant, trying in vain to hold back the rope-spill of her intestines; kindhearted Elvira Freeborn, in so many ways the sanest person there, who let her dying fall over her like a new sundress, a thing of razor and flame. And even the dead—Coach Hezel, the Atwoods, Irma Wilkins and the rest—even from these, Bucky felt the echoes of their suffering and, transcending time, seeped into their dying a thousand times over.

And then He rose over New Falls, did Bucky Vernon, feeling His holy tendrils reach into everyone who wept and wandered there. He knew at last the torment of his parents and the riches they'd lost inside themselves, and it made His heart throb with pain. Bucky rose, and, in rising, sank into every hurting soul in town, spreading Himself thick everywhere. And all was painful clarity inside Him. It grew and crackled, the misery, and still He rose and sank, moving like Sherman-Williams paint to engulf the globe, seeping deep down into the earth. Bucky wanted to scream. And scream He did. And His scream was the cause, and the sound, of human misery.

He tried to bring His hands to His face. To puncture

His eardrums. To thumb out His eyes. But they clung
like mules to the hard arms of the throne, not budging,
and His eyelids would not shut, and His earflaps sucked
all of it in like maelstroms of woe. Pockets of starvation
flapped open before Him like cover stories blown, and
each death-eyed Ethiopian became unique to Him—the
clench of empty stomachs, the wutter and wow of dying
minds.

Like dental agony, layer beneath layer surprising one
at the untold depths of it, Bucky's pain intensified and
spread, howling and spiraling off in all directions. And
after a while, it didn't exactly dull, nor did He get used to
it, but rather He rose to meet it, to yield to it as the
storm-tossed seafarer gives up the struggle and moves
into the sweep of the sea. He was the pincushion of pain,
He was the billions of screaming pins, He was the billions of thumbs pressing them down into flannel. He
suffered all of it, and knew Himself to be the cause of it
all. Caught in the weave, He *was* the weave.

He almost smiled, it was so perverse; but the smile
was ripped from His face by new outrage. There seemed
no end to the torment, no end to burgeoning pain. As
soon as He thought He'd hit bottom, the bottom fell out.
He began to wonder if the black woman had lied to Him,
if maybe He was trapped in this nightmare for all eternity. While He watched with eyes that could not close,
new births killed young girls, new deaths tore at mourn-
ers, new forms of woe were kennel-bred and unleashed.
Bucky was fixed in His firmament, and all was hell with
the world.

Plunged down the slippery slope of despair, He cast
His great eyes about, sought for pustules of resentment,
found them. The seeds of His redemption they were,

these seething souls. The black woman—Miriam Jefferson Jones—had, like her predecessor, been nursing others along, and now Bucky reached out to them and took up the whisper in their ears, the whisper momentarily stilled at the shift in deity. Heavens yes, Sean Flynn, he assured the young man leaned against the stone wall, huddled with his mates, it's only proper you elbow under their fuckin transport at night, fix old Mother Flammable there, crawl the hell out o' there, give it the quick plunge, watch all them limey bastards kiss the night sky over Belfast with their bones. And yes, Alicia Condon of Lost Nation, Iowa, it's okay to take your secret obsession with the purity of the newborn to its limit, it is indeed true that if you could wipe out a whole nursery of just-delivered infants before they hit that fatal all-corrupting second day of life, the Second Coming of My Own Sweet Son would indeed be swiftly upon the sinning race of mankind. And yes, oh most decidedly yes, Gopal Krishnan and Vachid Dastjerdi and Moshe Naveh, you owe it to your respective righteous causes to massacre whole busloads, whole airports, whole towns full of enemy flesh.

There were oodles of them walking the earth, ticking timebombs, and all of them He tended and swayed that way, giving with a whisper gentle nudges and shoves toward mass annihilation. New ones too, promising buds of bitterness, Bucky began to cultivate. Some one of them was certain to bloom any moment now—oh God, how Bucky prayed to Himself for it to be soon—at least one brave quarterback on this playing field of sorrow was sure to snatch that ball out of the sky and run for all he was worth, pounding cleat against turf, stiff-arming those who dared try to block him, not stopping till he crossed the forbidden line and slammed that bleeding pigskin down in triumph.

That was the hope, through agonies untold, that kept Bucky going. That was the hope that made things hum.

Robert Devereaux, a 1990 graduate of the Clarion West Workshop, has published short stories in *Pulphouse* and *Iniquities*. Two novels are forthcoming: *Deadweight* and *Santa Steps Out*.

PART FOUR
The Devil, Probably

Dumbarton Oaks

Barry N. Malzberg

 Middle management, that's what I am. Carry it up, carry it down. Put the best face on it, provide color and pizzazz for the masses, front for the higher-ups. Horns, a cloak, puff of brimstone, a muttering of curses, strokes of damnation, somersaults over the abyss. Sometimes a fool's cap and bells, horns for the uninitiated, perhaps a wisp of tail to be caught in the extinguishing light. There is something of a lack of dignity to the process but then again and as I am reminded, I do not have to make the serious decisions, hold the balance wheel, dwell at the curvature of Earth and abyss while trying to make the larger decision. Middle management suffers its humiliations, overworks from stress, pretends to an autonomy it can never have, but middle management also tends to lateral transfer, to the possibility of a lingering career. Hidden upper management, I am reminded, has the real responsibility and it is a long fall to the ground, a sickening vault through the scorching dark. Of course I do not really believe any of this. It is rationalization propounded by upper management to keep the fools at bay. In your heart you have always known—and so have I—that the real pain is felt by those of us who are truly exposed and that those behind the arras have no responsibility whatsoever.

Are you done ranting now? he says. Is that all of it?

I'm not ranting, I say, I am simply laying out the situation. I have a right to do that.

He smiles, not lovingly. My best angel, he says. As full of ideas as ever. Big ideas, warm heart. Don't let me interrupt you. The tilt of his mockery surges through me, makes me want to turn on him but of course in the stones and smoke of this wasteland such aggression is impossible, he would fling a vagrant thunderbolt, uncover a trapdoor beneath the mesquite and that would be the end of the discussion. Talk of vaults through the scorching dark. Tarshish, he says, Philadelphia. It's time to get on the move again. Unless you're otherwise occupied. Could that be so, Lucifer? I wouldn't want to inconvenience you.

There is no inconvenience, I say. Really, what else is there to say? Trapped in this abyss, unable to go up or down, in or out, I can only absorb the sound of his abuse until another idea emerges. None has emerged thus far, yet, and I have been at this a long time. Well, he says, be on your way, then. Unless you'd like to talk, as I said. I know you're full of ideas.

I'll just be on my way, I said. I was never the best-loved. This is a fiction propounded by public relations which attempts—who can blame them?—to put the best face on matters. Actually, he had it in for me from the beginning. The least benign of his imps, he called me, the only one with pretensions to some kind of inner life. Well he said, we'll just deal with *that*. We'll give you an inner life, all right. We'll give you a thread of consciousness to hang your dread on. Sodom, Gomorrah, that business with Bathsheba. Back and forth, in and out, a question of cosmic balances he instructed but at the end of it, always the same. Nothing changed, the contest between the corrupt and the deluded goes on and on. Of course that may be the point.

You will go to Tarshish, he says. You will reveal yourself there. Then, perhaps, you will want to show up in Nabucho's court. Give him just a glimpse of the brimstone before you disappear.

I've done that court, I said. That happens to be the truth. I have done the court and Bathsheba. I have also done Tarshish and Philadelphia, the spoils of Torquemada and the interiors of Auschwitz. Describe the place and I have camped within it. But then, as has been noted, there is essentially no end to any of this; one must replicate simply to keep the balance. This too has been explained to me numerous times, not that the explanations make any difference or ease the burning, the yearning. He makes a dismissive gesture. Be gone, he says, go on your way. Give a little color, a little *frisson* to the masses, that's what you're there for. That's what I'm there for too, he adds, not that you're interested in my problems or this is any concern of yours. Are you going? he says. I've really had enough of you. Enough of this, beloved, be on your way. I adjust my sandals, pick up the requisite anti-pentagrammatic devices, the stabilizers and the holographs and leave. There is really nothing at all to be done when he is this way. One could stand and argue the point but then the trapdoor would open and the smells and fires of the abyss would consume; he is absolutely merciless in his control of the conditions and I would not be the first to be consigned to the rack and the plague. From other lives, I have come to this; I have no desire to return. So I leave that strange and foliant garden, the stink of his perfumes full in my nostrils, pack my middle-management satchel with grief, loss and devices and head toward the standard oaths and imprecations hoping for better but knowing that—as always—it will simply be the colorless recursion.

So I go on to Philadelphia and search for Zephaniah. He is one of the minor prophets, of course, like Amos or Jeptha, James or the second Peter he can be seen as little more than a precursor, one who carries a certain clear apprehension of woe without the capacity to really make things any different; he lives if at all in the disasters and blandishments of prophets more demonstrative. Only Susanna the virtuous can compare to Zephaniah in intensity or superfluousness, nonetheless his oaths of damnation, his assurances that the Earth will be utterly consumed and destroyed have the ability to excite some of the lower masses. In this sense he is colorful and how can I not apprehend and have sympathy with this? I come to curse your righteousness, I say. Zephaniah is in a troubled sleep, he will remember this if at all as a tormented dream but the residue will eventually appear in his ravings. Your righteousness will get you nowhere. Are you prepared for the fires and the insects, the ravening plagues, the whitened bones of children, the cries of children, the murder of helpless infants in their mother's wombs? Have you truly understood the futility of bulwark? And so on and so forth. They live in close quarters, crude cultures here, peasants without facilities in tents staked up and down the desert in close file, the sandpits flowing with their waste, to be covered over by vagrant shovelfuls and left for the animals to snaffle. Of such rudeness, of such *crudity* have great reputations and writings been made but that too is the peculiar curse of middle management, to inflate the rudely circumstantial into the massive? Get up and face the dawn, I say, this is the judgment of evil. Oh, evil is upon the land.

Leave me be, Zephaniah says. He is an old man in this time, in his mid-forties and ravaged by illness and by the enormity of his terrible visions. I have done nothing. I have lived virtuously.

Virtue has nothing to do with it, I say. Virtue reaps evil in a time of trouble. Send them messages. Let them know the extent of the judgment. There is no mercy.

No mercy, no mercy, Zephaniah says. He claws himself out of sleep, curls to a crouch, heaves himself upright. You must grant us mercy. We have done nothing to deserve—

You have done too much, I say. One of the small and terrible pleasures of this assignment is to appear not in my true robes and function but disguised as an emissary of righteousness. He and I, in other times, have giggled about this simulation, about the way in which we have made ourselves collaborators. That is the theory of middle management, of course, one can go either way. I'm afraid that this is all for you, I say to Zephaniah. It is too late to turn to the path of righteousness. Judgment has been cast. This is more or less the message I have passed on through Jonah, Daniel, Torquemada, Goering, the victimizer as victimized, the torturer as tortured—more in pity and sorrow than in anger, folks—and it has never failed to work; every time this has been accepted as the genuine goods. Nothing else for you, I say, and show him a flicker of horn under the pristine robes, just a subliminal flash, enough to complicate and yet clarify the message. *Did I see that?* Zephaniah will ask himself later. *No, of course I did not see that. This is impossible. I saw an angel, an angel of the Lord.*

I will consume all things off the face of the Earth, I conclude.

I sweep away from the tent, leaving Zephaniah on the ground behind me. Perched on palms and knees he looks after me in the extinguished light, and I can imagine his fixed gaze as I move away grandly. At the outskirts of the wretched village I pause, take deep breaths, reacclimate myself, then head with enormous speed and force to Krakow where I observe the pogrom for a while, then to Warsaw where I whisper into the observant Eichmann's ear. He nods and nods. Back then, satisfied with the shape of the mission—carrying the word up, carrying it down—to the usual place where I find that he has abandoned quarters for a while, doubtless concerned with private affairs of moment far beyond mine. I look carefully to see that I am alone and unobserved, then mount the throne as I do occasionally, trying its seat, monitoring my own conduct and purchase as I move grandly upon its surface. Truly, it fits very well and there is no saying where in the custody of time it or I may go. Carry it up, carry it down. I prepare memoranda in my head, waiting for his return, clambering from the throne, of course, to perch submissively by its side. It is best to retain the appearance of humility, even in the intimation of its opposite. We will laugh. We will laugh again and again, the shrieks of our laughter beating like birds against the bowl of heaven.

1991: New Jersey

Barry N. Malzberg is the author of *The Destruction of the Temple, The Cross of Fire, Guernica Night, Herovit's World, The Falling Astronauts, Revelations, Beyond Apollo, The Remaking of Sigmund Freud,* the nonfiction *The Engines of the Night* and many short stories. He recently completed his eighty-third book.

Novena

Chelsea Quinn Yarbro

Novena: in the Roman Catholic rite, a devotion nine
days in duration to honor a specific saint or sacred
event; a recognized but optional observance.

 On the third day of battle, the bombing drove
Sister Maggie off the roof where she had taken
refuge in an abandoned dovecote; she returned to the enormous, wrecked hotel, dreading what
she would find in the four floors of pillaged rooms. Since
the local uprising—calling itself a revolution—destruction had escalated. In was worse than she feared: in what
had been the lobby injured children were left to their
own devices while their parents labored to shore up de-
fenses or joined various ragtag resistance movements,
nipping at the enemy with captured guns, with improvised weapons, with knives, with stones.

The smell was like a slaughterhouse in summer, pungent and heavy. A continual moan made up of all the
cries and whimpers and grunts of the wounded ebbed
and flowed through the pillared ruin. Most of the furniture had been broken up and now covered the large,

gaping holes that had once been windows. Two of the long couches had been pressed into service as examining tables. The village's midwife, usually shunned, was doing this work, practicing her own sort of triage.

Sister Maggie approached the old woman. "Let me help," she pleaded. "I am a nurse." She was reasonably certain she was the only person with clinical medical training for half a day's journey in any direction. It wrung her soul that no one in the village would accept her assistance: she was here to give it, yet remained ostracized.

The midwife pretended she did not understand, although Sister Maggie spoke her language expertly. The peasant-woman continued to pour vodka looted from the hotel stores over the jagged, puffy flesh of a shrapnel wound.

"You've got to take the fragments out first," said Sister Maggie desperately, wishing the clinic still existed. She could use the equipment there, and the antibiotics. "If you don't clean it, it will fester and he'll lose the whole leg. Or his life." She crossed herself and noticed two of the children waiting for help make a sign to ward off the Evil Eye as she did so.

Finally the midwife looked at her, deep-probing eyes lost in furrowed wrinkles. "You have no right here. Leave us."

"But I can help," Sister Maggie protested.

"You have helped enough," said one of the wounded children, a girl of fourteen who had lost an eye and whose body was starting to swell with her first pregnancy. Her resentment drove Sister Maggie away from her as a fire or a stench would have done.

Still caught in the intensity of the girl's stare, Sister Maggie almost tripped over a three-year-old with a savage scalp wound. The child, pathetically thin and breathing in fast, shallow gasps, was already sinking into coma; as Sister Maggie watched his breathing became more irregular. He would be dead in less than an hour without concerted treatment for shock. Without such intervention, he would die quickly, if God was kind. Sister Maggie paid no attention to the angry faces around her as she knelt to cross herself, and traced the sign of the cross on the boy's forehead, saying her prayers for him silently so that she would not be ordered to stop.

"Leave him alone!" shouted one of the old men guarding the place. In his arthritic hands he carried a rifle that was more than fifty years old.

"But I can help," Sister Maggie protested.

"No one can help him," the old man declared with the authority of age.

Sister Maggie moved away at once, leaving the dying child. She hoped God would understand and show His forgiveness, not only to her but to these people as well. There was so much she had asked Him to understand over the past five years, and always with the conviction that she would eventually be given the opportunity to make amends.

There was another boy, nine or ten, although he looked younger; everyone called him the Rat because he was the most adept thief and scavenger in the hotel, possibly in the entire village. He was especially good at raiding opposition materiel, but for this prized skill he was distrusted, too, and avoided. He was off in a corner of the lobby by himself, ignored and neglected. His right sleeve was stiff with dried blood. His huge eyes, a deep, soft brown, showed a cynicism that would have been troubling in a grown man; in this boy it was appalling. He watched the nun in the patched jumpsuit come toward him, saying nothing, his face expressionless, even of pain.

"Hello, Rat," said Sister Maggie, speaking his language with the ease of practice.

"Hello," he answered without emotion.

This would be difficult; she had been afraid he might not be willing to speak with her at all. She decided to behave as if the calamity around them were usual. "Has anyone had a chance to look at you yet? That arm could use—"

He regarded her with scorn. "Why would they look? What will they do?" He attempted to wave it, to show how minor a matter it was. His mangled hand flapped uselessly; unshed tears brightened his eyes, though he steadfastly refused to cry.

"Because they want you to keep stealing ammunition from the revolutionaries, and you need both hands working to do that," said Sister Maggie in her most reasonable voice. "Do you mind if I look at it?" She prepared herself for a rebuff and offered a short, inward prayer to the Virgin, hoping she could offer up the shame as well as her lost opportunity to serve.

"They don't care who steals the ammunition as long as someone does," the Rat said, but let Sister Maggie come over to him and cut away the lower part of his sleeve with the scissors of her Swiss Army knife. The only indication of his concern for his injury was in his reluctance to look at it. "There have been worse."

But not where a hand could be saved, thought Sister Maggie as she looked at what had happened to bone and muscle and flesh: an explosive had shattered half his hand and the lower end of the ulna. Fragile tendons showed above shattered bone. The Rat would be fortunate if he could salvage a thumb and the first two fingers, and that would require expert medical treatment. It was a grim prospect for the boy. What would he do with his life after such a loss? The possibilities were unbearably grim. "You should go to a hospital. You need help. You could lose . . ."

The Rat laughed.

"I mean it, Rat. You need a doctor, with drugs and medicines and machines to help him. That hand should be . . ." She made herself look away from the terrible damage. There had to be a way to save him. She had to do something. She wished she were not the only one left from the clinic—that the clinic was not a burn-scarred ruin.

"A surgeon could save your hand, or some of it, and it would work right afterward. There is a hospital at the army depot, isn't there? It's only two days from here."

"Two days if there's no fighting and the roads are open. But if I go to the army, they will not help me, they will arrest me. They will put me in a cell with other boys, or keep me to amuse an officer. The army is like that. The soldiers are given their choice of men or women, for rewards. You have light hair. You are a Sister. A lot of them will want you." His smile showed how completely he understood his predicament, and hers, and what little patience he had for her suggestion. "I won't go to the army."

"Where else can you find a doctor?" Sister Maggie asked helplessly. "There must be a doctor who is not part of the army, or who does not answer to the army. Not all the doctors live in fear of the soldiers, do they?" Since Father Kenster died two years ago, she had not been able to find anyone willing to take his place—the village was too remote and in a district where rebel and counterinsurgent bands roamed at will, taking what they could carry and burning the rest in the name of reform. "What about the . . . the town where they have the sheep market?" She could not remember the name, if she had ever known it.

"The sheep market?" The Rat made a contemptuous motion with his good hand, smiling without mirth. "Everyone thinks there are doctors at the sheep market. There are. For the sheep. None of them would touch me, or anyone like me."

"Then where?" Sister Maggie demanded.

"Nowhere, you idiotic woman." He let his voice drop, his face haggard. "There are no doctors for us. Doctors do not come here. It is only a lie to tell people when they get sick, so that they may be taken away when they are dying, and no one will make trouble about it. 'We are going to the doctor,' they tell the dying ones, and everyone is satisfied." At last the Rat looked at the destruction of his hand. Aside from turning white around the mouth, his face might have been set in cement for all it revealed.

"You need medical treatment." She said it more forcefully, watching the boy, wishing she still had even a few basic supplies. She wanted to know his blood pressure, body temperature, pulse rate; she wanted to monitor him for shock. But the last of the supplies had been lost when Father Kenster died defending the clinic.

"Your medicine is wrong. It would kill me." He stared at her. "I don't want it."

"But—" Sister Maggie squatted down beside the Rat. "You can't ask me to ignore you. I can't forget what's been—" She gestured toward his sleeve.

He swung away from her. "I will forget. I am forgetting already. *You* will forget. The others"—he jutted his chin toward the children lying in the refuse of the lobby —"will forget. It means nothing."

"I can't do that," she insisted. "I'm a nun. I took vows, Rat. I made promises to God and the Church, before you were born. I promised to help people." It was sixteen years ago, she realized distantly. The idealistic young nurse in her habit and veil and wimple was a third of the world and a third of her life away. It had seemed so wonderful, being a medical missionary, someone who could actually make a difference in the world, someone would could heal the body as well as the soul. Sixteen years ago, in Boston, it had all seemed so possible.

"God will not mind if you stop being a nun after so long," the Rat said with something like kindness, all he was capable of offering her. "Forget your vows. You cannot keep them here, and your Church has already forgotten you."

"You don't understand," said Sister Maggie, grateful for his attempts at softening the blow; steady, seductive despair tugged at her, tantalizing her with the balm of helplessness. "It would make me a . . . a fraud." The word was softer than the one she had chosen at first, but she doubted the Rat know who Judas was, or cared.

On the north side of the village the bombing steadily increased.

At dusk the next evening the Rat found Sister Maggie back on the roof in the remnants of her dovecote. He was looking pasty but for his wounded hand, which was ruddy and swollen, shiny of skin and hot to the touch; corruption had set in. "Not even the birds want to live here anymore. Why do you?"

"For peace," she said, refusing to be distracted by the tracer bullets against the northern sky. "It was this or the streets."

"But the bombs will ruin it. If not now, soon. At first it was just pistols, then rifles, but now they are serious. You could die." He was feverish, his eyes brilliant as broken glass. "It was stupid, getting hurt. I picked up a bomb. I couldn't throw it away fast enough." He laughed angrily, rocking with pain.

"Come out of the sun," said Sister Maggie, trying to lead the boy to what shelter remained of her dovecote.

"No." He lunged away from her. "Keep back."

She reached out to the boy. "Don't do this, Rat. Please don't do this."

"Why?" His voice broke. "Because it makes you unhappy? Because you don't have a way to stop it?" He could not swagger the way he liked but he was able to get an arrogant lift to his chin. "You came here! We didn't ask you, you came! None of us wanted you. We wanted help to kill our enemies. We didn't want a clinic, we wanted guns."

Hearing this from the infection-dazed boy, she had to struggle to maintain a little composure. "If you outlive your enemies, if you can live better than they do, then you triumph over them," she said patiently.

He spat. "They will come and take everything." He moved his good hand in an encompassing gesture. "The village will be gone before the year is out. Now that they have noticed us, there is nothing we can do to save it."

"They killed Father Kenster, and the other Sisters," said Sister Maggie, crossing herself as much out of habit as conviction. "May God forgive them for their sins."

"May God fill them with the plague that kills and kills

and kills, and rots their bodies to nothing for ten generations!" He stumbled and would have fallen if Sister Maggie not caught him. She settled him back gently onto the
sheet metal and planking that made up most of the roof.
"Get away from me," he muttered. "I do not want your
help."

"You will have to endure it, anyway," she said, almost
grateful to the boy for collapsing. At last there was a
chance—a slim one but a chance—to do something for
him, to expiate the many times she had not been able to
help. She did not want this boy to be like the others,
turning away from her. She might not have all the tools
she wanted, but she was a good nurse as well as a nun,
and neither of those callings had changed because her
circumstances had. As long as she had her skill, her training, and her faith, there was hope. The lessons learned
long ago were still with her. She went about her tasks
with the automatic ease of long practice. First she felt
the pulse in his throat, finding his heartbeat fast, not
quite regular; his forehead and palms were hot, dry; his
body had a meaty odor about it. She would get one of
her blankets to put over him, that was a start. When
night fell, she would give him her own blanket as well, so
that he would not be chilled. His feet ought to be raised
above the level of his head, to lessen the work his heart
had to do, but she had no means to accomplish this, and
abandoned the effort.

"I do not want your help," the Rat said again a little
later. He was distracted and remote. When he moved his
good arm it was in an aimless, swimming gesture.

Sister Maggie improvised a stethoscope made of a
small metal cone from a spent shell casing. She did what
she could to determine how ill the boy was, and was left

with only a few incomplete impressions that were more
distressing than helpful. She rocked back on her heels
and crossed herself, starting to pray for the Rat, and herself. For the time being it was the most she could do. He
needed to have his fever reduced, she was certain of that,
but there was no ice in the village, no aspirin, no cold
cellar or underground bunker where she could tend him.
There was no place to bathe him, for the water here was
rationed and guarded; none of it would be wasted on a
boy filled with infection.

Gunfire rattled in the street below, and occasionally
a heavier report thudded on the air. Once there was a
display of tracer bullets and the distant pounding of an
antiaircraft gun poking holes in the dark. Sometime after
the middle of the night a mine went off, and an instant
later the vehicle that triggered it exploded in a gasoline
inferno. Random shots from sniper rifles cracked in irregular observance of the passing hours.

By morning the Rat's arm was hard, more than twice
its normal girth, the lacerated flesh mounding out of the
wound, bright with red starburst patterns around it, radiating toward his shoulder. The smell of infection was
stronger and his mouth was dry, lips chapped and bleeding. Now he could not move his damaged hand at all.

Knowing it was a useless gesture, Sister Maggie began
to cut up her last set of sheets; she had salvaged them
along with two crates of bedding from the bombed-out
clinic. Now all that was left was this one pair of sheets
and three pillow cases. She began to roll pressure bandages, and methodically tied them in place above the
ominous red streaks. If she could do nothing else, she
might be able to hold the infection at bay for a little
while. "I should have done this last night," she muttered

as she bound the bandage in place with long strips of sheeting. "I ought to have done this when I first saw him. I should have insisted." She whispered a prayer for mercy as she knotted the strips on the boy's chest, taking care to be certain that the bandage would stay in place no matter now much the Rat tossed and strained.

At midday the desultory firing stopped and the streets grew still in the oppressive heat. There was no place on the roof where Sister Maggie could find shelter.

The Rat had begun to howl softly every time he breathed, plucking at the single blanket with the fingers of his good hand. There was no strength left in him.

Desperately, Sister Maggie took the second blanket she had wrapped around the Rat during the night and now spread it over the shattered frame of the dovecote. The tent that resulted was clumsy and inadequate, but it kept the sun off the child, and for that Sister Maggie thanked God in the prayers she offered for the boy, the village, herself.

By sundown there were three bullet holes in the blanket.

A sullen-faced young woman, no more than sixteen but with her face already marked by harsh lines, climbed onto the roof in the dusk, approaching Sister Maggie with an assault rifle in her hands. She had given up the traditional women's dress of the region for a soldier's fatigues; her manner was deliberately unfeminine. "You have to take that blanket down," she said without any greeting. "They're going to use it for a target. They know someone's up here. You can see that for yourself." She used the barrel of the rifle to point to the dry undergrowth at the end of the bomb-pocked road. "They're coming."

"Which group is it this time?" asked Sister Maggie, distressed that she should feel such animosity to the young woman for speaking to her. "Or do you know?"

"We think it's DRUY," she answered with a gesture of disgust. "We want no part of them. They're turds. But they're after us. They're coming here to find us. They'd been through the hills around here for the last six days, looking for us."

"DRUY," repeated Sister Maggie. "Whose side are they on?" She wanted to show the young woman she was interested, though she was unable to keep the various factions straight in her mind.

"Their own," said the young woman. "They're led by one of the generals, who was chucked out of the army, five years back. He thought they owed him something for all he was doing, so he took his best troops with him when he left, to get even. Supplies for them, too. They're better fighters than most of the others. They have better equipment, too." She patted her assault rifle. "We've been told they're getting money and supplies from outside."

"Who?" asked Sister Maggie, dreading the answer.

"Who knows?" The young woman shrugged. "The U. S. China. France. Tripoli. Venezuela. India. The Crimea. Ireland. Rhodesia. Who can tell? Saudi Arabia. Argentina. Korea. Brazil. What difference does it make? Their weapons are German and Japanese, but that means nothing. Who paid for them and brought them here? No one knows." She walked to the edge of the roof. "There are only three other safe buildings left in the village. Just three; that's all. If this battle lasts much longer, there won't be any."

Sister Maggie was busy holding the Rat down while he

thrashed in pain and delirium. It was a demanding task, for in these outbursts the weak child had the strength of a large grown man and fought without quarter. There was a bruise on the side of her face to attest to his demented fury. She hardly noticed when the young woman came over to look at the boy.

"He's dying," the young woman announced impersonally. "You might as well let him go. You can't save him. Don't make it any harder on him than it is."

"I have to try," said Sister Maggie.

"Why?" The young woman looked at the Rat with flat, pitiless eyes. "It only means that he suffers longer. Leave him at the other end of town."

"No!" Sister Maggie declared. "I will not leave a human being—let alone a child—on a refuse heap. Not this boy, not anyone. I told him I would do everything I can to save him." She put her hand to the Rat's forehead, knowing his temperature was much too high.

"You can't expect anyone to bury him, not with the DRUY coming. It wouldn't be safe. Anyone who can get out will be gone before midnight." She hunkered down beside Sister Maggie. "I'll help you get him off the roof. I'll try to get a place you can take him, somewhere you won't get shot, somewhere the pigs won't eat him. But don't try to hang on to him. He's lost already. All he has left is pain." She pulled out a brown cigarette and lit it with a wooden match. "Come on. Let's get to it."

"I can't abandon him to death," Sister Maggie persisted, reaching for new rolls of torn sheet in order to change his bandages. "I must do what I can to help him, as long as there is life in his body. And mine."

The young woman chuckled once, a sound like a pistol shot. "There isn't life in him anymore. There's infection, that's all." She stared at the Rat's sunken features. "He's gone, you foolish cunt. He's just breathing meat."

It was all Sister Maggie could do to keep from screaming. "He is not dead. Until he is dead, he is in my hands, and I have an obligation to do everything I can to keep him alive. I took an oath, one that most of you prevent me from keeping. I promised to heal the sick, for the honor of Christ. It is my sworn duty as a nurse." She hated the way she sounded, more pompous than devoted, but it was all she could do to keep her rage under control.

"Well, if you have to torture him—" The young woman shook her head once and stood up. "I'll help you get him off the roof. He won't broil down in the hotel."

This time the offer felt more like a threat, and after a brief hesitation Sister Maggie rocked back on her heels. "All right, but I need a protected place. I don't want you —any of you—near him."

"If we get to fighting at close range, you'll have more to take care of than the Rat. It won't matter where you're hiding then. They want the village, the group out there, DRUY. We don't know why. This place isn't important now that the clinic's gone." With that she ambled a short distance away, showing her indifference to danger. She took up a guard stance on the corner of the roof. She finished her cigarette while Sister Maggie pulled down the tented blanket and rolled it so that it could be turned into a sling-stretcher for the Rat.

When Sister Maggie had shifted the moaning boy onto the blanket, she signaled to the young woman. "He's ready. We can carry him down now."

"Fine," said the young woman. She took one last look around the roof, then came back to where Sister Maggie waited for her help. "You're a fool," she told Sister Maggie dispassionately as she knelt down to pick up one side of the blanket.

The shot tore through her shoulder and neck, spraying blood and tissue in sudden eruption. The young woman lurched, her arms suddenly swinging spasmodically. She half staggered a few steps, then collapsed, twitching, blood surging out of her destruction. Her assault rifle, flung away at the bullet's impact, clattered down the side of the hotel to the street below.

Sister Maggie made herself go to the young woman's side, though she knew there was no help left to her, not in the world. She knelt beside her, trying to block out the continuing violent tremblings and shudders of the young woman's body while she made the sign of the cross on her broken forehead, uttering the prayers of redemption and salvation; there was nothing else to do.

She knew the Rat was dead, but would not permit herself to admit it, not until she had reached safety for him, where he could lie in peace. The body in the improvised sling tied around her shoulders and across her chest was limp, flopping against her back as she made her way through the street in the first light of day. He would not be flexible much longer; he would become as rigid as carved wood. His shattered arm was bloated with the infection that had killed him; the stench of decay riddled his flesh.

A blackened bus lay twisted on its side, and Sister Maggie decided to avoid it—the wreckage had been there long enough to provide cover for one side or the other. It would give them no protection.

A helicopter fluttered overhead, searchlight probing

the long shadows as it hovered near the tallest rooftops in the village. From time to time its machinegun beat out a tattoo in counterpoint to the chatter of its blades. The morning light struck its side with glare; there were no identifying marks painted on it, no way to know whose it was or what it presaged. Once someone hidden in the old tannery took a shot at the helicopter, but the bullet missed and fire from the helicopter blasted the south face off the old building, setting the rest in flame.

As she walked Sister Maggie made herself pray, reciting the rosary although she had not held one in her hands for more than three years; people here regarded rosaries as bad magic, the tools of witchcraft rather than religion, and so she had not been surprised when hers—a gift from her grandmother—disappeared. She was on her ninth *Hail, Mary* when she heard the sounds of voices up ahead. As quickly as she could with her burden, Sister Maggie found a doorway and stumbled through it, seeking the dark corners where she could wait until the voices were gone. As she drew away from the light her lips continued to move in prayer, but now she made no sound at all.

More voices came, men's voices, and the sound of marching feet. This was more than a few resistance fighters returning from raids. Sister Maggie wished now that she had given more attention to the young woman who had been killed the evening before, to what she said about the DRUY, if that was who these men actually were. She felt the stiffening weight of the Rat's corpse drag at her shoulders, but she would not put him down, not here.

After an hour or so there was a flurry of gunfire from inside one of the buildings—the hotel? the school?—and some sort of heavy vehicle—more than jeeps and less than tanks—roared and lumbered down the streets, lurching through the blasted pavement to whoops of approval. There was one large explosion, and the impact of one of the vehicles hurtling into the side of the building where Sister Maggie hid, followed by several minutes of intense firing that left her with ringing ears. And then the remaining troop carriers were bouncing down the street again, and the men in them laughed and shouted their victory. Two of the officers posted men at the door to the old hotel, where the injured lay in the lobby, joking about the makeshift first aid station and the suffering children.

Sister Maggie shut out the coarse yells and bursts of laughter. She was fiercely thirsty, and she could feel the relentless heat growing as the sun climbed higher in the sky. The body she carried made breathing nearly unbearable, but she realized it provided her a curious protection, for the stench might keep the invaders away from this building.

"Later," Sister Maggie whispered, a promise to the Rat. "Later we'll make sure you have a proper grave, and a cross with your name on it. It'll take a while. I'm sorry. I'm sorry." She knew no name but the Rat, and she hoped he would understand when she wrote it. Perhaps, she thought, during the afternoon while everyone else was napping, then she might be able to sneak out of the village and find a place where the Rat could be laid to rest. She tried to think of an apology to offer the boy, to make amends for what he had endured. "It has to be done, for the sake of your soul, and mine. God is merciful, Rat. He understands," she said in an undertone. "God will welcome you, for your courage and your youth."

A ragged cheer rose up outside; she flinched at the sound. She inched closer to the door, crouching down as far as the body on her back would allow. The posture was uncomfortable and precarious, for if the corpse shifted Sister Maggie would be pulled off her feet. But it was most important to know what was going on. It was too risky to peek around the door, so she contented herself with listening. Soon she wished she had plugged her ears.

"What about this place?" one soldier called to another. "Worth holding?"

"No," the other answered from further away. "We'll mine it later. Don't leave anything for the terrorists to use. They've probably been given refuge here, anyway. Villages like this one—what can you expect?"

"Tonight?" His question was laconic, utilitarian.

"No rush. Not for a shithole like this. Tomorrow's soon enough." The indifference in his voice made Sister Maggie want to vomit.

Four villagers had been found and driven out of their shelters to provide the invaders with amusement. One was an elderly man, whose high, piping voice screeched with fear and wrath; one was a woman who wept constantly, begging for her life; one was a blind boy who used to play a hammered zither for coins but was now a beggar; the last was the retarded daughter of the last village leader, a sweet child who had no more reason than a puppy, and no recognition of danger.

"Make them run," suggested one of the invaders who stood not far from Sister Maggie's hiding place.

"Too easy," said his companion. "Look at them. No

sport in running these beasts." He clapped his hands several times for attention. "Is this the best the village has to offer? Those wounded are useless to us."

The old man hurled insults at the newcomers.

There was a short burst of automatic fire, and the unmistakable sound of a body falling. And then there was silence.

The retarded girl began to whimper.

"Think of something you can do to amuse us," said the second man, and his boredom made this a fatal pronouncement.

It was all Sister Maggie could do not to scream, to run from her protected spot and flail at these proud men. It was too much to bear. She felt it shiver through her, the enormity of her burden. She folded her hands and pressed her forehead against her fingers, as if faith could blot out what was happening just four strides away from her. She made herself remain still, thinking of the work she had yet to do for the Rat. If she were discovered she would not be able to help any of the villagers, she would only be able to join them in suffering and the Rat would be cast onto the refuse heap; she had vows and promises to honor, a purpose beyond the momentary and futile satisfaction of naming these DRUY soldiers as the murderous outlaws they were.

By midafternoon the soldiers had almost exhausted their three victims; they had tormented and tortured the villagers through the heat of the day and were beginning to run out of ideas. The woman had stopped crying some time before and now did little more than scream softly when a soldier threw himself on her. The blind boy no longer struggled but knelt passively, lost in a darkness greater than his eyes.

"Too bad the girl's dead," Sister Maggie heard one of the soldiers say; he was close enough that she could have stretched out her arm and grabbed his ankle. "But that's war, I guess."

What his answer might have been was lost in a sudden eruption of gunfire from the east side of the village.

The blind boy, his face streaked with blood and semen, stared up blankly at the sound. Then an antitank shell struck next to him and he vanished in a ruddy haze.

The DRUY troops bolted for cover, most of them swearing as they searched for shelter that provided a place to shoot from. One of the troop carriers went out of control and slammed into the entrance of the battered building where Sister Maggie crouched with the Rat, dead, locked in rigor mortis on her back.

For an instant Sister Maggie feared the troop carrier would explode, and then that fear was replaced by a more insidious one as she realized that she was now trapped inside the building. The thirst she had been able to hold at bay flared afresh, and hunger, which she had denied, sank into her body like a burn.

There were three helicopters overhead now, and the firing was constant, a rage of noise like the overwhelming shriek of a hurricane. Bits of stucco and metal and masonry flew into the street. The remaining shards of glass splintered in windows, crumbling sharp as diamonds. The wreckage of the clinic was broken again as mortar fire struck the one remaining section of roof.

The old hotel where Sister Maggie had lived in her dovecote took four direct hits and broke apart.

Sister Maggie was weeping, but she did not know it. She tried to pray for the children buried in the lobby, but the words stuck in her throat. If she were not so thirsty, she thought, then she could pray. If the guns were quiet. If she were not alone. She coughed in the acrid fumes of battle and tried again to find the words to heal the souls of that human annihilation, but could not utter them. Her eyes stung, her skin prickled and she realized how cramped her muscles were. "It's too loud," she shouted and could not hear herself against the clamor of battle.

The helicopters swung over the village, circled twice in their task of demolition. The remaining two sound buildings were their most obvious victims, one sundered from its metal skeleton, the other burning, toxic smoke blackening the remaining walls like a body in the sun.

The DRUY soldiers were cut down, their troop carriers shot and shelled.

Very deliberately Sister Maggie began to repeat the prayers for grace with which she had accompanied Father Kenster when he administered extreme unction, begrudging the few tears she shed, for she was so thirsty that even tears seemed too much precious moisture to lose. Her hands shook as she crossed herself.

And then it was quiet again, the helicopters slipping away to the east, following the rutted road that led to the next village.

"Spirit of Christ, give me life. Body of Christ, be my salvation. Blood of Christ, quench my thirst—" Sister Maggie gagged, then made herself continue. "Water . . . water from Christ's side, cleanse me. Suffering of Christ, enable me to suffer courageously. Merciful Jesus, hear me. Keep me always close to You. From Satan's wiles defend me. In death's hour, call me. Summon me to Your presence, that forever with Your saints I may praise you. Amen. Spirit of Christ, give me life. Body of Christ, be my salvation . . ." She did not know how many times she repeated the prayer; finally she realized it was nearly dark in the village, where the only brightness was the dying fire in the bombed buildings.

Insects had found the Rat's body; several long lines of them made their way across the ruptured floor slab to the now-flaccid figure that no longer seemed quite human—bloated and sunken at once. The endless, relentless minuscule armies moved industriously over the swollen corpse, searching out his wounds, his nostrils, his eyes.

Sister Maggie wrestled the blanket knots loose and flung herself away from the body, brushing her clothes to rid them of the multilegged vermin that bit and stung and wriggled on her flesh. As she clawed off her worn, filthy jacket she stared in horror at the ants and beetles and things she did not recognize making their way along the curve of her ribs, as if they did not know the difference between the living and the dead. She felt the raw and painful tokens the insects left for her; disgust, abhorrence went through her, leaving her retching and dizzy.

Thirst was the most overwhelming of her desires, a greed so pure that it filled her soul like prayer.

She dared not look back at the Rat, for fear of what she might do. The stench was thick in the air, and if she saw what she knew he had become she would be unable to pray for him, now or ever.

Water. Without that, she was no different from the Rat, just a little less ripe. Her body shuddered, in hurt or laughter she could not tell. There were no prayers left in her, no sworn duty to discharge. There was only water. Nothing else was real.

She approached the troop carrier blocking the entrance; it filled the doorway almost entirely, and what small areas it did not block could not provide sufficient room for escape. Sister Maggie shoved at it, trembling with the effort though it produced little force and no effect. Her vision muddied and blurred and she clung to the grille to remain upright. She had to find another way out, but she knew she would not be able to move much longer, and night was closing in.

There were stairs, but after the fifth one the treads were gone; Sister Maggie moaned with despair and felt her way along the hall, listening to the chittering and scuffling in the dark, her need for water making them unimportant. She was too consumed by thirst to be frightened. What was the more dangerous to her than her thirst? She was haunted by the sound of water falling —a faucet? rain? a river?—and it impelled her as nothing before had ever done. Water. Deep pools shimmered at the edge of her sight, brimming cups sloshed and squandered the precious stuff just out of reach. It was sacred. Her search went on though she was not able to think about what she was doing anymore.

The broken glass cut her hand, but she paid slight attention as she dragged herself out of the collapsed sliding door at the rear of the building. The ceiling showed gaping holes from the floor above, and occasionally there were bright eyes flickering in the darkness.

The storm was driven by high winds; lightning tore through the sky and thunder battered at it. Sister Maggie stumbled into the deluge, afraid that it was a continuation of her hallucinations. After her first shambling steps she fell, and the rain ran into her hair and ears. With the last of her strength she rolled onto her back and parted her cracked lips to the tumultuous sky.

By morning the rain was nothing more than a steady, pattering mizzle, likely to pass shortly as the day heated.

There were no more fires in the village. Nothing stirred. No voices called in greeting or warning or anguish. No screams or groans, no crying alarmed Sister Maggie. She sat on a fallen section of wall at what had been the jail when she had first arrived here to take up work at the new clinic, the hope of the region. Then the village was nothing more than the support to an old hotel where few tourists came. Her skin hurt, her eyes were hot in her head, her guts felt raw. The prospect of walking was hideous.

She made herself rise, then stood, wondering which way she ought to go. Which direction offered a haven? Where would she be safe? The sound she made was not laughter, though she had thought it would be.

Then she heard the crack of a rifle. She dropped into the mud and lay still, trusting she would be mistaken for dead.

The jeep that lurched into the village was ancient, its engine grating. The three men clinging to it were scruffy, the guns they carried old-fashioned.

"They said there was a clinic here!" one of them protested as the jeep wallowed down the main street.

"Where?" another asked in abiding cynicism.

"Shit," said the first. "What good's this place without a clinic?"

"Doesn't look like it's a place anymore," said the third voice.

"We need a clinic!" the first insisted.

"Well, there isn't one here," said the third. "We might as well leave it alone."

"God, look at it," said the second.

"It happens," said the third.

Then they were too far off and their faltering engine too loud for Sister Maggie to hear more. Within five minutes she heard the jeep labor out of the village, leaving it to the dying rain.

Were they right? she wondered as she got unsteadily to her feet. Had the medical team brought disaster to the village? The clinic did give the village a prize, something others might want, but it had been there to help them, all of them. If the clinic had not come, the village would have sunk into decay unnoticed. And no one, she told herself inwardly, would have bothered the village. They would have been free of war but the prey of disease. Many of the villagers had resented the clinic, and Father Kenster. And her. And when Father Kenster and the other Sisters had been killed, the villagers had not mourned them. Had they been right all along? Had she come here as an act of sacrifice or suicide?

She found a canteen and filled it with water. That was a beginning. She would have to eat soon or there would truly be another corpse in the village, one last— She pushed the thought out of her mind. Later, she told herself. Later.

In case there was someone listening—if only the Rat —she whispered, "Lord have mercy on us. Lord have mercy on us. Lord have mercy on us. Christ have mercy on us," as she walked away.

Chelsea Quinn Yarbro is the author of more than forty books, including a series about the legendary Count de Saint Germaine: *Hotel Transylvania, The Palace, Blood Games, Path of the Eclipse, Tempting Fate, The Saint-Germaine Chronicles* and *Darker Jewels*. Her work includes science fiction, fantasy, mystery, westerns, horror and the occult.

The Ghost Village

Peter Straub

1

 In Vietnam I knew a man who went quietly
and purposefully crazy because his wife wrote
him that his son had been sexually abused—
"messed with"—by the leader of their church choir. This
man was a black six-foot-six grunt named Leonard
Hamnet, from a small town in Tennessee named Archi-
bald. Before writing, his wife had waited until she had
endured the entire business of going to the police, talking to other parents, returning to the police with another
accusation, and finally succeeding in having the man
charged. He was up for trial in two months. Leonard
Hamnet was no happier about that than he was about the
original injury.

"I got to murder him, you know, but I'm seriously
thinking on murdering her too," he said. He still held the
letter in his hands, and he was speaking to Spanky Burrage, Michael Poole, Conor Linklater, SP4 Cotton, Calvin Hill, Tina Pumo, the magnificent M. O. Dengler, and
myself. "All this is going on, my boy needs help, this here

Mr. Brewster needs to be dismantled, needs to be *racked* and *stacked,* and she don't tell me! Makes me want to put her *down,* man. Take her damn head off and put it up on a stake in the yard, man. With a sign saying: *Here is one stupid woman."*

We were in the unofficial part of Camp Crandall known as No Man's Land, located between the wire perimeter and a shack, also unofficial, where a cunning little weasel named Wilson Manly sold contraband beer and liquor. No Man's Land, so called because the C.O. pretended it did not exist, contained a mound of old tires, a pisstube, and a lot of dusty red ground. Leonard Hamnet gave the letter in his hand a dispirited look, folded it into the pocket of his fatigues, and began to roam around the heap of tires, aiming kicks at the ones that stuck out furthest. "One stupid woman," he repeated. Dust exploded up from a burst, worn-down wheel of rubber.

I wanted to make sure Hamnet knew he was angry with Mr. Brewster, not his wife, and said, "She was trying—"

Hamnet's great glistening bull's head turned toward me.

"Look at what the woman did. She nailed that bastard. She got other people to admit that he messed with their kids too. That must be almost impossible. And she had the guy arrested. He's going to be put away for a long time."

"I'll put that bitch away, too," Hamnet said, and kicked an old grey tire hard enough to push it nearly a foot back into the heap. All the other tires shuddered and moved. For a second it seemed that the entire mound might collapse.

"This is my *boy* I'm talking about here," Hamnet said. "This shit has gone far enough."

"The important thing," Dengler said, "is to take care of your boy. You have to see he gets help."

"How'm I gonna do that from here?" Hamnet shouted.

"Write him a letter," Dengler said. "Tell him you love him. Tell him he did right to go to his mother. Tell him you think about him all the time."

Hamnet took the letter from his pocket and stared at it. It was already stained and wrinkled. I did not think it could survive many more of Hamnet's readings. His face seemed to get heavier, no easy trick with a face like Hamnet's. "I got to get home," he said. "I got to get back home and take *care* of these people."

Hamnet began putting in requests for compassionate leave relentlessly—one request a day. When we were out on patrol, sometimes I saw him unfold the tattered sheet of notepaper from his shirt pocket and read it two or three times, concentrating intensely. When the letter began to shred along the folds, Hamnet taped it together.

We were going out on four- and five-day patrols during that period, taking a lot of casualties. Hamnet performed well in the field, but he had retreated so far within himself that he spoke in monosyllables. He wore a dull, glazed look, and moved like a man who had just eaten a heavy dinner. I thought he looked like he had given up, and when people gave up they did not last long—they were already very close to death, and other people avoided them.

We were camped in a stand of trees at the edge of a paddy. That day we had lost two men so new that I had already forgotten their names. We had to eat cold C rations because heating them with C-4 it would have been like putting up billboards and arc lights. We couldn't smoke, and we were not supposed to talk. Hamnet's C rations consisted of an old can of Spam that dated from an earlier war and a can of peaches. He saw Spanky staring at the peaches and tossed him the can. Then he dropped the Spam between his legs. Death was almost visible around him. He fingered the note out of his pocket and tried to read it in the damp grey twilight.

At that moment someone started shooting at us, and the Lieutenant yelled *"Shit!"*, and we dropped our food and returned fire at the invisible people trying to kill us. When they kept shooting back, we had to go through the paddy.

The warm water came up to our chests. At the dikes, we scrambled over and splashed down into the muck on the other side. A boy from Santa Cruz, California, named Thomas Blevins got a round in the back of his neck and dropped dead into the water just short of the first dike, and another boy named Tyrell Budd coughed and dropped down right beside him. The F.O. called in an artillery strike. We leaned against the backs of the last two dikes when the big shells came thudding in. The ground shook and the water rippled, and the edge of the forest went up in a series of fireballs. We could hear the monkeys screaming.

One by one we crawled over the last dike onto the damp but solid ground on the other side of the paddy. Here the trees were much sparser, and a little group of thatched huts was visible through them.

Then two things I did not understand happened, one after the other. Someone off in the forest fired a mortar round at us—just one. One mortar, one round. That was the first thing. I fell down and shoved my face in the muck, and everybody around me did the same. I considered that this might be my last second on earth, and greedily inhaled whatever life might be left to me. Whoever fired the mortar should have had an excellent idea of our location, and I experienced that endless moment of pure, terrifying helplessness—a moment in which the soul simultaneously clings to the body and readies itself to let go of it—until the shell landed on top of the last dike and blew it to bits. Dirt, mud, and water slopped down around us, and shell fragments whizzed through the air. One of the fragments sailed over us, sliced a hamburger-sized wad of bark and wood from a tree, and clanged into Spanky Burrage's helmet with a sound like a brick hitting a garbage can. The fragment fell to the ground, and a little smoke drifted up from it.

We picked ourselves up. Spanky looked dead, except that he was breathing. Hamnet shouldered his pack and picked up Spanky and slung him over his shoulder. He saw me looking at him.

"I gotta take *care* of these people," he said.

The other thing I did not understand—apart from why there had been only one mortar round—came when we entered the village.

Lieutenant Harry Beevers had yet to join us, and we were nearly a year away from the events at Ia Thuc, when everything, the world and ourselves within the world, went crazy. I have to explain what happened. Lieutenant Harry Beevers killed thirty children in a cave at Ia Thuc and their bodies disappeared, but Michael Poole and I went into that cave and knew that something obscene had happened in there. We smelled evil, we touched its wings with our hands. A pitiful character named Victor Spitalny ran into the cave when he heard gunfire, and came pinwheeling out right away, screaming, covered with welts or hives that vanished almost as soon as he came out into the air. Poor Spitalny had touched it too. Because I was twenty and already writing books in my head, I thought that the cave was the place where the other *Tom Sawyer* ended, where Injun Joe raped Becky Thatcher and slit Tom's throat.

When we walked into the little village in the woods on the other side of the rice paddy, I experienced a kind of foretaste of Ia Thuc. If I can say this without setting off all the Gothic bells, the place seemed intrinsically, inherently wrong—it was too quiet, too still, completely without noise or movement. There were no chickens, dogs, or pigs; no old women came out to look us over, no old men offered conciliatory smiles. The little huts, still inhabitable, were empty—something I had never seen before in Vietnam, and never saw again. It was a ghost village, in a country where people thought the earth was sanctified by their ancestor's bodies.

Poole's map said that the place was named Bong To.

Hamnet lowered Spanky into the long grass as soon as we reached the center of the empty village. I bawled out a few words in my poor Vietnamese.

Spanky groaned. He gently touched the sides of his helmet. "I caught a head wound," he said.

"You wouldn't have a head at all, you was only wearing your liner," Hamnet said.

Spanky bit his lips and pushed the helmet up off his head. He groaned. A finger of blood ran down beside his ear. Finally the helmet passed over a lump the size of an apple that rose up from under his hair. Wincing, Spanky fingered this enormous knot. "I see double," he said. "I'll never get that helmet back on."

The medic said, "Take it easy, we'll get you out of here."

"Out of *here*?" Spanky brightened up.

"Back to Crandall," the medic said.

Spitalny sidled up, and Spanky frowned at him. "There ain't nobody here," Spitalny said. "What the fuck is going on?" He took the emptiness of the village as a personal affront.

Leonard Hamnet turned his back and spat.

"Spitalny, Tiano," the Lieutenant said. "Go into the paddy and get Tyrell and Blevins. Now."

Tattoo Tiano, who was due to die six and a half months later and was Spitalny's only friend, said, "You do it this time, Lieutenant."

Hamnet turned around and began moving toward Tiano and Spitalny. He looked as if he had grown two sizes larger, as if his hands could pick up boulders. I had forgotten how big he was. His head was lowered, and a rim of clear white showed above the irises. I wouldn't have been surprised if he had blown smoke from his nostrils.

"Hey, I'm gone, I'm already there," Tiano said. He and Spitalny began moving quickly through the sparse trees. Whoever had fired the mortar had packed up and gone. By now it was nearly dark, and the mosquitos had found us.

"So?" Poole said.

Hamnet sat down heavily enough for me to feel the shock in my boots. He said, "I have to go home, Lieutenant. I don't mean no disrespect, but I cannot take this shit much longer."

The Lieutenant said he was working on it.

Poole, Hamnet, and I looked around at the village.

Spanky Burrage said, "Good quiet place for Ham to catch up on his reading."

"Maybe I better take a look," the Lieutenant said. He flicked the lighter a couple of times and walked off toward the nearest hut. The rest of us stood around like fools, listening to the mosquitos and the sounds of Tiano and Spitalny pulling the dead men up over the dikes. Every now and then Spanky groaned and shook his head. Too much time passed.

The Lieutenant said something almost inaudible from inside the hut. He came back outside in a hurry, looking disturbed and puzzled even in the darkness.

"Underhill, Poole," he said, "I want you to see this."

Poole and I glanced at each other. I wondered if I looked as bad as he did. Poole seemed to be couple of psychic inches from either taking a poke at the Lieutenant or exploding altogether. In his muddy face his eyes were the size of hen's eggs. He was wound up like a cheap watch. I thought that I probably looked pretty much the same.

"What is it, Lieutenant?" he asked.

The Lieutenant gestured for us to come to the hut, then turned around and went back inside. There was no reason for us not to follow him. The Lieutenant was a jerk, but Harry Beevers, our next Lieutenant, was a baron, an earl among jerks, and we nearly always did whatever dumb thing he told us to do. Poole was so ragged and edgy that he looked as if he felt like shooting the Lieutenant in the back. *I* felt like shooting the Lieutenant in the back, I realized a second later. I didn't have an idea in the world what was going on in Poole's mind. I grumbled something and moved toward the hut. Poole followed.

The Lieutenant was standing in the doorway, looking over his shoulder and fingering his sidearm. He frowned at us to let us know we had been slow to obey him, then flicked on the lighter. The sudden hollows and shadows in his face made him resemble one of the corpses I had opened up when I was in graves registration at Camp White Star.

"You want to know what it is, Poole? Okay, you tell me what it is."

He held the lighter before him like a torch and marched into the hut. I imagined the entire dry, flimsy structure bursting into heat and flame. This Lieutenant was not destined to get home walking and breathing, and I pitied and hated him about equally, but I did not want to turn into toast because he had found an American body inside a hut and didn't know what to do about it. I'd heard of platoons finding the mutilated corpses of American prisoners, and hoped that this was not our turn.

And then, in the instant before I smelled blood and saw the Lieutenant stoop to lift a panel on the floor, I thought that what had spooked him was not the body of an American POW but of a child who had been murdered and left behind in this empty place. The Lieutenant had probably not seen any dead children yet. Some part of the Lieutenant was still worrying about what a girl named Becky Roddenburger was getting up to back at Idaho State, and a dead child would be too much reality for him.

He pulled up the wooden panel in the floor, and I caught the smell of blood. The Zippo died, and darkness closed down on us. The Lieutenant yanked the panel back on its hinges. The smell of blood floated up from whatever was beneath the floor. The Lieutenant flicked the Zippo, and his face jumped out of the darkness. "Now. Tell me what this is."

"It's where they hide the kids when people like us show up," I said. "Smells like something went wrong. Did you take a look?"

I saw in his tight cheeks and almost lipless mouth that he had not. He wasn't about to go down there and get killed by the Minotaur while his platoon stood around outside.

"Taking a look is your job, Underhill," he said.

For a second we both looked at the ladder, made of peeled branches lashed together with rags, that led down into the pit.

"Give me the lighter," Poole said, and grabbed it away from the Lieutenant. He sat on the edge of the hole and leaned over, bringing the flame beneath the level of the floor. He grunted at whatever he saw, and surprised both the Lieutenant and myself by pushing himself off the ledge into the opening. The light went out. The Lieutenant and I looked down into the dark open rectangle in the floor.

The lighter flared again. I could see Poole's extended arm, the jittering little fire, a packed-earth floor. The top of the concealed room was less than an inch above the top of Poole's head. He moved away from the opening.

"What is it? Are there any—" The Lieutenant's voice made a creaky sound. "Any bodies?"

"Come down here, Tim," Poole called up.

I sat on the floor and swung my legs into the pit. Then I jumped down.

Beneath the floor, the smell of blood was almost sickeningly strong.

"What do you see?" the Lieutenant shouted. He was trying to sound like a leader, and his voice squeaked on the last word.

I saw an empty room shaped like a giant grave. The walls were covered by some kind of thick paper held in place by wooden struts sunk into the earth. Both the thick brown paper and two of the struts showed old bloodstains.

"Hot," Poole said, and closed the lighter.

"Come *on,* damn it," came the Lieutenant's voice. "Get out of there."

"Yes, sir," Poole said. He flicked the lighter back on. Many layers of thick paper formed an absorbent pad between the earth and the room, and the topmost, thinnest layer had been covered with vertical lines of Vietnamese writing. The writing looked like poetry, like the left-hand pages of Kenneth Rexroth's translations of Tu Fu and Li Po.

"Well, well," Poole said, and I turned to see him pointing at what first looked like intricately woven strands of rope fixed to the bloodstained wooden uprights. Poole stepped forward and the weave jumped into sharp relief. About four feet off the ground, iron chains had been screwed to the uprights. The thick pad between the two lengths of chain had been soaked with blood. The three feet of ground between the posts looked rusty. Poole moved the lighter closer to the chains, and we saw dried blood on the metal links.

"I want you guys out of there, and I mean *now,*" whined the Lieutenant.

Poole snapped the lighter shut.

"I just changed my mind," I said softly. "I'm putting twenty bucks into the Elijah fund. For two weeks from today. That's what, June twentieth?"

"Tell it to Spanky," he said. Spanky Burrage had invented the pool we called the Elijah fund, and he held the money. Michael had not put any money into the pool. He thought that a new Lieutenant might be even worse than the one we had. Of course he was right. Harry Beevers was our next Lieutenant. Elijah Joys, Lieutenant Elijah Joys of New Utrecht, Idaho, a graduate of the University of Idaho and basic training at Fort Benning, Georgia, was an inept, weak Lieutenant, not a disastrous one. If Spanky could have seen what was coming, he would have given back the money and prayed for the safety of Lieutenant Joys.

Poole and I moved back toward the opening. I felt as if I had seen a shrine to an obscene deity. The Lieutenant leaned over and stuck out his hand—uselessly, because he did not bend down far enough for us to reach him. We levered ourselves up out of the hole stiff-armed, as if we were leaving a swimming pool. The Lieutenant stepped back. He had a thin face and thick, fleshy nose, and his Adam's apple danced around in his neck like a jumping bean. He might not have been Harry Beevers, but he was no prize. "Well, how many?"

"How many what?" I asked.

"How many are there?" He wanted to go back to Camp Crandall with a good body count.

"There weren't exactly any bodies, Lieutenant," said Poole, trying to let him down easily. He described what we had seen.

"Well, what's that good for?" He meant, *How is that going to help me?*

"Interrogations, probably," Poole said. "If you questioned someone down there, no one outside the hut would hear anything. At night, you could just drag the body into the woods."

Lieutenant Joys nodded. "Field Interrogation Post," he said, trying out the phrase. "Torture, Use of, Highly Indicated." He nodded again. "Right?"

"Highly," Poole said.

"Shows you what kind of enemy we're dealing with in this conflict."

I could no longer stand being in the same three square feet of space with Elijah Joys, and I took a step toward the door of the hut. I did not know what Poole and I had seen, but I knew it was not a Field Interrogation Post, Torture, Use of, Highly Indicated, unless the Vietnamese had begun to interrogate monkeys. It occurred to me that the writing on the wall might have been names instead of poetry—I thought that we had stumbled into a mystery that had nothing to do with the war, a Vietnamese mystery.

For a second music from my old life, music too beautiful to be endurable, started playing in my head. Finally I recognized it: "The Walk to the Paradise Gardens," from *A Village Romeo and Juliet* by Frederick Delius. Back in Berkeley, I had listened to it hundreds of times.

If nothing else had happened, I think I could have replayed the whole piece in my head. Tears filled my eyes, and I stepped toward the door of the hut. Then I froze. A ragged Vietnamese boy of seven or eight was regarding me with great seriousness from the far corner of the hut. I knew he was not there—I knew he was a spirit. I had no belief in spirits, but that's what he was. Some part of my mind as detached as a crime reporter reminded me that "The Walk to the Paradise Gardens" was about two children who were about to die, and that in a sense the music *was* their death. I wiped my eyes with my hand, and when I lowered my arm, the boy was still there. He was beautiful, beautiful in the ordinary way, as Vietnamese children nearly always seemed beautiful to me. Then he vanished all at once, like the flickering light of the Zippo. I nearly groaned aloud. That child had been murdered in the hut: he had not just died, he had been murdered.

I said something to the other two men and went through the door into the growing darkness. I was very dimly aware of the Lieutenant asking Poole to repeat his description of the uprights and the bloody chain. Hamnet and Burrage and Calvin Hill were sitting down and leaning against a tree. Victor Spitalny was wiping his hands on his filthy shirt. White smoke curled up from Hill's cigarette, and Tina Pumo exhaled a long white stream of vapor. The unhinged thought came to me with an absolute conviction that *this* was the Paradise Gardens. The men lounging in the darkness; the pattern of the cigarette smoke, and the patterns they made, sitting or standing; the in-drawing darkness, as physical as a blanket; the frame of the trees and the flat gray-green background of the paddy.

My soul had come back to life.

Then I became aware that there was something wrong about the men arranged before me, and again it took a moment for my intelligence to catch up to my intuition. Every member of a combat unit makes unconscious adjustments as members of the unit go down in the field; survival sometimes depends on the number of people you know are with you, and you keep count without be-

ing quite aware of doing it. I had registered that two men
too many were in front of me. Instead of seven, there
were nine, and the two men that made up the nine of us
left were still behind me in the hut. M. O. Dengler was
looking at me with growing curiosity, and I thought he
knew exactly what I was thinking. A sick chill went
through me. I saw Tom Blevins and Tyrell Budd standing
together at the far right of the platoon, a little muddier
than the others but otherwise different from the rest only
in that, like Dengler, they were looking directly at me.

Hill tossed his cigarette away in an arc of light. Poole
and Lieutenant Joys came out of the hut behind me.
Leonard Hamnet patted his pocket to reassure himself
that he still had his letter. I looked back at the right of
the group, and the two dead men were gone.

"Let's saddle up," the Lieutenant said. "We aren't doing any good around here."

"Tim?" Dengler asked. He had not taken his eyes off
me since I had come out of the hut. I shook my head.

"Well, what was it?" asked Tina Pumo. "Was it juicy?"
Spanky and Calvin Hill laughed and slapped hands.

"Aren't we gonna torch this place?" asked Spitalny.

The Lieutenant ignored him. "Juicy enough, Pumo.
Interrogation Post. Field Interrogation Post."

"No shit," said Pumo.

"These people are into torture, Pumo. It's just another
indication."

"Gotcha." Pumo glanced at me and his eyes grew curious. Dengler moved closer.

"I was just remembering something," I said. "Something from the world."

"You better forget about the world while you're over
here, Underhill," the Lieutenant told me. "I'm trying to

keep you alive, in case you hadn't noticed, but you have to cooperate with me." His Adam's apple jumped like a begging puppy.

As soon as he went ahead to lead us out of the village, I gave twenty dollars to Spanky and said, "Two weeks from today."

"My man," Spanky said.

The rest of the patrol was uneventful.

The next night we had showers, real food, alcohol, cots to sleep in. Sheets and pillows. Two new guys replaced Tyrell Budd and Thomas Blevins, whose names were never mentioned again, at least by me, until long after the war was over and Poole, Linklater, Pumo, and I looked them up, along with the rest of our dead, on the Wall in Washington. I wanted to forget the patrol, especially what I had seen and experienced inside the hut. I wanted the oblivion which came in powdered form.

I remember that it was raining. I remember the steam lifting off the ground, and the condensation dripping down the metal poles in the tents. Moisture shone on the faces around me. I was sitting in the brothers' tent, listening to the music Spanky Burrage played on the big reel-to-reel recorder he had bought on R&R in Taipei. Spanky Burrage never played Delius, but what he played was paradisal: great jazz from Armstrong to Coltrane, on reels recorded for him by his friends back in Little Rock and which he knew so well he could find individual tracks and performances without bothering to look at the counter. Spanky liked to play disc jockey during these long sessions, changing reels and speeding past thousands of feet of tape to play the same songs by different musicians, even the same song hiding under different names—"Cherokee" and "KoKo," "Indiana" and

"Donna Lee"—or long series of songs connected by ti-
tles that used the same words—"I Thought About You"
(Art Tatum), "You and the Night and the Music" (Sonny
Rollins), "I Love You" (Bill Evans), "If I Could Be with
You" (Ike Quebec), "You Leave Me Breathless," (Milt
Jackson), even, for the sake of the joke, "Thou Swell," by
Glenroy Breakstone. In his single-artist mode on this
day, Spanky was ranging through the work of a great
trumpet player named Clifford Brown.

On this sweltering, rainy day, Clifford Brown's music
sounded regal and unearthly. Clifford Brown was walking to the Paradise Gardens. Listening to him was like
watching a smiling man shouldering open an enormous
door to let in great dazzling rays of light. We were out of
the war. The world we were in transcended pain and
loss, and imagination had banished fear. Even SP4 Cotton and Calvin Hill, who preferred James Brown to Clifford Brown, lay on their bunks listening as Spanky followed his instincts from one track to another.

After he had played disc jockey for something like two
hours, Spanky rewound the long tape and said,
"Enough." The end of the tape slapped against the reel.
I looked at Dengler, who seemed dazed, as if awakening
from a long sleep. The memory of the music was still all
around us: light still poured in through the crack in the
great door.

"I'm gonna have a smoke *and* a drink," Cotton announced, and pushed himself up off his cot. He walked
to the door of the tent and pulled the flap aside to expose
the green wet drizzle. That dazzling light, the light from
another world, began to fade. Cotton sighed, plopped a
wide-brimmed hat on his head, and slipped outside. Before the stiff flap fell shut, I saw him jumping through

the puddles on the way to Wilson Manly's shack. I felt as though I had returned from a long journey.

Spanky finished putting the Clifford Brown reel back into its cardboard box. Someone in the rear of the tent switched on Armed Forces Radio. Spanky looked at me and shrugged. Leonard Hamnet took his letter out of his pocket, unfolded it, and read it through very slowly.

"Leonard," I said, and he swung his big buffalo's head toward me. "You still putting in for compassionate leave?"

He nodded. "You know what I gotta do."

"Yes," Dengler said, in a slow quiet voice.

"They gonna let me take care of my people. They gonna send me back."

He spoke with a complete absence of nuance, like a man who had learned to get what he wanted by parroting words without knowing what they meant.

Dengler looked at me and smiled. For a second he seemed as alien as Hamnet. "What do you think is going to happen? To us, I mean. Do you think it'll just go on like this day after day until some of us get killed and the rest of us go home, or do you think it's going to get stranger and stranger?" He did not wait for me to answer. "I think it'll always sort of look the same, but it won't be—I think the edges are starting to melt. I think that's what happens when you're out here long enough. The edges melt."

"Your edges melted a long time ago, Dengler," Spanky said, and applauded his own joke.

Dengler was still staring at me. He always resembled a serious, dark-haired child, and never looked as though he belonged in uniform. "Here's what I mean, kind of," he said. "When we were listening to that trumpet player—"

"*Brownie,* Clifford *Brown,*" Spanky whispered.

"—I could see the notes in the air. Like they were written out on a long scroll. And after he played them, they stayed in the air for a long time."

"*Sweetie-pie,*" Spanky said softly. "You pretty hip, for a little ofay square."

"When we were back in that village, last week," Dengler said. "Tell me about that."

I said that he had been there too.

"But something happened to you. Something special."

"I put twenty bucks in the Elijah fund," I said.

"Only twenty?" Cotton asked.

"What was in that hut?" Dengler asked.

I shook my head.

"All right," Dengler said. "But it's happening, isn't it? Things are changing."

I could not speak. I could not tell Dengler in front of Cotton and Spanky Burrage that I had imagined seeing the ghosts of Blevins, Budd, and a murdered child. I smiled and shook my head.

"Fine," Dengler said.

"What the fuck you sayin' is *fine*?" Cotton said. "I don't mind listening to that music, but I do draw the line at this bullshit." He flipped himself off his bunk and pointed a finger at me. "What date you give Spanky?"

"Fifteenth."

"He last longer than that." Cotton tilted his head as the song on the radio ended. Armed Forces Radio began playing a song by Moby Grape. Disgusted, he turned back to me. "Check it out. End of August. He be so tired, he be *sleepwalkin'*. Be halfway through his tour. The fool will go to pieces, and that's when he'll get it."

Cotton had put thirty dollars on August thirty-first, exactly the midpoint of Lieutenant Joys' tour of duty. He had a long time to adjust to the loss of the money, because he himself stayed alive until a sniper killed him at the beginning of February. Then he became a member of the ghost platoon that followed us wherever we went. I think this ghost platoon, filled with men I had loved and detested, whose names I could or could not remember, disbanded only when I went to the Wall in Washington, D.C., and by then I felt that I was a member of it myself.

2

I left the tent with a vague notion of getting outside and enjoying the slight coolness that followed the rain. The packet of Si Van Vo's white powder rested at the bottom of my right front pocket, which was so deep that my fingers just brushed its top. I decided that what I needed was a beer.

Wilson Manly's shack was all the way on the other side of camp. I never liked going to the enlisted men's club, where they were rumored to serve cheap Vietnamese beer in American bottles. Certainly the bottles had often been stripped of their labels, and to a suspicious eye the caps looked dented; also, the beer there never quite tasted like the stuff Manly sold.

One other place remained, farther away than the enlisted men's club but closer than Manly's shack and somewhere between them in official status. About twenty minutes' walk from where I stood, just at the curve in the steeply descending road to the airfield and the motor pool, stood an isolated wooden structure

called Billy's. Billy himself, supposedly a Green Beret
Captain who had installed a handful of bar girls in an old
French command post, had gone home long ago, but his
club had endured. There were no more girls, if there
ever had been, and the brand-name liquor was about as
reliable as the enlisted men's club's beer. When it was
open, a succession of slender Montagnard boys who slept
in the nearly empty upstairs rooms served drinks. I visited these rooms two or three times, but I never learned
where the boys went when Billy's was closed. They spoke
almost no English. Billy's did not look anything like a
French command post, even one that had been transformed into a bordello: it looked like a roadhouse.

A long time ago, the building had been painted brown.
The wood was soft with rot. Someone had once boarded
up the two front windows on the lower floor, and someone else had torn off a narrow band of boards across
each of the windows, so that light entered in two flat
white bands that traveled across the floor during the day.
Around six thirty the light bounced off the long foxed
mirror that stood behind the row of bottles. After five
minutes of blinding light, the sun disappeared beneath
the pine boards, and for ten or fifteen minutes a shadowy
pink glow filled the barroom. There was no electricity
and no ice. Fingerprints covered the glasses. When you
needed a toilet, you went to a cubicle with inverted
metal boot-prints on either side of a hole in the floor.

The building stood in a little grove of trees in the
curve of the descending road, and as I walked toward it
in the diffuse reddish light of the sunset, a mud-spat-
tered jeep painted in the colors of camouflage gradually
came into view to the right of the bar, emerging from
invisibility like an optical illusion. The jeep seemed to

have floated out of the trees behind it, to be a part of them.

I heard low male voices, which stopped when I stepped onto the soft boards of the front porch. I glanced at the jeep, looking for insignia or identification, but the mud covered the door panels. Something white gleamed dully from the back seat. When I looked more closely, I saw in a coil of rope an oval of bone that it took me a moment to recognize as the top of a painstakingly cleaned and bleached human skull.

Before I could reach the handle, the door opened. A boy named Mike stood before me, in loose khaki shorts and a dirty white shirt much too large for him. Then he saw who I was. "Oh," he said. "Yes. Tim. Okay. You can come in." His real name was not Mike, but Mike was what it sounded like. He carried himself with an odd defensive alertness, and he shot me a tight, uncomfortable smile. "Far table, right side."

"It's okay?" I asked, because everything about him told me that it wasn't.

"*Yesss.*" He stepped back to let me in.

I smelled cordite before I saw the other men. The bar looked empty, and the band of light coming in through the opening over the windows had already reached the long mirror, creating a bright dazzle, a white fire. I took a couple of steps inside, and Mike moved around me to return to his post.

"Oh, hell," someone said from off to my left. "We have to put up with *this*?"

I turned my head to look into the murk of that side of the bar, and saw three men sitting against the wall at a round table. None of the kerosene lamps had been lighted yet, and the dazzle from the mirror made the far reaches of the bar even less distinct.

"Is okay, is okay," said Mike. "Old customer. Old friend."

"I bet he is," the voice said. "Just don't let any women in here."

"No women," Mike said. "No problem."

I went through the tables to the furthest one on the right.

"You want whiskey, Tim?" Mike asked.

"Tim?" the man said. *"Tim?"*

"Beer," I said, and sat down.

A nearly empty bottle of Johnnie Walker Black, three glasses, and about a dozen cans of beer covered the table before them. The soldier with his back against the wall shoved aside some of the beer cans so that I could see the .45 next to the Johnnie Walker bottle. He leaned forward with a drunk's guarded coordination. The sleeves had been ripped off his shirt, and dirt darkened his skin as if he had not bathed in years. His hair had been cut with a knife, and had once been blond.

"I just want to make sure about this," he said. "You're not a woman, right? You swear to that?"

"Anything you say," I said.

"No woman walks into this place." He put his hand on the gun. "No nurse. No wife. No *anything*. You got that?"

"Got it," I said. Mike hurried around the bar with my beer.

"Tim. Funny name. Tom, now—that's a name. Tim sounds like a little guy—like him." He pointed at Mike with his left hand, the whole hand and not merely the index finger, while his right still rested on the .45. "Little fucker ought to be wearing a dress. Hell, he practically *is* wearing a dress."

"Don't you like women?" I asked. Mike put a can of Budweiser on my table and shook his head rapidly, twice. He had wanted me in the club because he was afraid the drunken soldier was going to shoot him, and now I was just making things worse.

I looked at the two men with the drunken officer. They were dirty and exhausted—whatever had happened to the drunk had also happened to them. The difference was that they were not drunk yet.

"That is a complicated question," the drunk said. "There are questions of responsibility. You can be responsible for yourself. You can be responsible for your children and your tribe. You are responsible for anyone you want to protect. But can you be responsible for women? If so, how responsible?"

Mike quietly moved behind the bar and sat on a stool with his arms out of sight. I knew he had a shotgun under there.

"You don't have any idea what I'm talking about, do you, Tim, you rear-echelon dipshit?"

"You're afraid you'll shoot any women who come in here, so you told the bartender to keep them out."

"This wise-ass sergeant is personally interfering with my state of mind," the drunk said to the burly man on his right. "Tell him to get out of here, or a certain degree of unpleasantness will ensue."

"Leave him alone," the other man said. Stripes of dried mud lay across his lean, haggard face.

The drunken officer Beret startled me by leaning toward the other man and speaking in a clear, carrying Vietnamese. It was an old-fashioned, almost literary Vietnamese, and he must have thought and dreamed in it to speak it so well. He assumed that neither I nor the Montagnard boy would understand him.

This is serious, he said, *and I am serious. If you wish to see how serious, just sit in your chair and do nothing. Do you not know of what I am capable by now? Have you learned nothing? You know what I know. I know what you know. A great heaviness is between us. Of all the people in the world at this moment, the only ones I do not despise are already dead, or should be. At this moment, murder is weightless.*

There was more, and I cannot swear that this was exactly what he said, but it's pretty close. He may have said that murder was *empty.*

Then he said, in that same flowing Vietnamese that even to my ears sounded as stilted as the language of a third-rate Victorian novel: *Recall what is in our vehicle (carriage); you should remember what we have brought with us, because I shall never forget it. Is it so easy for you to forget?*

It takes a long time and a lot of patience to clean and bleach bone. A skull would be more difficult than most of a skeleton.

Your leader requires more of this nectar, he said, and rolled back in his chair, looking at me with his hand on his gun.

"Whiskey," said the burly soldier. Mike was already pulling the bottle off the shelf. He understood that the officer was trying to knock himself out before he would find it necessary to shoot someone.

For a moment I thought that the burly soldier to his right looked familiar. His head had been shaved so close he looked bald, and his eyes were enormous above the streaks of dirt. A stainless-steel watch hung from a slot in his collar. He extended a muscular arm for the bottle Mike passed him while keeping as far from the table as he could. The soldier twisted off the cap and poured into all three glasses. The man in the center immediately drank all the whiskey in his glass and banged the glass down on the table for a refill.

The haggard soldier who had been silent until now said, "Something is gonna happen here." He looked straight at me. "Pal?"

"That man is nobody's pal," the drunk said. Before anyone could stop him, he snatched up the gun, pointed it across the room, and fired. There was a flash of fire, a huge explosion, and the reek of cordite. The bullet went straight through the soft wooden wall, about eight feet to my left. A stray bit of light slanted through the hole it made.

For a moment I was deaf. I swallowed the last of my beer and stood up. My head was ringing.

"Is it clear that I hate the necessity for this kind of shit?" said the drunk. "Is that much understood?"

The soldier who had called me pal laughed, and the burly soldier poured more whiskey into the drunk's glass. Then he stood up and started coming toward me. Beneath the exhaustion and the stripes of dirt, his face was taut with anxiety. He put himself between me and the man with the gun.

"I am not a rear-echelon dipshit," I said. "I don't want any trouble, but people like him do not own this war."

"Will you maybe let me save your ass, Sergeant?" he whispered. "Major Bachelor hasn't been anywhere near white men in three years, and he's having a little trouble readjusting. Compared to him, we're all rear-echelon dipshits."

I looked at his tattered shirt. "Are you his babysitter, Captain?"

He gave me an exasperated look, and glanced over his shoulder at the Major. "Major, put down your damn weapon. The sergeant is a combat soldier. He is on his way back to camp."

I don't care what he is, the Major said in Vietnamese.

The Captain began pulling me toward the door, keeping his body between me and the other table. I motioned for Mike to come out with me.

"Don't worry, the Major won't shoot him, Major Bachelor loves the Yards," the Captain said. He gave me an impatient glance because I had refused to move at his pace. Then I saw him notice my pupils. "God damn," he said, and then he stopped moving altogether and said "God damn" again, but in a different tone of voice.

I started laughing.

"Oh, this is—" He shook his head. "This is really—"

"Where have you *been*?" I asked him.

John Ransom turned to the table. "Hey, I know this guy. He's an old football friend of mine."

Major Bachelor shrugged and put the .45 back on the table. His eyelids had nearly closed. "I don't care about football," he said, but he kept his hand off the weapon.

"Buy the sergeant a drink," said the haggard officer.

"Buy the fucking sergeant a drink," the Major chimed in.

John Ransom quickly moved to the bar and reached for a glass, which the confused Mike put into his hand. Ransom went through the tables, filled his glass and mine, and carried both back to join me.

We watched the Major's head slip down by notches toward his chest. When his chin finally reached the unbuttoned top of his ruined shirt, Ransom said, "All right, Bob," and the other man slid the .45 out from under the Major's hand. He pushed it beneath his belt.

"The man is out," Bob said.

Ransom turned back to me. "He was up three days straight with us, God knows how long before that." Ransom did not have to specify who *he* was. "Bob and I got some sleep, trading off, but he just kept on talking." He fell into one of the chairs at my table and tilted his glass to his mouth. I sat down beside him.

For a moment no one in the bar spoke. The line of light from the open space across the windows had already left the mirror, and was now approaching the place on the wall that meant it would soon disappear. Mike lifted the cover from one of the lamps and began trimming the wick.

"How come you're always fucked up when I see you?"

"You have to ask?"

He smiled. He looked very different from when I had seen him preparing to give a sales pitch to Senator Burrman at Camp White Star. His body had thickened and hardened, and his eyes had retreated far back into his head. He seemed to me to have moved a long step nearer the goal I had always seen in him than when he had given me the zealot's word about stopping the spread of Communism. This man had taken in more of the war, and that much more of the war was inside him now.

"I got you off graves registration at White Star, didn't I?"

I agreed that he had.

"What did you call it, the body squad? It wasn't even a real graves registration unit, was it?" He smiled and shook his head. "I took care of your Captain McCue, too —he was using it as a kind of dumping ground. I don't know how he got away with it as long as he did. The only one with any training was that sergeant, what's his name. Italian."

"DeMaestro."

Ransom nodded. "The whole operation was going off the rails." Mike lit a big kitchen match and touched it to the wick of the kerosene lamp. "I heard some things—" He slumped against the wall and swallowed whiskey. I wondered if he had heard about Captain Havens. He closed his eyes. "Some crazy stuff went on back there."

I asked if he was still stationed in the highlands up around the Laotian border. He almost sighed when he shook his head.

"You're not with the tribesmen anymore? What were they, Khatu?"

He opened his eyes. "You have a good memory. No, I'm not there anymore." He considered saying more, but decided not to. He had failed himself. "I'm kind of on hold until they send me up around Khe Sahn. It'll be better up there—the Bru are tremendous. But right now, all I want to do is take a bath and get into bed. Any bed. Actually, I'd settle for a dry level place on the ground."

"Where did you come from now?"

"Incountry." His face creased and he showed his teeth. The effect was so unsettling that I did not immediately realize that he was smiling. "Way incountry. We had to get the Major out."

"Looks more like you had to pull him out, like a tooth."

My ignorance made him sit up straight. "You mean you never heard of him? Franklin Bachelor?"

And then I thought I had, that someone had mentioned him to me a long time ago.

"In the bush for years. Bachelor did stuff that ordinary people don't even *dream* of—he's a legend."

A legend, I thought. Like the Green Berets Ransom had mentioned a lifetime ago at White Star.

"Ran what amounted to a private army, did a lot of good work in Darlac Province. He was out there on his own. The man was a hero. That's straight. Bachelor got to places we couldn't even get close to—he got *inside* an NVA encampment, you hear me, *inside* the encampment and *silently* killed about an entire division."

Of all the people in the world at this minute, I remembered, the only ones he did not detest were already dead. I thought I must have heard it wrong.

"He was absorbed right into Rhade life," Ransom said. I could hear the awe in his voice. "The man even got married. Rhade ceremony. His wife went with him on missions. I hear she was beautiful."

Then I knew where I had heard of Franklin Bachelor before. He had been a captain when Ratman and his platoon had run into him after a private named Bobby Swett had been blown to pieces on a trail in Darlac Province. Ratman had thought his wife was a black-haired angel.

And then I knew whose skull lay wound in rope in the back seat of the jeep.

"I did hear of him," I said. "I knew someone who met him. The Rhade woman, too."

"His *wife*," Ransom said.

I asked him where they were taking Bachelor.

"We're stopping overnight at Crandall for some rest.
Then we hop to Tan Son Nhut and bring him back to the
States—Langley. I thought we might have to strap him
down, but I guess we'll just keep pouring whiskey into
him."

"He's going to want his gun back."

"Maybe I'll give it to him." His look told me what he
thought Major Bachelor would do with his .45, if he was
left alone with it long enough. "He's in for a rough time
at Langley. There'll be some heat."

"Why Langley?"

"Don't ask. But don't be naïve, either. Don't you think
they're . . ." He would not finish that sentence. "Why
do you think we had to bring him out in the first place?"

"Because something went wrong."

"Oh, everything went wrong. Bachelor went totally out
of control. He had his own war. Ran a lot of sidelines,
some of which were supposed to be under shall we say
tighter controls?"

He had lost me.

"Ventures into Laos. Business trips to Cambodia.
Sometimes he wound up in control of airfields Air America was using, and that meant he was in control of the
cargo."

When I shook my head, he said, "Don't you have a
little something in your pocket? A little package?"

A secret world—inside this world, another, secret
world.

"You understand, I don't care what he did any more
than I care about what *you* do. I think Langley can go
fuck itself. Bachelor wrote the book. In spite of his side-

lines. In spite of whatever *trouble* he got into. The man was effective. He stepped over a boundary, maybe a lot of boundaries—but tell me that you can do what we're supposed to do without stepping over boundaries."

I wondered why he seemed to be defending himself, and asked if he would have to testify at Langley.

"It's not a trial."

"A debriefing."

"Sure, a debriefing. They can ask me anything they want. All I can tell them is what I saw. That's *my* evidence, right? What I saw? They don't have any evidence, except maybe this, uh, these human remains the Major insisted on bringing out."

For a second, I wished that I could see the sober shadowy gentlemen of Langley, Virginia, the gentlemen with slicked-back hair and pinstriped suits, question Major Bachelor. They thought *they* were serious men.

"It was like Bong To, in a funny way." Ransom waited for me to ask. When I did not, he said, "A ghost town, I mean. I don't suppose you've ever heard of Bong To."

"My unit was just there." His head jerked up. "A mortar round scared us into the village."

"You saw the place?"

I nodded.

"Funny story." Now he was sorry he had ever mentioned it. "Well, think about Bachelor, now. I think he must have been in Cambodia or someplace, doing what he does, when his village was overrun. He comes back and finds everybody dead, his wife included. I mean, I don't think *Bachelor* killed those people—they weren't just dead, they'd been made to beg for it. So Bachelor wasn't there, and his assistant, a Captain Bennington, must have just run off—we never did find him. Officially,

Bennington's MIA. It's simple. You can't find the main guy, so you make sure he can see how mad you are when he gets back. You do a little grievous bodily harm on his people. They were not nice to his wife, Tim, to her they were especially not nice. What does he do? He buries all the bodies in the village graveyard, because that's a sacred responsibility. Don't ask me what else he does, because you don't have to know this, okay? But the bodies are buried. Generally speaking. Captain Bennington never does show up. We arrive and take Bachelor away. But sooner or later, some of the people who escaped are going to come back to that village. They're going to go on living there. The worst thing in the world happened to them in that place, but they won't leave. Eventually, other people in their family will join them, if they're still alive, and the terrible thing will be a part of their lives. Because it is not thinkable to leave your dead."

"But they did in Bong To," I said.

"In Bong To, they did."

I saw the look of regret on his face again, and said that I wasn't asking him to tell me any secrets.

"It's not a secret. It's not even military."

"It's just a ghost town."

Ransom was still uncomfortable. He turned his glass around and around in his hands before he drank. "I have to get the Major into camp."

"It's a real ghost town," I said. "Complete with ghosts."

"I honestly wouldn't be surprised." He drank what was left in his glass and stood up. He had decided not to say any more about it. "Let's take care of Major Bachelor, Bob," he said.

"Right."

Ransom carried our bottle to the bar and paid Mike. I stepped toward him to do the same, and Ransom said, "Taken care of."

There was that phrase again—it seemed I had been hearing it all day, and that its meaning would not stay still.

Ransom and Bob picked up the Major between them. They were strong enough to lift him easily. Bachelor's greasy head rolled forward. Bob put the .45 into his pocket, and Ransom put the bottle into his own pocket. Together they carried the Major to the door.

I followed them outside. Artillery pounded hills a long way off. It was dark now, and light from the lanterns spilled out through the gaps in the windows.

All of us went down the rotting steps, the Major bobbing between the other two.

Ransom opened the jeep, and they took a while to maneuver the Major into the back seat. Bob squeezed in beside him and pulled him upright.

John Ransom got in behind the wheel and sighed. He had no taste for the next part of his job.

"I'll give you a ride back to camp," he said. "We don't want an MP to get a close look at you."

I took the seat beside him. Ransom started the engine and turned on the lights. He jerked the gearshift into reverse and rolled backwards. "You know why that mortar round came in, don't you?" he asked me. He grinned at me, and we bounced onto the road back to the main part of camp. "He was trying to chase you away from Bong To, and your fool of a Lieutenant went straight for the place instead." He was still grinning. "It must have steamed him, seeing a bunch of round-eyes going in there."

"He didn't send in any more fire."

"No. He didn't want to damage the place. It's supposed to stay the way it is. I don't think they'd use the word, but that village is supposed to be like a kind of monument." He glanced at me again. "To shame."

For some reason, all I could think of was the drunken Major in the seat behind me, who had said that you were responsible for the people you wanted to protect. Ransom said, "Did you go into any of the huts? Did you see anything unusual there?"

"I went into a hut. I saw something unusual."

"A list of names?"

"I thought that's what they were."

"Okay," Ransom said. "You know a little Vietnamese?"

"A little."

"You notice anything about those names?"

I could not remember. My Vietnamese had been picked up in bars and markets, and was almost completely oral.

"Four of them were from a family named Trang. Trang was the village chief, like his father before him, and his grandfather before him. Trang had four daughters. As each one got to the age of six or seven, he took them down into that underground room and chained them to the posts and raped them. A lot of those huts have hidden storage areas, but Trang must have modified his after his first daughter was born. The funny thing is, I think everybody in the village knew what he was doing. I'm not saying they thought it was okay, but they let it happen. They could pretend they didn't know: the girls never complained, and nobody ever heard any screams. I guess Trang was a good-enough chief. When the daughters got to sixteen, they left for the cities. Sent back

money, too. So maybe they thought it was okay, but I
don't think they did, myself, do you?"

"How would I know? But there's a man in my platoon,
a guy from—"

"I think there's a difference between private and public shame. Between what's acknowledged and what is not
acknowledged. That's what Bachelor has to cope with,
when he gets to Langley. Some things are acceptable, as
long as you don't talk about them." He looked sideways
at me as we began to approach the northern end of the
camp proper. He wiped his face, and flakes of dried mud
fell off his cheek. The exposed skin looked red, and so
did his eyes. "Because the way I see it, this is a whole
general issue. The issue is: what is *expressible*? This goes
way beyond the tendency of people to tolerate thoughts,
actions, or behavior they would otherwise find unaccept-
able."

I had never heard a soldier speak this way before. It
was a little bit like being back in Berkeley.

"I'm talking about the difference between what is ex-
pressed and what is described," Ransom said. "A lot of
experience is unacknowledged. Religion lets us handle
some of the unacknowledged stuff in an acceptable way.
But suppose—just suppose—that you were forced to
confront extreme experience directly, without any medi-
ation?"

"I have," I said. "You have, too."

"More extreme than combat, more extreme than terror. Something like that happened to the Major: he *en-
countered* God. Demands were made upon him. He had
to move out of the ordinary, even as *he* defined it."

Ransom was telling me how Major Bachelor had

wound up being brought to Camp Crandall with his wife's skull, but none of it was clear to me.

"I've been learning things," Ransom told me. He was almost whispering. "Think about what would make all the people of a village pick up and leave, when sacred obligation ties them to that village."

"I don't know the answer," I said.

"An even more sacred obligation, created by a really spectacular sense of shame. When a crime is too great to live with, the memory of it becomes sacred. Becomes the crime itself—"

I remembered thinking that the arrangement in the hut's basement had been a shrine to an obscene deity.

"Here we have this village and its chief. The village knows but does not know what the chief has been doing. They are used to consulting and obeying him. Then— one day, a little boy disappears."

My heart gave a thud.

"A little boy. Say: three. Old enough to talk and get into trouble, but too young to take care of himself. He's just gone—*poof*. Well, this is Vietnam, right? You turn your back, your kid wanders away, some animal gets him. He could get lost in the jungle and wander into a claymore. Someone like you might even shoot him. He could fall into a boobytrap and never be seen again. It could happen.

"A couple of months later, it happens again. Mom turns her back, where the hell did Junior go? This time they really look, not just Mom and Grandma, all their friends. They scour the village. The *villagers* scour the village, every square foot of that place, and then they do the same to the rice paddy, and then they look through the forest.

"And guess what happens next. This is the interesting part. An old woman goes out one morning to fetch water from the well, and she sees a ghost. This old lady is part of the extended family of the first lost kid, but the ghost she sees isn't the kid's—it's the ghost of a disreputable old man from another village, a drunkard, in fact. A local no-good, in fact. He's just standing near the well with his hands together, he's hungry—that's what these people know about ghosts. The skinny old bastard wants *more*. He wants to be *fed*. The old lady gives a squawk and passes out. When she comes to again, the ghost is gone.

"Well, the old lady tells everybody what she saw, and the whole village gets in a panic. Evil forces have been set loose. Next thing you know, two thirteen-year-old girls are working in the paddy, they look up and see an old woman who died when they were ten—she's about six feet away from them. Her hair is stringy and gray and her fingernails are about a foot long. She used to be a friendly old lady, but she doesn't look too friendly now. She's hungry too, like all ghosts. They start screaming and crying, but no one else can see her, and she comes closer and closer, and they try to get away but one of them falls down, and the old woman is on her like a cat. And do you know what she does? She rubs her filthy hands over the screaming girl's face, and licks the tears and slobber off her fingers.

"The next night, another little boy disappears. Two men go looking around the village latrine behind the houses, and they see two ghosts down in the pit, shoving excrement into their mouths. They rush back into the village, and then they both see half a dozen ghosts around the chief's hut. Among them are a sister who died during the war with the French and a twenty-year-old first wife who died of dengue fever. They want to eat. One of the men screeches, because not only did he see his dead wife, who looks something like what we could call a vampire, he saw her pass into the chief's hut without the benefit of the door.

"These people believe in ghosts, Underhill, they know ghosts exist, but it is extremely rare for them to see these ghosts. And these people are like psychoanalysts, because they do not believe in accidents. Every event contains meaning.

"The dead twenty-year-old wife comes back out through the wall of the chief's hut. Her hands are empty but dripping with red, and she is licking them like a starving cat.

"The former husband stands there pointing and jabbering, and the mothers and grandmothers of the missing boys come out of their huts. They are as afraid of what they're thinking as they are of all the ghosts moving around them. The ghosts are part of what they know they know, even though most of them have never seen one until now. What is going through their minds is something new: new because it was hidden.

"The mothers and grandmothers go to the chief's door and begin howling like dogs. When the chief comes out, they push past him and they take the hut apart. And you know what they find. They found the end of Bong To."

Ransom had parked the jeep near my battalion headquarters five minutes before, and now he smiled as if he had explained everything.

"But what *happened*?" I asked. "How did you hear about it?"

He shrugged. "We learned all this in interrogation. When the women found the underground room, they knew the chief had forced the boys into sex, and then killed them. They didn't know what he had done with the bodies, but they knew he had killed the boys. The next time the VC paid one of their courtesy calls, they told the cadre leader what they knew. The VC did the rest. They were disgusted—Trang had betrayed *them,* too—betrayed everything he was supposed to represent. One of the VC we captured took the chief downstairs into his underground room and chained the man to the posts, wrote the names of the dead boys and Trang's daughters on the padding that covered the walls, and then . . . then they did what they did to him. They probably carried out the pieces and threw them into the excrement-pit. And over months, bit by bit, not all at once but slowly, everybody in the village moved out. By that time, they were seeing ghosts all the time. They had crossed a kind of border."

"Do you think they really saw ghosts?" I asked him. "I mean, do you think they were real ghosts?"

"If you want an expert opinion, you'd have to ask Major Bachelor. He has a lot to say about ghosts." He hesitated for a moment, and then leaned over to open my door. "But if you ask me, sure they did."

I got out of the jeep and closed the door.

Ransom peered at me through the jeep's window. "Take better care of yourself."

"Good luck with your Bru."

"The Bru are fantastic." He slammed the jeep into gear and shot away, cranking the wheel to turn the jeep around in a giant circle in front of the battalion headquarters before he jammed it into second and took off to wherever he was going.

Two weeks later Leonard Hamnet managed to get the

Lutheran chaplain at Crandall to write a letter to the Tin
Man for him, and two days after that he was in a clean
uniform, packing up his kit for an overnight flight to an
Air Force base in California. From there he was connect-
ing to a Memphis flight, and from there the Army had
booked him onto a six-passenger puddlejumper to Lookout Mountain.

When I came into Hamnet's tent he was zipping his
bag shut in a zone of quiet afforded him by the other
men. He did not want to talk about where he was going
or the reason he was going there, and instead of answering my questions about his flights, he unzipped a pocket
on the side of his bag and handed me a thick folder of
airline tickets.

I looked through them and gave them back. "Hard
travel," I said.

"From now on, everything is easy," Hamnet said. He
seemed rigid and constrained as he zipped the precious
tickets back into the bag. By this time his wife's letter
was a rag held together with scotch tape. I could picture
him reading and rereading it, for the thousandth or two
thousandth time, on the long flight over the Pacific.

"They need your help," I said. "I'm glad they're going
to get it."

"That's right." Hamnet waited for me to leave him
alone.

Because his bag seemed heavy, I asked about the
length of his leave. He wanted to get the tickets back out
of the bag rather than answer me directly, but he forced
himself to speak. "They gave me seven days. Plus travel
time."

"Good," I said, meaninglessly, and then there was
nothing left to say, and we both knew it. Hamnet hoisted

his bag off his bunk and turned to the door without any of the usual farewells and embraces. Some of the other men called to him, but he seemed to hear nothing but his own thoughts. I followed him outside and stood beside him in the heat. Hamnet was wearing a tie and his boots had a high polish. He was already sweating through his stiff khaki shirt. He would not meet my eyes. In a minute a jeep pulled up before us. The Lutheran chaplain had surpassed himself.

"Goodbye, Leonard," I said, and Hamnet tossed his bag in back and got into the jeep. He sat up straight as a statue. The private driving the jeep said something to him as they drove off, but Hamnet did not reply. I bet he did not say a word to the stewardesses, either, or to the cab drivers or baggage handlers or anyone else who witnessed his long journey home.

3

On the day after Leonard Hamnet was scheduled to return, Lieutenant Joys called Michael Poole and myself into his quarters to tell us what had happened back in Tennessee. He held a sheaf of papers in his hand, and he seemed both angry and embarrassed. Hamnet would not be returning to the platoon. It was a little funny. Well, of course it wasn't funny at all. The whole thing was terrible —that was what it was. Someone was to blame, too. Irresponsible decisions had been made, and we'd all be lucky if there wasn't an investigation. We were closest to the man, hadn't we seen what was likely to happen? If not, what the hell was our excuse?

Didn't we have any inkling of what the man was planning to do?

Well, yes, at the beginning, Poole and I said. But he seemed to have adjusted.

We have stupidity and incompetence all the way down the line here, said Lieutenant Elijah Joys. Here is a man who manages to carry a semi-automatic weapon through security at three different airports, bring it into a courthouse, and carry out threats he made months before, without anybody stopping him.

I remembered the bag Hamnet had tossed into the back of the jeep; I remembered the reluctance with which he had zipped it open to show me his tickets. Hamnet had not carried his weapon through airport security. He had just shipped it home in his bag and walked straight through customs in his clean uniform and shiny boots.

As soon as the foreman had announced the guilty verdict, Leonard Hamnet had gotten to his feet, pulled the semiautomatic pistol from inside his jacket, and executed Mr. Brewster where he was sitting at the defense table. While people shouted and screamed and dove for cover, while the courthouse officer tried to unsnap his gun, Hamnet killed his wife and his son. By the time he raised the pistol to his own head, the security officer had shot him twice in the chest. He died on the operating table at Lookout Mountain Lutheran Hospital, and his mother had requested that his remains receive burial at Arlington National Cemetery.

His mother. Arlington. I ask you.

That was what the Lieutenant said. *His mother. Arlington. I ask you.*

A private from Indianapolis named E. W. Burroughs

won the six hundred and twenty dollars in the Elijah Fund when Lieutenant Joys was killed by a fragmentation bomb thirty-two days before the end of his tour. After that we were delivered unsuspecting into the hands of Harry Beevers, the Lost Boss, the worst lieutenant in the world. Private Burroughs died a week later, down in Dragon Valley along with Tiano and Calvin Hill and lots of others, when Lieutenant Beevers walked us into a mined field where we spent forty-eight hours under fire between two companies of NVA. I suppose Burroughs' mother back in Indianapolis got the six hundred and twenty dollars.

Peter Straub is the author of the novels *Marriages, Under Venus, Julia* (filmed as *The Haunting of Julia*), *If You Could See Me Now, Ghost Story, Shadowland, Floating Dragon, The Talisman* (with Stephen King), *Koko* and *Mystery,* as well as the collections *Wild Animals* and *Houses Without Doors* and two books of poetry, *Open Air* and *Leeson Park and Belsize Square.* His new novel is *The Throat.*